The Name I Choose

D1461400

The Name I Choose

Holly Brough

Library of Congress Control Number:		2022908344
ISBN:	Hardcover	978-1-6698-2369-8
	Softcover	978-1-6698-2368-1
	eBook	978-1-6698-2367-4

Note from the author - This is a work of historical fiction. Some names, characters, and places are real and certain events actually happened. In other instances, names, characters and events are a product of the author's imagination to enhance the drama of the story.

Print information available on the last page.

Rev. date: 07/12/2022

To order additional copies of this book, contact:
Xlibris
844-714-8691
www.Xlibris.com
Orders@Xlibris.com
835421

For my mother, who loved books

SPAIN

Santander

Pamplona   Benas

Lleida

Barcelona

Madrid

Murcia

Lorca   Cartagena

Puerto
Lumbreras   Aguilas

Cadiz

Ciutadella

Es Mercadal

Mahón

MENORCA

ACKNOWLEGMENTS

SINCE THIS STORY begins in Spain, a place I had never been until recently, there were many people who helped me integrate the Spanish language and culture into my book. I would like to thank Bill (Guillermo), Mayra, Adam, and Jarom for their assistance. There were others who gracefully accepted the task to read the first drafts of my book and give their feedback. Thank you to Karen, Connie, Angel, Dee, Joni, Michelle, Kiersten, Kathi, Meredith, Ryan, and my sweet husband, Rob. I'm grateful for my family, especially my children, who sacrificed time with Mom to let her write. I love you. To Perry and Maria for their constant encouragement and selflessly sharing their connections to make my dream a reality, thank you. And lastly, to my editor, Chersti and her team, I owe a debt of gratitude for their passion for this story and encouragement through the arduous process of editing my first book. I have learned a great deal from the team at Writer Therapy. And lastly, a thank you to John Hruby for his priceless insight and professional direction. What a journey!

A good name is rather to be chosen than great riches.

—Proverbs 22:1

PROLOGUE

Somewhere in España
1823

LUCITA LABORED TO lift her eyelids. Musty air filled her lungs. Nothing around her felt familiar. The ache in her bones and muscles told her she'd been sitting on the cold cobblestone floor for some time. The last thing she could recall was Anton pressed against her back, caressing her neck with his kisses, his arms cradling her belly.

Drip . . . drip . . . drip.

Her eyes finally opened to an unfamiliar room with water dripping down roughly hewn stone walls. Shivers ran through her. The reek of urine and feces hit her like a fist, causing involuntary convulsions to torment her sore body. Lucita tried to shield her nose from the smell, but ropes held her hands to a wooden post at her back. The bitter taste of bile burned the back of her throat, and she coughed.

Water. I need water. "Help. Is someone there? Help."

A movement just out of sight caught Lucita's attention. She craned her neck, and her breathing turned to gasps of panic. The bruised body of her fiancé dangled from the ceiling directly behind her. Sweat-drenched curls clung to his forehead.

"Anton?" she said.

An unexpected voice spoke from the shadows. "How good of you to join us, mi amor."

Lucita froze.

Manuel Tudó appeared out of the shadows, casually wiping the moisture from his brow and patting down his disheveled hair. She struggled fiercely with her bonds.

He paced the room like a restless cat, his obsidian eyes piercing through her. When they first met during Carnival in Águilas, Manuel's self-assured demeanor and stimulating conversation drew her to him. Smartly dressed, his manner easy and genial, Manuel won people over with his straight-toothed grin, that ever-present confident sneer. There were times, however, when he'd turned on her, violently, behind closed doors. Lucita came to know Manuel as a deceptive manipulator who played games with his victims like a cat would a mouse. She'd chosen kind, gentle Anton instead.

Lowering himself to one knee, the rejected suitor took Lucita by the shoulders and lifted her to stand. She flinched at his touch, wishing she could shield her belly from him.

"I'm sorry for your discomfort, mi amor, but I'm afraid it is necessary for the moment," he cooed.

"Stop calling me that. I am not your love."

Manuel chuckled as he removed something from his belt. "That is why we are here. Isn't it, Anton?" He walked behind her, blocking her view from what happened next. Swinging chains rattled. A sickening thud. Anton screamed.

"Stop! Stop it," Lucita begged.

Before she could mutter another word in protest, Manuel stuffed his soiled handkerchief into her mouth. Gently brushing a tear from her cheek, he said, "This is your fault, mi corazón." Moving close enough to lean his body against her, he inhaled her scent and caressed her middle. "The ultimate betrayal is evidenced in your blossoming figure. What would people think if they found out you were unwed and carrying Anton's child? I thought you and I shared something special." He paused. "Of course, *I* am not completely unforgiving. Others would shun you, but I would protect you, Lucita."

Lucita bit on the cloth in her mouth and scrunched her eyes shut as he prowled around her.

"We could still be together. A quick visit to Father Arnold, and no one else needs to know what you have done."

She shot a glance toward Anton. Manuel moved past her, there was a flash of movement, and Anton cried out again. The suffocating cloth gagged her. Lucita screamed through her sobs. *God help us.*

Manuel ignored her. He considered the fresh blood on his leather boots. Yanking the handkerchief from her mouth, he wiped at the stains. "Love is such a filthy business." He lifted Lucita's chin with the ornate handle of his handmade flail. "It is a childish fantasy to think you can be with him now. He is going to die. You must see the mistake you made choosing a coward like him."

Uncontrollable tears streamed down her ashen face. Lucita wanted to escape the agony of Anton's deafening moans, but she knew she deserved to suffer. She'd chosen Anton knowing that Manuel, incapable of forgiveness, would take revenge, but she never considered something so heinous as this.

Manuel carefully set his tool of torture aside and wiped her tears with his bloodstained handkerchief. "Shh, mi amor."

Lucita whispered, "I am not your love. I could never love you."

A growl started low in his gut. His dark eyes flashed, and he heaved his flail at Anton. Only a faint protest escaped her fiancé.

"Stop. Por favor."

Watching her gasp for air between sobs, Manuel spoke, "You could make his death mean something. You could agree to be my bride. What is your decision?"

Lucita shook her head in defeat. *I hope you can forgive me, Anton, though I will never forgive myself. I cannot accept him—not even to save you.*

"I would rather die than marry you."

The malicious assassin didn't hesitate to continue his unrelenting torture. Anton's cries went on and on, each cutting away a piece of Lucita's heart. Finally, the cruel pounding ceased. She strained to hear Anton's labored breathing. One more breath and then another and then . . . silence. She couldn't bring herself to look toward his motionless, broken body.

The father of her unborn child was gone—murdered. That reality drained Lucita of her strength. Her knees buckled, taking her to the ground where she lost the contents of her stomach. *God, keep sweet Anton and give me strength. Somehow, I must protect our child from this demon.*

Manuel rushed from the shadows to lift Lucita to her feet and clean the sick off her chin and blouse.

"Such things the pure in heart should never experience. I'm sorry you had to be a part of that, but you mustn't work yourself up, mi amor. Think of our child. I will be a good husband to you. A good father."

Flushed with anger, she spit in his face. "You are a coward and a fool. I could never love a fool."

The hard flesh of Manuel's elbow collided with the back of Lucita's head. Stars erupted in her vision, but she had enough presence of mind to feel his excitement pressing against her side. She felt him tugging at her hair. Manuel braided a small section of it, produced a knife, and cut his plaited trophy at the nape of Lucita's neck.

"This is something I've wanted for a long time."

Lacing his fat fingers into her thick locks, he pulled her head back and ran his tongue from the hollow of her neck to the corner of her mouth. Lucita strained away in protest.

"Look at me, bonita." She didn't, so he pulled harder. "Look at me."

Lucita glared at him to convey her hatred.

Manuel loosened his grip and smiled. "How brilliant your green eyes shine when kissed with a few tears. You are truly my greatest prize." He licked his lips and caressed her cheek with his thumb. "We will be together and raise our child, mi amor. We will be a family."

It took every ounce of self-control not to swing her head forward and ram him in the nose. Lucita wrenched her head away. *Never. I'll die before I let you anywhere near my child. If I lose my life, God will find a way to protect you, sweet bebé.*

Black Cumin

CHAPTER 1

Sixteen Years Later
Near Puerto Lumbreras, Murcia, España
1839

"HOW MANY TIMES have I told you I cannot eat this oily food? All I ask is a nice cup of coffee. Why do you insist on provoking me?"

Amalia's discontented mother dropped the sugar-coated churro back onto her plate. The pouting, middle-aged woman wore a frilly, colorful gown and fluffy updo. Slightly overweight, Luisa Maritimo, a fussy, self-centered woman, expected to be catered to all hours of the day, and Amalia didn't know who was more overindulged, her mother or the queen.

Amalia took the plate from her with a frustrated sigh. "I never know . . ."

"Don't huff at me, ungrateful child."

The door to their meager dwelling opened, and her father interrupted, "Amalia, the carriage is outside waiting for you. Go pack your things."

The patriarch of their home, Gordon Maritimo, short, pudgy, and reeking of cologne, stood at the head of their worn kitchen table with his hands in his pockets, eyes bloodshot and weary from the long, sleepless night. His thick, disheveled hair and thin mustache were his charming features. Often pleasant but grossly insecure, Señor Maritimo secluded his family on a ten-acre farm and slaved to keep his wife happy.

"A carriage for me? I thought we decided I would stay," Amalia said.

"*You* decided you would stay. I decided you would go." Her father took a handkerchief out of his pocket and wiped his brow. "Don't stand there like a dumb animal. Vamos."

An unnatural wail came from her mother's throat. Señor Maritimo gave a heavy sigh, shook his head, and shooed Amalia up the stairs before taking his wife by the arm to their bedroom.

Amalia wiped her hands on her tattered apron and tossed it in the corner. Staring at the moldy, peeling walls over the stove, she wiped a tear and made her way up the uneven stairs her father built to the two bedrooms the eight children shared. Amalia and her three younger sisters—Josephine, Maria, and Jacqueline—slept in the larger room to the left overlooking the front yard, and the boys slept in the room set against the mountain with no window.

"This isn't right," a kind voice said.

Gordy, her twin brother, unfolded his muscular arms and met her at the top of the landing. He had been Amaia's constant companion in their younger years, but they'd been forced apart by daily rituals. Once plump and playful, a chiseled, careworn Gordy stood in front of her without his usual smile. Apart from their doleful expressions, the two looked nothing alike. Gordy towered over Amalia's petite frame. His brown eyes and straight black hair stood in stark contrast to her brilliant green eyes and curly, rich brown locks. Despite the differences, they shared a unique bond, like most twins.

He plucked the stick holding her hair up. Gordy's warm eyes held her as he tried to hold his composure. Failing a smile to lighten the mood, Amalia took the hand-carved stick from him and twisted her hair back up.

"I'll never forget the day you gave this to me. Papa scolded you for spending so much time on it when you should have been harvesting mulberries."

Biting the insides of his cheeks, Gordy looked away.

"Maybe I won't go. The way Mama has protested Papa's arrangement, she could insist I stay, though I would never have guessed she cared for me that much."

"Even if she did insist, why would you want to stay? No matter how hard you work, it's never enough for her. I can't watch Papa turn a blind eye anymore when Mama treats you with such contempt."

"You've always been my truest friend."

"As soon as I get the chance, I'm leaving," Gordy continues. "I want to have a say about my future."

"Speaking up for me at supper last night was very brave."

"It made no difference."

"It made a difference to me." Desperate for his undivided attention, she took his large hands in hers. "I have an important question to ask you before . . . before I forget. Last week, while I was skimming through Mama's old Bible, I came across a list of all the family members recorded on the front pages. I don't know why I never noticed it before, but my name wasn't under yours. The things he's said, the way he's been talking—do you think Papa always planned to send me away?"

Gordy pulled his hands away. "How should I know? I don't look through Mama's Bible because, if you remember, it is *forbidden*."

"I got tired of reading the only other book in the house."

Her brother didn't respond.

"Gordy, you must promise me something. Watch over Thomas? You know how he gets into trouble. Protect him from Mama."

Gordy nodded, wiped his nose on his sleeve, and brushed past her to go down the stairs. In their fifteen years together, Amalia couldn't remember the last time she'd seen him close to tears.

She crossed the short distance to her room and gathered her meager belongings. The sunlight streaming through their small window beckoned to her. Amalia wandered over to peer down at her future parked in front of their small, two-story dwelling. The carriage looked worn and unimpressive. Though she'd never met the man who would be her employer, her father praised his grand nobleness and high connections incessantly the night before.

Someone tugged at Amalia's elbow. Five-year-old Thomas stood at her side with puffy eyes and a runny nose. She pulled him onto her lap in an embrace.

He whispered, "I want to go with you, Ama."

Voices from downstairs floated toward them—their parents.

"I don't understand why you are acting like this," her father said. "I explained everything to you last night. You knew this day would come, Bonita. She was destined for this."

Mama wailed, "How will I ever live without my Amalia? She is everything to me. You should have given me more warning."

Amalia perked up.

"Ama?"

"Shh, machito, I want to hear."

Thomas fell silent and nuzzled her neck.

Her father's voice softened. "Luisa, we will be more comfortable in a larger house and have special privileges—things you have longed for. I can finally provide for you the way you deserve. Our patience has paid off."

Patience about what?

". . . agreed to this long ago. We have been blessed with many lovely children to help us start our new life. Everything will work out, you will see."

Agreed to what? What is he saying?

Thomas started to sob. Amalia ran her fingers through his light-brown hair and rocked to calm him. "Thomas, look at me."

"Do you think Mama will change her mind and let you stay?" he asked.

Amalia dared not hope.

More arguing distracted her.

"Por favor, mi amor, as long as we have each other, we will be happy, no?" her father said.

"You know nothing!" Mama screamed.

Amalia set Thomas down and rushed to the top of the stairs. "Papa, clearly Mama wants me to stay. Think about the children. This isn't the right time to send me away. I suggest we wait a few months before making a final decision."

"The decision *has* been made!" Señor Maritimo yelled from beyond the kitchen. "Your mother doesn't want you to stay."

Amalia's heart pounded. "But she just said . . ."

Her father appeared at the base of the stairs with a red face and sweat running down his temples. "You need to listen to my words, Amalia. You're only valuable to your mother because she—"

"Because I have trained a perfectly adept housekeeper and nursemaid and cook." Her mother yanked on Papa's arm, forcing him to face her. Finger close enough to pick his nose, she said, "I have worked tirelessly for years to train Amalia to be the very best of housekeepers, and now you want to give her away to a man who is a deceptive manipulator, a man who has done nothing to benefit our family. He has charmed you into this farce by promising you more land and social position just so he can get what he wants and reap the rewards of my hard work. It's completely unfair. With her gone, all the work will fall on me. None of our daughters have a single ounce of usefulness."

Señor Maritimo ran his hands through his thick hair, exasperated. He took her shoulders into his hands. "Your cousin assured me you will have a housemaid to attend to your needs. There is nothing you need worry about." He kissed her. When Mama didn't pull away, he kissed her again. Amalia turned her back, numb from the latest revelation. *I really am good for only one thing. I'm a servant in my own home. She's never loved me.*

Realizing the truth in her father's hurtful words, Amalia walked back to her room to find Thomas curled up on her bed, sniffing back more tears.

"Who is going to cook for us? You always make sure I get something to eat, and you keep my food from touching on the plate."

"Shh. Gordy will help you."

"But who will make my hurts better? He and Antonio are busy helping Papa. No one wants to play with me, not Jacqueline or Diego.

Maria and Josephine always push me away. They only talk to me in French because they know I can't understand."

Amalia sighed. "I know."

Their mother never taught her French. Even if she did want to learn a different language or play the harpsichord like her sisters, she didn't have the time to devote to it. Since Amalia was five years old, Mama turned the cleaning over to her, as well as the laundry, and a child always needed attending. By the time she was seven and could hold a skillet with one hand, she took over the cooking too. Maybe it was better for her to go, but leaving Thomas behind took all the pleasure away from a potentially exciting new adventure.

"I think you are old enough to start helping on the farm, Thomas."

"You do?" Thomas looked at her with his big brown eyes. Since the day he came into this world, he preferred Amalia to anyone else. She suspected their mother held a grudge against their closeness, and that's why he suffered the brunt of her foul moods.

Maybe if he is busy on the farm, he won't have occasion to play tricks and cause trouble for Mama. "Si. You are growing up."

Señor Maritimo yelled up the stairs, "Thomas, get your siblings and meet in the front yard!"

Tears stung Amalia's eyes, so she pulled him into an embrace. "Machito, I must go. I will visit you whenever I can." Her heart pricked. *How will I find my family after they move? How will I visit?* "Try harder to be good and stay out of Mama's way. No more hiding little critters for her to discover. She doesn't like them."

"Si, Ama." He kissed her cheek.

Amalia buried her face in his hair, breathing in his familiar scent. *How can I leave him? He needs me.*

"You promise to come visit?"

Amalia swallowed hard and pulled back to look into his eyes. "Every chance I get." A smile grew on his face before he bounded off to find the others.

She grabbed her bag, made her way down the stairs, and dashed out the side door unseen. Stepping outside, the clucking of chickens and snorts of pigs greeted her as they did every day of her life. Shading her eyes from the sun, she approached the leaning shed her father and the boys had built to find Gordita, the family workhorse, a dapple-gray Spanish-Norman, lazily chewing on hay. Amalia gave her a carrot and rubbed her nose.

"Something sweet for my sweet friend." She kissed the horse's velvety-soft nose. "I couldn't leave without saying good-bye. I will miss you, querido amigo."

Gordita nodded her head and flapped her lips at Amalia. Grabbing her jowls, Amalia pulled Gordita's forehead to hers and rested for a moment, relishing their closeness. "I'll see you again, I promise."

Amalia made her way to the front yard to find her father and four brothers standing in a line under the shade of the portico. Her mother and sisters must have decided to miss the farewell ceremony.

Wasting no time, she approached Gordy and their younger brother by a year, Antonio. "Os amo, brothers. I will see you soon, I hope." She leaned into Gordy and kissed him on the cheek. "Take care of Thomas. You promised."

Gordy cleared his throat, but no words escaped him. He nodded and looked away. Antonio held the hand of the baby of the family. Diego was too young to know what was happening. Amalia squatted next to him. He pulled his hand away from Antonio and placed both arms around Amalia to receive her kiss.

"Be a good niño."

Finally free of his captor, Diego giggled and ran off toward the shed.

Last was Thomas, who held to Señor Maritimo's leg.

Amalia knelt and took Thomas into her arms, kissing his cheek. "You will never be far from my thoughts. Be good, Machito."

Rising to face her father, she said, "I will miss our adventures together, Papa. Hopefully, I will get a chance to see everyone again soon, but we never talked about where you are taking the family. How will I find you?"

His ears turned red before he spoke. "Ah . . . well, the terms of our agreement are that you will stay with Señor Tudó from now on."

Amalia's breath caught. "I can never come home?"

"No."

She shot a glance at Thomas. He reacted by sending up a howl and grabbing at Amalia.

"You promised to come see me. You promised, Ama!"

"I know, Thomas. I know." She looked at her father with searching eyes. "Why? Did I do something to make you hate me?"

Señor Maritimo pulled Thomas from her.

"Papa?" she squeaked.

Thomas cried, "Take me with you, Ama. Don't leave me!"

Amalia tried to take him, but Señor Maritimo held him back. He nodded to the coachman, who took her by the arm and led her to the carriage.

"No." Her voice cracked as she yelled over her shoulder, "Thomas, te amo. Don't forget me." The driver pulled her toward the carriage. Amalia called out to her twin, "Gordy?"

He stared after her, hands in his pockets, tears creeping down his tortured features. Though he stood up for her the night before, he remained silent as she stumbled toward her uncertain future.

Shoved into the carriage, Amalia lost her balance and fell to the rough black floor between the red velvet seats, skinning her knees. The door slammed behind her. The lock clicked.

Thomas's cries intensified when she disappeared from his view. Amalia struggled to the window only to witness him squirm out of Señor Maritimo's arms and run after her.

Amalia pounded on the window to warn him as the carriage started moving. "No, Thomas. Go back."

"Ama, don't go! Don't leave me. Por favor, come back!" Thomas's little legs ran so fast he caught up to the carriage. Gordy yanked him out of the way before the wheel caught hold and rolled over him.

Amalia shoved a fist into her mouth to keep from crying out. She crumbled to the floor and pressed her head between her hands to block out the desperation in Thomas's eyes as he chased after her. Finally, she cried as loud as she wanted, releasing all her anguish for sweet Thomas, for the love she never felt from her mother, and for her father's betrayal.

Bougainvillea

CHAPTER 2

I T DIDN'T SEEM like more than a couple of hours passed when the carriage slowed. Amalia sat up and looked out the window to witness a beautiful city, and the ruins of a castle high on a hilltop. Built close together, small, neatly kept homes came into view. They were made of adobe or stone and red tile roofing. Planted where they could get the best sun, quaint little herb and vegetable gardens graced each yard. The pleasant scene suggested a sense of community, and Amalia longed to be a part of such a neighborhood.

The aroma of freshly baked bread introduced Amalia to the center of town. Her stomach growled. She searched out the small window in anticipation of what she would see—the local market. On her travels with her father, Amalia visited many small towns along the southeast coast of España. It was the only time she experienced the rich culture of her country.

The carriage had arrived at the perfect time, when all the tables and booths with an assortment of delicious vegetables, fruits, cheeses, breads, and meats from the local area and imported were set out for people to sample and purchase. Her favorite—tables filled with colorful spices— dotted the square. People of all ages milled about. Young children ran under and through the many displays, merchants yelling after them to be more careful.

The carriage jerked to a stop. Amalia heard the latch click, and the door swung open to reveal the driver who had forced her into her current prison. He was a tall, middle-aged man with obsidian eyes and straight, thick hair, cut short and neatly combed. His hat and cloak had been removed to reveal a slightly plump physique. Offering his hand, the driver smiled a white, straight-toothed grin and helped her from the carriage. "I hope your ride was comfortable."

Taken aback by his pleasant smile, Amalia almost forgot to speak. "It was fine, gracias."

"We will stretch our legs here before heading on."

"Where are we?"

"Lorca."

"So this isn't our destination?"

"No, señorita. You are going to a trade school in Murcia before coming back to Lorca."

"Trade school? I've been trained my whole life to keep house and cook and care for children."

A sour look crossed the driver's features. "Si. It is Señora Carolina's wish you receive training before joining her household."

"Is she the master's wife? Do you know the señora, señor?"

"Let us not be so formal. You may call me . . . Manuel." Amalia nodded and looked toward the market.

He followed her gaze. "The market is very busy today."

"I love the market. I have visited many different markets with my father over the years to sell our produce, mulberry wine and preserves. It's where I get new ideas for recipes."

"Would you like to take a look?"

Amalia's heart felt heavy, but she agreed. "Is there time?"

"I'm sure we can make a small exception at this stop. It will be our little secret, but first you may want to take a private moment. I'll point you the way."

Upon returning, Manuel offered his arm to escort her down the street. He held her tightly to him, too tightly for her comfort, so she attempted to put some space between them. His grip did not loosen. Trying not to be alarmed by his familiarity, she concentrated on the sights and smells of the fresh flowers, spices, and food on display instead of the uneasy feeling welling within her. Along their path, people stopped and nodded in her guide's direction.

"Are you from Lorca? Everyone seems to know you," Amalia said.

"Sí."

A canopy of dangling scarves brushed at her face, and she chuckled. Manuel responded with a laugh. She fingered a bright red-and-orange scarf with turquoise beaded tassels. *I wonder how Thomas is doing.*

"Would you like a scarf? This would look lovely on you."

Amalia stuttered, "I-I don't have the money for such finery."

"I'll buy it for you." Manuel reached for the scarf.

She pulled back. "No . . . That is kind of you to offer, but I would have little occasion to wear it." Amalia tried to relax from the tension building inside her at his presumptive offer.

He smiled his straight-toothed grin and continued to the next row of stands.

They walked past fragrant fruit and vegetables before stopping by the bakery. Amalia's stomach growled.

She covered her belly. "I would like to buy some bread and cheese, por favor. I haven't eaten since early this morning."

"Of course. I'll be just a moment."

Amalia reached out to catch his arm. "Wait. I have money."

"I insist on paying for your meals. Stay here." The tone Manuel used startled Amalia out of objecting. He was back quickly with a paper bag of bread and hard cheese.

"Gracias."

"Is there anything else you would like to see before we journey on?"

"I'd like to go to a spice table. Smelling the fresh herbs and spices inspires me with new ideas for meals."

"I doubt you'll ever have a use for those skills again."

That's quite a supposition. His manner suggested he was master of all things, not humble and reserved like Amalia assumed a servant should behave.

"Do you work for Señor Tudó?"

"He is a powerful man. Everyone works for him."

Because of this Señor Tudó, I'll never see Thomas again, and I hate him for it.

Manuel broke the silence. "You loved your family."

"Shouldn't everyone love their family?"

Manuel laughed. "I never really cared for my family. My father was always in pursuit of a way up or a way out, and my brother, well, he died young. My mother was the only one dear to me."

Amalia didn't comment. They stopped at a spice stand, and she lowered her head over the saffron.

"You were close to your brothers?" Manuel asked.

I don't want to talk about my family. "Si, I was closest to my twin brother, Gordy, and my little brother Thomas." Amalia faced Manuel. "Do you know what my responsibilities will be at the Tudó estate?"

"Not entirely."

"Then I may need to cook, which would be a good thing because I am an excellent cook."

Taking her arm and pulling her away, he said, "They already have a cook, señorita. I suggest you get these silly ideas out of your head and stick to what you are good at."

Amalia mulled the comment over in her head. *He knows nothing of my abilities. I am good at many things.*

The next stretch of her journey lasted torturously long. Left only to herself, haunting thoughts of the strange man who drove her to Murcia and then being sent to work for a master who cared for no one other than himself kept her from falling asleep. Several hours passed before the carriage stopped. Amalia spent the final thirty minutes with her thighs clenched tightly together to keep from losing her water.

They stopped in a small town called Totana for a short break, just long enough to get some relief and eat la merienda. Amalia did little to hide her discomfort around Manuel. He tried to make genial conversation, but Amalia didn't encourage him.

Almost to the carriage, Manuel smiled. "The next stop is six hours away. Try to get some rest. I had a cushion and blanket set in the carriage to help make the journey more comfortable. If you need to stop for any reason, knock on the back walright there."

Amalia mumbled, "I wish I had known that earlier."

"Pardon me?"

"Nothing. Gracias." Amalia stepped inside the coach and closed the door before he could do it for her.

Night fell, and the countryside darkened, making it difficult for her to watch the blossoming trees and flowers pass by. Thankful for the cushion and blanket, she finally drifted to sleep.

The carriage jerked to a stop, startling Amalia awake. She didn't recognize her surroundings. Manuel's disconcerting grin greeted her upon opening the carriage door.

"We are here, pequeña."

The way he called her *pequeña* made the hairs on the back of her neck stand on end. Amalia paused before taking the hand he offered, and Manuel's black eyes flashed with something—anger, perhaps—before turning neutral. She tried to control the shiver that ran through her, but he'd noticed her reticence, and his manner hardened.

With Amalia's bag in hand, Manuel took off at a quickened pace toward a drab, gray building. The massive dwelling didn't appear welcoming, and Amalia felt tears sting her eyes.

This is my home for the next six months. I've traded one prison for another.

Manuel dropped her bag on the steps before knocking the rapper on the massive doors. "Buenas noches, señorita." He tipped his head and left her standing at the door, wide-eyed and alone.

She yelled after him, "But wait, what do I say? Are there any instructions for me?"

He ignored her as he climbed back onto the carriage and drove away.

Chamomile

CHAPTER 3

AFTER A WASTE of six months training Amalia things she already knew, she was on her way back to Lorca in what seemed to be the same well-used carriage, only a different driver held the reins. The thought of her previous driver made her skin itch, and she hoped to never see him again.

Amalia dreaded meeting the man who had changed her life and separated her from Thomas. Growing up in Puerto Lumbreras, Amalia's life was as consistent as the rising and setting of the sun, but with the changes and new experiences she faced, it was a struggle to keep her nerves under control. The circles under her eyes affirmed her apprehension.

The journey was arduous and long. Finally, a massive fortress appeared, the same grand fortress she saw when traveling through Lorca. Taking a sharp turn through the opening of a massive stone wall, the carriage entered the estate grounds.

Amalia sat up with anticipation. On either side of the carriage stood rows of manicured cypress trees like pillars reaching to the sky. She grabbed a tool to pry open the windows. Fresh air brushed her face. She took in a deep breath, and a mixture of flora tickled her senses, making Amalia laughed with delight. Vibrant colors dotted the grounds.

First impressions are everything. Maybe my new life will be better than I imagined.

Farther up the gravel road, bushes of blooming lavender, ivy, and a variety of ferns replaced the cypress trees. The gardens were skillfully accented by crafted clay pots overflowing with reds, yellows, and purples. The carriage rolled past a large vineyard and up a slight incline.

Amalia's mouth fell open when the grand house came into view. A white rock structure flanked by an old olive grove cascaded up the mountainside; the magnificent structure featured three archways leading to a heavy wooden door with two large windows on either side. Red tile roofing stood in wonderful contrast to the pale rock, and Amalia counted eight windows, with individual balconies, lining the second floor.

An open balcony at the upper end of the house ignited her imagination. Featuring another set of three archways overlooking the immaculate grounds below, it was the perfect scenery for evening parties in the warmer months. Amalia's heart fluttered picturing herself leaning over the railing in an elegant, pale dress—her face lit by soft candlelight—and a wealthy young man beckoning from below, seeking her favor.

Loud commotion near the carriage wheels drew her back to the present. A papa goose chased after the horses, honking at them to stay away from his family, who'd taken up residence near a small pond to the right of the estate. Amalia smiled and looked to the other side of the carriage to watch the grand entrance of the house disappear from view. They pulled around the side of the manor below the arched balcony, and a well-dressed young man opened the door to help her down.

An older gentleman stepped forward and introduced himself. "I am Señor Luis Valdez, the butler." With perfect decorum, a straight back, and steely regard, he motioned for her to follow. "Vamos, señorita. Your coach is late, and the Tudós have been waiting for your arrival."

A woman waited just outside the side entrance. Señor Valdez nodded at her, then turned to Amalia. "This is the housekeeper, Señora Morales.

You will report directly to her." He instructed the footmen behind Amalia to take her bag to her room, then turned back to the stately, older woman. "I will leave you to it," he said and walked inside.

Looking like she'd just eaten a lemon, Señora Morales considered Amalia before saying, "Follow me, por favor."

The housekeeper's demeanor was stern and intimidating. She appeared to be in her late forties with only a few smile wrinkles at the corner of her eyes and mouth. Her hair was dark and perfectly coiffed. She wore a black dress, pleated down the front with a white scalloped collar.

A small flight of stairs greeted them as they entered the residence. They descended to a large hallway, and it took some time for Amalia's eyes to adjust to the dimly lit area leading to the kitchen and servant common area. A girl about her age with mousy brown hair, a cleft chin, and a lovely smile stood perfectly straight, hands folded gracefully in front of her. She appeared to be waiting for Amalia, who couldn't help but smile back at her.

"Señorita Maritimo, this is Sonia Vela. She arrived here last week. You will be sharing a room together. Though your responsibilities are vastly different, hers is the only other room with a vacancy. You will just have to adjust to the difference in your daily schedules."

Amalia could comfortably look Sonia in the eye. She wore the uniform of a scullery maid, and a pang of jealousy shot through Amalia. She'd learned at the trade school she would be attending the Tudós' two young daughters.

Señora Morales continued addressing Amalia, "The señora of the house, Señora Carolina, insists she inspect you after you are cleaned up. This way to your room."

They ascended the stairs to the servant's floor in the back of the house. Señora Morales paused for Sonia to retrieve a small bundle from an armoire. At the end of the hall, Sonia opened the door to a small room to reveal two beds divided by an accent table with a single brass candleholder. One dresser with six drawers stood opposite the door. It seemed they would share that as well. The only other furniture in the room was a small vanity for washing.

"Quickly change and freshen up before meeting me back in the hall near the servants' common area for introductions."

The girls curtsied and waited until the housekeeper left.

"This is your uniform," Sonia explained. "I am responsible to help you with your schedule and teach you the rules of the house. Let's quickly go back down, so you can make a good first impression."

Sonia had been hiding her hands from view, and Amalia realized why when she handed her the bundle and saw them chapped and raw. Sensing Sonia's embarrassment, Amalia pretended not to notice. "Good idea. I think we will have a great adventure here. This could be our chance to gain a better life."

"Not likely. Neither of us will ever realize a better situation than this. Don't forget your training. We are only servants and must remain invisible."

Amalia frowned and looked away.

Sonia straightened her back, hands fisted by her side, and lifted her dimpled chin. "I have never been treated nicely by people of wealth and prominence. This place is no different. I plan to become a housekeeper like Señora Morales, maybe replace her here. That is the only realistic advancement I'm expecting. You should follow my example."

"I'm sorry. I know I should listen to you, but I've always dreamed of living like this someday. I guess I'm just enchanted by this house and its possibilities."

A crease formed between Sonia's brows.

"Don't look so concerned. I know my place," said Amalia.

"I would appreciate it if you didn't ruin my chances by nurturing those daydreams."

Amalia took a deep breath and finished tying her apron. "There. How do I look?"

"Exactly as you should. Vamos."

Amalia smiled at her, and a smile flitted over Sonia's pale face as she led the way.

The girls scampered down three flights of narrow stairs, Amalia pinching Sonia the whole way.

"Stop it." Sonia tried to swat her away.

"You are too stiff. Relax a little. This is exciting."

Sonia scowled. "Maybe for you."

When they neared their destination, Sonia stopped to compose herself by straightening her apron and cap. "Amalia, it is now time to behave. Remember, how you conduct yourself is a reflection on my tutoring."

Amalia rolled her eyes. Together, they stepped around the corner to come face-to-face with the housekeeper.

"Well done, señoritas. I'm impressed. The señor and señora will be here shortly."

Señor? That's unusual. Usually, it's just the señora who meets the staff. Maybe they don't hold strictly to protocol. That would be a relief.

Señora Morales led the girls into the large space between the servants' dining room and kitchen. Filled with restless anticipation, Amalia found it extremely difficult to stand at attention. It took footsteps approaching for her to freeze. A regal couple glided into the room together. The señora was a real beauty—lustrous, dark hair and deep brown eyes. Her complexion was flawless, but her ruby red lips pursed like she smelled something unpleasant.

She leaned her ear toward her husband, who engaged her attention with a low whisper. Tall and a bit plump around the middle, the man's strut was proud, his manner familiar. When he turned his obsidian eyes toward Amalia, she recognized him immediately.

"Manuel?" she said.

The Tudós stopped abruptly. Señora Carolina stared wide-eyed at Amalia, but Señor Tudó looked at her with a smirk on his face as if laughing at her folly.

"What did you say?" Señora Morales asked.

Amalia lowered her eyes.

Señora Carolina's glare seared through Amalia. Shifting her attention to her husband, the señora said, "I see now why you insisted on *this* additional housemaid."

He looked at her with false innocence. "I only think of you, mi amor."

Bitterness flitted over her face, then was gone. She turned to Señora Morales and mumbled something, and the señor sauntered over to the girls. It didn't escape Amalia how he looked at poor Sonia with disgust, but when he walked up to Amalia, he licked his lips and winked at her. Anger boiled inside her, and she challenged his gaze.

"Aw, you dare look me in the eye." She said nothing.

He chortled. "I see your mother's familiar fire in you already."

"You know my mother?"

"Really, did you learn nothing in your training?" Señora Carolina had pulled away from her conversation to confront Amalia. "You do not speak unless given permission."

"Well said, mi cielo," Señor Tudó cooed.

"Si, señora, forgive me." Amalia curtsied and lowered her eyes.

When the woman turned back to Señora Morales, Señor Tudó stepped closer to Amalia. He yanked the cap off her head and pulled the neck of her blouse down to reveal the tops of her shoulders.

Her breath caught.

His hands lingered on her skin. Tudó walked behind her, took a handful of her hair, and breathed it in. Amalia tried to put some distance between them, but he had a strong hold on her.

Is no one seeing this?

Getting the attention of his wife, he held up the cap he'd removed. "Mi cielo, should we not allow this one to keep her hair down instead of up in these miserable caps? It would be such a disappointment not to have her long tresses admired by our many esteemed guests."

Señora Carolina's eyes flitted over Amalia, ignoring the difference in her uniform. Amalia tried to act calm but risked a look at the señora, hoping for mercy.

Por favor, say no.

An almost imperceptible look of pity flashed in the señora's eyes before she waved her husband off. "As you wish."

He had triumphed. Señor Tudó chuckled in Amalia's ear before walking to his wife, offering his elbow, and leaving the room.

Amalia glanced sideways at Sonia, disappointed to see her staring at her toes.

HOLLY BROUGH

"Now." Señora Morales fixed Amalia's blouse and clapped her hands for attention. "You will quickly organize your things before we meet again in thirty minutes at the side entrance where you first arrived. I will take you on a tour of the house and grounds and explain your duties. Señorita Vela, you may join us. A month from now, the family will be leaving for an extended holiday to Madrid. We have much to do before their departure." Amalia and Sonia scurried off.

As soon as they were out of earshot, Sonia asked, "What happened to your blouse?"

"The señor was touching me and smelling my hair."

Sonia looked shaken. "I saw him put his hand to your neck out of the corner of my eye, but I didn't notice anything amiss until Señora Morales adjusted your blouse. I told you not to draw attention to yourself."

"I didn't do anything to draw attention to myself. I just stood there, like you did."

"No, you spoke out of turn."

"Señor Tudó was my driver to trade school. He told me to call him Manuel. The way he spoke to me and the things he said led me to believe he served the señor, so when he walked in, I was surprised and responded as any confused person would."

"You aren't anyone. You're a servant, and the señor has shown a strange interest in you," Sonia said.

Amalia bit her bottom lip. "Did you hear him mention my mother?"

"If the señor knows your mother, that could explain why you got this position."

"Maybe . . . I vaguely recall hearing my mother complain about a dishonest man who did nothing to benefit our family and him reaping the rewards of her hard work. Sounds like him."

They reached their room, and Sonia held open the door for Amalia. "After what happened today, I think you should avoid him."

Amalia stepped into their shared room and stopped in her tracks. Sonia ran into her.

"Ouch. Why did you . . ."

Amalia walked to her bed and carefully picked up a red-and-orange scarf with turquoise beaded tassels. "I told him I didn't want this."

"Told who?"

Amalia dropped the scarf back onto the bed. "Manuel—er—Señor Tudó. We stopped here in Lorca and visited the market. I saw this, and he offered to buy it for me. I refused."

"You can't accept it now."

"I know, but what do I do with it?"

"We need to hurry. Put the scarf in this drawer." Sonia opened an empty drawer. "My things only filled one drawer. You may use the rest of them if you need."

Amalia rubbed the gooseflesh on the back of her neck, not moving from her spot.

Sonia picked up the scarf, tossing it in the drawer, out of sight. "Wake up, Amalia. We need to get downstairs."

Daffodil

CHAPTER 4

SEÑORA MORALES WAS waiting for the girls at the side entrance when they arrived. She gave them a nod. "Bueno. We will start in the living quarters." The señora paused. "Señorita Maritimo, are you feeling well?"

"I'm fine."

She considered Amalia for a moment. "Very well. All the rooms are located in the front of the house on the second floor with the exception of the master's rooms, which face the olive grove in the back of the house. As you may have noticed, the servants' quarters take up the third floor at the back of the house. This way, por favor."

Amalia concentrated on the intricate tile floor leading to stairs near the front of the house.

Señora Morales spoke over her shoulder. "Señorita Maritimo, when you are not needed in the nursery, you will help with the housework. Each room you see today must be freshly made up as soon as it is vacated and dusted once a day whether someone is using it or not. Make it your duty to know when guests are out, so you can clean their rooms immediately. There is an assignment board in the servants' common area."

At the top of the stairs was a long hallway lined with doors. Señora Morales showed them each room in turn as they passed.

"These first three rooms belong to the Tudós' young daughters, Señoritas Matilde and Josefa. The bedrooms are joined by this large nursery." Señora Morales showed them into the nursery.

Amalia marveled at the grandeur of the room. Admiring the space, she stubbed her toe on something and stepped back into Sonia.

"Oh, sorry. I almost stepped on this." Amalia bent down and picked up a type of glass doll. "It's beautiful. I've never seen such a lovely toy."

Señora Morales took the doll from Amalia, brushed its silk gown straight, and placed it at a miniature table with chairs. "It's a porcelain doll from China. They are very fragile."

Amalia looked around the room to see it filled with toys. *All of these toys for just two children. If I had just one of these to share with my siblings, entertaining them would have been so much easier. Look at all the books.*

Sonia had to pull Amalia out of the room when it was time to move on, and Amalia noticed Sonia's red, chaffed hands again. She wanted to say something about them, but the housekeeper continued.

"This is Señora Carolina's private suite. Of course, she shares the master's suite, but the lady of the house insists on her own personal space." Señora Morales opened the door for the girls to peek in. Amalia didn't just peek. She pushed through to the center of the room and turned full circle, taking in every elegant piece of furniture.

Sonia's jaw dropped, and Señora Morales put her hands on her hips. "Really, señorita. You forget yourself."

Amalia felt no remorse. She merely smiled as they continued the tour across the hall.

"A chandelier and beautiful hand-painted roses on the walls, can you believe it? A velvet chaise by the window! It's perfect to curl up on and read a book," Amalia said behind her hand to Sonia.

Sonia shook her head and mouthed for Amalia to pay attention.

She turned to hear, ". . . master suite. The señor likes to have their bed turned down each evening before they retire. Fresh water should be brought up twice daily and the biscuit jar filled. Some of our staff are on holiday. Señorita Maritimo, you will be responsible for that assignment."

Amalia shuddered. "Si, señora."

The master suite overlooked the olive grove just as Señora Morales had said. Heavy curtains hung on the two windows to block out the morning sun. The bed was large, and two overstuffed leather chairs sat in front of a stone fireplace.

They walked across the master suite through another door to a smaller room. A single bed, dresser, and washing table were the only furnishings.

"This room is reserved for Señor Tudó. No one but his valet is allowed in his private chambers." She looked at Amalia until Amalia nodded. "Vamos, we still have much to go over."

Amalia turned to shut the door and noticed some green gems partially exposed out of a black velvet bag tucked behind the wash basin. The curtains were drawn so the outdoor light hit the color perfectly, making the stones sparkle on the wall. Her curiosity was piqued, and she paused a moment.

Señora Morales cleared her throat, pulling Amalia out of her trance.

"Coming." Amalia shut the door behind her.

They walked in silence to the end of the hall. Beautiful brass candelabra sconces divided what Amalia assumed were family portraits, the largest of which faced them on a sizable wall of the grand staircase landing. It displayed a naked woman lounging provocatively across a velvet chaise. Amalia stared wide-eyed at the painting. Sonia turned a shade of pink.

Señora Morales noticed their expressions and offered some information as though she, too, was embarrassed by the work of art. "That is a portrait of Señor Tudó's mother, Pepita Tudó. I believe it belongs in a museum and not a family home."

Amalia looked at Sonia and mouthed, "His mother?"

Sonia shook her head and followed down the grand staircase to the main level of the house.

"Oh my. It sparkles like a thousand stars," Amalia said.

Sonia stifled a laugh.

Señora Morales stopped to admire it too. "Si, it is exquisite but a terrible burden to clean. This chandelier will have to be cleaned when the family leaves for Madrid. The chandelier in the Tudós' Paris mansion is almost twice the size, which can actually be lowered from the ceiling, thank goodness. But *this* one takes two days to clean because we use a ladder and lower each individual crystal down to be cleaned." Señora Morales let out a deep sigh. "It is tedious work."

The small party visited the sitting room, Señor Tudó's study, which was attached to the library—Amalia promised herself to frequent the library often—and the dining room. The house was immense, and Amalia was just beginning to realize how much work it would take to keep it clean.

"As you were taught in your training, the house is to stay in pristine condition for the family and their guests," the housekeeper said.

Amalia was about to ask if there was other help when Señora Morales answered her question, "In addition to you two girls, there are two other housemaids, two footmen, a nursemaid for the girls, and another scullery maid residing here at the estate."

That's a relief. "Where is everyone?" Amalia asked.

"They are on holiday or attending to their responsibilities. The family travels often in the summer, so only a minimal staff is necessary."

Sonia pinched Amalia to keep her quiet, but Amalia would not be dissuaded. "We haven't seen anyone on our tour."

Señora Morales stopped and faced her. "That should be no surprise to you, Señorita Maritimo. We have been touring the living quarters of the estate. You are to stay out of sight of everyone. I believe you were also taught *that* in your training. If not, it is a strict rule of the señor's."

Amalia bit her lower lip. "Si, I must have forgotten."

"Now you are reminded. See that you don't forget." The housekeeper waved them on. "We will now tour the grounds."

Amalia didn't follow. Sonia hissed at her to move, but Amalia was stuck in place with a puzzled look.

"What is it, señorita?" Señora Morales was losing her patience.

"If they already have a nursemaid and two other housemaids . . ." She couldn't finish the sentence.

"Why would they need you?" Scrutinizing Amalia, the señora continued, "That is a very good question, indeed."

Amalia's heart sank to her belly. *They didn't want me at home. I left Thomas for nothing and came to this horrible place. If they don't need my services, why am I here?*

"Enough of this. Let's continue."

Fresh air greeted the women, and Amalia perked up. She tried to whisper to Sonia how lovely it was outside, but Sonia ignored her.

The middle-aged housekeeper flourished her arm at the view. "As you can see, there are several paths to various places throughout the estate. We will take the one on the left. There is an enchanting flower garden the señora frequents. You are not to be seen in the garden without permission or while guests are visiting, understood?"

Both girls answered, "Si."

Amalia could smell vanilla and separated herself from the others to follow the uneven stone path to a delightful gazebo. It was woven with green ivy and tiny white flowers that gave off a wonderful fragrance. She took a handful of blooms and put them to her nose. Some movement in the corner of her eye gave her pause, and she looked around for the culprit. Nothing but bright bougainvillea graced the flower beds surrounding the gazebo and foot paths.

She heard another noise ahead of her. The strong smell of sweat permeated the air, and the hairs on the back of her neck stood up.

Amalia caught up to Sonia. "Did you see anyone else out here, like a man?" Sonia shook her head.

Amalia's focus shifted when she noticed her favorite flower, the golden gorse, growing under the most distinct cypress trees she'd ever seen. Trimmed to look like giant green cauliflower heads, they were the crowning feature of the garden.

"Charming, isn't it?" Señora Morales smiled.

She's pretty when she smiles.

"Señora Carolina designed this garden herself. It took only a few weeks to import the plants and have them ready for display, so meticulous were her instructions. The señora has a gifted eye for design." Motioning them on, she continued, "Our next stop is the horse stables. I don't know how familiar you señoritas are with horses, but these horses are thoroughbreds and kept on a strict diet."

Stables was all Amalia heard, and she rushed forward to get there first, but Sonia grabbed her arm in time to save her the embarrassment of moving ahead of the housekeeper. When the señora turned to address the girls, she found Amalia only inches away from her. She took a step back to create a comfortable distance.

"It seems you have an appreciation for horses, Señorita Maritimo?"

Amalia's smile grew. "Si, señora. I love horses."

"Seven horses reside here, but four of them took the family to their dinner party in Tiata."

Sonia kept her distance, but Amalia walked closer to the stalls.

"Would the stable hands allow me to help brush them down or feed them or muck out their stalls? I would enjoy helping," Amalia asked.

"I will speak with the stable master, but I don't foresee any reason why you wouldn't be permitted to help once in a while, as long as your main duties are taken care of first." She gave Amalia a firm look.

"Si, si. Of course, I will do my duties first. Gracias. I've missed my horse." Amalia could hardly contain her joy.

"I'll make the arrangements. It will take only a moment. You two may look around for a few minutes and become familiar with this area."

Amalia grabbed Sonia's hand to pull her closer to the nearest stall. Sonia took in a sharp breath and pulled her rough, cracked hand away.

"Sorry," Amalia said. "Are you alright?"

"Si. I'll stay right here." Sonia put her hands under the front of her apron.

Amalia approached the first horse, a black Andalusian mare. Sonia stared with wide eyes as the beautiful animal walked up to Amalia and nodded her head several times. Amalia placed both hands on the horse's jowls to steady her, then ran her hand along the mare's forehead and down the soft, velvety tip of her nose so she could sniff Amalia's hand. Moving closer, Amalia lightly blew into the horse's nose.

"Why did you do that?" Sonia asked.

"So she will learn my scent." The mare flapped her lips at Amalia, and she laughed. "I love the smell of fresh hay. I feel so at home here." She strode past several stalls until the last where the final horse was eyeing her. "Oh, you are wonderful. Hmm. That's strange."

"What is it?"

Amalia stood on her tiptoes to get a better look. "Señora Morales, this horse is saddled. The family has been gone for some time. Is there a reason the groom hasn't attended to him?"

The housekeeper shot her head around the stables. "It is time to end the tour. Before you retire to your room, you should be aware the Tudó family will arrive late in the evening after you have gone to bed. Señorita Vela, you know the routine, five o'clock sharp in the kitchen. Señorita Maritimo, Señora Carolina won't need your services until eight o'clock in the nursery. The young girls like to sleep in. Cook should have a meal prepared for you two in the kitchen, so go there first, then off to your rooms. It's been a long day. Vamos."

The saddled horse, a breed Amalia wasn't familiar with, flipped its head and caused her to stumble back. She quickly patted the horse on its nose and hurried back to the house with Sonia.

"That was strange. I've never seen her act so . . . I don't know, shaken," Sonia said. "The señora is always an example of calm deportment. I wonder what upset her."

"Maybe that horse is Señor Tudó's and someone neglected to care for the poor animal."

"Maybe."

Amalia lay on her back, staring at the ceiling in the dark. "Are you awake?" she asked.

"Sí."

"I can't sleep."

"Me either." Amalia heard Sonia turn under her covers and scratch the lye-damaged skin on her hands. "What are you thinking about?"

"The scarf," Amalia said.

"Don't think about that. It's put out of sight." After a pause, Sonia said, "We didn't get to talk much today about your time at trade school. You were there for six months like me, but I was a few weeks ahead of you, and our tasks are so different we never crossed paths. How did you like it?"

"I had a hard time adjusting to the rules." Sonia chuckled.

"For as long as I can remember, I was the one who enforced the rules and ran the house. Going to classes on things like making a proper bed, ironing a shirt, and dusting a table or candelabra were a waste of time. I already knew how to do those things, as well as care for children. I practically raised my five youngest siblings, but Señora Carolina insisted I attend the trade school before coming here." Amalia changed the subject. "Did you have a break before coming to the estate?"

"Si. I was able to go back home for a few days."

Amalia took a deep breath. *Don't think about Thomas.*

"It was nice to see my parents again."

Amalia scrunched her eyes to stay the tears.

"Didn't come straight here after training?" Sonia asked.

"Si."

"You must miss your family terribly."

"There were some things I enjoyed . . . at the trade school, I mean. I'd never been to Mass before. The service was confusing but nice. I mostly enjoyed the singing."

"You've never been to Mass?"

"No. I used to sneak my mother's Bible and read it, so I understood some of what the preacher was saying, but our family never went to church. We lived on the outskirts of town where we had little contact with anyone."

"Oh."

Amalia sighed. "The festivals they held in Murcia were the best part of living there. I loved the music and watching people dance in the plazas."

"I loved the Iglesia Catedral de Santa María. I felt such peace there," Sonia said.

"I thought the building was beautiful, especially the bell tower, but I don't understand why we worship Mary, who is a mortal. I thought we were supposed to worship God."

Sonia sat up in her bed. "Mary is the *mother* of God. She should be revered and worshipped. She is the most holy woman to ever walk the earth. We should pay homage and worship her as often as we can."

"I'm sorry, Sonia. Obviously, I know little of what I am talking about."

"It's fine. Noches."

Apparently dismissed, Amalia turned her back to Sonia and muttered, "Noches."

It seemed they'd been asleep only minutes when their bedroom door clicked. Amalia sat up, wondering if Sonia had already left for the kitchen.

"Sonia?"

No answer, but she could hear Sonia sleeping restlessly in the bed next to hers. Like so many times since she met Manuel Tudó, the hairs on the back of her neck stood up. The same pungent smell from the garden filled the air, or did it? She shivered involuntarily. Lying back on her pillow, Amalia tossed the rest of the night.

Poppy

CHAPTER 5

EIGHT O'CLOCK CAME too soon, but Amalia was at the nursery to meet Señora Carolina on time. Wearing a flowing muslin gown of pale mauve, the woman was even more beautiful in the morning. *She probably slept well last night.*

Señora Carolina sighed at the sight of Amalia as if seeing her was bothersome. She clapped for her daughters' attention. "Niñas, this is Señorita Maritimo. I present my two daughters, Señorita Matilde and Señorita Josefa."

Amalia curtsied, and the girls curtsied in return.

The older one, Josefa, said, "But where is Anita?"

"She is on holiday with her family for the next few weeks. She will meet us in Madrid."

Señora Carolina turned to Amalia. "Have the girls ready and in the gardens by eight thirty."

"Si, señora."

Señora Carolina gracefully walked away, leaving Amalia alone with the girls.

"Shall we do your hair?" Amalia asked, but the girls ran away from her. "Señoritas, por favor, come to the vanity so I can do your hair."

They were giggling and playing tag with each other. "Señoritas!" Amalia resorted to chasing them around the nursery. "Your mother will not be pleased if you aren't in the gardens soon."

Finally catching Matilde, Amalia forced the squirming girl onto her lap to braid her hair. As soon as the brush started moving through her hair, Matilde calmed down. Her shrewd hazel eyes studied Amalia in the mirror as she intricately plaited Matilde's thick, wavy tresses.

"How old are you, niña bonita?" Amalia asked.

"Three."

Josefa noticed their interaction and stopped running. "Do my hair like that."

Josefa looked to be about six years old. She had coarse jet-black hair, straight as a pin like her father's, and deep brown eyes like her mother's. With round cheeks and pouty lips, Josefa had the same entitled attitude as Amalia's own mother, especially when she walked to Amalia's side and waited her turn with folded arms and tapping toes.

"I would be happy to, señorita, if you sit nicely and wait until I am done with your sister's."

Josefa slumped down in an overstuffed chair built perfectly for her size and scowled at Amalia.

Matilde smiled. "I like this. It doesn't even hurt."

"I'm glad to hear it. I have little sisters of my own, so I've learned to be careful." "Oh." Matilde was well-mannered, and Amalia already liked her.

By the time Josefa was ready, they had to rush to the gardens to be on time. Sensing the urgency, the girls happily led the way to where Señora Carolina and Señor Tudó sat under an umbrella canopy in comfortable chairs surrounded by vibrant vegetation.

Amalia could feel Señor Tudó watch her every move as he always did. His beady black eyes skimmed over her body, making every inch of her skin crawl. "I'm sorry we are a little late. It took longer to get the girls' hair done than I expected," she said to the señora.

"I am not interested in your excuses, señorita. You may go."

Señor Tudó watched Amalia leave before excusing himself. "I will only be a moment, mi cielo."

Amalia heard him beg his pardon, knowing full well he was leaving to find her. She quickened her pace, finding the nearest large bush off the path to hide behind and holding her breath. He passed her three times before giving up the chase and returning to his family.

The night of Amalia's first dinner party, everything was abuzz in the kitchen. With most of the staff gone, everyone, even the housekeeper, Señora Morales, followed Cook Dulce's instructions and prepared trays. Cook and Sonia would remain downstairs, but everyone else rushed to serve the guests.

The meal went off without incident. Everyone convened in the upper gathering room and balcony for more wine and cigars. Amalia made her way around the grand room and into the open air, collecting empty wine glasses and giving Señor Tudó a wide berth.

The host himself stood in the middle of the parlor, drink in one hand, a cigar in the other, braying like a donkey with his comrades. Comments made behind hands and glances toward Amalia haunted her even when she tried to ignore them.

The footman, Ambrose, stood by the exit door, waiting for a full tray to take to the kitchen. Walking toward him, she smiled. "Here is another one. I don't know how much more they can drink."

"They will drink all night as long as the decanters and wine bottles keep coming."

"Ambrose, I don't think you're aware, but your lapel has a stain on it. You better take care of that before the señor notices."

"Gracias, señorita. I owe you one."

Amalia took an empty tray from him and made her way around the room again. The smoke-filled air agitated her lungs, and Amalia struggled to keep the tray steady and clear her lungs at the same time. Making her way to the parlor door to transfer her burden to Ambrose, she saw Sonia there instead. Forgetting her vigilance, she walked near Señor Tudó and felt someone grab her buttocks and squeeze. She jumped out of the way, tossing the tray toward Sonia, who reached out to grab it. It was no use. Too many glasses, some of them half full, flew through the air before shattering or tumbling to the imported Persian rug, staining the intricate design and cream tassels.

The women nearest the scene screamed. Señor Tudó and his comrades laughed at the girls' expense.

Amalia whispered to Sonia, "I'm so sorry. The señor grabbed my backside! I was completely—"

Without warning, Señora Morales appeared and grabbed Sonia by the ear, dragging her to the hall and reprimanding her in full view of the guests.

"How dare you come up here in your scullery uniform! You can imagine my outrage to see you mingling among the guests, causing a scene, and ruining the señor's imported rug. What were you thinking?"

"I couldn't find you. Ambrose needed to change his uniform, and we are so understaffed, I did what I thought a housekeeper would do. I took the responsibility upon myself to bring a tray up for Amalia, so the service wouldn't be interrupted."

"Well, you were wrong. Clearly, you lack good judgment, a virtue all housekeepers must possess."

Amalia rushed to Sonia's side. "Señora, it was my fault. I was the one who told Ambrose to change his uniform."

"That is not the point. Señorita Vela made a terrible judgement call. She is a scullery maid. Look at this mess."

Amalia tried not to look in the señor's direction. "I-I lost my balance and dropped the tray. Sonia was just trying to help me clean it up. She isn't to blame." Amalia could feel Señor Tudó's eyes on her, and she felt the need to rub the back of her neck.

"You must learn to follow orders, Señorita Vela. I have never been so disappointed. You will never improve your station, not if I have anything to do with it." Thrusting her arm toward the stairs, she added, "Finish cleaning up the kitchen, then off to bed. Out of my sight. Vamos." Sonia wiped a tear from her cheek and rushed away.

"As for you, Señorita Maritimo, I suggest you get Ambrose and clean up this disaster immediately."

"Si, señora." As Amalia left the area, she overheard the housekeeper apologize to the guests for the chaos and invite them to mingle on the balcony while the wine was soaked up and broken glass cleared away.

Amalia found Sonia in their room, wetting her pillow with her tears. She sat on Sonia's bed next to her. "I'm sorry about tonight."

"I just wanted to help. I have been so diligent in following the rules. She embarrassed me in front of everyone. Now I will never realize my dream of becoming a housekeeper. I really thought this was my chance. Nothing I did for my last employer pleased them, so I tried extra hard to do well and follow the rules here. It's gotten me nowhere."

Amalia got up and retrieved something from the dresser. "I have something for you. I made this with Cook's help after I noticed your hands. My mother had me make this for her sore, cracked feet. It will soothe your sores." She took one of Sonia's hands in hers and rubbed some cream into her tender, damaged skin.

Sonia took in a sharp breath but soon relaxed. "That's nice. Gracias. What is it made of?"

"Just oats, olive oil, water, and saffron."

"And Cook let you have all of that?"

"Well, I told her I was at her service for anything she needed."

"You did that for me?"

Amalia smiled. "It's hardly a sacrifice. I love being in the kitchen."

Fresh tears started down Sonia's cheeks.

"Am I hurting you?"

"No. I haven't been very kind to you since you arrived."

"It doesn't matter. I know you were doing what you thought was right."

Sonia offered her other hand and smiled. "I guess I know better now. It doesn't matter what I do, I'll never be more than a scullery maid to them."

"I think you and I should create our own destiny."

"How can we do that?"

"I don't know." Amalia paused. "Maybe we keep our eyes open for opportunities."

"What opportunities?"

"We'll know when we see them."

Amalia entered the garden room the following day, tray in hand, ignoring the smirk Señor Tudó wore as he watched her pour the coffee. She handed a cup to Señora Carolina first. When she handed the señor his cup, he caressed her hand until she pulled away, nearly dropping the cup in his lap.

"Where are my daughters?" the señora asked.

"In the nursery, señora. Did you want to see them?"

"No. Let them play."

"I propose another dinner party before we depart, mi corazón," Señor Tudó said.

Señora Carolina looked up from her letter. "We just had one. After last night's disaster, I wonder if that is a good idea. We leave in less than a fortnight."

"Nonsense. All the more reason to have one. Señorita Maritimo, you may go and inform Señora Morales of our plans. We'll set it for a week hence." He winked at her before waving her off.

Sonia was peeling the wax off the candelabras in the upper hallway when Amalia approached her. "Another dinner party has been arranged for a week from now."

"What? We just had one," Sonia said.

"I know."

Sitting down on the floor, Sonia wiped the perspiration off her forehead. "We have prepared so much food. I didn't know it was possible to entertain this often. Before you arrived, we only had a picnic with visiting dignitaries. The instructors at trade school never mentioned how difficult it would be to feed large parties. There is *one* good thing about it, though."

"The meal scraps," they both said in unison.

Amalia sat on the floor next to Sonia, her back against the wall. "I'm tired of hearing the señor tell his friends I am the most beautiful housemaid in all of España. The men look at me like I am a juicy chunk of meat. I can't do another party."

Rubbing her fingers, Sonia said, "I know."

"Your hands look better already."

"They feel better." She smiled.

The week went by without incident. Amalia took care of the children and made certain she was never alone with the señor though it had become harder and harder to think clearly with no sleep at night. Mistakes were certain to be made. Before Sonia left to help organize the food for the dinner party set to arrive, she spoke to Amalia in calming tones to help her relax and clear her head.

"You will avoid going anywhere near the señor and be deliberate in your responsibilities so no confusion can make you flounder. You will be fine if you follow the plan."

But after the last dinner party when the señor fondled her backside, Amalia didn't feel confident at all, so she sat on her bed gasping for air and praying for strength before heading down. No matter the encouraging words Sonia said to her, every inch of her skin crawled. Amalia rocked back and forth, laboring to numb her brain.

"What are you doing in your room, señorita?" Señora Morales stood at Amalia's door.

Amalia jumped to her feet. "I . . . I . . ."

"Are you ill?"

"No."

Taking her by the arm, the housekeeper said, "Señor Tudó has been asking for you. I need you serving tonight."

"Por favor . . ."

"Take a minute to gather yourself, then go down to the parlor."

The housekeeper left. Amalia wiped at her eyes, rolled her shoulders, and pulled her back straight before making her way to the kitchen. With a tray of wine bottles, Amalia made the climb up the stairs. After unloading her burden, she weaved in and out of groups of guests engaged in animated conversation, gathering empty glasses.

At least a hundred candles lit the richly furnished room. Elegant gowns and debonair black suits confronted her at every turn. Several guests were drinking wine and conversing, their host nowhere to be seen. Amalia took a deep breath and concentrated on performing her duties. Having acquired a tray full of empty goblets, she passed it to Ambrose, who quickly turned to leave. An unexpected arm took Amalia by the waist and pulled her behind the curtains, out of sight of the guests.

Amalia yelped, but a sweaty hand quickly clasped over her mouth.

His hot breath in her ear and his excitement against her hip, Señor Tudó whispered, "You look most beautiful tonight, señorita. I could hardly stand to admire you from a distance."

Amalia tried to shift so they weren't touching, his body odor almost suffocating her.

"I'll release my hold if you promise not to make a sound."

She nodded her agreement, and he slowly lowered his hand.

Avoiding his eyes, she said, "Señor Tudó, I have guests to attend."

"I think you can be spared for a few moments, no?" He brushed a loose strand of hair from her forehead.

Anger at his intimate gestures snuffed out Amalia's fear, and she moved to leave. "No. I don't like the way you are touching me. Let me go."

Señor Tudó gripped the back of her hair and wrenched her head back, pulling her off balance.

"Never speak to me that way again, do you understand? You are mine, señorita, and there is nowhere you can go that I won't find you." Tudó pulled her head back so far she couldn't speak, though she tried.

He pulled harder. "I can't hear you. What did you say?"

She croaked, "Si, señor."

Leaning in closer, he breathed in her fragrance. "That will be all. Get back to work." He shoved her head forward and stiffly walked from their hiding place.

Rubbing the soreness out of her neck and scalp, Amalia paused a moment to calm her breathing. She wiped away a stray tear before entering the large gathering room. Scanning the room, hoping no one would notice her agitation, she caught Señora Carolina's eye. The woman looked curiously at her for a brief moment before a stately woman at her side said something to draw her attention away.

Amalia stepped out of sight behind a group of conversing men until she spotted an empty tray. Grabbing it, Amalia searched the room for an open refuge against the wall, somewhere she could become invisible.

A space near a small group of young ladies who were having a lively conversation looked to be the perfect spot. Each held a glass half full of sangria. As soon as they were finished with their refreshment, Amalia would be there to take their glasses. Attention forward, hands holding the tray flat and low against her legs, she immersed herself in the indulgence all young women enjoyed—gossiping.

"Say what you will, but I think he is quite handsome." A pouty, plump señorita wearing a full pale-blue dress fanned herself as she continued, "I hoped he would be here tonight. Can you imagine? A duke taking holiday here in Lorca."

A tall, slender señorita wearing a rich burgundy gown and tight ringlets in her hair said, "But surely, Valeria, you find his eccentric behavior offensive, if not humiliating."

"On the contrary, Mariana, he is wonderfully endearing and ever so kind," the plump Valeria protested. "My last visit to Cádiz, I was enjoying a nice stroll when my parasol wouldn't open. I found the glare from the sun too much to bear, and he noticed my discomfort. The duke took me by the arm and quickly escorted me to some lovely shade."

That got an eye roll from everyone standing in their circle, including Amalia. *Couldn't she find her own shade?*

Señorita Mariana said, "I understand the duke is keeping to himself while he is traveling. I personally don't care. The way he waves his hands and holds his chin between his fingers as if entranced by your conversation, unbearable. And his voice is too high." Another girl standing close to Mariana giggled behind her gloved hand as her friend imitated the duke's theatrical behavior. "His expressions are far too dramatic. Just being in his presence gives me a splitting headache. He is not a man, he is a fop."

Señorita Valeria turned red in the face. A tantrum was likely to surface, so Amalia offered to take their glasses and extricated herself from the area. She'd had enough eavesdropping for one night, though she did find the duke's description intriguing.

The moment came, the one she dreaded at the end of every week. Amalia sat, staring at her hands as the names were read. She couldn't bear to look at anyone when Señor Valdez failed to call her name again. "Ambrose, Vela, Martinez, Soto. That will be all." Finally, he was finished and excused himself. Señora Morales followed after him, and the staff slowly filtered out of the servants' dining room after her. Only Sonia remained.

She leaned across the table. "Another week without pay?"

"Sí."

"Why don't you talk to Señora Morales while she is in her office? She won't mind."

"I don't know."

Sonia walked around the table, pulled Amalia to her feet, and pushed her toward the door. "Go."

Amalia brushed her skirt straight and pulled her shoulders back. Finding the housekeeper at her organized but cluttered desk reading a letter, she tapped on the open door. "Señora Morales, may I speak with you?"

With a sigh of exhaustion, the housekeeper removed her glasses and motioned for Amalia to take a seat. "You may. What is it?"

Amalia chose to remain standing. "I hope you can tell me why . . . I never receive any wages."

"I have asked that question as well, and the only answer I can give you is that your family received a large parcel of land and a spacious home in trade for your services, so they have been paid in full."

"They have been paid, but I am doing the work. How am I to purchase things I need with no income?"

"I wish I could help, but it seems you are inescapably reliant on the kind graces of the señor and his wife."

"For how long?"

Señora Morales paused a long time before answering. "I don't believe there is an end to your contract."

Amalia whispered, "So I'm a slave." Heat rushed to her cheeks, and she turned away and wiped at her tears.

"Amalia . . ."

Surprised to hear her Christian name, she turned back to see a softened expression on Señora Morales' face. "I'm sorry."

Eyes down, Amalia barely muttered "gracias" before exiting and rushing up the stairs to avoid anyone else. No escape in sight, her existence depended on the mercy of her oppressive employer. *Maybe that is what he meant when he said I was only good for one thing.*

Sonia stood when Amalia entered their room.

"It wasn't good, was it?"

"No. I can't live like this! I need sleep. I can't even think straight." Amalia slumped onto her bed. "Again, I have no choices. I am completely reliant on the Tudós' *kindness*."

Sonia straightened her back and stood resolute. "Not completely. I will help you, Amalia." She motioned for Amalia to take a seat on the edge of the bed. Sonia gently brushed through Amalia's thick hair to braid it. "I am happy to let you use my things, and when you need something, I'll get it. We'll share everything."

"I couldn't ask that of you. Besides, don't you send most of your money home?"

"Si, but we will find a way. I want to do this. You are like a sister to me, and I have always wanted a sister."

"I don't understand why you would do this."

"We're in this together."

Amalia's eyes burned, but it wasn't for shame. Sonia was a true friend.

Buttercup

CHAPTER 6

A MALIA BARELY SUPPRESSED a giggle. She had convinced Señora Morales to let her walk the grounds while the others took siesta. It was a brief but much needed reprieve from the constant vigilance it took to avoid Señor Tudó.

Practically skipping toward the stables, Amalia hadn't yet become acquainted with the horses. The sun filled the sky; only a few clouds dotted the vibrant blue. She passed the gazebo Señora Carolina had designed, pausing briefly to smell the clematis woven around the columns.

Her heart leaped with joy when the sizable stables came into view, and two horses grazed in the open corral next to them. Having permission from Cook to take some carrots from the kitchen, Amalia presented one of her gifts, hoping they would approach her at the fence. A gray Arabian accepted her offer first and nibbled the carrot out of her palm.

"There you go. You are very handsome, aren't you?"

She ran her hand down his nose and blew. He bucked his head back, then turned to look her in the eye. Seeing her reflection mirrored back in his black pupil, Amalia was startled to see another figure standing behind her. She spun around, dropping her carrots, to come face-to-face with Señor Tudó.

Holding her startled gaze, he approached Amalia slowly and bent down to pick up her offerings without breaking eye contact. The señor flashed his perfect smile. "How lovely to see you out enjoying the sunshine this fine day, señorita. You have met my Encantador. He's a superb animal, wouldn't you say?"

Amalia had difficulty finding her voice. Señor Tudó continued to smile, waiting patiently for her reply with no hint of the aggression she'd seen in him before.

"He . . . he *is* a superb animal."

Señor Tudó stood with his hands behind his back, keeping a polite distance. "Do you like horses?"

"Very much."

"Did you have horses growing up?" He held out a carrot for her to take.

Timidly, Amalia took it from him. "Si. I was very attached to our Spanish-Norman, Gordita."

"Ah, Spanish-Norman. They are excellent workhorses. I can understand your kinship." The señor sauntered over to Encantador and scratched behind his ear.

Amalia tilted her head at the comment.

"What I mean to say is you're a hard worker. I see how much effort you put into making my daughters happy and how respectful you are of the house."

Trying to hide her astonishment at his puzzling behavior, she turned toward the Arabian and watched the other horse approach. He was white with freckled brown along his girth, bleeding into solid brown down his back and haunches.

"Ah, here comes my pride and joy, Majestad."

Amalia couldn't believe the kind man next to her was really the same man she'd had the misfortune of working for. He handed her the last carrot, which she accepted and offered to the stallion.

"I've never seen his most unusual coloring before. I'm not familiar with this breed."

"This is a Spanish Jennet, the smoothest ride you will ever experience. All the nobility owns at least one of these fine creatures." Señor Tudó puffed out his chest and welcomed the horse to his touch.

"Amalia?"

They both turned to see Sonia staring wide-eyed at the two of them. She curtsied and mumbled, "Forgive me, señor. I was sent to fetch Amalia for the señora."

A shadow flitted over his face before he turned to Amalia and waved his hand forward. "After you, then."

Amalia hurried past him and followed Sonia back to the manor, neither one saying a word to the other, both acutely aware the señor was not far behind.

The young señoritas prepared for la merienda in their ruffled, satin dresses, hair neatly plaited on their heads. Amalia was about to take them down to their parents when she heard whimpering coming from Señor Tudó's personal chambers. The sound was female.

"You señoritas start downstairs. I'll be with you in a moment."

Concerned but uncertain if she should investigate, Amalia paused just outside the señor's door to see it slightly ajar and peeked in. The bed covers had been turned down, and a robe lay across it. Fresh water and hand towel lay undisturbed. No one in sight, she turned to leave, but a familiar, low voice stopped her.

"Did you need something, señorita?" Señor Tudó stepped into view from behind his door.

Putting some distance between them, she stuttered, "N-No, sorry. I thought I heard someone crying and wanted to see if I could help."

"How very kind of you. It just so happens that there *is* someone crying." He pulled Sonia into view, her hair disheveled and a bruise forming under her left eye. Tears streamed down her face.

"Oh no! Are you alright?" Amalia reached for her.

Sonia's eyes shot between her and the señor.

Señor Tudó spoke. "It seems she tripped on a fire poker and hit her head. Why don't you take her to the kitchen and get some ice for her poor cheek?"

"Your daughters are waiting for me to take them down."

"I'll take them," he said.

"Si, señor."

Amalia pulled Sonia to her and escorted her away.

Señor Tudó out of sight, Amalia asked, "Did he hurt you?"

Wiping an errant tear, Sonia said, "I fell, like he said. I'm so clumsy sometimes."

Amalia wasn't convinced. "Shh. It's alright now. We'll get you some ice and a drink of water, and you will feel much better, I promise."

Only two days before the family left for Madrid, Señora Morales found Amalia in the library dusting the books. "The señora has decided your services will not be required in Madrid, so you will stay and work here."

Though she tried to hide it, relief washed over her and a smile brightened her face. "Gracias, señora. I am happy to do whatever I can to help."

"Bueno, señorita, because that is your job."

Sleep finally overcame Amalia. It was the night before the family left for their holiday when Amalia woke to the sound of their door clicking shut. Certain she wasn't dreaming, she lit the bedside candle. Sonia slept soundly in the next bed. Amalia looked around to see if anything was amiss, and to her horror, cut strands of her hair lay next to her on the pillow.

"Sonia. Wake up. I think someone was in our room."

Groggy and red-eyed, Sonia sat up. "What? What are you talking about?"

"Look at my hair." She picked up some hair from the floor.

Sonia gasped. "Let me see."

Amalia turned her head from side to side.

"Stop that." Sonia seized her head. "A small section of your hair has been cut shorter, right here." She tried to show Amalia.

"Who would do this?"

Amalia shook her head.

"Did you see someone?"

"No, the sound of our door shutting woke me. I think I am going to be sick." Gasping for air, she held on to her friend. "Tell me it wasn't Señor Tudó. One of the other housemaids might be playing a trick on me, no?"

Sonia sat next to her silent and somber.

Amalia's mouth had gone dry. Trying to gather her voice, she whispered, "I need to tell you something. The same thing happened before. I mean, I woke up to what I thought was our door clicking shut my first night here. I didn't tell you because I wondered if it really happened. I heard your steady breathing and decided it was nothing."

Sonia almost yelled, "Why didn't you tell me? Did you speak to Señora Morales?"

"Why? What could I tell her when I didn't really know for certain if someone had come into our room? I thought it might be my imagination."

Taking the cut hair from Amalia's pillow, Sonia said, "Well, now you know it wasn't your imagination."

Rose

CHAPTER 7

TO AVOID ANY encounter with Señor Tudó, Amalia didn't see the horses again until the family left for their holiday. Her favorite walks among the olive trees stopped too when she noticed the curtains in the señor's window shift. But now, with the family gone, Amalia got permission, not only to see the horses whenever she wanted, but also to venture beyond the grounds of the estate during siesta.

That particular day, the wind danced through Amalia's hair, breathing new life into her troubled soul as she wandered along the vineyard past the front of the grand house. She stopped, closed her eyes, and pulled her head back, soaking in the feeling of freedom. Amalia made her way past well-groomed gardens until she reached the unkempt shrubbery of the countryside. The smell of wild daffodils filled the air, and beautiful buttercups lined her path in their abundance. To her delight, she spotted some deep-purple blossoms her father called sand viper's bugloss. While studying the flora, she discovered a strange bee, large and black, buzzing from flower to flower. Amalia committed to ask the gardeners what they were called.

Distracted by the beauty of her surroundings, Amalia walked and walked until she noticed the terrain become unfamiliar. She'd gone farther than she'd planned, but to her delight, just in the distance on top of the highest hill stood the Fortress of the Sun, the Moorish castle she'd seen glimpses of on her journey to the estate. Amalia had wanted to find it and wander along the paths and among the gardens. The castle had only been abandoned for twenty years, and she imagined it was still in good condition, its story written throughout its walls.

The hike to the castle was extensive, and large rocks hindered her path, but Amalia found her way around and over the rocky terrain, her skirt getting stuck on a broken branch only once. Reaching the walls to the fortress, she ran her hand along the rough stone until she found the opening to a courtyard. Overgrown flower gardens, a path of pomegranate trees—unpruned but still bearing fruit—and olive trees dotted the landscape. Her favorite, however, was a large carob tree, its red flowers in full bloom. She sat comfortably against its trunk and, using a large rock as her table, unpacked a small basket of apples, bread, and cheese she'd brought with her.

The pangs of hunger gone, Amalia ventured toward the walls of the spacious castle to explore. Of the two towers, she decided to visit the tallest to the south. Past a roughly hewn archway, she found remnants of a heavy door and bars to fortify it. She walked up a slight incline to reach the tower doors and pushed with all her strength to open them.

The musty entryway featured two steep staircases, one leading up, the other leading down. She decided to investigate the lower level first. Scorch marks covered one of the walls, indicating she'd found the kitchen. Memories of her kitchen at home flooded her mind—the black soot creeping along the cracked, moldy stucco above the stove she used.

Amalia climbed the stairs to the main level, then up to the living quarters. Fading frescos depicted a life of leisure and opulence. She could picture lavish rugs, tall candelabras, tapestries, and comfortable chairs filling the space. Enormous windows opened on each side of the square structure, overlooking miles of rolling hills. The view took her breath away.

Taking the staircase to the very top of the tower, Amalia could see the whole valley. Fresh air greeted her with a gust. The sun had moved closer to the horizon, and Amalia knew it was time to head back.

HOLLY BROUGH

Enchanted by her discovery, she committed to visiting the fortress every day.

A week later, while nearing her favorite spot under the carob tree in the shadows of the fortress, Amalia heard voices coming from the grounds near the south tower. Creeping closer to investigate, she crouched behind a large rock and craned her head around its edge to find the source of the commotion. There were *one, two, three—*

"Hola, who might you be?"

Amalia jumped to her feet and turned. *Four!* In front of her stood a dashing young gentleman dressed in tan breeches, an untucked white shirt, and leather shoes. His muss of dark, curly hair stopped at the nape of his neck, and his brown eyes scrutinized her. Amalia saw his amusement at her surprise when he failed to stifle a chuckle under his hand. She put her guard up, and he cocked his brow like a triumphant lion considering his prey.

Clutching her chest to quiet the rapid beating of her heart, she swallowed and took some deep breaths before speaking, but before she could mutter a word, he said, "Pardon me, señorita, were you spying on us?"

Amalia straightened her back. "Pardon *me*, señor, but I discovered this spot days ago and haven't come upon anyone in this area. Until now, I thought it my own personal refuge."

Giving her a crooked smile, the gentleman responded, "Well, it wasn't our intention to intrude on your *refuge*. We were just having a bit of fun and couldn't resist this spot to play a game of cat and mouse. There are so many marvelous places to hide." Shifting his weight and looking around, he continued, "Shall we leave you, then? Or . . . would you like to join us?"

Amalia heard a noise behind her and turned to find one of the other gentlemen standing several meters away. He considered Amalia before looking past her to nod at her curious lion. Out of the corner of her eye, she saw him wave his comrade off.

Turning her attention back, she said, "It seems that I have disrupted your fun. Perhaps it is I who should leave."

He took a step toward her and touched her arm. Amalia's heart flipped, and she forgot to breathe.

The young man lowered his voice. "Oh, no, no, querida, being with you would be far more stimulating than being with those three fellows." He waved the back of his hand in the direction of his comrades, who were gathering to wait for him. He shot them a glance and motioned them away.

Unsure of what to do next, Amalia smoothed her skirt flat for the second time, breaking his hold on her arm. She immediately missed its warmth. He chuckled and reached his hand to her face, hesitated, then softly brushed a wisp of her hair from her forehead. Gooseflesh erupted on her arms, and she quickly moved to cover them.

They stood for a moment in silence before she finally spoke. "May I ask your name, señor?"

He laughed through his nose and turned to walk away.

"Are you leaving?" He kept walking.

Was it something I said? Amalia looked after him, surprised she felt lonely for someone she didn't know.

There was another muffled chuckle. He turned back, gave her a wink, and motioned with his head for her to follow before sprinting toward the fortress. Without hesitation, she lifted the front of her skirts and ran after him. Even when he darted around bushes and over large rocks, Amalia kept up. She'd become very familiar with the terrain over the past week. He laughed, and she giggled when she caught hold of his shirt, but he twisted away, and she stumbled. By the time she righted herself, he was out of sight. Amalia tried to call out for him, but she didn't know his name.

Since they were playing cat and mouse and she chased him, she yelled, "Where are you, ratoncito?"

No reply. After searching for a while, Amalia was certain he'd left without a farewell. Breathless from the chase, she sulked to her basket under the tree, pulled out an apple, and took a bite. A loud thump sounded at her side, startling her into throwing the apple, which hit the gentleman in his gut. That earned a blast of laughter from him.

Still stunned, she looked up into the tree to see where he'd jumped from. The young man, not waiting for her acquiescence, took her arms and pulled her to her feet in a wonderful embrace. Amalia melted into him, taking the opportunity to explore his athletic frame with her hands. She breathed in his cologne—cedar and bergamot.

His warm breath tickled her ear. He didn't stop there but brushed his soft lips along her earlobe, sending a shiver down her spine.

Oh my!

Joyously light-headed, she clung to him as a leaf clings to its branch in autumn. Amalia rested her chin on his collarbone and savored the way he caressed her back and played with the hair that had fallen loose at her neck. Unfamiliar feelings of excitement and warmth filled her as they swayed to their own music. Amalia ran her hands along his shoulder blades and the muscles along his spine, feeling his heartbeat unite with hers.

What am I doing? I don't even know him! She pushed him away and covered her flushed cheeks. "We shouldn't be alone like this," Amalia said, taking a step back and looking around.

"Then I shall go."

"Who are you? What is your name?" she blurted before she could stop herself.

He just smiled at her.

"Do you want to know who I am?" Amalia mumbled.

Leading her eyes to his, he declared, "I want to know all of who you are." Moving closer, he whispered in her ear, "You are exquisite."

Amalia sighed with pleasure.

He stepped back and ran his hand down her arm, stopping at her hand. "Never have I seen such beauty and felt such flawless skin. You smell like sweet cream and berries, and I long to taste you."

Amalia's breath caught. *What is happening to me? The way he touches me . . .*

"I . . . I . . ."

A bigger smile lit up his features.

"You . . . make me feel things I have never felt before," Amalia whispered.

He chuckled. "I feel something too, querida. I can tell from our little game that you are one I would gladly let catch me."

Amalia bit her lip to suppress a smile.

"And . . . I believe I heard you call me ratoncito. Now calm yourself, niña. This may come as a shock to you, but the fact is, I am the cat and you are the mouse. As you can see, I have caught you!" He grabbed her into another embrace and twirled her around before letting her loose.

She looked into the rich, mysterious eyes of her lion and, with a giggle, pushed him away, grabbed her basket and started toward the estate.

"I must go," she said over her shoulder.

In the corner of her eye, she saw his smirk grow into a full grin.

"See you tomorrow, I think," her dashing gentleman yelled after her.

Carnation

CHAPTER 8

WATCHING THE ENCHANTING señorita walk away from the fortress, Francis picked up her discarded apple, flicked off the dirt, and took a bite. He walked past the castle ruins and down the hill to a road that would take him to his rented residence in Lorca. His ever constant cousin, Adolpho, stood at the base of the hill, waiting for him.

"You've been waiting here this whole time? It's been over an hour," Francis said.

Using his foot to push off the tree he leaned against, Adolpho replied, "Si. Our two other friends got tired of waiting for you, but not me. The duke of Cádiz shouldn't be roaming the countryside alone. I am responsible for you, and you should heed my counsel."

Five years his senior, Francisco's cousin had taken it upon himself to teach him the ways of the world. Tall, muscular, with wavy black hair and charm enough to seduce anyone for anything, Adolpho had no trouble finding the best entertainment.

"I wasn't alone."

Adolpho gave Francis a knowing smile before motioning him to start walking.

Francis huffed in frustration. "I know you have more experience, and I am glad you volunteered to accompany me, but you can be so annoying sometimes." Using his shoulder, he bumped his cousin out of the way. "Don't keep too close an eye on me, or you might interrupt. I'm trying to have a little fun, and I can't do that if I think you are lurking in the shadows."

"Pardon me, señor. I am to safely deliver you to Madrid. You are not welcome home unless you secure the queen's affections." Adolpho held up a hand to stay Francis's protest. "After you have had some fun, I would like to get back to our holiday. I find I like our two friends' company."

Rolling his eyes, Francis replied, "Si, they are great fun, but I am quite enjoying my time with this beautiful bonita. She is petite and soft, and she smells delicious."

Adolpho smacked the backside of his head. "Keep your head where it belongs, Don Juan. Don't lose your heart to a peasant. Remember, this is just practice for the real thing. Work your charms and get out. That is your purpose, and the sooner the better. We don't have that much time before you have to report to Madrid and seduce Isabella into marrying you."

"We both know I don't have a chance. She prefers Enrique."

Grabbing his shoulder and pulling him to a stop, Adolpho said, "That doesn't matter. You are the oldest, and you will be king."

"What if I don't want to be king?"

Adolpho shook his head in frustration. "That also does not matter. You have a duty to fulfill, just like we all do. Mine is to watch over you and make sure you go where you need to go and be where you need to be, yours is to put the family on the throne. Don't forget that while you philander around with this señorita. I only agreed to this little holiday because you said you needed some freedom before committing to the throne."

Dreamily, Francis declared, "I don't think even you could turn a blind eye after she has looked deep into your soul with those green eyes like she did mine."

Adolpho sighed. "I'm beginning to think this holiday was a mistake."

Amalia couldn't get back to the estate fast enough. When she found Sonia dusting the bookshelves in the study, Amalia grabbed her and pushed her behind the heavy velvet curtains.

"Sonia, I have to tell you about my walk today. Come and find me as soon as you can, por favor. I'll be cleaning the crystal chandelier in Señora Carolina's bedroom. Hurry, I feel like I am about to burst!"

Confused, Sonia grabbed her arm before she could leave. "What happened? Was it good or bad?"

"Very good!" Looking around to make sure no one could hear, she declared, "I met someone."

Sonia gasped. "Where? I *knew* I should have gone with you today."

"At my favorite spot by the carob tree. Now, it will be my favorite spot forever and ever."

Señora Morales cleared her throat. "Will you kindly stop warbling like birds and get back to work, both of you? After the books are dusted, the silver needs polishing, and it won't polish itself."

Upbraided into action, they separated to complete their duties.

Amalia made her way up the grand staircase, past the embarrassing painting of the señor's mother, and into the señora's private chambers—the one room she enjoyed visiting—but cleaning the individual crystals of the many chandeliers throughout the house was proving to be tedious work. At least, in this room, Amalia could sit on the velvet chaise overlooking the gardens and daydream about her encounter with the adorable lion.

An hour later, Sonia joined her. "I am finally here. Tell me everything."

Amalia moved the crystals next to her to make room for Sonia to sit. "Oh, it was so wonderful and got more and more wonderful with each passing moment."

Sonia laughed and plopped her slight frame down on the floor next to the chaise.

"He is tall and handsome and has honey-brown eyes. When I look into them, I want to see what he sees. I want to be part of everything he does. I feel . . . I feel so . . ."

Sonia smiled and nodded her head in encouragement. "You feel so . . . silly, nonsensical?"

Amalia playfully shoved at her, making Sonia laugh.

"I feel so alive. Happy and in love, yet we only just met. Can you believe it?" Amalia added. "Each time he touched me, it was like fire spreading through my whole body. I've never felt like that before."

"He touched you?"

"He embraced me. He smelled so good."

Sonia's eyes were popping out of her head. "You are reckless. Give me a crystal and tell me more."

"We played cat and mouse, a sort of tag game. I lost track of him, and he jumped out of a tree. When he got close to me, close enough for a kiss, I walked away. It was such a thrill. I hope I don't regret leaving. He yelled after me to see him tomorrow."

Using a special cloth, Sonia rubbed a teardrop crystal in silence.

"Was it a mistake to walk away?" Amalia asked. "Do you think he will come back?"

Sonia looked up. "He will probably come back. I read a book about a woman who could draw men to her by flirting with them until they showed some interest. Then she would turn a cold shoulder, drawing them in more. Men like a little challenge, holding out for the possibility that, in the end, they will get what they want. The woman got burned by her own game when she fell for a man who left her as soon as he got what he wanted."

"What did he want?"

"You don't know?"

Amalia shrugged, not certain she *did* know but afraid to ask further.

Sonia took Amalia's hand. "My advice to you is *be careful*. You don't want to do something you will regret. This man sounds like trouble to me. You met him by chance, which is innocent enough, but meeting him unaccompanied is completely inappropriate. Do you think that wise? Who is he? Does this mysterious man have a name and a place to call home?"

Amalia paid extra attention to the crystal in her hand. "I don't know."

"Don't know? Did you ask?"

"Si, but we got distracted playing chase."

"What if he is a renegade?"

Amalia straightened her face. "Well, that would definitely make him more interesting."

"Amalia, you can't be serious. You don't know where he's from. You don't know his name. Those things are important things to know about someone you want to kiss."

Dreamily, Amalia sighed. "Oh, what's in a name?"

"There is *much* in a name."

"It's just a name. He is far more than any name."

Sonia put her crystal down. "Amalia, names help us know who people are and where they come from. Names are so much more important than you realize." Amalia gave Sonia her full attention.

Taking a deep breath, she continued, "When my mother was young, she thought joining a nunnery would help her fulfill her purpose in life. Serving others and devoting her life to God seemed the perfect way to find happiness. My mother's name is Alisa, which means 'great happiness.' My name means 'wisdom.' I have a book from her that gives the meaning of most names. I looked yours up. It means 'industrious, hard worker.'"

Amalia scrunched up her nose. "That sounds accurate."

Sonia chuckled at Amalia's reaction. "Shortly before my mother took her vows, she heard a sermon given by a young priest. His insights and passion stirred feelings inside her she never felt before. At that moment, she realized she wanted to marry and have children." Sonia's eyes lit up. "My mother said my father's voice was like 'a fountain of pure, clear waters.' A philosopher, he opened up vast, new worlds for her."

"The young priest is your father?"

"Si. My mother wanted to get to know him better, so she found opportunities to ask him questions, and they arranged secret rendezvous just to be with each other. Of course, after a while, they felt guilty being so secretive, so my mother went to the Mother Superior and confessed her sin and asked to be released from the abbey. My father, who was being tutored to become a member of the clergy, also asked for release. My parents were married soon after."

"I love that story."

"Me too. But what I was leading up to is my parents believed our names can define us in good and bad ways. Sometimes a name can hinder us from reaching our potential, and yet other names can give us the motivation we need to reach our goals. As I said before, a name can explain where we come from. Maritimo means 'mariner.' Did you know that?"

"That *is* interesting. My father was in the navy before he met my mother, but he said he didn't like being at sea for long periods of time, though he certainly loved all the places he got to see and explore." Amalia got the stepladder and started placing the crystals back on the chandelier. "He became a farmer instead, but he should have stayed a seaman. He was a terrible farmer. Growing things wasn't necessarily the problem, but he never stayed with one crop long enough to create a good product."

"You seem to know a lot about farming."

"I had to figure out ways to make our produce work for us, otherwise we would starve. Two years ago, my father decided there was good money in silk, so we planted only mulberry bushes on our small farm. When the silk worms created their cocoons, he told me to gather them and give them plenty of mulberry leaves to eat. I put them in big boxes with the leaves. Each day I checked on them, and each day the leaves went uneaten. After two weeks, they all turned into fluffy butterflies. He was so angry with me."

"That doesn't sound fair."

Amalia shrugged her shoulders. "I decided to take the mulberries and make wine, syrup, and preserves so we could make *some* money out of his blunder."

"That was a smart solution."

"It worked out well. Are you finished with those?" Amalia pointed at the crystals near Sonia's feet.

"Si, here." She stood and helped Amalia place the last crystals in position.

With their task done, the girls made their way to the master's bedchamber.

"I'm happy to share my book with you later, if you like," Sonia said. "But we need to talk about your mystery man. I don't think it is wise to meet with him alone. There is an art to courtship."

"Courtship? I just met him. And besides, I don't want to play games. If I don't act interested, I could lose him. Just the thought of that makes me sad."

Sonia sighed. "It seems you won't listen to me. You're lovesick."

"I didn't know that was a real thing." Amalia laughed.

Sonia said, "In your case, it is."

Gazania

CHAPTER 9

FIDDLING WITH HIS waistcoat, Francis took another deep breath.

"Are you well, señor?" his valet inquired. "You seem agitated. Would you like me to get you something to ease your anxiety?"

"No. It's nothing. I met a beautiful señorita today, and I am quite taken by her. Keep it to yourself, but I have plans to meet her again tomorrow, and I will require your help."

"Of course, señor, anything you need."

Francis clapped his hands together and rubbed them vigorously as he considered how to begin. "Bueno. Have my horse ready by eleven o'clock. I should leave by the back door so Adolpho won't have an opportunity to stop me. Your discretion is appreciated."

"Will there be anything else?" The older man looked at Francis's image in the standing mirror with a knowing smile on his face. "Perhaps some indulgences to woo her?"

"What would you suggest?" Francis turned to face his valet expectantly.

"I could never presume to be qualified to advise on such things, but I'm sure you have considered treating her to a unique experience—something you are particularly knowledgeable about."

Francis pondered for a moment. "I doubt she's ever tasted chocolate."

"A genius idea, señor. I'll have your horse ready at eleven sharp and inform Cook you will need a picnic basket filled with strawberries, cheese, and chocolate. Perhaps something to drink as well?"

"Si, the wine our family was gifted before I left Cádiz. I believe we brought a crate of it."

Amalia was nudged several times before she realized someone was trying to wake her. With sleep heavy in her eyes, she noticed it was light.

"What time is it?"

"It's almost nine o'clock, Amalia. I tried to wake you earlier and figured you would be up by now doing your chores, but after I got done in the kitchen, I couldn't find you anywhere in the house."

Amalia shot out of bed. "Oh no! Have I been missed? Tell me I'm not to be disciplined. I must be allowed to leave today."

Sonia pulled her into a hug. "Don't you fret. I covered for you, but you should quickly get dressed."

Sonia helped fix her hair. She handed Amalia a roll to eat as they made their way to the servant dining room to check the chore list, which was considerably shorter than the day before. Such things as taking the large curtains down and beating them dust-free or polishing all the silver pieces were finished. Of course, the chandelier crystals took the most time, but the many intricate mirror frames had been meticulously dusted, the fireplaces cleaned out, and the soot scrubbed away. Peeling the wax off the many sconces was the next major chore before the brass could be shined. With less work, the household siestas lasted longer, giving Amalia more time at the fortress.

Amalia turned to Sonia. "Let's go peel the wax off the brass in the large gathering room upstairs."

The girls found Señora Morales sitting at her desk.

"It is nice of you to join us, Señorita Maritimo," the housekeeper said when they entered her office.

"Sorry." Amalia curtsied. "We were hoping the brass was available in the upstairs gathering room for us to clean."

"No," the señora said. "I have a request for you to go to the stalls and help Ricardo muck them out and discard the old hay."

The girls stared at her wide-eyed.

"I thought you wanted to help with the horses," the old woman said.

"I do," Amalia finally said. "Is Sonia requested too?"

Señora Morales smiled at Sonia, who stood next to Amalia ashen-faced. "No, Cook would like you, Señorita Vela, to go into town with her to purchase some supplies."

There was an audible sigh of relief from Sonia. "Gracias."

"Señorita Maritimo, ask for Jorge. He is expecting you."

Amalia whispered to Sonia before they parted, "Normally, I would like this assignment, but I don't want to go to the fortress smelling like manure."

Sonia laughed. "See you later."

Amalia was later than usual to her tree. She had a quick wash and changed her clothes before taking her highly anticipated walk. Approaching her tree, she noticed a small bouquet of wilting wildflowers in the center of the rock under its shade.

A smile lit up her face. She picked up the bouquet and smelled the lovely fragrances of wild daffodils, sweet peas, and lavender. The temperature was warm, the breeze mellow and soft. Amalia looked around but couldn't see anyone. She moved closer to the ruins but saw nothing. Then she heard some rustling in the leaves and looked up to see someone preparing to pounce. She squealed with delight and ran toward the fortress to hide. Finding a place under a recessed archway, she crouched against the cool stone to steady her breathing. It was impossible to hear footsteps approach with her heart pounding in her ears.

Suddenly, her lion appeared at her side, and she screamed. He laughed as he took her into an embrace. Liking the thrill of his body against hers, she clung to him.

The excitement of having him so close took her breath away, and she was unable to conjure more than a whisper. "I see you have caught me again. Now what are you going to do with me?"

"A wonderful prospect, I think. Shall we sit under our tree and eat the treat I brought for you?" He pushed her to arm's length, his eyes alight with anticipation.

"A treat?" Amalia looked up through her lashes at him.

"Si. Have you ever tasted chocolate?" Taking her by the hand, he led her to the shade of the carob tree.

"Chocolate? I've never even heard of it."

"You will love it, cariño."

Amalia's heart leaped at her pet name, and she grinned. *He is so romantic.*

Producing a blanket from behind the far side of the large rock, he laid it out, inviting her to sit, then retrieved a small basket. Sitting next to her, he pulled out hard cheese, strawberries, and something wrapped in paper. Carefully pulling the edges of the paper away, he revealed something resembling mud and laughed. "I'm sorry it looks a bit messy. The heat makes the chocolate melt. I promise it is delicious." Dipping his finger into the soft, dark mass, he lifted it to her lips.

Amalia scrunched her face before opening her mouth.

He cocked his brow in amusement. "You will have to open wider if I am to put it in your mouth without getting it all over your face, cariño."

A thrill shot through Amalia at the intimate gesture, and she smiled before opening wider. He placed his finger on her tongue, and she carefully closed her lips to receive its gift. A sigh of pleasure escaped him, causing a rush of emotions to overcome Amalia. Trying to concentrate on the chocolate, she perceived notes of bitter nuttiness and earthy sweetness. Amalia savored the taste, as well as his closeness.

Pulling away, he put the same finger in his mouth to suck off the residue. Amalia couldn't pull her eyes from his mouth and realized she was licking her lips.

Her cheeks flushed, and she looked away. "That's delicious. I have never experienced anything like it."

"I hoped you would like it. I brought this with me from Cádiz. We have to keep the chocolate cool, or it gets soft like this. A Spaniard discovered chocolate. It comes from beans called cacao in the Americas. He brought it back to España. The people from there drank it."

"A drink? Sounds very rich."

"Si, a warm drink. Much better than coffee, I think. I don't like coffee."

Amalia covered her mouth and giggled. She reached out her finger to dip it in the chocolate. He moved it toward her. "Si, have some more."

"Gracias."

"For years, chocolate has been primarily enjoyed by the upper class. It doesn't surprise me you've never heard of it," he said.

Amalia felt a prick in her heart. *Is he nobility?*

"Only recently has chocolate been easier to produce and more available to everyone. I find I can't get enough of it. Chocolate gives me a boost of energy and elation. How does it make you feel?"

He ran his finger down her arm.

Gooseflesh erupted all over her. "I feel . . . warm inside." *Cádiz— where have I heard that before?*

"Try some of the cheese and strawberries with it. Together, the essence of these different flavors are enhanced."

He dipped a strawberry in the melted chocolate and raised it to Amalia's mouth. She took a small bite, not taking her eyes from his.

"Mmm. So good." She wiped the corner of her mouth and asked, "You are a connoisseur of food, señor?"

He ate the rest of the strawberry. "I enjoy eating it as much as I enjoy cooking it. I wanted to be a chef when I was younger. I know women are meant for the kitchen, but as a child, I would sneak downstairs to watch our cook make delicious dishes. I wanted to do what she could do. There is an art to cooking, and she was a master."

"I've never known a man who wanted to spend time in a kitchen but to eat the food. What are some of your favorite dishes?"

He leaned back on one elbow and said, "Simple dishes, nothing grand, but I enjoy making croquettes with fresh rabbit I've killed myself. I also make them with mushrooms and blue cheese. Just thinking about it makes my mouth water. I love bread pudding—not the bread pudding you may be familiar with, like torrejas, but English bread pudding with a rich, decadent texture."

Amalia watched his animated descriptions about an obvious passion of his, enjoying every detail, practically tasting the food as he spoke.

"I was cooking all the meals for my family by the time I was seven years old," Amalia said. "I made croquettes too, but I always made it with my black sausage. It was my father's favorite. Rabbit meat would definitely give it a nice, mild flavor. I would like to make it that way someday."

They sat in companionable silence, listening to the chirping birds overhead until Amalia found herself blurting out, "You may call me Amalia, if you like." Embarrassed, she focused on a thread that had come loose on her skirt before adding, "And I can call you . . ."

She could see from the corner of her eye that her mystery man scrutinized her a moment before finally saying with a flip of his hand, "My name is Francisco de Asís María Fernando de Borbón, the duke of Cádiz. Call me Francis—"

Amalia's countenance fell. *The dinner party . . . He is royalty, but he doesn't act eccentric or silly like the girls had intimated.*

"Actually, I would prefer Cisco. I've always wanted to be called Cisco. It's less formal." He popped some cheese in his mouth and smiled. When Amalia didn't respond immediately, Cisco stuttered, "T-That could be your special pet name for me. What do you think?"

"I would like that very much, Cisco. And maybe you could call me Ama," Amalia said.

He took her hand in his and kissed it. "I like Amalia better."

Her heart sank. *But Ama is what my little brother called me.*

Cisco looked at her, absently grinning.

Amalia summoned a smile. "Gracias for trusting me with your name. I heard about a duke who was here on holiday, though I didn't know it was you. Is it true you are trying to stay anonymous so you can enjoy some peace and quiet?"

Leaning back, he said, "Something like that. It is hard to find solitude when so many people are seeking my favor. I've wanted to escape the constant scrutiny of others and their expectations of me for a long time." With a heavy sigh, he continued, "However, I'm afraid I can only escape it for a short while. I have responsibilities that will not go away, and I'll have to return to that life again."

Amalia looked at her hands. *He's leaving. When? But if he has feelings for me, maybe he will take me with him.*

"But . . . not right now." Cisco jumped up and pulled her to her feet, then dashed off laughing toward the fortress before disappearing around a corner. Amalia bounded after him. They ran around and through ancient stone walls, painted frescos looking down on them. Cisco nowhere in sight, Amalia found herself in a dark corner of the spacious room on the second floor, her excitement peaked. The anticipation of him jumping out at any moment made the game a thrill, and her heart beat recklessly. She strained her ears for sound to echo off the floor. As if on cue, movement shot across her vision, and Cisco appeared from nowhere.

How does he do that?

Amalia yelped when he unexpectedly swept her into his arms and carried her down the stairs, through the spacious antechamber, and back to their sanctuary under the carob tree.

Barely out of breath, Cisco gently set Amalia down on her feet and pinned her arms to her side. "Now that I have you, mi querida, I will not let you go until I have devoured you completely." His maniacal laugh made Amalia giggle. With a throaty growl, he kissed her neck, and she shrieked with delight. But then he tasted her earlobe, and Amalia's breath caught. He slowly moved his lips along her jawline to her cheek, then her nose. She closed her eyes ready for their lips to touch, but he paused. His breath was warm, his lips only inches away, but nothing happened. Amalia opened her eyes to see his silly smirk.

He's teasing me?

Cisco took her chin in his hand and looked deeply into her expectant green eyes. Seeing his desire for her, she felt like she was on fire and started to lean into him, but he quickly backed away and let her go. His smile didn't fade.

"I'd hoped to have a wonderful time with you today. I am happy I met you, cariño."

Snapped out of her dream state, she realized he was saying goodbye. "I hope I will see you again tomorrow," she said with a subtle grin.

Cisco's eyes lit up. He leaned forward and kissed the corner of Amalia's mouth. "Until tomorrow then, Amalia."

"I prefer Ama."

He caressed her face with the back of his hand and winked at her.

Amalia kept hold of him until she was forced to let go. Longing to follow him instead of going back to the estate, she grudgingly turned and walked away.

Geranium

CHAPTER 10

AS THE GIRLS lay in bed waiting for sleep to take over, Amalia said, "He told me his name today."

"What is it?"

"Francisco de Asís María Fernando de Borbón, the duke of Cádiz." Sonia shot up. "He's a duke? What are you thinking, Amalia?"

"I didn't *know* he was a duke when I met him. It's not my fault he is interested in me."

"Don't be silly, Amalia. Why would a duke be interested in a housemaid?" Sonia asked.

A pit formed in Amalia's belly. She'd wondered the same thing but didn't want to believe there was anything between them but love.

"I hate to say it, but I believe he is just playing with your feelings. He could never be with a housemaid."

Amalia huffed, "Well, love transcends any title. What does Francis mean?"

"Let's look it up." She leaned over the side of her bed and felt for the book. Together, they skimmed through the pages. "Here." Sonia pointed to the name. "It means 'free one' or 'adventurous.'"

"That fits him."

"What happened today?"

Amalia got comfortable and recounted everything that happened between them, going into great detail about the chocolate Cisco brought. The girls stayed up way too late, but before blowing out the candle, Amalia promised to bring some chocolate back to Sonia if the duke brought her some again.

Amalia saw him leaning against their tree before he saw her. He was holding another bouquet of wildflowers.

"Hola, Cisco." Amalia waved.

"Hola, mi amor." Bowing, he presented the flowers. "These are for you."

"Gracias." Amalia curtsied with a smile, and he smiled back.

"Are you hungry?" Cisco asked. "I have another surprise for you today."

"Si, gracias. I didn't have time to pack myself a basket before I came." Amalia sat down on the blanket Cisco laid out for them.

"Have you heard of pâté? Or caviar?"

"I've seen caviar before but not pâté. I haven't tasted either of them."

"Bueno. That makes me very happy. If you've seen caviar, I'm sure you are aware there are different grades of caviar, some better than others. There are other types of pâté too, like ham, chicken liver, duck or wild turkey liver. I've even tried salmon pâté." Cisco pulled out several things from his basket—a small bowl with some sort of paste in it, another bowl of a beautiful silver substance, a variety of crisps, fresh strawberries, and a bottle of expensive-looking wine.

Amalia clasped her hands to her chest with a smile on her face. "This looks marvelous."

Cisco laughed. "Our cook is very skilled in the culinary arts."

He produced a small silver spoon and dipped it into what Amalia knew was the caviar, though she'd never seen it with a light, pearlescent color.

"Close your eyes and try this."

She gladly opened her mouth wide enough to receive the contents on the spoon. Several bursts of a salty, buttery flavor tickled her tongue.

"Mmm. Wonderful. I didn't realize it would be so flavorful."

"Our caviar grader said this is the best of all caviar. We don't eat it very often, but it is one of my favorite delicacies. Now, try this."

Cisco spread some pâté on a crisp and handed it to her. She took a bite and was pleased with the contrast of flavor between the sweetness of the crisp and the strong, spicy taste of the creamy paste.

"I have never tasted such rich food as you have shared with me these last few days, even with all the experimenting I did at home. I feel like I've been missing the best things in life."

Taking another bite, she asked, "What do you mean by caviar grader?"

"A caviar grader can tell by the sound of the eggs if they are the best quality. Listen."

Cisco moved the bowl in a circular motion near her ear, and Amalia could hear a faint humming.

"I can't believe it. They purr like kittens."

"You must have a musical ear. I can't hear anything," Cisco said.

She quickly finished the crisp before Cisco handed her a goblet of wine.

"Gracias. What is this?"

"This wine came from the Gutiérrez Colosía family, who are very good friends of my family. It's the perfect wine for what we are eating. You didn't get to try it last time we were together. Our cat-and-mouse game interrupted our culinary adventure."

Amalia had never indulged in drinking alcohol and wondered how it would affect her. She took the goblet and drank the contents. Cisco laughed when she drank the whole glass in one swallow.

"No, no, querida. You are supposed to sip it. Surely you know that."

She giggled. "Sorry, I'm overwhelmed with all this wonderful food . . . I wasn't thinking."

"I admit I'm enjoying the experience through you. None of this is new to me, and I like seeing your eyes light up at every new taste."

After her third glass, Amalia realized, to her detriment, wine and possibly all the rich, new food did not agree with her. "Oh no." She jumped to her feet and ran behind the carob tree.

Cisco was close behind with a handkerchief, which Amalia quickly accepted. She wiped her mouth but kept the cloth close to her lips to mask the smell.

I've humiliated myself in front of a duke. He'll never want to see me again. "I'm . . . I'm sorry." Amalia wiped at the moisture gathering in the corner of her eye.

"Don't think on it. A little vomit doesn't bother me in the least. Here, this cracker should help calm your stomach." Cisco looked at her with an endearing smile. "You are so charming and lovely."

Amalia blushed and turned the other way to eat the cracker. The bad taste in her mouth dissipated after a third cracker and drink of water Cisco offered her. They stood in silence for a few moments. Amalia grew acutely aware of the gurgling in her stomach. She backed away from Cisco to prevent him from hearing it too and bumped into the carob tree. He followed and slowly pulled her face to his, lightly kissing her on the lips. Amalia hesitated briefly before leaning in to kiss him back.

He chuckled, and she pulled away.

"Did I do that wrong?"

"No, it was nice. Just think of it as a dance. Let me lead and you follow." He kissed her again, a little longer, and she reveled in the softness of his lips. The moment didn't last long before he pulled away, gathered his things, and walked away with a smirk on his face.

The sky was overcast the next day, and the air was thick with moisture, but Amalia still ventured out to meet Cisco at the Fortress of the Sun. As she got closer, she had to make herself walk, not run. To her disappointment, Cisco wasn't waiting for her when she arrived. For several minutes, she looked around, but there was no sign of him. *Maybe he's just late like I was yesterday.*

Amalia sat at the base of her favorite tree and relaxed for a moment. The grass beneath her was welcoming and soft. Though the bark of the carob tree was rough, she leaned against it to daydream. Her eyes grew heavy listening to the birds warble in the tree overhead. After a while, she became aware of a tickle under her chin that wouldn't go away, even after brushing at it. Amalia opened her eyes to see a large blue-and-green feather waving in her face and, just beyond it, Cisco.

He gave her a brilliant smile. "It's the feather from a peacock. Have you ever seen a peacock?"

Amalia shook her head. "A kind of bird?"

"Si."

"A big bird?"

He squatted beside her on the ground. "Well, think of a large turkey, then put blue feathers on it and a fan of these kinds of feathers as a tail. The male is the most colorful, and when seeking a mate, he splays his tail feathers out to attract the female."

Cisco stood up straight and produced four more feathers. Holding them behind his back, he danced around like a chicken.

Amalia laughed. "Stop, stop, my tummy hurts. You look so silly."

"Are you not attracted to me and my impressive display?"

With tears blurring her vision, she asked, "Are you trying to impress a possible mate?"

Continuing his ridiculous strut, he replied, 'If you are interested, then si. If not, then I must try something different."

"You make an adorable bird. Now stop! I can't breathe." Joining in the laughter, he fell to the ground.

"May I hold one of those?"

Cisco knelt on one knee to present them. "You may have them, mi amor. I brought them as a gift for you."

"Cisco, these feathers are the most exquisite gift I have ever received. I don't deserve them. Gracias."

"Deserve them? You don't need to deserve something to receive something. I adore you."

Then he got up and reached for her hands. "That brings me to my next surprise. I was sure you would hear me when I came upon you, but you must have been very tired, mi cielo."

"I haven't been able to sleep lately."

"Me either." Cisco winked and led her toward the fortress, around a downward bend. In the shade stood a magnificent white horse nibbling on a few blades of grass.

Amalia took in a quick breath. "Oh."

"May I introduce you to my horse, Taddeo. He will take us to our entertainment for the day, if you like."

Amalia walked up to the stunning animal and carefully ran her hand up his nose and blew into his nostrils. Taddeo flipped his head, then nuzzled his nose to her face. That earned a giggle from Amalia; Cisco watched her interact with his loyal companion.

"He is an Andalusian, fifteen hands. Am I right?"

His eyes grew wide. "You are correct. I've never known a woman who knew so much about horses."

Amalia ran her hand through Taddeo's mane and said, "My father taught me. He's so brilliantly white. His coat just sparkles. I believe, kind señor, I am in love."

Cisco shook his head with a chuckle, joining her at Taddeo's side.

"What does Taddeo mean?" Amalia asked.

"Courageous."

Holding Taddeo's head in her hands, she asked, "Are you courageous? Do you live up to your name?"

Cisco ran his hand along the horse's neck. "He has never been tried in battle, but he is a good, loyal friend. I like to think he is courageous."

Amalia kissed Taddeo's velvety nose. "My friend says there is great significance in names. They can reveal who we are and where we come from. I think Francisco fits you well."

Cisco looked at her expectantly. "Maybe you can tell me what it means on our little adventure."

Amalia turned her attention to Cisco, a bright smile on her face. "Adventure? What sort of adventure?"

Running his fingers along her arm, he replied, "That is a secret, Amalia. I have something very special planned for us."

Amalia felt light-headed and almost giddy. *He said my name.* Cisco's touch lingered long after his fingers left her arm. He slowly backed away with her hand in his and led her to mount Taddeo's saddle. "Vamos, or what little time we have will be spent looking at this beast. Shall I help you up?"

"Si, gracias," Amalia replied breathlessly.

Cisco placed his hands on her waist and easily lifted her onto Taddeo before deftly mounting the horse behind her. He pulled her closer to him, holding tight as he urged Taddeo forward. Amalia's heart fluttered when she got a whiff of his cologne again and wanted to lay her head back on his shoulder.

Leaning in for a whisper, he said, "You are warm and soft. I want to feel you next to me always, cariño."

Heat rushed through her despite the cool of the shade.

Cisco led his courageous steed through the outer fortress wall and down a path dense with trees and lush vegetation.

"Green is my favorite color. Look how alive everything is around us. It's so fresh," Amalia said.

"Tell me what my name means and why you think it fits me."

"Francisco means *free one*. You love adventure, and you long to be free."

"Si, that is true. What does your name mean?" Cisco asked.

Amalia grimaced before answering, "My name isn't glamorous or astounding. It simply means *work* or *labor*. I have worked all my life, and I've learned to enjoy it. Whether I like it or not, Amalia fits me well."

"I think your name is beautiful. You are stunning."

Amalia closed her eyes and smiled at the compliment.

They approached the base of the closest mountain. A path of pink and red rose petals appeared before her eyes, and she gasped. "Cisco, look. Where does it lead?"

Cisco pulled his horse to a stop, hopped down, and tied Taddeo to a tree. Then, lifting Amalia down, he took her hand in his.

"Cisco?" Amalia said.

He smiled and led her up a slight incline to a large natural cave hidden by overhanging branches. A cotton blanket lay just inside the opening, a bouquet of wildflowers set in the center as a welcome. *This took a lot of thought and effort. Did my lion really do all of this for me?*

Cisco pulled Amalia close and slowly took the comb out of her hair, releasing her thick, dark tresses down her back. He placed his arms around her waist and nuzzled her neck. "How is it you always smell of berries and cream?"

Amalia giggled. "Because you are a connoisseur of food, señor. That is all you think about."

Cisco threw his head back with a blast. "You know me so well!" He kissed her cheek. "I think you have somehow missed my desire for you. I would go without food if it meant I could have you instead."

Chills ran up her arms at the warmth of his breath on her face. She reached around his neck and wrapped a curl of his hair around her finger. Being close to him was thrilling, almost dangerous, and she wanted so much more.

They slowly rocked to their own music, turning in a circle around each other. Cisco brushed his cheek against hers and caressed her jaw with his lips. Amalia sighed at his touch, encouraging him to continue. She moved her hands around his back and took fists of his shirt, clinging to him as he tugged at the strings closing the neck of her blouse and lowered it below her shoulders. A delicate breeze skimmed over her skin in perfect harmony with his kisses. Amalia felt her knees weaken, but Cisco had already whisked her into his arms. He gently lowered her to the blanket set out to catch her. He knelt above her and gently brushed wisps of hair from her eyes to clear the way for a kiss to her brow. He moved to her cheekbone, her jaw, her nose. Amalia craved more of him—more of them.

His lips inches from hers, she watched them, anxiously awaiting him to bridge the distance. The anticipation of his mouth on hers drove Amalia to seize his cravat and pull him to her. Cisco tasted her lips, igniting a desire in her she never knew. She sighed with pleasure at the warmth of his breath at her ear. The few whiskers he was nurturing into something more substantial tickled her cheek and made her giggle. Cisco mimicked a growl, and Amalia laughed with delight.

He found her lips again and kissed her freely and deeply. Amalia heard her own voice declare, "I love you," which caught her by surprise, but Cisco didn't reply. He was fully absorbed in the moment, and the passion between them knew no bounds. Feeling thoroughly desired, Amalia gave in to him completely, but when the pleasure was short-lived and their moment ended abruptly, she found herself wanting for more.

After they parted, Amalia lay still, wondering if she'd done something wrong. Cisco pecked her on the cheek, shrugged on his breeches, and walked out of the cave, out of sight. Cold and self-conscious, Amalia pulled the blanket over her and contemplated the feelings of disappointment and confusion running through her. *Is that all?* Cisco seemed to enjoy himself, but nothing really happened for her except a little pain. She closed her eyes tight, trying to stay the tears. *Don't overthink it or you'll ruin the moment you just shared.*

Cisco came back, still half dressed, holding a ceramic dish with a thick cloth. The wonderful aroma of cinnamon and sweet cream wafted through the air toward her when he set the tray down to reveal his surprise.

"Mmm." Amalia's mouth watered.

He chuckled. "This is the torrejas I told you about. I had my valet bring it up while we were . . . occupied."

Amalia's stomach dropped, and heat rushed to her cheeks.

Cisco acted like it was of no consequence and proceeded to scoop out a large helping of his special dish. "It's delicious, I promise. I even added raisins."

"I'm no longer hungry."

He kissed her softly. "Don't worry, Amalia. My valet is very discreet. He has to be. There is nothing you need to be ashamed of. Vamos, while it's hot. I had it made to my specifications especially for you, with day-old bread soaked in fresh milk and spiced with cinnamon and nutmeg."

She would have reveled at the sound of her name on his lips, but she wanted to hide under a rock.

"Vamos, cariño."

Amalia reluctantly took a bite, and her hunger returned. She enjoyed his gift, while Cisco's eyes swept over every inch of her. She didn't mind the silence between them. His eyes were extremely telling. She smiled; he smiled in return, leaning in to kiss her bare shoulder.

"You've made me very happy, Amalia."

She felt her smile grow. *He said it again.* Amalia loved hearing him say her name. She laid her head on his shoulder as he ran his hands through her hair. When she finished the last bite, Cisco took her by the waist and pulled her to him, kissing her and licking off the crumbs left at the corners of her mouth.

"I cannot seem to satiate my want, my need for you. Your skin is as soft as the petals of a rose, and after I have loved you, you glisten like the dew in the morning sun."

Enraptured by his words, Amalia wanted to feel more of his passion for her, so she initiated their closeness the second time, reveling in Cisco's pleasure. It didn't hurt as much the second time. She focused on following his movements, like he'd mentioned when they shared their first kiss. *Follow his lead.*

His ecstasy ended, she whispered. "Promise me this will never end."

Cisco laid his head on the ground to rest and catch his breath. "I wish things could be different. This has never happened to me before."

"You haven't been with another woman?"

"Of course, I've been with other women."

Amalia's face burned red, and she turned away.

Cisco laughed it off. "Cariño, I'm nobility. It's expected of me to gain experience. But I've never been in love before. I believe I am in love with you."

Amalia didn't say anything. It was her first experience being with a man. How could she possibly compare to *other women*? Tears rolled down her cheeks.

Finally, Cisco showed some concern. He pulled her to him and whispered in her ear. "Did I hurt you? Why are you crying?"

"I . . . I'm so embarrassed. I have never been with another man. I don't know if . . . if . . ."

"If you did everything right? Are you worried about what I think of you compared to other women?"

Amalia nodded. "How many other women?"

"Two. But you don't need to worry about that. You are exquisite. I loved every moment with you. Those things don't matter when you love someone." He paused. "Do you love me too?"

"Yes, I do love you."

"Then we share this first love together. What could be more binding?" Cisco kissed her deeply, with what seemed to be all the emotion he could express in that one moment.

Somehow, she knew it was true; they would always be bound to each other. Amalia lay on her back next to him and looked at the sun. It was getting low. "Cisco, it's late, and I need to get back. How I wish we could just be together."

Cisco became somber. He turned to her and said, "Me too, mi amor. Me too."

The next several days slipped into a comfortable rhythm. Amalia took her daily walks, desperate to find Cisco waiting for her near their tree, holding a bouquet of wildflowers. The way he casually leaned against the tree in his white shirt and fitted breeches made her heart skip every time she saw him. He brought indulgences for her to try, and she willingly tasted every new concoction. Cisco would turn on his theatrical persona and quote poetry, snorting his nose amidst a silly laugh to show how he discouraged ladies trying to secure his affections. Amalia's stomach hurt from laughing at his antics.

Each day ended with a wonderful game of cat and mouse followed by velvety kisses and dreamlike passion. For Amalia, life couldn't be more perfect—unless, of course, Cisco whisked her away to a life they could share together.

"I vow to be the one to catch you tomorrow, ratoncito," Amalia giggled as they said their goodbyes yet again.

A look of annoyance flitted over Cisco's face before he replied, "I cannot come tomorrow. Maybe in a day or two. I have responsibilities to attend to."

Amalia's heart sank. "Oh, si. Of course, well, that would be nice. I'll see you in a day or two." Saddened by his quick dismissal, Amalia was filled with foreboding. *Maybe Sonia was right. I've given myself to him. Has he lost interest in me?*

Cisco got up and gathered his things. He pecked her on the cheek and left, her eyes following him down the hill, past the fortress, and out of sight. He didn't look back.

Ivy

CHAPTER 11

THOUGH CISCO TOLD Amalia he wouldn't be coming to the fortress, she went hoping to see him anyway. After two days of his absence, she could hardly drag herself out of bed in the morning.

Sonia came into the room in a huff the third day. "Get up and get dressed. You kept me up all night with your sniveling, and I'm tired of your irrational behavior. It's a waste of good daylight to pine over a silly boy. Let's get you cleaned up and in some fresh clothes. Nothing is better at raising one's spirits than a good washing and something to busy the mind. Up with you!"

Sonia grabbed Amalia and pulled her out of bed, taking her by the hand and leading her to the servants' washing room, at the end of the hall, where a warm bath waited for her.

"I had Ambrose bring up the hot water, and I added some rose oil because I know it is your favorite. Your clothes are on the chair there, coffee and sweet breads over here." She pointed to a small vanity. "Call for me when you're finished."

Though Amalia protested, as soon as her body hit the warm water, she relaxed and new life brightened her features.

Sonia greeted her as soon as she exited the washroom. "See? You feel better with clean clothes and some food in your belly."

"You're right. Gracias. Sonia, what do you think of the name Alejandro? It means 'protector of men' . . . I like to add the word *women* also."

Sonia shrugged. "It's nice. Why do you ask?"

"No reason. I just remembered it from your book and liked it."

"Would you like to go with me to the stables today?"

Amalia knew it was Sonia's attempt to keep her close. "I need to go to the fortress. Cisco might come back today."

"No, you can't go. Stay here. We can find a book to read after we dust them off. Por favor, don't go."

"Do you want to come with me?"

Sonia grimaced. "No. What would I do with myself if he *is* there?"

"Bueno, I will see you in a few hours."

Sonia's brow furrowed when Amalia walked away.

Amalia's heart almost choked her when she saw a small bouquet of wildflowers on the rock under the carob tree. *He came back!* She snatched it up, looking around and up in the tree but couldn't see him.

Walking toward the fortress, she yelled, "Cisco, where are you?"

Her fingers touched her lips in anticipation of finding him. Standing in the shadows of the grand archway leading to the inner courtyard of the fortress was Cisco. He stood deep in thought, studying what appeared to be a letter. Amalia snuck around to the other side of him as quietly as possible and, from her vantage point, could make out some of its message.

Enough time philandering about . . . Tomorrow and you will be ready . . . Time to do your duty to our . . .

Amalia jumped out and grabbed him. Cisco swung around and shoved her away. His face was filled with rage.

Surprised by his reaction, she apologized, "I'm sorry. I was only playing."

Cisco came to himself, and his face softened. "You startled me. It seems you remembered your promise to catch *me* this time."

"I fear I may have interrupted something important." Amalia watched his eyes grow distant.

"Oh, it's nothing. A letter I just received."

He casually put it in his pocket and motioned her to join him as he walked out of the courtyard. Brooding filled his countenance. Wanting to lighten the mood, Amalia grabbed his hand and started to run toward their tree, but Cisco pulled back.

"I don't feel like playing today, Amalia."

"What's wrong? Did I do something to upset you?"

Cisco said nothing.

"I have looked forward to seeing you for three days. I have something I need to tell you."

She reached up and gently turned his face to hers and ran her thumb along the fine little whiskers on his upper lip. Leaning in, Amalia kissed his cheek. He sighed as he moved to find her lips. They kissed each other with desperate emotion, Amalia wanting Cisco to feel her love, Cisco receiving it like the dry, cracked desert floor drinks up the rain. She sensed the duke's sadness grow more fervent with each caress; such emotion emanating from him, it broke her heart. Wanting to close the chasm that seemed to have grown between them, she told him she loved him. In return, he whispered unintelligible things in her ear, rocking her back and forth to their own melancholy tune.

Cisco grabbed her upper arms and led her toward the fortress wall, pushing her against the stones to steady her. A lump in the rock lodged in her spine, and Amalia cried out. He didn't stop but tightened his hands uncomfortably around her.

"Cisco, you're hurting me."

She tried to squirm out of his grasp, but he was pressing firmly against her. Releasing his hold to pull at her blouse, Cisco used his legs to guide her toward a boulder jutting from the wall. Amalia shoved at his hands.

"Stop. What are you doing?"

He pressed his full weight on her to lay her back. As he fumbled with his pants, she took that moment to create some distance between them.

"Cisco, don't do this."

His eyes were wild as though he wasn't seeing her anymore.

Trying to snap him out of his frenzied state of mind, she said, "Francisco, you're scaring me."

Through his teeth, he growled, "Quiet, señorita! You are ruining the moment." Pulling her to him, he warned, "Stop fighting me."

Cisco separated her legs with his and became more violent as he thrust toward her. Amalia shoved with all her strength and rolled out from under him, but he immediately gave chase.

Running as fast she could, she started to cry. "What has come over you? Are you playing a cruel joke?"

Cisco tripped over his trousers and nearly fell but quickly regained his footing and charged after her. Amalia outran him, finding a hiding place beneath a bush to catch her breath, but his feet appeared in front of her, and she yelped. Hands heaved through the foliage and jerked her to stand.

"Cisco, why are you acting like this?"

"Shut up, puta!"

Amalia stiffened and slapped him. "How could you?"

Momentarily stunning him, Amalia pushed past Cisco and ran again. She could hear his heavy breathing behind her, so she sprinted as fast as she could. A broken branch lay in her path. Amalia lunged for it and turned around with the broken end toward him. Closer than she realized, Cisco collided with it, and a wail of agony rent the air. He crumpled to the ground. His moaning almost ripped her heart out, and Amalia crawled to his side.

"Cisco, I'm so sorry. I never meant to injure you. Show me where you're hurt."

"No, get away from me," he whimpered.

Blood soaked the ground around them, and Amalia turned pale with terror. He didn't resist her when she pulled him over. She saw the source of the blood and fell backward in utter shock. The stick had punctured his groin.

Amalia screamed, "Cisco, you need help. What should I do? Tell me what to do!"

Cisco gasped for air. All color drained from his face. Slowly, he rolled away from her and lost everything in his stomach. Amalia sobbed.

Should I leave him to find help? What if he dies? Oh, Lord, have mercy. We need help.

As if in answer to her whispered prayer, Amalia heard a voice calling for Cisco. She got to her feet and frantically searched for the voice. *Is it real? Yell again.*

She yelled back, "Hola? Help! We need help. Anyone? Is someone there?" A man walked in their direction.

"Francis, Francis, where are you? Your uncle has arrived. I've been sent to fetch you."

The gentleman stopped in his tracks when his eyes fell on Amalia. Then his gaze lowered to Cisco curled up at her feet. Rushing toward them, he yelled, "No, what happened?"

Cisco mumbled, "Adolpho, help."

His eyes searched for answers. Gently shaking him, Adolpho asked, "Francis, can you move?"

He didn't respond. Adolpho tugged at him and flinched back in horror when he realized where the blood came from.

"I need to slow the bleeding. This looks really bad." He removed his cravat.

Amalia stuttered, "I-It's my fault. I'm so sorry. He was acting crazy, and I was frightened. I only meant to hold the stick out for a defense when he ran into it. Por favor, I'm so sorry. Is he going to be alright?"

Realizing his cravat wouldn't do, Adolpho cast it aside and tore off his bolero coat, waistcoat, and shirt. Using his shirt, he wrapped Cisco's groin like a diaper; cries of pain filled the air. Putting his coat back on, Adolpho carefully lifted him up.

"Amalia," Cisco whispered.

She rushed to him. "I'm here, Cisco. I'm here. I'm so sorry."

HOLLY BROUGH

Cisco reached his hand to her face and brushed his thumb over her lips. Then he looked into her eyes and hissed, "I hate you for what you have done."

Using the rest of his strength, he shoved her head, causing her to stumble backward. Hurt and confused, Amalia regained her footing just in time to get a face full of spittle from Adolpho.

"You heard him. Stay away." He rushed away with Francisco, the duke of Cádiz, unconscious in his arms.

Amalia fell to her knees, wiping at the spittle on her face. After a long cry, she stumbled back to the estate in a numb stupor, unable to fully accept Cisco's last words to her. It wasn't until she neared the house that she noticed blood on the hem of her skirt. Thanking God one more time the Tudó family was still on holiday, she rushed to the stables and used the water from the trough to rinse it out. More blood stained her sash, which meant blood probably smudged other places she couldn't see without a thorough inspection. Praying no one would notice before she could properly wash it, she sneaked from corner to corner, successfully dodging the staff, until she found refuge in her room.

Adolpho got Francis into the house and to his quarters without alerting the entire staff. Finding his valet, Adolpho asked him to quietly summon a doctor.

"What has happened?"

"Francis had another mishap, but this one is serious. You need to hurry, then come straight to his room. Don't speak to anyone."

"Right away, señor."

There was no way to keep their uncle from discovering Francis's latest catastrophe. Adolpho waited for the valet to return before searching out their uncle, all the while determining a convincing lie.

Finding the intimidating man looking over some papers in the study, Adolpho cleared his throat and knocked on the open door. "Uncle Carlos, I am relieved to find you. Francis is here, but I am afraid he is indisposed at the moment."

His uncle suffered from a receding hairline and bulging, bloodshot eyes—the result of overindulgent wine.

"Indisposed? I demand to see him at once." He stood from the fine upholstered chair he was sitting in and yanked his waistcoat over a generous middle. "I'm outraged at your audacity, leaving without telling me where you were taking Francis. I've had a hell of a time catching up to you here in Lorca. My brother gave me strict orders on his deathbed to ensure his eldest son take the throne. There are serious consequences at stake here, and *you*, of all people, know that as well as anyone."

"Si, Uncle, I take full responsibility. I just felt Francis couldn't experience true freedom under constant scrutiny."

"You have taken too much liberty, señor! That was not your decision." Adolpho created some space between him and his uncle.

"When I allowed you to be a companion to Francis, I believed, or rather hoped, you would keep him out of trouble. You're five years his senior, and yet I believe he is the more sensible of the two of you, and that isn't saying much."

"That's unfair, Uncle. If you knew half the things I have done to keep Francis on the road to the throne, you would not be so unforgiving."

Uncle Carlos downed the last of his drink. "I'll see my nephew now. Where is he?" For such a large man, he could cross a room in two strides.

Adolpho rushed to the door and thrust out his arm to head him off. "Uh, before you go to him, you need to know something."

His uncle's face turned red with rage.

"Francis had an accident today. He was having a little sport with a señorita earlier and fell out of a tree."

"That damned fool. Will he ever stop acting like a monkey? What did he break this time?"

"I think it is worse than that . . . He seems to have punctured his groin."

"What?!" Uncle Carlos stormed past him, throwing Adolpho against the doorframe.

He sprinted after his uncle up the stairs. "I don't know how bad it is yet. The physician is probably with him now. We should know more soon, I'm sure."

They both entered Francis's room in time to see the doctor examining the damage under a bloody sheet. Uncle Carlos put his fist to his mouth and turned away.

Noticing the two men enter the room, the physician addressed them. "Ah, señors. I am Dr. Garcia. Your nephew has had a most unfortunate accident. I have successfully sedated him, and he is peacefully resting. I'm afraid, however, I will need to perform some minor surgery to repair his scrotum."

Uncle Carlos looked at the man, wide-eyed.

"I apologize for my candor, but I feel it is best to be perfectly forthright."

"Si, *perfectly.*" With a wave of his hand, he said, "Do what you must. However, I'm not familiar with you, Doctor. I'm sure I don't need to stress the importance of your professional discretion on this matter. I will have your license if I hear the slightest rumor of my nephew's condition. Do I make myself clear?"

Dr. Garcia stuttered, "S-Si, of course."

"That goes for all of you."

A housemaid and Francis's valet nodded their heads in unison.

Uncle Carlos took Adolpho by the arm and escorted him out. "Who is this señorita you mentioned? Did she see the accident?"

"I believe she did, but I don't think she realized how badly he was injured. She ran off when she saw me."

"Does Francis have feelings for this girl?"

Chuckling as if the question was ludicrous, he replied, "Of course not. She was just a little diversion before committing himself to the crown."

"If hear even a whisper about her, Nephew—"

"Si, Uncle. Not a whisper."

The two men made their way to the parlor to await the doctor's news. It took two hours before they got the devastating diagnosis. Dr. Garcia cleared his throat, then took a slight step back when Uncle Carlos rose to his feet at his entrance.

"Sí?"

"I'm afraid the duke will never father his own children." Dr. Garcia pulled at his collar.

"I beg your pardon?" Uncle Carlos sank into his chair.

"There is nothing that can be done. I'm sorry."

After escorting the doctor out, Adolpho slumped in the seat opposite his uncle, ran his hands through his once perfectly styled hair, and rested his head in his hands. "Francis has told many convincing lies in his life, but this one may be too difficult, even for him."

"Mmm." Uncle Carlos swirled a new glass of liquor. "He can still charm the queen into marrying him. She won't know of his *disability* until after the wedding."

"But what about the wedding night? There are witnesses to the consummation."

"You let me worry about that. Our family's prosperity depends on him taking the throne. It's his right, and I will not let my late brother down. Francis will be king of España."

Lavender

CHAPTER 12

D USTING THE FURNITURE of an empty house for yet another day, Sonia couldn't listen to Amalia's heavy sighs for another second.

"Amalia, I don't think you should go to the fortress anymore. You've gone every day for almost three weeks with no sign of Cisco."

"I can't stop."

"But you aren't well. You haven't been well for weeks. You can't get up in the morning. You eat very little and what you do eat, you can't keep down. I think you need a doctor."

Amalia sat on the freshly made bed and leaned her head on one of the bedposts. *Should I tell her?* "Sonia."

Sonia brushed a wisp of her mousy brown hair into her cap and looked at her expectantly.

"What if . . . What if he's dead? What if I killed him?" Amalia wiped a tear from the corner of her eye.

"If you killed him, the Civil Guard would have come for you by now." Sonia sat next to her friend. "Amalia? There's something you need to know." Sonia waited for the response that inevitably came with every conversation lately.

As if on cue, Amalia burst into tears. "What is it?"

Sonia took a deep breath and pulled Amalia into an embrace. "There is a rumor Cisco is traveling to court to secure Queen Isabella's hand soon. It's possible he's already left."

No . . . "He is going to Madrid? But he doesn't want to be king. Who told you this?"

"The stable boy, Ricardo."

"How would he know this? He's just a stable boy."

"It seems our stable master, Jorge, is interested in the same stallion as the duke, and that is how Ricardo overheard the conversation. He goes into town regularly with Jorge."

Amalia stood and frantically looked about the room. "Why haven't you told me about this?"

"Until now, there wasn't anything to tell."

"I need to write to him immediately. Does anyone know where he is staying? Does Ricardo?" Rushing out the door, she vaulted down the grand staircase with renewed vigor.

Sonia followed. "He won't respond. He hasn't sought you out in weeks. He obviously doesn't want to see you. You are acting desperate, Amalia."

Amalia spun around, hands in the air. "I *am* desperate."

She carelessly rushed into the study, bumping her elbow on the door jamb. A howl escaped her as she pushed past stuffed leather chairs to get to the desk. Unceremoniously opening and closing several drawers, she found some paper and lead and penned a short note. Amalia set out to find Ricardo at the stables, almost knocking Sonia off her feet as she shoved past. "I'm going to the stables."

The tall, chubby eleven-year-old was whitewashing the stable walls when Amalia approached him.

"I understand you brought news of the duke."

Ricardo looked up from under his wide-brimmed hat.

"Do you happen to know where he is staying?" Amalia asked.

The young boy wiped his disheveled hair out of his eyes and nodded.

"If I promise to finish whitewashing this wall for you, will you take this letter to him right now for me?"

Ricardo's brown eyes lit up. "Si, señorita."

"Gracias, machito."

He ran off with the letter in hand and not a glance back.

As Sonia predicted, no reply was sent in return, so the next day Amalia sent another letter, promising Ricardo all her desserts for a month. It continued for a week. With the family still on holiday, the freedom she had acquired over the last ten weeks was a luxury. Some days, Amalia sent more than one letter. All went unanswered, so when Ricardo timidly walked into the study to interrupt Amalia perusing a book on horse breeding, she startled him with her abrupt approach.

"Did he send for me?"

The poor boy hung his head, his hat held in front of him as if in mourning. "Pardon, señorita. I have been told to stop bringing letters. The duke"—he sniffed and wiped his nose on his sleeve before continuing—"is leaving for Madrid in the morning."

Amalia crouched to his height. "Why are you crying, machito?" Amalia asked through a tightening throat. "This isn't your fault." Ricardo shrugged his shoulders.

"Were they abrupt with you?"

He shrugged again and averted his eyes.

I've got to go to Cisco myself. If he knows I'm carrying his child, he'll know why we are meant to be together and take me back. Amalia took a shuddered breath. "I need to know how to get to his house. Will you tell me?"

Ricardo hiccupped through the directions.

"You have been a true friend to me, and I'm grateful you delivered my letters despite the distance. I will never forget your kindness, machito. You may go now."

As soon as the boy left, Amalia went to Señora Morales's office. Like always, the housekeeper was at her cluttered desk, reading through papers.

Amalia knocked on the door to make her presence known. Señora Morales didn't look up but said, "You want to go on your daily walk. How many times do I have to tell you that you need no permission when you leave the manor at siesta?" The woman finally lifted her head.

Amalia smiled. "Si, señora. And if I am a little longer today?"

"No more than an hour."

"Gracias."

It took an hour for Amalia to find the residence where Cisco was staying. Several people pointed in her direction, whispering things behind their hands. She kept her head down, tucked in the loose strands of her hair, and casually wiped at the dust on her skirt. Approaching the white stone building and intimidating mahogany door, Amalia lifted her hand to ring the bell but paused.

Feeling a fit of nausea coming on, she pushed the button and stepped back.

Thinking twice about her plan, she moved to leave, but the butler answered before Amalia could turn and walk away.

"Si?" He looked down the tip of his nose at her.

Amalia smiled through her discomfort. "Buenas tardes, señor. I am Señorita Maritimo. I am here to inquire about the duke. Will you let him know I am here, por favor?"

His expression didn't change when he motioned her just inside the door. "Wait here."

Hands clasped behind her back, Amalia nibbled on her lower lip as she looked around the cavernous, unwelcoming entrance hall and its gray marble floors. Hastened footsteps drew closer, and she brought her hands to her chest to quiet her pounding heart.

He's coming.

In walked the love of her life, looking as dashing as ever in his crisp black breeches and burgundy tailcoat. She flushed at the sight of him. Cisco's face lit up when he saw her, but Amalia's happiness dissolved into apprehension when his behavior suddenly turned cold.

Was he expecting someone else?

"Si, señorita, you called?"

Amalia blurted, "I am so relieved you are well. You can't imagine—"

Cisco lifted his hand to stop her. His eyes softened for only a fleeting moment before he averted his gaze. "Did you say there was something you needed?"

Amalia reached for him. "Cisco, look at me, por favor. Let me take you away from here. You told me you don't want a life at court. Let's go away and grow old together."

His eyes shifted fearfully toward the hall from where he came before pushing her off. "Do not address me like a plebeian, señorita. I have no knowledge of what you speak." Turning his head away from her, he continued, "Now if you will excuse me, I am in the middle of some very important business. I have no time for such frivolous nonsense." He fluffed one of his lacy cuffs before waving the back of his hand for her to leave.

Amalia stood speechless, hands clasped at her belly, searching for the man she'd come to love. She whispered, "Is someone listening? Cisco, I . . . I'm . . . I need you."

Cisco lifted his gaze to her. He finally looked at her like he had so many times before. Recognition filled his eyes, some kindness and maybe regret, but then a door slammed in the distance, and it disappeared. *Probably just my wishful imaginings.* Quick as lightning, the foppish behavior he'd adopted when trying to discourage girls at court replaced his compassion. He coughed a dainty cough and brushed his eyebrows flat with his pinky. Many times she'd seen him revert to that behavior to make her laugh. He'd taken on the role of the joker again, but this time, it was no joke.

After some uncomfortable silence, Amalia dared to ask, "Do you feel nothing for me?"

He looked bored as he examined the ruby ring on his finger, huffed on it then shined it on his black velvet lapel. A facade had replaced the Cisco she thought she knew. When he again looked at her fully in the face, an undeniable loathing permeated his features. The air sucked out of her. She couldn't breathe. It felt as if someone had punched her in the gut. Amalia realized it was over.

"So be it," she said. Rallying as much dignity as she could, Amalia willed the moisture in her eyes to stay put, opened the heavy door, and walked out. The lump in her throat threatened to choke her, but he would not know it. She held her chin high and didn't look back. Oh, how she wanted to take one last look, but she wouldn't give him the satisfaction of knowing how deeply he'd hurt her.

Not until she rounded the tall hedges at the corner of the dusty road did she hasten her pace and allow her tears to flow. The waterworks streamed down her cheeks, momentarily obscuring her vision, and she collided into someone. If he hadn't reached out to catch her, she would have fallen to the ground, but instead, Amalia came face-to-face with Cisco's friend, the one who'd rescued him.

His amused dark eyes regarded her. "You should watch where you are going, señorita."

"Pardon me," Amalia said, fiercely wiping at the tears on her face.

His strong hands still held her close to him. "You are Amalia. Allow me to introduce myself."

"I don't care to know who you are, señor." Notes of cedar and musk filled her senses.

"I can tell you're upset. I am Francis's best cousin, Adolpho." He laughed at her surprise. "There is no reason why we shouldn't be on familiar terms, seeing as you are no lady."

Amalia raised her voice. "Let me go."

"Sí, cariño. I'm happy to let you go, but you should know some things before we part." Loosening his grip slightly, he said, "Pardon me if I am making an incorrect assumption, but I dare guess you have just seen your beloved *Cisco*. Am I correct?"

Amalia said nothing but lowered her eyes to stare at his perfectly tied cravat instead of his rich, chocolate eyes and condescending smile.

Unable to stand the silence, she said, "I don't understand how he could dismiss me so easily. I thought we were in love." Her voice trailed off. Even to her, the words sounded absurd.

Adolpho shook his head, tsking his tongue as if she were a puppy with a thorn in her paw. Amalia bit her lip, still avoiding his gaze, and waited for the answer she already knew in her heart.

"You really are quite a fetching creature, aren't you?"

That brought her eyes back to his. *He knows I am suffering. He is mocking my pain.*

As if already disinterested, Adolpho continued, "You don't understand, do you? Amalia, if you were a lady of noble birth, the duke of Cádiz would never have acted with the lack of decorum as he did. He is a noble destined for the highest court of España. This holiday was his opportunity to enjoy uninhibited freedom and promiscuity, and you gladly obliged." Adolpho released her, stepped back, and flourished a mocking bow. "He wouldn't have looked at you otherwise."

Amalia felt her consciousness slipping. Numbness took over her limbs. She almost wished Adolpho hadn't let go of her.

"You damaged him in a way that has altered his life forever. He will never forgive you for that."

Amalia's mouth dropped open, her hands intuitively cradling her belly. "I don't know what you mean."

"Come now. You know what happened. Is it really that hard to understand how he could truly despise you, that he would never want to see you again after what happened? He wants to forget your short romance ever happened. And you. Think of the shame if anyone found out you were merely a toy for the duke—a toy he grew bored of and tossed aside. No honorable man would want anything to do with you."

He's right. Not even a decent man could want me after what I have done.

Adolpho and Cisco were so alike, vicious and callous. Anger boiled inside her, giving her the drive to shove past Cisco's cruel cousin and walk away. The numbness in her limbs became unbearable pain. Starting in her chest, it spread like wildfire throughout her body. To escape the burning anguish, she ran over rocky terrain, tall grass, and up steep hills, pushing her legs and lungs past their limit, but it did not numb her pain. Amalia gasped for air amid racking sobs, sobs that grew in volume at the sight of her destination—the very carob tree where she and Cisco met.

Stumbling into the rock that collected his gifts of wildflowers, she crumbled to her knees and allowed the tears to flow. All the hurt, anger, and frustration she'd bottled up over the past year came flooding back. Her father betrayed her, sending her from sweet Thomas to a hateful, abusive master. Then there was Cisco . . . His soft, tender kisses forced their way into her mind, bringing the scorch to its apex. Amalia ground her nails into her arms to channel the memories from the intimate moments they shared. She slipped to her backside and kicked at the rock and screamed until her voice gave out. No amount of exertion lessened the pain.

"Let the darkness consume me!" she pleaded. "Por favor, God, no more!" *I've been so naive. How could someone like him truly love someone like me? And now I am ruined.*

Her head pounding, she lay down and looked into the tree Cisco pounced from. Cries turned to moans. The pressure in her heart crippled her lungs, and she turned to her side to throw up. *If I can't breathe, maybe I will die right here or maybe the baby will. No child should have to endure a stupid woman like me.* Amalia squeezed her legs to her chest until light slipped from her vision, and she lost consciousness.

Paprika

CHAPTER 13

WHEN AMALIA GREW aware of her surroundings, darkness cloaked the sky, and the terrain seemed unfamiliar. Like a gust of wind, her memories came back. Again, she felt like she was drowning in despair. Willing herself to stand, she made her way to the estate. Searing pain accompanied every step. Fresh tears streamed down her dirt-crusted face.

All of this agony because I allowed myself to be seduced by a charming man. How pathetic I turned out to be.

When Amalia entered the back door, a barrage of questions from the kitchen staff accosted her.

"What happened to you?"

"You look terrible. Are you hurt?"

"Why are your clothes covered in dirt?"

Before Amalia could say anything, Sonia pushed through the group and pulled her aside. "Leave her alone."

With everyone out of earshot, Sonia asked, "Where have you been?"

"I went to see . . . him."

"What? Did he hurt you?"

Amalia lied, "I had a bad fall and hit my head. I think I may have blacked out, but I'm fine now. I just need to go to bed." Amalia excused herself and walked to their room, despite the persistent pleas from Sonia to eat something before turning in.

After two more days of moping and avoiding others, Amalia went to bed as soon as supper was concluded, only to receive an unexpected visit from Señora Morales. Quietly opening the door, the woman stood in the doorway, wringing her hands with uncertainty.

Amalia sat bolt up, hid the book she was reading, and pulled the covers to her chest.

"Are you ill?" Señora Morales asked.

"No." Amalia frantically wiped at the tears on her face. "Did I do something wrong? I finished all my work. You said I could retire early if I finished my responsibilities."

"It's not that." The housekeeper stepped into the room.

"Where's Sonia? Is she alright?" Amalia stood and replaced Sonia's name book under her pillow.

"Si, si. Let me finish. Señor Tudó has arrived from his summer holiday and requested your company." The housekeeper's hands shook slightly as she tucked a loose strand of hair behind her ear.

Amalia felt the color drain from her face. "My company? I don't understand. I didn't think they were expected back for another week. It is late, señora." Searching the woman's eyes, she continued, "I don't mean to be disrespectful. I am just so tired."

"I've noticed, and I've had the doctor summoned for tomorrow morning."

I can't be seen by a doctor.

Amalia tried to protest, but the señora cut her off. "I have made my decision, señorita. You don't seem quite yourself. Despite your ailments, however, I'm afraid I must request you make yourself presentable and meet the señor in his study. Vamos. He isn't a very patient man."

Sonia bounded into the room and stopped short when she saw Señora Morales standing just inside the door. "Oh, pardon me. I didn't know you were here. Should I go?"

"I'm leaving." Turning to address Amalia, she said, "See you in a moment, señorita. Don't be long. And Señorita Vela, Cook has some things for you to attend to right away. See to it before retiring for the night."

Sonia stood silent in the doorway for a moment, watching Amalia struggling out of bed to put on her uniform. She puffed a loose strand of hair out of her eyes and jumped to assist her.

"You must have heard that Señor Tudó came home early from his summer holiday."

"Si. That's why Señora Morales was here. Señor Tudó has asked for my company, and I'm trying to understand what's going on. So . . . he came home without his family?"

Sonia's brows were knit together with concern.

"That means Señor Tudó is alone in his study. I'm frightened, Sonia. I don't want to be alone with him."

She tied the bow to secure Amalia's apron. "I know. Just keep your distance and don't make eye contact. Ask him if he would like some coffee and offer to get it for him. I'll try to be close, so I can interrupt if need be."

"You know how well that went last time. It's not safe for you either." Amalia quickly pulled her black shoes on.

Sonia finished brushing and rolling Amalia's hair with pins so it was up under her cap. They hugged, and Amalia took a deep breath to calm her nerves before leaving. She saw Sonia slump onto the bed and clasp her hands in prayer. *God be with me,* Amalia offered too.

Nearing the study, she overheard Señor Tudó ask after her. "What is taking the lovely angelita so long? I asked for her twenty minutes ago."

Señora Morales said, "I had to get her out of bed, señor. She isn't feeling well. Perhaps tomorrow would be better."

"Do not presume to deny me. I want her now!"

"Si, señor, I'll go check on her." The housekeeper nearly ran into Amalia as she exited the room. "I'm sure you heard the señor," she whispered. "He has been waiting too long and already had too much to drink."

Amalia pulled her blouse closer around her neck and walked into the study.

Señor Tudó was sitting in the overstuffed leather chair set by the fireplace, his cravat untied and the top buttons of his shirt undone. Holding a glass in one hand and an empty decanter in the other, he stood when she entered.

"Señorita, it has been months since I last saw you. Come, sit over here by me and relax for a moment. Would you like a drink to refresh yourself?" His eyes were glazed and his words slurred.

Amalia took a step back. "No, gracias. Are you expecting guests? I am happy to ask Cook to prepare a tray of sweet breads and coffee."

"No, I don't want coffee. You are my guest, and I want you to sit with me. I have offered you a drink, señorita. It is impolite to refuse my offer."

Amalia looked toward the door and noticed someone closed it. When she turned back, Señor Tudó had sidled up next to her, breathing down her neck. The smell of tobacco and alcohol turned her stomach, so she stepped back and covered her nose to block the odor. He caught her by the waist and pulled her to him, reached up, and yanked the cap from her head. Amalia's hair came loose and fell down her back.

"I thought I told you not to wear these stupid caps."

"Señor, I am not feeling well. Por favor, let me go."

Grabbing a handful of her thick hair, he brought it to his nose and took a long whiff. "I like it when your hair hangs down. Now, querida, I will not ask again. Sit with me. I have spent many weeks thinking about a moment alone with you."

Her voice quivering, she asked, "Should we be expecting your family soon?"

"Enough of this!" Señor Tudó lifted Amalia off her feet and carried her to the sofa, forcing her onto his lap.

"Let me go." She kicked and hit with all her strength, but he was stronger.

"Stop struggling, señorita. You're making this harder than it needs to be." The señor easily pinned Amalia's legs beneath one of his legs, so she couldn't flee and held her wrists in one hand, pulling her head toward his with the other. Amalia opened her mouth to scream, but he put his mouth on hers. The taste brought on a sudden gag, and she threw up in his open mouth and down the front of his unbuttoned shirt.

"Ah!" Señor Tudó threw her off and kicked at her as she instinctively crawled away and sheltered her growing belly from his rage. Gagging himself, he wiped at the mess to no avail. "You filthy puta! The devil take you!" He kicked at her more before storming out of the room.

Amalia lay curled up on the Persian rug at the base of the desk, unable to silence her sobs. Vomit crusted her face, her hair, and her uniform, but that was a minor inconvenience compared to the throbbing in her legs and back. Acutely aware of the danger she faced if she stayed, the time to run had come.

The footman, Ambrose, showed up and lowered to his knees next to her. "Oh, poor pequeña. Can you walk? I'm sorry. I should have appeared sooner, but *my* pitiful carcass would be found in a ditch come morning."

Once on her feet, Amalia shoved Ambrose away. "Where is Sonia?" He shrugged and moved to wrap his arm around her.

"Leave me be. I can manage on my own."

Amalia limped to her room, fresh tears streaming down her face. A plan of escape had been formulating in her mind for weeks. She'd waited too long to say something to Sonia. With a doctor coming in the morning, she didn't want to think what would happen if the señor found out she was with child. Leaving immediately was her only option.

Amalia winced as she removed her soiled uniform and washed off all the sick. She dug her old carpetbag out from under her bed and emptied the drawer that held the few things she owned. She then started gathering Sonia's things. *Where is she? We don't have much time.*

Just then, Sonia burst through the door. Amalia immediately pulled her in and closed the door behind her. "We have no time. Hurry."

"What happened? Señor Tudó almost trampled me with his horse. He rode off like a wild man."

"He tried to force himself on me, but I vomited in his mouth. Where is your travel bag?" Amalia found her brush and tossed it on top of her underclothing. "I can't stay here any longer, especially after humiliating him." She took Sonia's hand in hers. "Come with me, por favor. You can't stay here either."

Sonia gathered the clothes Amalia had set on her bed and began putting them away. "I can't leave. My family depends on my earnings. And . . . we have no money. Where would we go?"

"I don't know."

Silence weighed heavily between them. "Sonia . . ." Amalia paused. *This is not the time to tell her of my condition. It will only make her worry.* "There are so many things I wish I could tell you. Why does life have to be so hard?" Both girls gave in to tears.

"We live in a world of men, and we have no control over our lives," Sonia said.

"Then let's take control, right now. It's not fair that we have to part because a man can't check himself. Come with me."

"I can't."

"Why?"

"You know why."

Amalia wiped at her tears and pulled Sonia into a hug. "How can I leave you? You're the only friend . . . family I have."

"I wish things could be different."

"I have to leave before Señor Tudó gets back. Stay away from him as much as you can. I'll try to send word when I'm finally settled. Te amo, Sonia."

Amalia didn't wait for a reply. Her heart was breaking, and she couldn't leave fast enough. Sneaking from shadow to shadow, she gathered things she needed. In Señora Carolina's room, she picked one of her more conservative dresses with plenty of room in the front to hide her belly. She then rushed to the master suite, not really knowing what she should take but frantic to find something of value to ensure her and her child's survival.

Nothing grabbed her attention. With only a small candle for light, she scurried through Señor Tudó's personal chamber and noticed a sparkle on the vanity. The green gems, she'd discovered the first day she toured the estate, lay half exposed from a black velvet bag. Amalia shoved the treasure into her carpetbag and tiptoed down the servants' stairs, through the kitchen, and out the back door, but not before taking some scraps from the evening's meal, fruit and a loaf of day old bread with her.

Pomegranate blossom

CHAPTER 14

AMALIA LUMBERED ALONG the road as fast as she could. Absently rubbing her belly, Amalia considered the two emotions fighting within her. Did she want the evidence of Cisco's love, or did she hope the pregnancy would terminate on its own? Of the men she had known in her life, all had betrayed her. From now on, she would be the one to use them for her purposes and not be taken advantage of again. *My heart belongs to my child now.*

Noises in the dark scared Amalia into creeping along the road near the foliage, careful not to trip on protruding roots and prickly brush. Every misstep made her side and legs hurt where she'd been kicked, but she had to keep going.

The road she followed led to the small seaport town of Águilas. Just thinking about the way Cisco dismissed her so carelessly turned her stomach. She'd proven herself a simpleton, running to him and thinking he'd take her back.

Another stupid choice was taking the jewels. Now that she'd had time to think about it, how could they benefit her? He might give up the chase over a minor slight from a servant girl, but valuable jewels were an entirely different matter. How could she sell them without someone thinking it suspicious? Coming up with a new name was the only thing she did right.

Lea Tavio, tired eighth. I will refer to myself as Lea from now on.

Amalia whispered her new name over and over and practiced introductions until it sounded natural. She ate all the bland food she had commandeered from the kitchen to curb the insatiable hunger she felt, but it did little good. Nothing tasted appetizing and rarely stayed down. Picking up her pace after a short break, Amalia held her swollen breasts while she ran along the path to keep their pain to a minimum.

Horses could be heard approaching, so she scurried behind a nearby bush. Crouched out of sight, Amalia pulled her skirt beneath her and allowed herself to relax and concentrate on the low voices moving her way. The words were difficult to understand at first, but the friendly banter told her the men were comrades—English comrades.

One of them said, "We will arrive in Águilas in just over ten kilometers. Then you can treat me to a nice meal and some lively entertainment."

"I treat you? *Captain* Channing, with your recent promotion, it is you who should treat me. Plus, I saved your life twice this week."

"It's not *captain* yet, and what do you mean, saved my life? Those women were harmless."

Laughing, the other man said, "They were most certainly not harmless, and they had their hooks baited for you. For someone whose job is in intelligence, I'm surprised you've survived this long. You're lucky I made it back to our table when I did, or you'd have been skinned alive and fileted for supper."

Joining in the jest, Channing conceded, "Perhaps you are right. I am a sucker for beautiful women, and they were both *very* beautiful. Come to think of it, one of them couldn't keep her hands off me."

"That one, I believe, was trying to lift your coin purse. You should be more selective when pursuing a woman's affections."

The laughter faded, and so did Amalia. The few words she understood were *Águilas* and *ten kilometers*. Pleased with the twenty kilometers she had traveled, she rolled up her shawl for a pillow and curled up on her side for a short respite.

Before she knew it, light shone through her eyelids and warmth kissed her skin. Realizing she no longer had the cloak of darkness, Amalia scrambled to get her bearings and listen for voices. She shadowed her eyes with her hand to determine the angle of the sun—late morning—and she still needed to cover several kilometers. Amalia's belly vehemently protested its neglect. Hurrying her pace and staying in the cover of roadside vegetation, Amalia finally came to a beautiful house that appeared to be just on the outskirts of town. A lovely two-story adobe structure with red tile roof featured a charming balcony overlooking a white lattice archway and herb garden. Everything looked so inviting that she felt emotions well up inside of her.

What is wrong with me? She never used to be this emotional. She finally understood why her mother was so unbearable each time she had a baby. *Por favor, God, don't let me be like her.*

Amalia finally made it to a small cluster of cork trees near the beautifully kept herb garden. Grateful for the shade, she started to strip the clothing of her servitude and transform into a lady of station when a tantalizing aroma of fresh biscuits wafted past her. Her stomach growled. Sweat dripping down her temples from the excursion of the morning, Amalia noticed her hands shaking and the ground shifting under her feet. *I need to eat.*

The back door hung open, so she pressed her back against the adobe and sneaked her way to peek in. On a worn wooden table in the center of the modest kitchen sat a hot tray of golden brown biscuits. A whisper of a moan escaped her as she gingerly picked a hot biscuit off the tray and placed it in her mouth. A rich, buttery flavor seized her taste buds, and Amalia's eyes welled up with tears again. Anxious to grab another and stuff it into her mouth, she placed three more in her apron and moved to run out of the house before she was discovered.

She heard a *humph* behind her. The back door just in reach, Amalia was horrified she'd been caught and turned slowly around to see a plump, older woman standing just inside the kitchen door, hands on her hips and a puzzled look on her face. After getting a good look at her intruder's cheeks full of bread, the woman's eyes grew big, and she gripped her chest as if alarmed.

Dropping her contraband, Amalia rushed out the back, tripping on the base of the doorframe and falling to her hands and knees. She retched up the bread she had consumed and sobbed.

The woman hurried to her side and knelt down, wrapping her arm around Amalia's shoulders. "Oh, cariño, you poor thing. Now, now, we need to get you cleaned up and properly fed." Taking the corner of her apron, she wiped Amalia's tears away and said with a soft voice, "Shh. Stop your crying. Everything is going to be alright. Vamos."

Is this woman offering me help? Maybe God hasn't forsaken me.

Once on her feet, the white-haired, rosy-cheeked old woman assessed the damage. Her knees were scraped and bleeding, her black skirt torn at the hem but nothing appeared to be broken.

The kind woman pulled Amalia toward the house, but Amalia pulled away. "Por favor, señora, my bag is behind those trees. I must retrieve it."

"You go into the kitchen and sit at the table. I will get it for you."

"But . . ." *What if she looks into my bag and discovers the jewels?*

"Don't you fret. I will only be a moment . . . My, how you remind me of my daughter when she was your age." Brushing hair out of Amalia's face, she said, "You may call me Abuela. I had hoped to be one at this stage of my life." Abuela's smile faded, and sadness seeped into her mossy green eyes before she walked away.

Amalia felt better after eating another fresh biscuit and some vegetable broth. Abuela moved skillfully around the well-stocked, cozy kitchen, drawing water to put on the stove. She then prepared a fizzy drink and handed it to Amalia. "Drink this. It will refresh you." Amalia put her nose over the lip of the glass and sniffed. The bubbles tickled, and she quickly wiped the sensation away. She took a tentative sip, and the liquid seemed to lift a heavy burden from her shoulders. "Gracias, Abuela."

"Bueno. Now let's get you cleaned up."

The kind woman led Amalia to a room off the kitchen where a beautiful copper tub sat. An overstuffed chair was situated in the corner, where Abuela encouraged Amalia to sit until she filled the tub. "Not long now, and I believe you will feel more like yourself again."

When the water was ready, Amalia stood in the tub with a cotton sheet around her bare body while Abuela used a sweet-smelling soap to wash her and her long hair. Luxurious warm water ran over her sore limbs to rinse away the suds. Though covered, Amalia knew her petite frame revealed a growing belly and deep bruises on her legs and back, but Abuela was kind enough not to say anything. Instead, the elderly woman tenderly cared for Amalia as she'd imagined a mother would care for her daughter. Fresh tears slipped down her cheeks.

"There, there. Are you in pain?"

Amalia shook her head.

"What is your name, cariño?"

"Oh." *Oh dear. What was it again?* To stall, Amalia wiped at her tears. "I'm . . . Lea Tavio."

With a look Amalia knew all too well, Abuela clicked her tongue. "No, niña. You must say it with conviction." She held out a towel and helped Amalia step from the tub.

Heat rose to her cheeks. *Good heavens, will it always be this difficult to lie to people?*

Settling at a lovely vanity near a window with sheer curtains, Amalia said, "I *am* Lea Tavio. A very good friend of mine told me my name means *tired*. As you know, *tavio* means *eighth*, and it just so happens that I am the first of eight children. Perfect, no?"

Pulling a brush through Amalia's long hair, Abuela said, "Too perfect, I would say."

Amalia sat silent, avoiding her reflection in the mirror, while Abuela finished plaiting her hair.

"Let's get some clean clothes out for you, shall we?" The old woman picked up the used towels and wet linen sheet, carried them to the kitchen, and set them in the basin.

Not moving from her place at the mirror, Amalia watched Abuela situate herself in a chair opposite her and handed Amalia the bag she'd brought with her. Hands trembling slightly, Amalia took her bag and carefully pulled out a rich burgundy dress adorned with pearls at the neck and lace on the sleeves.

Abuela's eyes grew wide only for a moment. "Come, I may have something more suitable for you to wear during the day." Taking her hand, Abuela led Amalia through the kitchen into the entrance hall and up some stairs to a small room on the second floor, all the while, Amalia clinging to the cotton towel she had wrapped around her bare body.

Opening a large wooden chest at the base of a single bed, Abuela pulled out a pretty lavender muslin dress. "What you need is some clothing that makes you look less like a young niña who is trying to dress up like a woman of influence. The gown from your bag is too grownup for someone as youthful as you. This was my daughter's. I think it is just your size, maybe a little outdated, but let's try it on, shall we?"

Amalia turned her back to Abuela and lowered the towel draping her. Once the gown was fastened in the back, Amalia turned to face her. It mostly fit, but her bosom was flowing out of the bodice.

Abuela smiled. "Nothing my skill with a needle can't fix. I'm afraid all the other dresses will fit the same. Here, wear this for now." She pulled out of the chest some underclothing—a long blue skirt and full white blouse much too large for her.

Amalia grimaced when she held them up.

"No one will see you. This was mine when I was expecting my daughter, Lucita. I know it is big, but it will have to do until I can create some more room for your blossoming figure in this other dress."

Turning a shade of pink, Amalia bit her lip and looked in the standing mirror against the wall.

"Why don't you help me in the kitchen?" The kind woman twirled Amalia around and unfastened the muslin gown for her to put on the oversize clothes. "I think you should be Lucita instead of Lea, in honor of my daughter. How would you feel about that?"

Following Abuela down the stairs, Amalia said, "You speak of changing a name like it is something people do every day. Changing one's name shouldn't be so nonchalant."

"Why did you do it?"

"I didn't change it."

Abuela shook her head. "Si, you did."

"Why would you say that?"

Pulling out a bowl of dough starter, she said, "I have my reasons. Will you go into the pantry and get the flour on the shelf directly in front of you? That door there." Abuela pointed to her left.

Amalia did as she was asked.

"Do you trust me to help you?" Measuring a portion of the starter into a separate bowl, Abuela took the flour and added two cups, a pinch of salt, and a couple spoons of sugar.

"What makes you think I need help?"

"A mother sees many things that others think are hidden. Before anything else, you need a more suitable name, one that is believable."

Considering for a moment, Amalia admitted, "Lucita is a lovely name. What does it mean?"

Abuela handed Amalia a chunk of dough, sprinkled some flour on the counter, and they kneaded separate pieces in unison. "It means *light*. My daughter was the light of my life, and I see that same light in you. What is your real name, amorcito? I know your name is not Lea. It does not suit you."

"The tired part does."

Abuela took Amalia's chin in her flour-crusted hand. "You may *feel* tired, but being tired does not define you. You have a strength and vigor about you that is refreshing. To me, you look strong and healthy, despite feeling sore and sick." Patting her cheek, she continued, "I promise you won't feel tired and sick forever. You have a vibrant future ahead of you. Life is all about overcoming our challenges and enduring well. You can do anything you put your mind to."

Amalia didn't know what to say.

"I'm sure your given name suits you better," Abuela added.

Amalia nibbled on her lower lip for a moment before she finally admitted, "My real name is Amalia Maritimo, but you must keep that a secret. A powerful man tried to force himself on me, and I offended him. He turned violent, so I ran from his employ late last night while he was gone. I had to get away from him."

Abuela opened her mouth to say something but appeared to have thought better of it and turned back to her dough. "You made a wise choice. What a blessing you came to me. You are safe here." After some companionable silence, Abuela continued, "You should choose a name that will define your potential or give you courage to reach your goals."

"My friend said something similar to that."

"Wise friend. Do you have goals for yourself? What is it you want, niña?" Abuela waited patiently for Amalia to consider her question.

"Well, I've never really put it into words, but . . . I've always wanted a friend, someone I can count on who will accept me for who I am. I found that in my friend Sonia, but . . . I had to leave her behind."

"I'm sorry."

"We worked together for nearly a year, and she became family to me. She was the one who taught me the importance of names." Amalia wiped at a tear with the back of her hand. "I worry about her safety too."

"That must have been so hard to leave her behind."

"Si."

"Tell me more about your dreams, Amalia."

Sniffing back more tears, she said, "I . . . I'd like to be part of a community. My family lived in the country on a farm away from everyone else. We never participated in worship or festivals. I could see the colorful lights in town from our home and wondered what they were celebrating. When I went to trade school in Murcia, we got to go to worship services and festivals in the square by the Iglesia Catedral de Santa María, and it was magical—all the bright banners and colorful people. I feel like I have missed so much in my life. And . . . it might sound silly, but I want to do something meaningful, be a positive influence in the world. I'm failing so far. I do stupid things and trust the wrong people. So far I have made a mess of things."

"Those are wonderful goals, and they take time. You'll have to work hard for what you want, Amalia, but I believe you can do it with His help. I think God is more concerned about the direction we are traveling than the speed. Be patient with yourself. You've already made a difference in my life." Amalia's face lit up, and Abuela smiled back. "Your dough looks perfect. I daresay you have worked in a kitchen before."

"All my life."

"Muy bien. What you need now is rest. This is a fine start for la merienda. Time for siesta." Abuela shooed Amalia up the stairs and down the short hall. "I hope you don't mind if you stay in my room with me. I wasn't expecting company, and the other rooms aren't made up properly for such lovely company." She removed several small embroidered pillows and pulled the eyelet lace bedspread down. "You remind me so much of my Lucita. I feel like a part of me has come back to life with you here."

Amalia's eyes brimmed with tears. "I'm sorry. I can't seem to control my emotions."

Abuela picked up a nightdress from the base of the bed. "You have been through a great ordeal. Of course, you are tired. Put this on and get some rest."

Amalia shed the oversize blouse and skirt and slipped on the fine chemise offered. The soft sheets welcomed her weary body. Sleep overcame her quickly.

Saffron Crocus

CHAPTER 15

"BUENOS DÍAS, AMALIA." Abuela entered the room with a tray. "You must have been very tired."

"What time is it?"

"It is nine in the morning. Here, drink this tea. It will settle your stomach."

"Gracias."

Amalia had a chance to look about Abuela's room for the first time. A large painting of a young child in a white gown adorned the wall beyond the foot of the four-poster bed. A chubby cherub face framed by dark, curly hair looked down at her with its brilliant green eyes.

"Is that Lucita?"

"Si, very much like you. That is my angelita."

"She's beautiful."

"Gracias." Abuela handed her some vegetable stew and said, "When you feel up to it, meet me in Lucita's room to help me with the dress I'm working on."

Amalia finished her meal and wandered over to the large window overlooking the herb garden. At that window, Abuela would have had a perfect view of Amalia sneaking around the house the day before. *If she could see me, who else could see me?*

Finding Abuela, Amalia skipped across the room to hold the billowy fabric in her fingers.

"It's so light and soft."

"I'm glad you like it, but it's not quite finished yet. Put on the gown you brought with you."

She didn't hesitate. "I've been wanting to see how it looks on me. Isn't it lovely?"

Examining the moiré, burgundy dress, Abuela suggested, "I can make this more practical if I remove the lace on the sleeves and the pearls along the neck. What do you say?"

Amalia nodded. "Would it be alright with you if I wear it just the way it is for a while? I dream of wearing many dresses like this someday."

Abuela chuckled. "Of course, but there are things to be done in the kitchen. You'll need to wear an apron so it doesn't get soiled."

"Si, gracias." Amalia giggled. She twirled the dress in front of the mirror. The deep burgundy brought out the brightness of her green eyes. A wide velvet ribbon tied just above her growing belly, but the fabric was gathered generously in front to hide it.

Abuela wrapped what looked like a sheet around Amalia and stood back with her hand on her chin. Amalia looked at her reflection, wondering how she would maneuver around the kitchen in so much fabric and burst out laughing. Abuela joined in.

"You look like you're wearing a tent."

Amalia countered, "You don't like it? How about when I twirl like this?" She grabbed both sides of the sheet and twirled from side to side, lunging to the left and right like a dancer.

"Ah, when you pose like that, you look quite lovely." Abuela took Amalia into an embrace before leading her to the kitchen.

"Will you tell me more about your daughter?" Amalia asked.

"My sweet Lucita was just a little older than you when she was tragically taken from me. For years after, I couldn't make her favorite churros or put a bouquet of sweet lavender and daffodils on our table without crying." Abuela got out the vegetables and handed Amalia a knife. She could see the woman's mind drift to the past, to a time of sadness.

"She was so beautiful, so much like you that I thought I was seeing a ghost when we first met in this kitchen." Abuela wiped a tear from her cheek.

"You don't have to continue."

"I want to tell you. Our daughter caught the eye of a wealthy gentleman several years her senior who resided here for a time to oversee his growing business, but Lucita was in love with a nice, local boy named Anton. They grew up together. Unfortunately, this gentleman—his name was Manuel—wouldn't take *no* for an answer. He was cunning and manipulative, giving her gifts and priceless jewelry to seduce her, but she still refused him."

Amalia knew that kind of a man well: Tudó, Cisco, *and* her father. All three men did terrible things to get what they wanted with no regard for others. They all seemed to have the same motto: "Damn the consequences."

Abuela continued, "He persisted, of course. Lucita was eventually softened by the gifts—young bonitas are vulnerable, and Lucita was no different. Poor Anton could not afford to give her such extravagant things, and his heart broke when she considered accepting Manuel. The promise of a life of privilege, never wanting for anything, tempted her. Not many can resist such an offer."

That sounds all too familiar. I am guilty of that very thing, and now look at me.

"Not much time passed before we lost all control of Lucita. She sneaked out late at night, not returning until early the next morning. You can imagine her surprise when she found my husband, Don Sebastián, and me waiting for her arrival one morning. To our horror, a bruise covered her left eye and red welts blotched her neck. Don Sebastián rushed to her side. I was too stunned to move from my place. How could this man treat our little angelito like that?"

"What happened?"

"Lucita explained she made her decision to be with Anton, and the wretched Manuel lost his temper. Seeing her father's rage frightened her, and she tried to tell us he didn't hit her, that she had fallen, but we knew the truth. How else do you explain the hand marks around her throat?"

"That's terrible."

"No mother can endure such abuse of her child. Don Sebastián vowed to make Manuel pay. He left immediately to challenge him to a duel. I begged him not to go. My sweet husband was a hidalgo—a man of honor and very skilled with a saber—but in a fit of rage, anything could happen. He could be killed."

"A hidalgo? Why live here in such a small town as Águilas?"

"After his heroic years of service to King Carlos and King Ferdinand, and a difficult injury, we were allowed to retire here. We love this town. Our connection with Lucita's Manuel was through his father, Manuel Godoy, who also served under both kings. Godoy is a manipulative man, who lied and cheated his way up the ranks, even seducing the queen to get favor at court. They called Godoy the Prince of Peace if you can believe it. He was anything but, and he lined his pockets with blood money, craving power with no concern for consequences, which was his ultimate downfall. His son, Manuel Tudó, is just like him."

Amalia gasped and slumped into a nearby chair.

"Are you well? You look like you have seen a ghost, niña?"

Amalia tried to swallow. "I'm fine, gracias. I think I'm just tired."

"You know this Manuel Tudó, don't you?" Abuela couldn't hide her grief.

Amalia nodded. "What happened when Don Sebastián went after him?" *Don't say Señor Tudó killed him.*

"Being the coward Manuel is, to my great relief, he chose to run instead of meet my husband. Lucita and Anton disappeared the following day. At first, we assumed they ran off together—at least that was the rumor. But we didn't hear from them for months. We thought that after they were married, they could come back to us. Seven months, two weeks, and four days later, Lucita was found on the cobblestone path between our house and the marketplace. A terrible, blood-crusted gash spread across the back of her head. We knew she'd been murdered. Her body had been placed behind some bushes in a sitting position, as though she was napping against a tree trunk, her hands cradling a swollen belly." Abuela paused, looking at Amalia with new eyes. "Oh, how blessed I am that you came into my life, Amalia."

Amalia wiped the moisture from her brow. "Men are evil."

"Don Sebastián was a wonderful man. And so was Anton. There are good men out there."

"I've never met a good man. I don't think they exist."

"You will meet a good man someday. I promise."

"It won't matter. I repudiate all men and plan to be an old maid."

Abuela chuckled. "Tell me about your family, your . . . what was it, seven other siblings? What about your parents?"

Grateful for the change of subject, Amalia said, "I didn't get along with my mother very well, but she taught me everything I know about how to take care of a house and several children. I was even her midwife when she gave birth to four of my younger siblings."

"You couldn't have been very old."

"I think I was five when I cut the umbilical cord of my sister Josephine."

"Five. That is astonishing."

Amalia laughed. "I was running the house entirely on my own by the time I was seven. I hated it at first because my siblings were free to play and learn music and French. Of course, my twin brother, Gordy, and my second brother, Antonio, had to work with my father on the farm when they were old enough, but my sisters had it so easy."

"You had a twin?"

"Si. He was slower in development than me, but by the time we were three, he had caught up. My truest friend until my father sold me into servitude. Sweet Thomas was the one I hated leaving behind. Gordy can take care of himself, but Thomas . . . the moment he took his first breath, we connected, like he was mine. My mother resented it. He could do nothing right, and she neglected his needs. He was desperate for her attention and often left his favorite little critters for her to find. That only earned him more lashings. I did everything I could to protect him, but when I was sent away, I feared for him the most."

"Oh dear."

"The worst experience happened just a few weeks before I was sent away. Thomas found a particularly large toad he wanted as a pet. He showed me his prize, but I had dinner to get on. I insisted he put the toad back where he found it. Later that evening, my mother retired to her room to find a bloated toad under the covers in the middle of her bed. A shriek alerted everyone in the house that something bad had happened. We all ran to see the source of her excitement—everyone except Thomas. He knew he was in trouble."

"That seems harmless enough."

"It would have been, but my father poked at it with a stick to get it to move, and it exploded. Evidently, it died and swelled up in the heat. There were toad insides everywhere—on my mother, sisters, all over the bed. It was a mess. Thomas got a horrible whipping that evening. After I cleaned up the guts, I tended to Thomas's welts. Some lashes had broken skin. My heart ached for him, so I told him if he behaved and went to bed without complaining, I would give him a surprise in the morning."

"That's sweet. What was it?"

"I had discovered that one of our cats birthed a litter of kittens. I'd hidden them away, but I trusted Thomas would take good care of a kitten if he felt it was his special responsibility to protect and nourish it. The next morning, he chose a kitten and named it Ama, after me. He is such a sweet angelito."

"You sound like you are wonderful with children."

"Gracias."

Abuela paused before voicing her question. "Is Manuel Tudó the father of your child?"

Wrapping her arms around her belly in protection, Amalia blurted, "No."

Abuela seemed relieved. "I didn't mean to upset you, niña, but I had to ask. There is something I must tell you, but I need you to remain calm."

Amalia's eyes grew big.

"Tudó is looking for you and has posted a reward for any information as to your whereabouts."

Amalia took in a sharp breath. "No. How long have you known? Why did you keep this—"

Holding up her hand, Abuela continued, "I found out last evening while you were sleeping, and I feel we should pack your things and get you ready, in case you need to leave in a hurry. I will keep you safe."

"Por favor, he must not find me. I took some things from him and vomited all over him when he . . . when he tried to force himself on me. I did not tell you because I was afraid. Por favor, don't let him find me. What should I do?" Amalia's whole body shook.

"What did you take, Amalia? Besides the dress, I mean."

"I will show you."

She walked up the stairs to retrieve the jewels. Abuela followed. Amalia produced a velvet bag and revealed the emerald jewelry, inadvertently pulling out a folded slip of paper that fell to the floor. Clutching her heart, Abuela steadied herself against the bedpost.

"I know. I shouldn't have taken them."

"No, cariño, you shouldn't have." The old woman gingerly took the jewels from her.

"I grabbed them from his room on a whim. Maybe I could sell off the gems to support myself."

"That will not do. These are a well-known heirloom of the Tudó family, and the jewels Manuel offered Lucita in exchange for her hand. They belonged to his mother, Josefa de Tudó, first Countess of Castillo Fiel, but most people called her Pepita."

"I've seen a painting of her."

"I know of the one you speak." Abuela gave her a disgusted look. "She is a beautiful woman but tawdry. Pepita was Manuel Godoy's mistress until he secured a divorce from his wife and married her. I'm afraid Señor Tudó will never stop looking for these jewels. This is more serious than I thought."

Amalia bent down and picked up the folded paper. "What is this?"

"Let me see that." Abuela took it from her and unfolded it.

"It looks like me, except this nose seems bigger, and I have no dimple in my chin." Amalia pointed at the differences.

Abuela examined the portrait, then looked at Amalia with tears in her eyes. "This is my Lucita, my sweet angelito."

The resemblance to me is remarkable.

"Where did it come from?" Abuela asked.

"I think from this velvet bag."

Nodding her head in understanding, she said. "Let's talk about a plan of escape. Hopefully it won't come to that, but it is best to be prepared, I always say. First, we need to hide these, so no one will ever find them. You certainly can't be running around with them in your possession. Come, I have the perfect place."

Abuela took Amalia's arm to lead her back down the stairs.

Amalia asked, "But how will I take care of my bebé, and what if they find out you have them? You could be in danger."

Abuela pulled her in close. "Don't worry about me. I will never be the victim of that man again. These jewels almost cursed our home once before. It seems they are destined to remain here. I will be fine, and all will be well."

"Abuela?"

"Si?"

"I have never felt so loved. You have shown me kindness I can never repay."

"Hush, niña. It has been my greatest pleasure. You are a gift and a blessing." Abuela led Amalia through the kitchen to the pantry where she moved a bag of flour and pulled up a loose board in the floor. She got on her knees and placed the jewels deep inside the hole along with the drawing. There was a knock at the front door.

"That will be the morning produce. Stay here. I won't be a moment."

Amalia heard Abuela open the door and say, "Buenos días. Where is Roberto this morning? I was expecting him to bring me some fresh tomatoes."

A young man answered, "Si, señora. He is helping his father today, and I was sent in his place. I have everything you requested."

"As well as the spices?"

"Si, señora."

"Gracias, el joven. Come in. I just need to retrieve my coin purse in the other room."

Amalia peeked around the corner to see the young man step just inside the door and look around the house. She slipped from view before they made eye contact. He looked no older than her brother Antonio.

When Abuela returned, the young man was looking anxiously over his shoulder.

"Is anything the matter?"

"No, no. I just need to get back. Gracias, señora." He took the money and hurried out the door.

Sand Viper's Bugloss

CHAPTER 16

LATER THAT AFTERNOON, a pounding on the door interrupted the ladies upstairs. Both women stood in alarm. Abuela bit a thread off the lavender muslin gown she'd been altering and threw it into Amalia's bag. Unceremoniously shoving Amalia toward the back stairs, Abuela said, "I should have insisted you take that dress off earlier." She tore the rest of the lace off the left sleeve, put her finger to her lips, and whispered, "Go down this way and out the side door. You know the plan. Stick to the thick foliage near the house—no one can see you from the street—then make your way to the harbor. If we're lucky, a ship will still be at anchor off the shore. I know the captain and commander of that ship. I saw them a few days ago. Do what you can to find passage out of España. When walking in the open street, walk with purpose and don't bring attention to yourself. You have the money?"

Amalia nodded.

"Bueno. I'll distract whoever it is. All will be well, amorcito." Abuela hastily kissed Amalia's forehead and sent her off. Amalia felt like she needed to say something before they parted, but she couldn't find the words. Abuela nodded, left the room, and descended the stairs to answer the door.

"Buenas tardes, señors. What is all this impatience? I am an old woman. It takes me a little longer to get to the door." Abuela's smile faded a little when she noticed a shadowed figure in the distance, but a blink and it was gone.

The younger of the two men spoke first. "Buenas tardes, señora. We are with the Civil Guard. I am Guillermo Duranté, and this is Juan Engaños."

His comrade, a tall man with protruding eyeballs and derisive sneer, said nothing but craned his neck to look into the house.

Señor Duranté continued, "We received word that a criminal was seen here. Forgive the intrusion, but we are required to search these grounds for a señorita by the name of Amalia Maritimo. She is short and slender with dark hair and green eyes. She was a servant at the Tudó estate until recently."

"Oh my, a criminal, here? What is the crime? Is she dangerous?"

"She could be very dangerous if she becomes desperate," Señor Engaños said.

"I am happy to help in any way I can. My señora is on holiday for another few days, but you are more than welcome to search the grounds."

Abuela motioned them in, and the men searched the house, the garden, the cellar, finding no trace of Amalia. They made ready to leave.

Turning on her motherly charm, Abuela offered, "May I interest you in some coffee and fresh biscuits? You work so hard for the citizens of this town."

They looked at each other. Señor Duranté shrugged his shoulders as if to say, *We could use a break.*

Señor Engaños rolled his big eyes. "Perhaps we can have one biscuit before we leave."

Abuela noticed he shot a warning glance toward Señor Duranté before they both followed her to the kitchen at the back of the house.

"Oh, I am pleased. It must be such a grueling task running around town trying to find a woman who probably doesn't even exist." She smiled and motioned them to take a seat at her small table. Her plan had worked.

The young Señor Duranté removed his gloves and hat and relaxed in his chair. "That is what I think. We've had many people claiming to have seen someone fitting this señorita's description, and I suspect it's because of the reward Señor Tudó has offered for her capture. But we keep coming up empty. Personally, I think the old man is crazy." He stuffed a second biscuit into his mouth, eager to accept another.

Engaños caressed his pointed beard and said condescendingly, "You are new to the Guard, Duranté, and you know little of what you speak. Señor Tudó is a very powerful man. He commands respect and gets what he wants."

Duranté countered, "Si, well . . . he said he knew this had to be the house Señorita Maritimo was hiding in, yet she is nowhere to be found, is she?"

Abuela's heart skipped. "What do you mean he knew the girl had to be here hiding?"

Duranté assured her, "No need to worry, señora. She is not here. We did a thorough search."

Color drained from her face. "Why would Señor Tudó insist she was at this house?"

Engaños sat back and folded his arms as though content to listen to the conversation. His beady eyes watched Abuela closely.

Duranté took another bite of biscuit. "I don't know. He just said if a nice old lady answered the door, we had found the right place. He said you and he have a past. Are you related? Why would he think you would harbor a fugitive?"

Abuela laughed uncomfortably. "Harbor a fugitive? Do I look like someone who would willingly let a criminal into my home?"

Putting down his biscuit, he asked, "Your home? You said your señora was on holiday. Why would you lie about that?"

Abuela shot a glance over at Engaños, who sat profoundly silent with a smug look on his face.

"I didn't mean to be deceptive. I'm just in the habit of saying that to people so they will leave me alone. If they think I am not important and the important people are gone, then I have my peace. To answer your other question, Señor Tudó and I are very personally connected. I believe he is the reason my daughter is dead."

The young Guard looked astonished. "You accuse him of murder? That is a very serious claim, señora."

Engaños broke his silence, annoyed by the conversation. "It is an old unsolved case, but they cleared Tudó of any wrongdoing. He wasn't even in España at the time your daughter's body turned up."

Abuela lost control of her temper, rose from her chair, and leaned across the table. "How dare you defend that evil, manipulative man? You are speaking of my daughter, señor. How can you turn a blind eye like so many others when you are supposed to protect this community?"

Silence followed. Only an insolent sneer came from Engaños.

"Why did she and that sweet boy, Anton, suddenly disappear the day after she refused Manuel Tudó?" Abuela continued. "And only Lucita was found several months later? Anton hasn't been heard of, and he was to inherit his father's business. Why would he go away, never to return, when his future looked so bright? He wouldn't. Anton loved his family and my daughter. Everyone knew Tudó had it out for him. Witnesses saw him attack Lucita when she gave the Tudó family jewels back. He is the reason she is dead. And probably Anton too." Clarity hit her in the gut, making her breathless. "Oh, Lord in Heaven, what of the babe she was carrying in her belly?"

Engaños's jaw muscles tightened, and she knew she'd gone too far. For years, she'd stayed quiet. As families came and went in their little town of Águilas, fewer people knew her or the terrible tragedy surrounding her daughter's disappearance and death. She believed, over time, if she let it go, spoke no more of Tudó, he wouldn't haunt her anymore. But Engaños undoubtedly served Tudó and knew everything about her and her daughter, probably knew her husband died a few years ago, and she only employed a young man to run errands and help with things around the house. Somehow Tudó had entered her life again, but this time she was alone. Wiping at the tears in her eyes, Abuela sighed with a smile. "Oh well, it is all in the past. How are your biscuits? Would you like more coffee?"

Duranté watched the exchange intently. He passed his cup for more, but Engaños stood, abruptly forcing Duranté to stand as well. "We have disturbed your peace far too long, Doña Eulalia. Justice must be served. We will leave you now. Gracias for your hospitality. Buen día." Engaños clicked his heels, gave a stiff bow, and showed himself out the front door.

More considerate, Duranté took her hand in his and bent over it with a compassionate smile. "Your biscuits are delicious, Doña . . ."

With a crack in her voice, she replied, "Por favor, call me Abuela, for that is what I'd always hoped to be at this point in my life."

"Very well, Abuela. Your biscuits are better than my own mother's, but that must remain a secret between us." With a wink, he turned and followed after his comrade.

Sweet Amalia. Por favor, Lord, safely bring my granddaughter back to me.

As instructed, Amalia stuck to the trees, keeping in their vast shadows on the outskirts of Águilas, but the trees spread farther and farther apart as houses clustered closer together, and the thought of Abuela peering down at Amalia from the second floor of her home and knowing someone else could be doing that same thing frightened her.

Once she entered town, the streets narrowed, and visibility beyond the next bend became impossible. Horror struck when she came face-to-face with herself at the end of an alley.

> *Reward for any information about this woman, who goes by the name of Amalia Maritimo. Dark hair, green eyes, short in stature, and slender. Last seen wearing the uniform of a housemaid. She is in the possession of precious emerald jewelry belonging to the Tudó family. Report any information to the Civil Guard.*

Amalia's heart pounded. Her feet felt numb. She rushed through streets, catching only brief glimpses of the next turn. Coming to a high wall and nowhere to go, Amalia turned, praying no one would stop her. Few people looked up from their conversations, and she kept her eyes averted. Peeking over her shoulder to make sure no one was following her, she took a left and barreled into something solid but soft.

She yelped in surprise.

Strong hands set her right. She made eye contact with a short, stout man, possibly in his late twenties, dressed in military uniform, his soft brown eyes wide with surprise.

Not a moment later, a taller gentleman appeared at her side, taking her elbow and turning her so her back faced the open plaza and any curious bystanders. Out in the harbor sat the most beautiful ship she'd ever imagined. He wrapped his cape around her shoulders.

"Be gentle, Hastings," the shorter gentleman said in English.

"I was very gentle. You help her, then." The tall officer walked a short distance away, but his hawklike eyes canvassed the area. They both wore English Royal Navy uniforms complete with navy tails and gold tassels on their shoulders. *Could these officers be the ones I overheard on the road to Águilas or the ones Abuela told me about?*

Uncertain why the handsome officer abruptly walked away, Amalia flashed her prettiest smile at the other gentleman and spoke slowly in Spanish. "Pardon me, is this your ship?" She prayed he understood her.

He removed his hat and replied in near-perfect Spanish, "Buenas tardes, señorita. Allow me to introduce us. I am Commander Gilbert Channing, and this is Captain Joshua Hastings. We are at your service." The commander lowered over her hand and kissed it.

Captain Joshua Hastings.

The captain quickly glanced at Amalia, then looked away.

"Hastings?"

He rolled his eyes and mustered a stiff bow. "Buenas tardes."

Amalia's face brightened when she recognized his voice. As a result, Captain Hastings's mouth fell open, and she had to cover her own to hide a laugh at his reaction. He adjusted his broad shoulders, and her eyes followed their taper down to a narrow waist accentuated by an ornate belt. His crisp uniform emphasized his muscular frame, making Amalia's commitment to stay away from men teeter dangerously. His impeccable physique was as mesmerizing to her as her smile seemed to be to him.

"Hmm, hmm . . . And you are?" Commander Channing said.

Pulling her eyes from the captain, she replied, "Oh, si, pardon me. I am Am—um . . . I apologize, I was distracted. My name is Lea Tavio."

A lopsided smile and raised eyebrows revealed Captain Hastings's amusement at her stutter.

Did they notice my blunder? Amalia smiled through her long eyelashes at him, hoping to cover up her mistake, but blushed at the attempt. Feeling like a fool, she lost some of her courage and looked down at the cobblestone.

"You are in luck, Señorita Tavio. This *is* our ship," Commander Channing said.

"I would like to purchase a ticket, por favor. When will you be casting off?" she said a little too eagerly.

"Our ship is leaving in a few hours, but we don't often ferry civilians when delivering cargo and supplies. However . . ." Channing looked at Hastings, who gave him a slight nod. "I believe we can make an exception this one time for a nominal fee." Amalia felt some nausea settling in.

"Señorita, are you well?" Commander Channing asked.

Trying to act confident, her voice squeaked, "What is the price?"

"You haven't asked where the ship is going," Captain Hastings said.

Taken aback by Captain Joshua Hastings' perfect Spanish, as if it were his native tongue, Amalia stared at his polished teeth as his lips glided over them. She forgot to respond.

Oh dear, what was the question?

There was a chuckle from the commander.

"Where is it going?" Amalia quickly asked. Nerves on edge, she tried desperately not to look around for the Civil Guard. With one man in front of her and the other nearly behind her, they kept her hidden from suspicious eyes, but she felt anxiety at not being on the ship yet.

Commander Channing again spoke for the captain. "We are traveling to the charming island of Menorca."

"Perfect. That is just where I need to go."

Captain Hastings coughed in his hand to stifle a laugh.

Leading her in her lie, Commander Channing asked, "Ah, going to visit family?"

"That's exactly right, my aunt . . . Sonia." Amalia forced a laugh. "I haven't seen her in ages. She probably won't even recognize me."

Captain Hastings stepped around her and took his comrade by the elbow, turning their backs to her for privacy. "Will you excuse us a moment?" Hastings said over his shoulder.

Amalia lost a touch of her smile. "Of course, I'll be right here." *Don't leave me alone.*

Captain Hastings lowered his voice and spoke in English. Commander Channing looked amused.

Leaning closer to hear, Amalia heard the captain say, "These bulletins posted all over the town, we need to get her off the street, Gil. You know what a womanizer Tudó is. I don't trust him."

"I've never met him," Channing replied.

"Well, he is the worst of men. I suspect she's one of his victims."

Commander Channing had a twinkle in his eye. "Yes, and it has nothing to do with how charmingly beautiful she is either."

"Don't be ridiculous. Of course it has nothing to do with that. I mean . . . never mind. And you need to start referring to yourself as captain. Yes, I noticed."

Channing laughed. "That's ridiculous. I'm not a captain yet. Why would you bring that up *now* when there is a damsel in distress?"

Hastings said nothing.

"Shall I go make the arrangements?"

Hastings shot a glance toward Amalia, then dismissed himself. "I'll go."

Channing surveyed the area as his comrade walked away. "Captain Hastings will make preparations for you to join us." He offered his arm. "Shall I escort you to the ship, then?"

"Oh, gracias, Commander. I've never been on a ship before. It looks so big." Beads of perspiration formed on her brow. Practically pulling him toward the ship to distract herself from an upset stomach, she referred to his uniform. "Have you been in the navy long?"

"I was recruited four years ago to serve with Captain Joshua Hastings. When we return to England, I'll be promoted to captain. England is where Hastings and I met—at school, Eton College. His family has a beautiful estate on Menorca where we are sailing today."

Amalia searched the streets as they walked, though she desperately wanted to run. "He speaks Spanish like it's his native tongue."

It's hard not to be captivated by her bright green eyes and dark, wavy hair. No wonder Hastings lost his cool demeanor. Channing tried to hide his joy at finding a weakness in his friend's otherwise impenetrable armor. So focused on his career, rarely did a woman catch his eye. In the ten years he'd know Hastings, not once had he been rattled by a woman until this señorita came along. *What is it about her?*

Amalia insisted on a rushed pace, so it took only minutes to reach the frigate. Channing motioned to their pride and joy, freshly painted and repaired from years of wear and tear.

"Here we are." Facing Amalia, he said, "I almost forgot. I must collect the fee for your passage."

"Fee for what?" She kept looking over her shoulder.

He pulled at his collar. "To board the ship. You must pay to board the ship."

"Oh, si. I, um, just a moment." She rummaged through her bag.

Channing turned a shade of red.

Amalia hurried to explain, "I'm afraid I'm a bit flustered. Por favor, I must leave this place as soon as possible."

"Is there something amiss, señorita?"

"Oh, no, nothing like that." A bead of sweat dripped down her forehead. "Pardon me." Amalia dropped her bag and ran to the water before losing the contents of her stomach.

Channing rushed to her side with the bag in hand and a ready handkerchief.

"Gracias." She wiped her mouth, tears pooling in her eyes, and struggled to keep her hands steady as she successfully fished out a purse of coins. Amalia chanced a look into Gilbert Channing's face.

He couldn't fully hide his misgivings. "It isn't safe to be carrying such a large sum of money on your person. Some people wouldn't hesitate to hurt you for it."

Amalia stuttered, "I-I left in such a hurry, I didn't think about that. It's my inheritance, and I wasn't sure what the cost would be to travel to my aunt."

"I understand. Just six reales, por favor, then we can be off."

"That would be bueno. I am most anxious."

With a look of concern, Channing replied, "Si, you've mentioned that. What, if you don't mind my asking, would you have done if we hadn't met and offered you passage to Menorca?"

"I guess I'd have to swim my way there."

That earned a chuckle. He accepted the coins, disappointed he hadn't seen the jewels in her possession when he chanced a look in her carpetbag. Bowing with a flourish, he waved her up the gangway. "After you." Channing grabbed his lapels and puffed out his chest when they boarded the ship. The crew was bustling around a clean deck. Though it looked like chaos, there was a beautiful rhythm to it.

"Commander Channing, what are the flags?"

"Ah, that is the Union Jack flying above you, and the other one identifies us as a merchant ship. Welcome to the frigate *Santa Sabina*. I believe Captain Hastings has arranged your lodgings for the journey. If you will follow me?" He was loud enough for Joshua to hear, and that earned him a distasteful look, but Channing didn't care. They would retrieve the jewels from Amalia, and she would be safe from a man Hastings claimed to be the worst of men. *A good day for us would-be heroes*, Channing mused. It felt good to save rather than destroy, which happened all too often at sea, especially during the war. After the war ended, he and Hastings spent the rest of their commission ferrying goods between España and England.

The war had changed them. Rarely did Hastings share his thoughts on the subject. Though a deep thinker, Hastings usually kept his opinion to himself, unless solicited—sometimes not even then. A fantastic listener, adept at assessing a situation and then acting on his vast knowledge and understanding, he rarely made a decision without giving it a great deal of thought. That was not to say Hastings didn't have remarkable reflexes, as well as the ability to act spontaneously under pressure. He just wasn't as comfortable doing things that way.

This woman, Amalia, had caught him off guard. Gil knew Hastings hadn't expected her to be so speechlessly disarming, but he sensed there was more to it than that. His friend was rattled. Though he was usually a man of few words, Joshua's inability to put more than a few words together was unusual. Consequently, Joshua left the duty of conversing with Amalia to Gil, which he didn't mind. He enjoyed putting the fairer sex at ease. Though his physique leaned more to the cuddly side, he made up for his less than stellar appearance with his charm and quick wit. He didn't have fantastic wavy hair or the incredibly intuitive blue eyes that all the ladies claimed saw "deep into their very souls" like Hastings, but he had other great qualities. *Oh, who am I kidding? Hastings is, by far, the better man in every arena. Good thing we're best mates.* Gil laughed at himself.

Amalia couldn't help but giggle at Commander Gilbert Channing's gallantry. He had a wonderful way of helping her relax. Relief washed over her the moment she set foot on deck. Following her splendid new friend toward the front of the ship, dodging crew members performing their well rehearsed duties, she noticed Captain Hastings eyeing her. He didn't seem to like her, but Amalia had sworn off men, so she didn't like him either.

HOLLY BROUGH

"Follow me, señorita." Channing ushered her down some steps to a private room. "You should be comfortable enough to rest in here." Channing opened a door to a large room that looked like a study. Ahead of her was an unkempt desk. She walked up to the dark, rich wood and ran her finger along a spot of unencumbered smooth surface.

"What is this?" Amalia picked up a triangular object with tiny, colorful glass pieces and moving parts.

Carefully taking it from her, he said, "That is a Hadley's quadrant, a navigation tool. It helps us know where we are going. Captain Hastings's grandfather gave it to him when he joined the Royal Navy."

Pencils and crumpled parchment riddled the surface of the mahogany desk. Amalia touched the corner of a colorful drawing held in place by a bottle of sangria and wine cup.

"This looks interesting."

"Have you never seen a map of the world before?"

Color rushed to Amalia's cheeks. She ignored the question and pretended she'd lost interest by looking about the rest of the room.

"This way, por favor." Channing motioned her to a door on the right, which opened to a smaller room with a bed, apparently where she would rest during the voyage. "We should arrive in Menorca tomorrow morning." He bowed out the door.

Amalia sat on the bed and looked around the quarters. Unlike the office, everything was in order. A blue glass ball hung suspended from the ceiling near an armoire, and a saber leaned against the armoire. A small vanity with a washing bowl, pitcher, and shaving kit occupied the other side of the room. Amalia walked over to the basin and poured some water to splash on her face. Looking in the mirror nailed to the wall in front of her, she noticed a beautiful painting of Captain Hastings with three people she assumed were his parents and brother. His mother, a lovely woman with dark hair and deep brown eyes, seemed familiar to Amalia. *What is it about her? The smile, perhaps?* She stared at the painting until her stomach churned again. *Oh no, not again.*

Spanish Bluebells

CHAPTER 17

AMALIA FOUND HERSELF retching over the *Santa Sabina*'s newly painted railing before they'd even left port. Channing attended to her as best he could, standing ready with a clean handkerchief when she had a reprieve from being sick. His kindness reminded her of Abuela, and she wanted to cry.

Captain Hastings kept his distance. Nothing seemed to escape his notice, however. Hands clasped behind his back, he proudly watched from his perch at the front of the ship like a hawk. Amalia caught herself unintentionally gazing at him, admiring his handsome light-brown hair neatly tied at the nape of his neck. When he walked, he walked with purpose. Head held high, the brim of his hat shadowed his dark, mysterious eyes, making it impossible for Amalia to discover their true color, though she'd tried several times. Captain Hastings avoided her gaze, and she wondered if he knew her secrets.

His opposite, Commander Channing could charm a tiger. He, too, kept his hair tied at the nape of his neck. His light-brown eyes were kind and inviting. A head shorter than his comrade, Channing wore his round belly with pride. Confidence beamed through his smile. His jovial, somewhat foppish character made for wonderful conversation.

Always quick with an amusing remark, the commander didn't take himself too seriously, and she found that refreshing.

"You see how Captain Hastings looks slightly out of the corner of his eye at us? He suspects we're conspiring against him," Channing said behind his hand.

"Why would he think that?" Amalia asked.

"He says I'm 'spending too much time with our guest and not attending to my duties on the ship.' The nerve! Can't he see you need my undivided attention?"

"I apologize for that. I don't mean to be such a burden."

"You are not a burden. You are a damsel in distress."

"Conspiring against the captain?" She smiled.

"He probably thinks you are trying to manipulate me into commandeering the ship and sailing beyond the unknown."

Amalia's eyes grew wide. "Commandeer . . . what does that mean?"

"It means you intend to steal the ship from him."

Amalia laughed. "Me, steal a ship? I like that idea. Shall we make a plan, then?"

"Of course."

Amalia leaned in and whispered, "How do we begin?"

"We need a destination. Where would you like to go?"

"I've never considered it before. Until a year ago, Puerto Lumbreras was the only place I would ever live. My father says China is beautiful. Maybe America. Where would you go?"

"I'd like to go to America. So . . . your father was a sailor?"

"He was in the Spanish Armada for six months. Why does Captain Hastings always look cross?"

"Oh, that's just his gastritis." Channing laughed, and Amalia joined him. "Tell me more about your family."

Joshua watched her. When he and Channing first came upon Amalia, it didn't escape his notice her figure showed signs of a delicate condition. Before they boarded the frigate, she turned sick, became flush. Channing must have realized too, which would explain the inordinate amount of attention he paid her. *Unless, of course, he fancies her.* Oddly, the idea bothered him.

Turning his thoughts to the other concern they had, Channing informed him the jewels weren't in her travel bag, but she did carry a large sum of money. *Perhaps she already sold them. Blast, this girl is a mystery. Is Tudó the man responsible for her condition?* The idea twisted in his gut. Joshua paced, frustrated with his emotions. He couldn't shake them. There was no denying Amalia was hauntingly familiar. She looked like the Lucita of his youth.

Pulled from his thoughts at the sound of Amalia's laugh, Joshua scowled at his friend for making a fool of himself. *What is he doing?* Just because they had a guest onboard didn't mean Channing could shirk his duties. There was a meal that needed to be prepared. Had he even thought about giving orders to have that started? And yet there he was, cavorting with a wanted criminal. *Hmm. That's probably a little too harsh. She isn't a criminal, and he is my loyal friend. Damned weather isn't cooperating.* Turning his back to them, Joshua rolled his shoulders to relax.

Their journey continued through the night, the weather completely uncooperative. The *Santa Sabina* wouldn't reach Menorca for another day if the wind didn't pick up. Thankfully, Amalia's sickness seemed to improve by evening. He worried she'd become so dehydrated the physician would need to attend to her. As he stared absently at his maps and papers by candlelight, Joshua heard muffled whimpering in his quarters and quietly moved toward the door, leaning his ear against it to listen. After a moment, he opened it a crack to see a single candle illuminate Amalia's shaking form under the covers.

"Pardon me, señorita. Are you well?"

Amalia sat up and pulled the covers to her chin. "I am fine, gracias."

"Can I get you anything? Are you hungry? Thirsty?"

After a long pause, she said. "I'm afraid to eat." Her face twisted as if trying to stifle another sob.

Joshua tentatively moved to her side and knelt by the bed. *She smells like roses. I love roses.* "You would feel better if you had a crust of bread and a little water. Would you like to try?"

Amalia didn't answer right away. "Si, I would like to try."

"I'll only be a moment."

True to his word, Joshua presented a small roll from their evening meal and a cup of water. "Don't feel bad if you get sick. A lot of people get sick on the ocean."

"Gracias, Captain."

"I'll only be in the next room if you need anything else. Here is a bucket if you need it." He left as quietly as he came.

Maybe she would relax with some music. Finding his mandolin tucked in a forgotten wood chest, Joshua tuned the strings and strummed a few notes to warm up his fingers. An hour passed before he noticed the early morning lights appearing over the horizon and his fingertips throbbing from lack of use. *I am out of practice, but it feels good to play again.*

Not until late afternoon did their destination appear on the horizon. Amalia liked how Captain Hastings directed the swarm of chaos on deck like a well-rehearsed dance. Throughout the day, her mind drifted back to when Hastings came to her aid in the middle of the night. He treated her with such gentleness. After he left, the tune of a mandolin calmed her so completely that she fell asleep to its lovely melody and traveled to a magical place where flowers danced on the breeze and wild horses ran free.

Amalia's attention turned to the gorgeous turquoise water lapping along a golden shore. Soon, Port de Mahón could be seen clearly from where they sat on the water. It bustled with activity. Buildings clustered together; people scurried every which way. Two other ships waited at port, so the *Santa Sabina* lingered in the bay. After finally making port before the sun set in the west, Amalia felt relief knowing some distance lay between her and Tudó.

Bag in hand, Commander Channing prepared her to disembark. Looking about the ship, Amalia couldn't help feeling disappointed Captain Hastings hadn't joined them to send her off. Taking a deep breath to steady her heart, Amalia looked toward her new home.

"There she is—Port de Mahón. You have everything?" Channing asked.

"Si. Gracias for helping me get here. It has been *mostly* a pleasure," she teased. "Sorry to be such a nuisance."

With a wink and a slight bow, Commander Channing bent over her hand. "It wasn't *that* bad. In truth, you have been a delightful companion. Good luck to you, señorita."

Amalia looked past Channing one last time.

He followed her gaze. "I apologize Captain Hastings isn't here to bid you farewell, but he is currently overseeing preparations for our delivery."

"Oh, no, I wasn't looking for him. I just wanted to see the ship one last time." Amalia smiled at him, and he offered his arm.

"We hope your aunt is well and receives you with joy."

"What? Uh, si. Gracias." Amalia squirmed inside.

Her heart leaped when she finally spotted Captain Hastings atop his perch at the front of the ship, watching her with his all-seeing eyes. She turned and walked with purpose, pretending not to have noticed though she could feel his glare on her back as she disembarked. A pit formed in her stomach when she stole a quick look and noticed a crease wrinkling his brow. *He hates me. Where is the kind Joshua Hastings I met last night? He is a mystery to me.* Amalia waved, hoping to convey some confidence in her step as she walked into the unknown.

Joshua wasn't comfortable sending Amalia away, not knowing if he'd ever see her again. After watching her leave the ship, he gave some final orders and prepared to go ashore himself.

Finding Gil, Joshua anxiously confided, "I don't feel comfortable throwing Amalia to the wolves. I don't believe she has any experience dealing in the world. What if something happens to her?"

Gil shook his head. "I agree that she doesn't know the world like we do, but she certainly knows how to work her charms for her benefit. She'll be fine. I'm not quite sure why you're concerning yourself."

Why am I concerning myself? Though it was brief, we had a connection—that's why. But she's gone now, out of my life, and there is nothing I can do about it. "You're right. There's no reason to give it a second thought."

Gil eyed him for a moment, waiting for more, but there was nothing. "You know, she told me some interesting things about her father."

"Which father?"

"What do you mean, which father?"

"The father who raised her or her birth father?"

"I don't understand."

"There is a lot I don't understand either. So much more is going on here than a case of stolen jewelry."

"Well, I'll tell you about the only father she seems to know about then. Evidently he up and left the Spanish Armada six months after he joined *because he didn't like it.* If she is who you suspect she is, how did she come to live with a traitorous father? He may not even be a Maritimo."

Joshua continued to look after Amalia, though she'd disappeared from view.

"You won't let this go, will you?" Channing said.

No reply.

"I guess I'll just have to wait patiently for you to decide the next move, eh, Hastings?"

Pushing off the railing, Joshua said, "Shall we go? I'm quite famished."

"You don't need to ask me twice. After you, then? I believe it is 'age before beauty.'" Gil motioned for Joshua to lead the way.

With a princely flourish of his arm, Joshua urged Gil forward with a counter reply. "Actually, I believe the saying is 'ass before horse.'"

That earned a boisterous laugh. Gil cocked a brow. "Very funny. Did you come up with that yourself?" Wagging a finger at him, he said, "You need to stick to philosophy and stargazing, Hastings. Leave the jokes and charm to me."

"It's too bad you don't have the looks to go with it," Joshua said in jest.

"I resent that. Women like my physique. I'm extremely cuddly, and my height is perfect. The ladies can look straight into my eyes and actually see my sincerity."

Joshua scoffed. "And you know this, how?"

"Pure logic, my fine fellow. Pure logic."

Basil

CHAPTER 18

AMALIA MANEUVERED THROUGH the narrow streets of Mahón. The familiar scent of fresh spices wafting in the air led her toward the town square, where displays of the many foods and wares attracted patrons from all over. Business as usual, people haggled to get a fair price. Delighted to experience something familiar, Amalia happily watched young children gather crumbs of food and make a small picnic for themselves under a table near the edge of the plaza.

A new sense of freedom enveloped Amalia, the excitement mesmerizing her. She lost track of time until darkness brought with it a new sense of confusion. The buildings and avenues all looked the same, and she strained to get her bearings.

Amalia considered taking one street, but an awful foreboding turned her in the opposite direction. It soon became apparent that her choice set her on a street in the poorest part of town. Three children, filthy from head to toe and wearing nothing but tattered shirts, pulled at her dress, begging for food. Having purchased a small loaf of bread earlier, Amalia gave them what she had left and rushed away. No sooner had she entered another alley, a woman, baby at her breast and a toddler in tow, stopped her.

"Pardon me, señora. Por favor, can you help me? I have nowhere to go, and my child is starving," the pungent woman begged. Her left eye was swollen shut, and dried blood crusted her hands.

Amalia's future flashed before her eyes. She stuttered, "I-I'm new here. I don't know how I can help you."

A fat, filthy man stepped out of the darkness and took Amalia by the wrist. "Where are you going, señorita? You look a little lost. Let me help you."

"No, leave me alone." Panic threatened to choke her.

He pulled her closer, but she swung her bag at him, knocking him off-balance. Amalia stumbled into a brick wall and scraped her shoulder as she tried to find her feet to run. A tavern presented itself at the end of the alley, and she hurried toward it.

A curvy, brazen woman halted Amalia at the door. "Buenas noches, señorita. Are you lost?"

Amalia mumbled, "No, I was just looking for a place to stay."

Scrutinizing her up and down, the stout woman said, "Welcome to the El Comienzo Tavern. This is my place." She wore a ruffled dress and colorful shawl. Her blouse hung low in front to flaunt a full bosom.

"I am very weary from my travels."

"Where did you travel from, señorita? Are you running to or from something?"

Heat rose to Amalia's cheeks.

The overbearing woman pulled her into an embrace, laughing. "You shy little thing . . . Oh—" Pushed to arm's length, Amalia knew her secret was out when the foul woman groped her middle. Amalia opened her mouth to speak, but nothing came out.

"Hmm. There is more to you than a fancy dress, no? Where is your man? Why isn't *he* securing you a place to stay?"

The sweet, rancid smell of spoiled milk accompanied every word the overbearing woman spoke. Amalia wanted to run the opposite direction, but the image of a beaten woman with an infant at her breast cemented her to the spot.

"Clearly, I am the only hope you have. Vamos. I was just telling my partner we could use some extra hands around here. You may be just what we're looking for."

Choking from the foul stench surrounding them, Amalia turned away to retch behind her hand and swallow her sick. She took a deep breath to calm her nerves, but standing in such close proximity to the plump woman was suffocating. Amalia's eyes teared from the strain, and the woman took it as a sign to comfort her with another embrace.

"It can't be that bad. You leave everything to Señora Consuela. What is your name?"

Amalia pulled away. "Lea . . . Lea Tavio."

Señora Consuela wore too much makeup. Her buck teeth protruded so far forward they pushed her lips out when they were closed. "Bueno, Señorita Tavio. I want to make some introductions. Follow me. Then I will show you to a room."

When Señora Consuela opened the door, a rank burnt smell hit Amalia like a tidal wave, an altogether different odor than what she'd just escaped. She covered her nose and took gulping breaths of thick smoke through her mouth. The room was filled with drunken patrons who laughed and taunted each other while barmaids served charred remains and drinks. They walked to the bar at the back of the room where a large, gruff man stood leaning against the wall. His eyes moved around the room as he assessed the ruckus going on, not unlike a certain captain she observed on the *Santa Sabina*.

Señora Consuela said, "Señor Guerra, I've invited this young señorita to stay here. She needs our help since she is in a delicate way."

The señora casually tossed her most personal information to a perfect stranger. Mortified, Amalia stood before the intimidating man, trying not to show her embarrassment, though she wanted to crawl under a rock and disappear.

Señor Guerra glanced over Amalia before grumbling, "She looks fine to me, but we don't have any positions open."

Amalia's heart sank. She didn't know where else to go and realized she would rather stay at the tavern than try to find another place in the dark, unfamiliar streets. She just needed to rest.

Señora Consuela spoke up. "Señor, she is a perfect fit for our tavern. I believe our place is just what she needs to get her feet back under her. We have a vacancy, and when she is feeling better, I believe she is eager to help around here to earn our hospitality."

"Por favor, I'm a hard worker."

Señor Guerra waved them away. "I don't care. Leave me be." He walked over to a group of people starting a scuffle.

Amalia's head was spinning. "Señora, I need to lie down. You mentioned a room I can rent?"

The repugnant woman merely nodded as she took Amalia by the arm and led her up some stairs and down a hall to a small room far away from the noise and smells. Relief swept over her weary body as she whispered a prayer of gratitude.

A single bed with pink patchwork quilt beckoned her. Lace curtains framed the window, but a heavier curtain hung beneath them to keep the morning sunlight out. With a small fireplace, a chair next to it, and a vanity for her convenience, the room suited Amalia just fine. She barely said "gracias" before falling onto the bed.

The next morning, Amalia got up early and readied herself for a day of introductions and instructions. El Comienzo Tavern was too stuffy and smelly for her to endure long term, so she decided to only stay until she could find a better place of employment.

Staring at her reflection in the mirror, dark circles framing her green eyes, Amalia wore the lavender dress Abuela altered for her. Hoping not to ruin it before she could purchase something more suitable for the tavern, she moved to open the door, but the señora beat her to it. She boldly walked in, holding a tray of food.

"Uh . . . Buenos días, señora," Amalia said. "I am ready for my introductions and instructions. I'm anxious to earn your hospitality."

Setting down her offering, Señora Consuela said, "Si, si, all in good time. I have brought you some food to help build up your energy and settle that stomach of yours."

Amalia's eyes grew big.

"I saw how sick you were last night. There isn't much these eyes don't see. Now, after you have eaten, I will take you downstairs to meet our cook, Señor Rana. You met my other partner, Señor Guerra, last night. They are both agreeable men if you stay out of their way and do as you are told. I must inform you, however, we will not require your help until the sickness has passed. You'll stay in this room until then."

"What?"

"It's probably only a few more weeks."

Amalia protested, "A few weeks? What am I to do in this room that whole time? I would rather die. How do you expect me to pay for my room by sitting around doing nothing? I think maybe I should look elsewhere for employment."

"You can't do that. You're only a woman, unwed and expecting. You wouldn't last a day—well, maybe two—out there. If you and your child are to be protected, pequeña, you must live by our rules. That is the deal. We'll put you to work, don't you worry about that. Just a few weeks."

"But—"

Señora Consuela put up her hand to stop her. "We can't have you getting sick in front of the patrons."

Amalia lost her resolve and gave in to the señora's logic. After a few bites of overcooked sweet bread and watered-down coffee, Amalia followed Señora Consuela's lead down a different staircase they used the night before to reach the inner workings of their business. They passed a few doors, then a small washroom for cleaning the linens—the pressing table piled with debris, implying it hadn't been used for a long time, if ever. They stopped at a door leading into an office.

"The master would like to see you," said Señora Consuela.

Behind the desk stood a short, pudgy man whose face resembled a toad's. At his side sat a muscular, cleaner man she recognized as Señor Guerra.

"Gentlemen, I would like to present to you our newest guest, Señorita Lea Tavio. She will be under our care out of the goodness of our hearts."

Amalia winced at the tone of the señora's voice and the look of pleasure on the men's faces. Already, she found herself in another situation where she had no choices and felt obligated to stay.

THE NAME I CHOOSE

"Lea, may I introduce you again to Señor Guerra, who is the manager of our fine establishment." The man nodded his head at Amalia. She curtsied.

Motioning to the other man, Señora Consuela continued, "And this is Señor Rana, our cook. We three started the El Comienzo Tavern several years ago. It is our pride and joy, and we expect all who stay and work here to behave with honor and decorum. Do you understand?"

Amalia nodded her head, confused. Had she imagined the deplorable odors and riotous crowd the night before?

"Vamos. Back to bed you go."

That was fast. Amalia was escorted back to her room and instructed to rest.

Once the señora closed the door behind her, Amalia spoke to her belly. "Sweet bebé, te amo. We will stay here for a while, and when I am well and able, I will take you from here to a more suitable place to grow up. I promise, amorcito." *I miss Abuela.*

For weeks, Amalia stayed in her room, struggling to keep her wits about her. She wearied the señora with her constant begging for something to read. Finally, a book called *Livestock, Herbs, and How to Make Tonics for Physical Ailments* appeared at her door. Amalia already knew how to make a good tonic for pain—something useful she learned from her mother. Other things in the book made Amalia laugh out loud, gratefully diverting her from suffocating in her forced confinement.

Thoughts of Thomas haunted her. Where was he now? Did Gordy keep his promise to protect him? And Sonia . . . was she safe? Would there ever be a day when Tudó didn't plague their lives? What about Abuela? Amalia tried to occupy her mind by reading aloud to her bebé. Cisco made his way into her mind often, which frustrated her to tears. Amalia tried counting her blessings. They were few. She had a bed and a nice window to open, but she could only open it at night when the air cooled and the stench cleared. Miles separated her from Tudó, but thoughts of Tudó led to thoughts of Commander Channing, which led to thoughts of Captain Hastings, the handsome, mysterious man who helped her escape. Amalia tried to suppress thoughts of the captain and his comrade, supposing *she* hadn't crossed their minds since parting.

Black Cumin

CHAPTER 19

"HASTINGS, WAS THAT your mandolin I heard you playing last night? I thought you lost that thing years ago," Channing said.

"No, I just put it away."

"What made you want to start playing again?"

No answer. Joshua Hastings was in no mood for conversation.

"You haven't stopped looking behind us since we set sail to Águilas." Channing followed his gaze toward Menorca.

"Hmm?"

Gil sighed. "As I was saying, you haven't played it in years. Why are you playing again?"

"No reason." Joshua turned his attention toward their destination.

Hastings's constant friend kept talking. "I can't put my finger on it, but something has changed about you, old friend. Ever since we met a certain señorita last week . . ."

"Look." Pointing his finger toward the Spanish coast, Joshua asked, "Channing, what do you suppose that is?" He didn't wait for an answer but barked orders to his crew to raise another sail.

Gil chased after him. "The smoke, you mean? I can't quite tell. It appears to be in Águilas. Very unusual, I must say. Good thinking to have the crew pick up our pace. Always to the rescue, eh, Hastings?"

Grimacing at the remark, Joshua replied, "Let's hope we get there in time to lend a hand."

"Indeed."

Once they reached port, Joshua called out more orders before he and Gil ran down the plank toward the commotion. As they got closer, Joshua broke into a sprint. Abuela's house was completely ablaze, the front entrance blocked by refuse.

"Channing, see what you can do. I'm going to the back of the house to find a way in!"

He watched Hastings run around the house before jumping into action. The heat sucked all the moisture out of the air. People were running everywhere, falling over each other to grab buckets of water to throw at the blaze. Pulling his handkerchief out of his pocket, he wrapped it around his face as a shield from the scorching heat.

Searching the chaos for someone in charge of the rescue, he finally spotted a Civil Guard and pulled the man around. The poor chap looked pathetic, his face and hair matted with blood and dirt.

"What happened to you? Is everyone out of the house?"

Channing received no reply, only silence. Shaking him, he said, "Come on, amigo, pull yourself together. Are you hurt? Can you hear me?"

The young man nodded.

Shouting over the noise, Channing yelled, "Is anyone still in the house? Answer me."

"I . . . I don't know."

Dragging a few people farther from the flames, Channing realized there wasn't much he could do. The house was a complete loss. Hoping Hastings had more success than he did, Channing ran to the back of the house.

HOLLY BROUGH

Dread almost consumed Joshua when he saw a lone figure just outside the back door lying on the ground. *Please, God, let her be alive.* He ran to Abuela's side and turned her over. Blood covered her face from a gash over her brow. Her once-white blouse was covered in blood and soot. Carefully lifting her body away from the house, he listened for a heartbeat and felt for breath.

Slowly, she opened her eyes and focused on Joshua's face.

"You must retrieve the jewels, Hastings. Hurry! They are under a wood plank in the pantry. You'll know the one. Vamos." She closed her eyes again.

"Abuela? Abuela!" Joshua shook her, but she didn't respond. Her chest rose and fell. She was still alive.

Joshua ran into the house. The heat took his breath away. Rushing to the familiar pantry, he pulled out his handkerchief to help him breathe but ran into the center table and tumbled to the floor. *Lud, she must have rearranged things in here.* Joshua stayed down and crawled along the floor until he found the pantry. Moving things out of the way, he felt along the floor, snagging his right hand on a nail.

Blast it! Where is it? Abuela wouldn't ask this of me if it wasn't important.

Whispering a quick prayer, Joshua moved to the corner of the pantry. A thunderous noise sounded above him, and he impulsively ducked. Timber was falling.

His heart pounding faster, Joshua yanked on a whole in the wood, and it came loose. He thrust his injured hand into the hole. There was a bundle of fabric just at the base. He felt around for anything else, grabbed it and stuffed them into his military jacket.

Fire had reached the kitchen. Joshua could see a figure wandering in the smoke. He lunged toward it, realized it was Gil, seized his arm, and rushed toward the door, tripping on the doorframe on the way out.

On his knees, Joshua gasped for air. Fits of coughing racked his body.

A familiar voice scolded him through ragged coughs, "What were you thinking? You could have been killed."

Joshua couldn't reply. He needed air.

Gil tried to help him up. "Come on. The old woman is over here. We need to get clear of the house. It will come down soon."

Sucking for air, Joshua trudged toward an old cork tree and slumped near Abuela. It felt like forever, but he got more air in his lungs, and his coughing slowed. He became aware of his surroundings and moved closer to Abuela while Gil fetched some water for them.

"Abuela?" Joshua gently nudged her. His hand hurt, but it was covered in dirt; he couldn't discern how much damage had been done. "Abuela, can you hear me?"

"Si."

"Do you feel stable enough to walk?"

"Si, I believe I can walk. Did you get them?"

"I did. I also grabbed a small book."

"Bueno, Hastings. Your mama would be proud."

"I am so sorry about your house."

"Si, but we are alive to see another day, gracias to you."

Joshua pulled at the bundle, holding the jewels to see what they were. He noticed a green emerald peeking between the folds of velvet.

Somewhat alarmed, he asked, "Why do you have these jewels in your possession?"

Gil arrived, and Abuela replied, "Put those away. We cannot talk here. There is much to tell you." She looked at Joshua's companion with uncertainty.

Turning to see his best mate, Joshua assured her, "This is my trusted comrade, Gilbert Channing. We have no secrets."

"That may be so, but I am not ready to talk about anything, especially here. We are not safe. There are eyes and ears everywhere."

Gil scanned the trees around them.

Joshua lowered his voice. "I understand, but you are safe now." He nodded for Gil to help her up as he struggled to his feet. "We can discuss things somewhere privately. We won't let anything happen to you."

Reaching her hand to his face, she smiled. "I know, angelito."

Gil and Joshua carefully walked Abuela to a small inn on the opposite side of the town square where she could clean up and rest. Gil called for the physician to attend to her head and the gash in Joshua's hand. Both needed several stitches.

After the doctor left, Abuela held a mirror in front of her face to see the damage. With tears in her eyes, she looked up at Joshua.

He took her hand in his and kissed it. "Don't worry, Abuela. No amount of stitches could mar your loveliness."

"Hear, hear!" Gil clicked his heels and bowed.

She took a deep sigh and closed her eyes. "I am a vain woman. So much has been lost today, and people were hurt trying to help me."

"You judge yourself unfairly," Joshua said.

Abuela said nothing. Her eyes were full of sadness.

He motioned for Gil to join him. "I can see you need some rest."

The two men retreated to their own rooms across the hall; answers to their questions would have to wait until morning.

Before they parted, Gil said, "I thought your grandmother had passed away."

"Doña Eulalia Domingo is my mother's second cousin. I call her Abuela because she has always been like a grandmother to me. I spent many winters here with her in my youth. I will always protect her."

"She is a dear woman. I will help you keep her safe."

"Even if it means we take her back to England with us when our commission is up in a few weeks?"

"Of course, that goes without saying."

"You never disappoint, Channing. I appreciate your support more than you know."

Gil cocked a brow and posed, belly out, fists on his hips. "Honestly, Hastings, what would you do without me?"

Joshua rolled his eyes and stepped forward to offer his hand. "Always the peacock strutting his feathers."

"What do you mean? I was completely serious."

"I know."

Lifting the torn fabric on Joshua's sleeve, Gil said, "You look terrible. We'll talk in the morning about a plan."

"I hope I can talk in the morning. This cough is destroying my voice."

"Well, gentlemen, Doña Eulalia is recovering nicely. She will make a full recovery, but she shouldn't travel for a few more days. You may see her now. As for you, Captain Hastings, you did terrible damage to your lungs staying in that house for so long and will cough up soot for a few weeks, I'm afraid."

It was late morning, but Joshua felt like he hadn't slept for days. Offering his hand, he said, "Gracias, Doctor."

He and Gil entered Abuela's small apartment to find her sitting on the embroidered settee near the window, resting her eyes. A cotton blanket adorned her shoulders. *She's lost all her lovely lace shawls. She's lost everything.*

Crossing the tile floor to her side, Joshua knelt and whispered, "Abuela, it's Hastings." Her eyes flicked open.

"Abuela, do you have the strength to speak with us about last night?"

"Ah, Hastings, mi angelito. Si, let us talk. Are we alone?"

Joshua nodded to the other side of the room where Gil stood near the fireplace. "You remember Commander Channing from last night? He and I went to Eton together. We also served in the Royal Navy during the end of the war. You can trust him."

Channing bowed. "Most Illustrious Lady."

Abuela nodded to him with a somber smile. Looking at Joshua, she patted the seat next to her. "You will think me a visionary woman when I say I believe I have met my granddaughter. But I sent her away, and now I have lost everything, príncipe. He has won."

Joshua offered his handkerchief. "A granddaughter? What are you saying? Who has won?"

"That snake, Manuel Tudó."

Joshua's heart thumped against his ribs.

"A couple of weeks ago, my beautiful granddaughter came to me. She was running from Tudó. Oh, you should have seen her, Hastings. She looked just like my sweet Lucita. I thought I had seen a ghost when I caught her stuffing her little face with my butter rolls. So beautiful, an

HOLLY BROUGH

angel." Abuela's shoulders sagged. "But to protect her, I sent her away when two Civil Guards pounded on my door the day after she arrived. I had warned her about the bulletin, but I never told her I suspected she was mine, and now I don't know where she is or if I will ever see her again." Abuela wept until coughing took over.

Joshua put his arm around her and glanced toward Gil wide-eyed. "Shh. Calm yourself. What is her name?"

"She called herself Lea Tavio, but her real name is Amalia."

Joshua sat back in the chair with a silly grin on his face.

"What is it?" Abuela asked.

"We escorted her to Menorca. It must have been the same day you sent her away that we ran into her on the docks. She is in Menorca somewhere. We lost track of her after she left the *Santa Sabina*, but I am sure we can find her again." Joshua was so happy he chuckled.

"Oh, could it be true? She found you, then?" Abuela clapped her hands to her heart, and light filled her countenance. "I hoped you were still in port, but I didn't know for sure. You must bring her back to me. You must."

"Do you think Tudó could be Amalia's father?" Joshua braced himself.

"I pray no. And we must protect her from him the rest of her life."

With a whisper, he asked, "Is he the father of her child?"

Abuela looked into Joshua's eyes. "She says no."

"Child? What are you talking about?"

"Honestly, Channing, you say you know women."

"What? I—"

"Amalia is expecting."

"Lud. I mean . . . oh. Sorry, Most Illustrious Lady. I didn't mean to be crass."

Abuela nodded her head and smiled. "My ears are not so innocent. I was married to a hidalgo for most of my life."

Channing asked, "Did you get the names of the Civil Guards?"

"Sí. Guillermo Duranté. He looked like a kind machito, but the other one, Juan Engaños, I could tell, was up to no good."

"How could you tell?" Gil asked.

"Señor Engaños jumped to Tudó's defense when I told them about the murder of Lucita. He became agitated, and I lost my temper, saying some things about Tudó I shouldn't have. By the way Señor Engaños abruptly left, I knew I had gone too far.

"When they forced their way into my house yesterday. I could tell Señor Duranté was distressed. I stepped in front of Señor Engaños to stop him from going farther into my house, but he shoved me, and I lost my balance, hitting my head. The next thing I knew, my house was on fire. I felt large hands lift me to my feet and push me in the direction I should go, but a timber came crashing down between us. I barely made it out before I collapsed. Whoever helped me probably died in the house. Have you heard anything? Oh, I am so blessed you found me, mi angelito."

Getting emotional, Joshua touched his forehead to hers and whispered, "I am so grateful I found you when I did. If we hadn't come that day, I cannot imagine . . ."

Taking his face in her hands and guiding his eyes to hers, she said, "Don't think about it. All is well. See? I am fine. The doctor says I will be fine. I just need some rest."

Straightening up, Joshua wiped his eyes and sniffed. Channing pretended to inspect some dust on the mantle.

"When you are well enough, it is time for you to leave this place. You have refused in the past, but the time has come for you to go to my mother. You will be safe in England."

Abuela tried to protest, but Joshua stopped her, "Abuela, you know you are not safe here anymore, but we can protect you. I'm afraid I must insist."

She closed her eyes and nodded. "This has been my home for almost sixty years, and it will be a difficult change for me. But . . . you are right. My granddaughter must be found. Here, you need to see something."

She retrieved the velvet bag from her pocket and pulled out the sketch of Lucita. "Amalia thought this was a portrait of her, but you can see it is my Lucita. Their resemblance is impossible to dismiss, no?"

Joshua took the paper and examined it before passing it to Gil, who said, "Her nose is different, but her eyes and the curve of her lips are unmistakable."

She looked at Channing and nodded. "Pass me that book there, Commander." Then to Joshua, she said, "I'm glad you saved this along with the jewels, Hastings."

Channing placed the book in her outstretched hand.

"This is my financial ledger. I want you to settle my accounts before we leave, por favor. I have been living very humbly these past few years, so there should be enough to settle comfortably in England."

"You don't need to concern yourself about money. I will provide for you." Joshua was insistent as he gently took the ledger from her.

"A very generous offer, machito, but I have taken care of myself for many years and will not be a burden on others."

Joshua wanted to make it clear she was no burden, but Abuela held up her bruised hand. "I will hear no more of it, Joshua. I must rest." Abuela rarely used his Christian name.

With a smile, Joshua kissed her on the head. "Your family is in England, and you will find happiness there, I promise. We will leave you now. There is much to arrange."

Quietly closing the door behind them, Joshua took a deep breath. "Of course it was Tudó. I *despise* that man. And Amalia . . . I wondered the first time I saw her if she could possibly be Lucita's daughter, like seeing a ghost from my past. I am anxious to know her connection to Tudó."

"If you think Amalia is his daughter, why would she be working for him as a housemaid?"

Joshua rubbed his tired eyes. "I don't know. What I *do* know is he needs to pay for his crimes. I have to protect Amalia at all costs, and I cannot allow his treachery to continue."

"What are you planning, Hastings? This isn't something *we* can take into our own hands. I think we need to find this Duranté chap."

Bougainvillea

CHAPTER 20

J OSHUA'S HAND WAS a nuisance, and his lungs still hurt after inhaling so much smoke. The pain and the memories of Abuela lying on the ground near the heat of the fire chased all hope of sleep away. After a fitful night, Joshua rose early. He needed to find Tudó and get some answers.

A couple nights previous, he and Gil assured Abuela they would return the jewels to their rightful owner. If Amalia wasn't Tudó's daughter, they all agreed to stop their pursuit once Tudó had his priceless jewelry back. However, Joshua secretly wished to confront the degenerate himself, with the possibility of taking him out for good. Wrapping the jewels in a nondescript box to avoid suspicion, he left his room with package in hand.

Having reached the stables, he saddled his horse and mounted to leave when a Civil Guard stepped in front of him and took the reins. Joshua's horse pulled up short, and he immediately dismounted.

"Unhand my horse and step away, señor. You have no business here." Joshua could see the young Guard's head was wrapped with a bandage under his hat. Dark circles framed his light brown eyes.

Looking toward the different stalls to establish no one else could hear, the Guard put his hand to his lips to quiet Joshua's outburst and closed the gap between them. "Shh, señor, I'm here to warn you. I've been asked to keep an eye on you."

Joshua flinched back and forced the reins out of the man's hands. "That's captain to you, and what do you mean, keep an eye on me? Asked by whom?"

"Señor Engaños, head of the Civil Guard office here in Águilas," he replied before offering his hand. "Allow me to introduce myself. I am Guillermo Duranté."

Recognizing the name, Joshua offered his hand in return. Lowing his voice, he said, "Señor Duranté? I have been meaning to ask you about the incident a few days ago. You were at the scene of the house fire, si?"

"I am ashamed to say I was there."

"Ashamed?"

"Just following orders, señor, but it was not my wish to hurt the kind abuela who lived there."

"You are the one who harmed the doña?"

"No. Not on purpose." Señor Duranté looked terrified. "I watched my comrade, Juan Engaños, set fire to her house and did nothing. I was a coward. It didn't take long for the fire to engulf her house entirely. When I heard screaming, I ran in to help her, but we were separated when the ceiling fell." He removed his hat. His voice cracked when he spoke. "I have been eager to inquire about her health. I thought she was dead. Will she recover?"

Letting out a deep sigh, Joshua assured him, "Si, she will be fine. She has a nasty gash over her eye and breathing is difficult, but the physician believes she will make a full recovery."

Duranté reached up and touched the bandage on his head. "I got out of the house with a few scrapes, but it's nothing compared to my despair thinking Abuela might die, and I could have prevented it from happening."

Joshua felt the heat of the fire as he listened to the young man's account. His horse nipped at his sleeve, pulling him out of his nightmare. "Easy now. Why do you call her Abuela, señor?"

"She asked me to. She said it is what she hoped to be at this point in her life." Joshua smiled slightly.

"Señor . . . Captain . . ." Duranté shuffled his feet, embarrassed. "When I became a Civil Guard, I thought I was going to help people, not hurt them. When I heard Señor Engaños wanted you watched, I volunteered because I hoped you could help me make amends for what I have done. I will do anything you ask."

Joshua could feel his sincerity. "Does anyone know where you are right now?"

"Si. They think I am watching your place, but no one cares. Only Señor Engaños says you can't be trusted."

"Really."

"Señor Manuel Tudó told him you are nothing but trouble. I didn't believe him because I saw the care you gave that kind woman. I know from personal experience sweet Abuela is a saint, not a menace like he would have us believe."

"I'm going to Tudó's estate to confront him right now."

Duranté's eyes lit up. "I'd like to go with you, Captain. I can wake one of the Guards, tell them there has been no movement, and ask them to take over while I get some sleep."

Joshua didn't hesitate. "If you hurry, I will wait for you. I need to tell my comrade someone is watching our rooms."

Señor Duranté immediately left. Joshua tied his horse and went to inform Gil of the latest development.

He knocked and muttered through the doorframe, "Channing, wake up. I'm on my way out."

The door opened not a moment later. "I still don't like the idea of you going alone."

"I'm not. As luck would have it, I met Señor Duranté at the stable. He is going with me."

"You think he can be trusted?"

HOLLY BROUGH

"I do. Listen, there is a Guard watching our rooms. Try not to draw attention to yourself."

Wiping the sleep from his eyes, Channing said, "I make no promises."

"Thanks, Channing. Hopefully things will go quickly, and I'll bring him back in chains."

"If you don't kill him instead."

Traveling up a long gravel road hedged by tall cypress trees and immaculate grounds to the Tudó estate, Duranté and Hastings observed an older man in traveling suit dragging a squealing housemaid from the three-story manor. Both instinctively spurred their horses faster.

In one fluid motion, Joshua pulled his horse to a stop and dismounted, holding his hand up for Duranté to stay on his horse. Other servants sat in several overcrowded coaches, anxiously watching the confrontation.

"Señorita, you are trying my last nerve," growled the man.

Making his presence known, Joshua interrupted. "Pardon me, señor. I am Captain Joshua Hastings, and this is my comrade, Señor Guillermo Duranté of the Civil Guard." He waved in Duranté's direction.

The gentleman immediately stopped towing the girl toward a carriage. "I'm the butler of this estate, Señor Luis Valdez."

The young girl broke free and sat on the ground to shake some pebbles from her shoe.

"May we be of assistance?"

Straightening his waistcoat and smoothing his disheveled black hair, Señor Valdez said, "No, gracias. As you can see, we are trying to leave, and this selfish señorita is inconveniencing our entire party because she is convinced her stupid, ungrateful friend will return." Looking down at Sonia, he said, "She's gone. She's never coming back. Get it through your tiny head."

"Forgive my impudence, but may I ask who you are referring to?"

"Just another servant girl. Why do you ask?"

A woman approached. "Señor Valdez, may I help?"

"Sí, señora, I would be most appreciative. Pardon me while I go explain the reason for our delay to the staff." Señor Valdez bowed out of the conversation and walked to the overstuffed gilded carriages.

"I am the housekeeper, Señora Morales. Señorita Vela here and Señorita Marítimo, the housemaid who left us, were quite attached to each other. Thick as thieves." The housekeeper bent down to help Sonia up. "Come, señorita. It is past time to go."

"Is Señor Tudó accompanying you, then?" Joshua asked.

"No. He left last week."

"I see. Pardon me." Joshua walked a short distance to the butler. "May I speak to the scullery maid privately?"

Señor Valdez huffed, "If you must, but we are on a tight schedule. Why one scullery maid is worth all this trouble, I'll never understand."

"Gracias. I won't be long." Joshua tipped his hat and approached Sonia. "I'd like to speak with you, señorita. Over here, por favor." He led her under the balcony overlooking the ancient olive grove. Señora Morales looked on, and Duranté continued watching from his saddle.

"Señorita, I am Captain Hastings."

Tears running down her face, Sonia trembled. "Called in the Civil Guard, have they? I will not leave. I am such an insignificant part of their staff . . . Why can't they just let me stay?"

Offering his handkerchief, Joshua asked, "Why would you want to stay?"

Sonia searched his eyes, hesitating before speaking. "I can't go, señor. My friend had to . . . leave suddenly. I should have gone with her, but I was afraid. Now I don't know where she is. I know it is foolish of me to think she would send word of her whereabouts, considering everything that happened, but what if she does, and I am not here to receive it? I'll never know."

"Is your friend's name Amalia?"

Sonia's eyes grew big. "Sí, señor. You . . . you know her?"

It was his turn to pause. He wondered what to say, knowing he didn't have a satisfying answer. "Si, I know her. I'm trying to find some answers about her past. Maybe you can help me."

Sonia said, "Amalia and I trained at the same trade school in Murcia before meeting each other at this estate."

"Do you know how she came to be in Señor Tudó's employ?"

"No. We wondered if there was a relationship between the señor and Amalia's mother because of a comment he made when she first arrived, but we never found out anything."

Joshua couldn't hide his disappointment.

"I'm sorry, Captain." Sonia looked afraid.

"It's not your fault."

She watched him closely, as if sizing him up. *Sonia doesn't trust me. I need to prove to her I'm a friend.*

He heard someone approaching and noticed the butler, with the housekeeper not far behind. Turning to Sonia, he said, "You've got quite a predicament. May I speak on your behalf to Señor Valdez and Señora Morales? Maybe this can be resolved in a very simple and beneficial way for everyone."

Before she could respond, Joshua turned and addressed the sour-faced man. "Señor Valdez." He bowed with a subtle flourish. "Would it be too bold of me to take this señorita off your hands if she refuses to work for the Tudó household any longer?"

Señora Morales gasped at the suggestion.

Joshua continued, "I only ask if you are willing to release her from her contract. It is inadvisable for her to stay here alone with no way to care for herself."

"We never intended to let her stay." Señor Valdez looked offended.

The housekeeper leaned her head closer to Señor Valdez and muttered a few words. Perhaps Sonia had worn them down, and they were willing to compromise.

It didn't take long for the butler to voice his decision. "If this inconsiderate child refuses to honor the contract she signed, there is a fine of twenty escudos to be released from our employ, and she will receive no references."

Sonia took in a sharp breath. "But I don't have twenty escudos."

Señor Valdez firmly repeated, "Twenty escudos, or you leave with us now. Make your choice."

Sonia started crying again. "I cannot pay you that amount of money."

Señor Valdez lost his patience. "Then get in the carriage." He pulled Sonia to the closest carriage and shoved her toward the door, but it wasn't open to receive her. Crashing into it, she fell to the ground.

Señor Duranté jumped from his horse and moved between Sonia and the butler. Joshua rushed to her side, but it was Señor Valdez who helped her up. "I didn't realize the door wasn't open. Dust yourself off and get in the carriage."

Sonia looked at Joshua, pleading. *I have found another lost puppy, it would seem.* Twenty escudos was a prohibitively large amount of money for Sonia to have to pay, but there had to be some consequence for breaking her contract, principled as it was. He could not bail her out completely.

Joshua spoke up. "If I may provide another option?"

Everyone turned to him.

"Señorita, have you saved any money?"

"Si, a little. Most of what I earn goes to my family," she replied.

"If you give Señor Valdez all you have saved and I pay the remainder . . . Señor Valdez, you can release Señorita Vela to my employ with the understanding she will have to work off her debt to me. Is that agreeable to you all?"

Sonia spoke up immediately. "Señor, it is difficult for me, in good conscience, to allow you to pay such a sum, but I have eight escudos saved. I will gladly give you all that I have and work to pay off my debt."

Looking somewhat astonished but relieved, Señor Valdez and Señora Morales both agreed in unison, "Si."

The butler held out his hand, waiting for Sonia to dig through her carpetbag for the coins. Joshua handed him the balance. As soon as the sum was paid, Señor Valdez waved his hand in the air and yelled for the caravan to start moving.

Joshua rushed to stop him. "Pardon me, señor, will you deliver this package to Señor Tudó, por favor? It is very important he receive this." Remembering he had jotted down a message of warning in case the slippery snake eluded him again, he reached into his pocket and included it with the package. "This too."

With a forced smile and nod of his head, he agreed, "Si, señor, he shall have it upon our arrival in Paris."

"Gracias, señor." Turning to Sonia, Joshua offered his arm. "Señorita, it is time for you to leave this place."

"But what about Amalia? There is no other place she can find me but here."

Glancing at Duranté, Joshua replied, "If Amalia hasn't sent you word of her destination, it must not be safe to do so."

Wiping a tear from her cheek, she took his arm.

"Maybe you can tell me what happened the night Amalia left." Motioning to his horse, he added, "I apologize for our current mode of transportation."

Sonia assured him, "Señor, you will hear no complaint from me."

Before mounting, Joshua said, "Forgive me. I have been thoughtless. May I introduce you to my friend, Señor Duranté. He has quite an interesting story to tell as well."

Sonia smiled with a blush at the handsome Guard when he tipped his hat before mounting his horse. Joshua helped Sonia up and joined the saddle behind her.

"Why are you so interested in Amalia?" she asked.

"At first, it was because I know Tudó to be a deceitful, manipulative man. When I met Amalia, I knew right away she had become the latest victim in one of his little games. But recently I've discovered Amalia is very likely my distant relative, my mother's cousin's granddaughter."

Joshua saw Duranté's reaction of surprise and knew it mirrored Sonia's as well.

"I don't understand? How is Amalia related to you?"

After a deep sigh, Joshua admitted, "I'm not certain how the pieces all fit. Por favor, tell me of the night Amalia fled."

"Señor Tudó came back early from his summer holiday. She hadn't been feeling well and already retired to bed, but the señor had Señora Morales summon Amalia to the study. Both of us feared for her safety. Señor Tudó came back without his family. He was alone. I told her I would be close if she needed me, but Cook requested my help in the kitchen. Not a half hour later, when I was fetching more water from the well, the señor almost ran me over with his horse. I found Amalia in our room, frantically packing her bag. She told me the señor had tried to force himself on her, and she threw up all over him. He beat her pretty bad before he left."

Joshua cursed under his breath. *Was that the first time he tried to force her?*

"Amalia asked me to go with her. Señor Tudó had lifted a hand on me too. We were both so scared, but I couldn't leave. My parents relied on some of my wages each week. I promised not to tell anyone I helped her, and she told me she would eventually let me know where she settled."

"She suffered so much," Joshua muttered.

"It's worse. Before the señor came back, Amalia experienced a terrible heartbreak."

"What do you mean?"

"A few weeks previous to Señor Tudó's return, a careless, selfish boy stole her heart and then threw it away. She loved him, really loved him. When he turned his back on her, she was so devastated that it made her physically sick. Señora Morales insisted on sending for a physician if she didn't improve. She could hardly get through a day's work."

Some of the pieces came together. The confrontation with Tudó may have solidified her decision to run away, but if a doctor was summoned and her condition discovered, the consequences would have made things far worse for her.

"Who broke her heart?"

She didn't speak.

"Señorita?"

"I apologize, but it is not for me to say."

Blast. She is a good friend. "Señorita Vela, I helped Amalia escape to the island of Menorca a few weeks ago. It is there that I lost track of her, but I am determined to find her again."

Sonia gasped. "Are you sure it was her?"

"Si, I am sure."

"You must find her. I need to know where she is, that she's alright."

Joshua felt as anxious as Sonia sounded. "I quite agree. I will not rest until she's found and safe from Tudó. I'm only too sorry I couldn't confront him today."

Sonia asked, "May I go with you?"

Joshua smiled. "No, señorita. Our immediate destination is to retrieve another of Tudó's victims, and then to England."

"England? You would have me go to England?"

"Si. We'll need to send word to your family about the change of employment."

"Both my parents died a month ago. I just received word last week."

"I'm so sorry."

"I don't think I've accepted it yet. So much has happened. I feel so emotional all the time."

"You will always have a place with my family. You're safe now."

Chamomile

CHAPTER 21

SEÑOR DURANTÉ ENTERED Águilas a separate way than Joshua to avoid suspicion. Prior to that, the men had come up with a lie to cover for his absence of half the day. After learning more about the treacherous nature of Manuel Tudó, Duranté expressed his interest in working at the Guard and secretly help Joshua's quest for justice against the man.

Joshua led an anxious Sonia up a flight of stairs to Abuela's small apartment. They entered the well-lit room, curtains pulled wide to welcome in the evening sunlight, to find Channing occupying a chair near the hearth and the lovely woman seated properly on a floral settee, reading the daily bulletin. Channing stood at their arrival.

"You look radiant today," Joshua said.

"Gracias, amorcito," said Abuela. "After a good night's rest, I feel much better. Who do we have here?" Abuela smiled kindly at the petite, somewhat disheveled scullery maid.

"It is my pleasure to introduce you to Señorita Sonia Vela, who was, until recently, employed by Manuel Tudó." Turning to Sonia, he said, "Señorita Vela, this is my mother's cousin, our Most Illustrious

Lady, Doña Eulalia Domingo, but we call her Abuela. And this is my comrade, Captain Gilbert Channing."

"Commander," Channing said.

Abuela reached her hands out to Sonia. "Come here, niña. You look like you have had a very long day. Tell me about yourself."

Joshua loved how Abuela made everyone feel welcome.

"Hastings, may I have a word?" Channing motioned him to the door.

"Pardon us a moment, ladies." Joshua bowed and followed Channing into the hall.

"Am I right in assuming you have rescued *another* poor soul?"

"I know what you are thinking . . ."

"You have no idea what I am thinking. What are *you* thinking?" Channing asked.

"I couldn't leave her there. She was miserable. She's Amalia's closest friend."

"What are you going to do with her? She's a housemaid."

"Actually, she's a scullery maid but very intelligent. The señorita has more potential than cleaning dishes." Joshua pulled at his cravat. Under Channing's disapproving gaze, he continued, "In exchange for her freedom from the previous contract she had with Tudó, I have hired her, but for what, I don't know."

"Sometimes, I really don't understand you. You can't rescue everyone." Channing shook his head. "Do you ever think before you act?"

"Yes, and I've regretted it my whole life."

"That was years ago. I thought you'd put that behind you."

Joshua looked away. "It's ever present."

"Listen, I don't know if this is good advice, but maybe Señorita Vela can be Abuela's lady's companion. That could be her purpose for joining our growing party."

Patting Channing on the back, Joshua chuckled in relief. "That is a genius idea, Gil. Thank you."

"Well, I'm not just a pretty face, Hastings. There's more this head can do than grow thick golden curls."

"I never doubted it."

The men reentered the room to the music of giggling women.

Joshua interrupted, "Señorita Vela, may I speak with Abuela for a moment?"

Sonia quickly got up. "Certainly."

Channing motioned for her to sit in the overstuffed chair he'd recently occupied near the fireplace.

Joshua joined Abuela on the settee and asked, "How would you feel about Sonia becoming your lady's companion? I need something for her to do, and I think it could be good for both of you since we will be leaving for England soon."

Abuela didn't hesitate. "I like the idea, príncipe. Gracias for thinking of our happiness."

Joshua kissed Abuela's cheek. "Brilliant." Motioning for Sonia to join them, he said, "I have a proposition."

"Si?"

"We"—pointing to Abuela and himself—"would like you to be the doña's lady's companion."

"I'm only a scullery maid, Captain." Sonia looked terrified.

"Señorita, we are leaving for England in a few days, and I believe this will serve to help you both adjust to a new life. Abuela needs a companion, and so do you. Your responsibilities are simple. Whatever Abuela needs, you take care of. You will help her dress, groom, and keep her company."

Sonia slowly nodded her head in acceptance and committed her service. "As you wish. I will do my best, but por favor, be patient with me. I have much to learn."

Abuela joined in the conversation. "This will be a wonderful friendship, bonita. I already feel a kinship. Come sit with me."

"I hope you will not be disappointed. I have little to offer and will never amount to much more than what you see—a humble, scrawny disappointment."

Abuela chuckled and patted Sonia on the knee. "You are too hard on yourself. I think you will find, niña, that a simple candle shines just as brightly as a gilded one. You shine your light, Sonia. You're wonderful as you are."

With constant encouragement, Sonia learned her duties quickly. Within two days, she and Abuela were getting on so well; they spoke for hours about everything, especially their favorite topic—Amalia. Joshua purchased some cross-stitch for them to do together, and Abuela appeared to relish the opportunity to teach Sonia something new.

One evening, as the men quietly played cards at a small table, Sonia answered Abuela's questions. "Amalia escaped into books. Many times, after a dull day of peeling wax off of candelabras or dusting furniture, I would find her curled up in the corner of the library with a book. Sometimes, she would sneak a book to our room just so she could finish it by morning."

"What were some of her favorite books?" Joshua asked.

"That's a good question. All books would be the accurate answer, but to be specific, I have a book about names, and their meanings we read together often. Though it isn't a story book, she enjoyed the time we spent together looking up different names. She also loved *Don Quixote*. I don't know how many times she read that book. Señor Tudó kept several books on horses. Amalia read all of them. She claims a person can see forever in the eye of a horse if they are allowed to look long enough. I wouldn't know. Horses scare me."

"Ha ha, Hastings. I beat you again! That never happens. I believe that is three times in a row."

Joshua threw his cards on the table and got up to pour himself a drink.

"You know, when Amalia first took a tour of the grounds at the Tudó estate, she seemed enchanted by its grandeur. They have a large stable, which became her favorite destination until she discovered the Fortress of the Sun. Every day, she walked to the ruins after she met her true love, but then he ended up being a heartless rake. Perhaps if I had accompanied her, I could have saved her from such heartache." She looked at the small party. "Have you been to the ruins before?"

All three nodded in unison.

Channing took the glass Joshua offered. "Who was this *heartless rake?*"

"The duke of Cádiz," Sonia offered without thinking and promptly covered her mouth with her hand.

Both Channing and Joshua choked on their drinks. Abuela sucked in a sharp breath.

"You mean the duke who is to marry Queen Isabella II?" Channing used his handkerchief to wipe at the mess he'd just made.

"The very same. I shouldn't have told you. It wasn't my place." Sonia nibbled on some bread.

No one spoke.

"I warned her to stay away from him, but Amalia has a rebellious streak in her."

Joshua rubbed his lips. *Is she carrying the duke's child? Does he know?*

Realizing the others looking at him, Joshua set his glass down and cleared his throat. "Señorita, are you aware Amalia is expecting?"

"Expecting? You mean she . . ."

"Sí, she is with child," Abuela said.

"I thought she couldn't get up in the morning or eat her meals because of a broken heart. How could I be so stupid?"

Joshua moved closer, hands clasped behind his back, and asked the question haunting him most. "Is there any possibility the child could be . . . could be Tudó's?"

Sonia didn't seem alarmed by the question. After a moment's thought, she said, "No, Captain. The señor went on holiday to Madrid for three months. Amalia didn't start getting sick until a few weeks before he came back." She took a deep breath. "I should have prevented this."

He rolled his shoulders as if relieved from a terrible burden. "Gracias, señorita. It is late, and I believe you ladies could use a good night's sleep."

The ladies looked at each other, and Abuela nodded her consent.

"Buenas noches, Captain and Commander." Sonia stood and curtsied.

"It's been a delightful evening. Buenas noches." Joshua gave Abuela a kiss on the cheek and a quick bow to Sonia before both men retired to their rooms.

He overheard Abuela say, "You shouldn't feel responsible for Amalia's choices, Sonia. Making choices, good or bad, helps us grow. That is our purpose—to make choices and learn from them. Think if you had not chosen to leave the Tudó's employ, I would not have you in my life, and you are already so dear to me."

After the door closed behind them, Channing asked, "What do you think of the latest news?"

"I think Amalia is giving birth to a child of noble blood. I know I should not even think it, but I'm relieved her child is the duke's."

"Relieved?"

"The night Amalia fled Tudó's employ, he tried to force himself on her. I've been worried that wasn't the first time he attacked her."

With the luggage secured on the large black carriage the Earl of Huntingdon sent to retrieve their party from Portsmouth, England, Joshua made ready to travel on horseback alongside Channing. The ladies comfortably sat on royal blue velvet cushioned seats. Light-blue and silver upholstery decorated the ceiling and walls of the spacious cabin.

Channing pulled up next to Joshua and asked, "Shall we go, then?"

"We have no other choice."

"Come now, how long has it been since you visited Hodcott House in Berkshire Downs?"

"A few years."

"You seem in a foul mood, Hastings? We're finally home and finished with our commissions."

"At least you have something to look forward to." Joshua motioned for the carriage to move.

"The official presentation, you mean? They're only making me a captain because they hope I'll take on my own ship. It's pointless. I'm not signing another commission."

"Why would you pass that up?"

"Enough about me. We're home, Hastings. Surely you are happy to breathe in English air. It clears the sinuses."

Joshua had to admit it felt good to be on English soil, just not as his true self, the heir to the Huntingdon earldom. "I'm just tired, that's all." Honestly, he couldn't get Amalia out of his head. He needed answers, but he was stuck in England, where he would be thrust into the social scene, prominently on display, upon arriving home.

Channing chuckled about something.

"You are entirely too jovial today," Joshua said.

"I don't understand why you *aren't*."

"You know how I despise the social scene, and it will only get worse when we travel to London for the season."

"Take heart, Hastings. It is only for a month or two or three. Surely you can grace the halls of the most prominent Englishmen for a short while. How else will they know what a handsome, noble gentleman looks like?"

"They have ample opportunity among themselves. I cannot stand to watch them strut about, their peacock feathers splayed open, manipulating their way higher up the ladder."

Channing got serious. "Hastings, I understand you're dissatisfied with the system, so it falls on you to show your peers what it is to be noble and fair and true. I have never known a better man."

The compliment embarrassed Joshua. He neither deserved nor wanted such praise.

"You're the one who should be in Parliament, prattling on as you do." He spurred his horse faster, leaving Channing behind.

Daffodil

CHAPTER 22

SEÑORA CONSUELA BURST through Amalia's door, threw off her covers, and plopped herself on the bed.

"What's going on?" Amalia wiped the sleep from her eyes.

"I would like to know when Your Highness feels like earning her keep around here?"

Your Highness? Amalia raised her voice in frustration. "You've insisted on keeping me cooped up in here. I've always been ready and willing to work for my support." A glint of contempt flashed in the señora's eyes, so Amalia took a deep breath and asked, "When can I start? I would love to do something other than sit in this room all day."

"Music to my ears." Señora Consuela slapped her knees and stood. "What things are you good at? It needs to be something you can do out of sight of the patrons. We really can't have you traipsing around the tavern looking like that. You have a fine melon sprouting there."

Amalia pulled her blanket to her chin.

Laughing it off, Señora Consuela asked again, "What can you do? Do you clean? Cook? What?"

Thinking she might enjoy the kitchen, Amalia stated, "I cook well, actually. May I work in the kitchen?"

Surprise and delight lit up Señora Consuela's face. "Bueno. Get up and get dressed. I'll introduce you to the kitchen. Cook could use a refresher on how *not* to burn food. I'll wait for you outside your door."

Amalia quickly dressed in some of the clothes Señora Consuela had collected for her. The blouse was a little big, but it covered her belly well. Amalia pulled her hair up with the stick her brother, Gordy, carved for her and looked in the mirror one last time. Her cheeks were rosy, and her eyes sparkled. Excitement filled her heart for the first time in a long time.

The kitchen was located near the back of the tavern. She stopped just inside the entrance and stared at the dirt and blood smears staining the walls and preparation table in the center of the spacious room.

"When was the last time this kitchen was cleaned?" Amalia asked.

Señora Consuela ignored her and walked to the cook, who was standing behind an enormous pan with a chunk of lard skating on its hot surface.

"There you are, Rana. We have been looking for you. Señorita Tavio is ready to help you in the kitchen."

He used his hand to wipe his nose, then wiped it on his filthy apron before holding it out for Amalia to take. She reluctantly took it, not wanting to offend him on her first day out of confinement.

He bent over her hand with a sloppy kiss and said, "Señor Rana. Welcome to my kitchen."

Amalia discreetly wiped her hand on her skirt. He grabbed what appeared to be a chunk of meat wrapped in dough and made a splash tossing it into the fat. Sparks ignited on the stove, causing Amalia and Señora Consuela to jump back.

"We'll leave you to your preparations for the day," Señora Consuela said, "and I'll put her to work out of your way."

Cook grunted before tossing another hunk of something in the lard. Amalia's tummy flipped when she thought of all the food she'd eaten in the last few weeks.

"What's the matter?" Señora Consuela asked. "Are you going to be sick? Don't you dare try to get out of this. You gave me your word you would help around here, and Señor Guerra and I don't take kindly to liars."

Amalia assured her, "I'm fine. No, I'm happy to work in the kitchen. Where would you like me to begin?"

"Well, if you look around, there are several pots and pans that need scrubbing. You should probably start there. I'll show you the well and pump out in the back and a place to clean. You'd better hurry. The morning rush is in less than two hours."

Greeted by the happy sounds of farm animals milling around, Amalia spotted a well in the middle of a large backyard. To the left was a barn with pigs, chickens, a few cows, and two horses. Happiness filled her until she saw a cat run across their path. The thought of sweet Thomas pricked her heart, and a sudden fit of emotion threatened to overwhelm her.

Where is he now?

Focusing her thoughts, she noticed a slaughterhouse to the right, and between that and the barn, a beautiful garden of colorful vegetables brightened the area. Amalia couldn't help but notice the stark difference between the filthy kitchen and immaculate backyard. *Someone other than Señor Rana must be responsible for keeping it.*

Shoving an apron at her, Señora Consuela said, "Stop standing there like a statue and get to work. Time is wasting."

Amalia made her way back to the kitchen to fetch the dirty pans and immediately felt the cluttered oppression of being indoors. If she was going to spend her days in the kitchen, things needed to change. Amalia transferred the pots and pans to the well. After spending several weeks in her small room, it felt good to work her muscles and be productive. Soon, she caught herself humming a favorite tune in the open air. She breathed new life into her lungs and reveled in its cleansing power.

It took over an hour to see some progress, but finally the basin and counter were clear of clutter. The cooking implements clean and drying, Amalia got some rags and started washing down the walls and counters. There was rotten food and garbage everywhere. Along with streaks of blood, grease, kernels of rice, and flecks of dried dough peppering the walls, the lower cupboards collected dead mice and fecal matter in the crevices. Bugs littered the shelves, and spiders built their homes in all the corners above and below. Amalia covered her nose and mouth with a rag and found an empty bin to catch all the garbage as she meticulously made her way around the kitchen.

That chore nearly completed, Amalia retrieved the pots and pans and hung them on the hooks above the preparation table in the center of the kitchen. It was then she noticed a young man—maybe fourteen years old, the same age as her brother Antonio when she was sent away. He was sitting in the corner. He had light red hair and golden eyes. Horribly pocked skin pitted his face, and burn scars ran up and down his arms.

Amalia stepped over to Cook and asked, "Excuse me, Señor Rana, who is the boy at the counter cutting vegetables? I didn't notice him before."

Scarcely taking his eyes off his task, he said, "That's Leonardo. We call him Leo. Just leave him be. He works better without distraction."

After Amalia observed him for some moments, she was pleased to see Leo move proficiently from place to place, in and out of the kitchen with practiced precision. He knew what to do without being told, but the boy didn't speak or make a sound. Amalia wondered if he was mute.

"Hey, señorita! What have you done with all of my pots?" Cook hollered.

"They are hanging above the preparation table."

He walked over and pulled one down. "What happened to these?"

"I scrubbed them clean."

"You ruined them! They were perfect the way they were."

A little disgusted, Amalia replied, "They were filthy."

"What is wrong with a little grime? It adds flavor."

Amalia felt a gag coming on. "I can't believe I've been eating your food."

That earned a blast of laughter from Señor Rana.

"Well, you're still here, aren't you? You haven't died. Get out of my kitchen and help Leo outside."

She happily walked out the back door and found Leo hoeing the ground in the garden between perfect rows of vegetables. He hummed a calming melody.

Amalia was pleased. "Hola, Leo." He nodded.

"You may call me Amalia." Catching her mistake, she quickly corrected herself. "Oh, excuse me. I'm sorry. Call me Lea. I'm Lea Tavio." She nervously looked around to see if they were alone. *Stupid! It's been weeks. My new name should slide off my tongue by now.*

He looked confused, but he just shrugged his shoulders and went back to work.

Amalia didn't know what to do, so she stood there for a moment, watching him. He worked the soil with a skilled hand, picking and pruning the plants.

"You have a wonderful gift for gardening. How can I help?"

Leo looked up at Amalia with a smile. His grin featured a large gap separating his upper front teeth, but she found it charming.

"Por favor, will you get a large basket from over there to fill with vegetables for Rana?"

Amalia smiled at the sound of his deep, rich voice. She retrieved a basket and filled it with peppers, tomatoes, carrots, onions, and corn he had set aside.

"What have you done to my space? I don't know where anything is! How am I supposed to cook any food around here?" Cook exclaimed from the back door.

"I organized your spoons, spatulas, and knives in the drawers under the cupboards. Your flour, lard, and spices are above the knife drawer."

"Damned señorita meddling in my business."

She and Leo looked at each other a moment before laughing.

"How old are you, Leo?"

"Almost sixteen."

"You have a gift for growing vegetables. I imagine they would taste delicious if cooked properly." She winked at him, and he chuckled. "I'll take these to Cook." Amalia hefted the basket inside. "Here are the vegetables. Is there anything you need from me before I start cleaning out the drawers on this side of the kitchen?"

Cook winced the way a child does when slapped. He mumbled something incoherent, lifted his cleaver, and hacked through a thick hunk of meat.

"Very well, then. I'll be over here if you need me," she said.

By the end of the day, every muscle in Amalia's body cried from exertion, but it felt good. The next two weeks, though rough at the beginning, slowly took on a sort of rhythm. Leo prepared the food, Señor Rana cooked the food, and Amalia cleaned. For the most part, their system worked well, but to Amalia's frustration, Cook would burn a simple dish and still serve it. Amalia saw the food before Cook got a hold of it, but by the time the patrons received their meal, the dish was unrecognizable.

After hurting her hand trying to scrape the burnt food off yet another pot, Amalia suggested, "Señor Rana, I happened to notice that some of your best food is getting . . . well, crispy."

"So what's it to you?"

"I just thought if you didn't get the stove as hot and shook the pan to move the meat around, it would cook more evenly. You are the expert, of course, but maybe Leo could tend to the rice and vegetables while you stir the meat."

She braced herself for a spoon to be thrown her way, as it had several times that week when she offered a word of advice or simply made conversation.

To her relief, he just yelled, "Leo doesn't cook! Attend your own business and leave me to mine."

However, the next time Amalia observed him, Rana was jiggling the pan to separate and spread the meat out evenly. He motioned for Leo to join him and whispered something that sent Leo over to the other stove to stir the rice. That day, Cook received a compliment and proudly repeated it for them to hear. Leo glanced Amalia's direction with a knowing smile, and she couldn't help but smile back. Wiping her brow with the back of her hand, she took in a sharp breath. Red and peeling, her hands were raw from cleaning. Amalia sought out the señora, who she found seated at a back table in the dining room chatting with Señor Guerra.

"I'm about to retire and wondered if I could have some salve to rub on my hands? They won't hold up much longer without it." She held them out for the señora to see.

"They don't look bad to me. You'll be fine by morning. Buenas noches."

"But . . . señora, if you don't have some, may I go to the apothecary or use a few ingredients in the kitchen to make my own? My hands aren't used to the harsh lye I've been using to clean the cooking utensils. I can't close them without splitting my skin open."

Señora Consuela grabbed Amalia by the arm and pulled her out of sight of Guerra and the patrons. "Do you presume to know better than I do? You are not allowed to leave the tavern, and you can't just use the resources we have for your own benefit. If you challenge me again in front of Señor Guerra, your rent will double."

"Double? I hardly make the money I pay for rent now."

"Then you will keep quiet and stop complaining. Buenas noches." The señora shoved her hard enough to cause Amalia to stumble.

Tears of frustration stung her eyes, but she kept them at bay and stomped up the stairs to her room. Sitting by her fireplace, she contemplated her dilemma. *With no access to the kitchen supply or the apothecary, my hands will never heal. Por favor, God, help me. I can't sleep with this pain.* Amalia rubbed her hands together, and some of the scabs opened.

Staring at the charred remains of her fire, she got an idea. Using the shovel, she gathered a small pile of fine ash on the tile. Adding drops of water, Amalia worked the ash into a paste and rubbed it on her hands. The cooling effect was instant.

Gracias, Lord. Gracias.

Poppy

CHAPTER 23

A MALIA MADE HER way to bed after yet another exhausting day. Approaching the stairs, she overheard muffled voices in the small room off Señor Guerra's office and stopped when her pseudonym, Lea, floated through the door.

The audacious señora spoke excitedly. "Señorita could be a gold mine. She's the reason why the food is better, I just know it. We should have her help Rana with the food. Leo can clean the pots and pans. Rana can learn some new dishes to make, and we can charge our customers more. Think of it. You've seen the increase of business. More and more will come, you listen to Consuela. We could even afford to get new dishes and linens. We've needed to do that forev—"

"I'm in charge here," Señor Guerra interrupted. "Don't forget your place, señora. If any changes are made, it will be me who makes them."

"But . . . but think of all the money coming in," Señora Consuela tentatively continued. "If we have Lea start cooking with Rana, it could change everything."

"I don't want to hear any more."

"But—"

"Leave me."

Amalia quickly took her leave up the stairs and out of sight. *What if I get to cook?* With the possibility on the horizon, her brain started devising a plan to contact the smithy across the road to have some hollow posts made for the first dish she'd introduce to Señor Rana. Despite her exhaustion, ideas came flooding in, but as soon as her head hit the pillow, darkness overcame her.

Perhaps a bit premature, Amalia woke before the cock crowed the next morning and jotted down a note to the smithy. She put it in her apron pocket just as the señora barged into her room.

"Bueno, you're up." Closing the door behind her, Señora Consuela added, "I'm here to tell you that you are going to start cooking with Señor Rana and teach him everything you know about food. We want to make some changes, and he needs new ideas." Stepping toward Amalia and taking her hand, she tsked. "Your hands look appalling."

Amalia looked at them too. Her nails were chipped and broken, but her hands looked better than they did the week before. "They'd heal quicker if I could get some salve for them. It would only take a moment for me to walk to the apothecary. I'm happy to go." *If I am given permission to go to the apothecary, I can drop off the request to the smithy myself.*

Señora Consuela shook her head. "You know the rules, señorita. Why do you continue to ask me the impossible?"

"Why is it impossible?"

"Enough of this. I will send someone to get the salve for you. We can't have you walking around Mahón looking like that. You can't hide your condition now that you are, what, seven months along? You're such a petite thing. I doubt you'll carry him full term."

"Him? We don't know if it is a *him* or a *her*."

"You are having a boy, señorita. I can tell by the way you are carrying him. You also have dry skin, and you prefer to eat a lot of meat and cheese. All of those things indicate you are having a boy. He is going to be a big boy too, hard delivery."

Amalia's eyes grew big.

The señora laughed. "You are afraid, are you?"

"No, I've seen six babies born. I know what happens. And I don't believe in your old wives' tales. They never predicted the correct gender of any of my siblings." Uncomfortable with the subject, Amalia asked, "I don't know how we got off the subject of helping Cook in the kitchen."

"You need salve." Patting her hand, Señora Consuela moved to leave. "I'll have someone get it for you. But right now, you're needed in the kitchen. Make me a list of ingredients you need for the recipes you will be teaching Señor Rana."

Amalia smiled.

"Don't be proud and prance around about it either, and don't think for a second that because you are helping Cook now, you will ever amount to anything. If I hadn't been the one to insist on this change, you'd never be more than a scullery maid. Because of your poor choices, you should thank me for taking pity on you." Consuela moved to leave, but then added, "And don't make a spectacle of yourself and embarrass us because you're overzealous."

Amalia was speechless. *I have made poor choices, true. But that doesn't mean I can't achieve anything. I'm smart, and I've been trained well. I know I can make a good go of this new opportunity.*

"Stop standing there all sullen. Get me that list." Señora Consuela closed the door.

Amalia yanked her hair up in a bun as ideas for meals and recipes flowed through her mind. First, she needed to find Leo.

Reaching the bottom of the stairs, she saw him entering the kitchen from the gardens. "Leo, will you help me with something?"

He look at her.

"I have a request for the blacksmith across the road and wondered if you would give him this note for me, por favor."

He took the paper from her and nodded.

"Gracias, Leo. I appreciate your help."

Leo left his garden tools and disappeared around the back of the tavern. Amalia continued to write down ingredients and the different processes of cooking each meal.

When he returned immediately, she asked, "Did you get a response?"

"No."

"Did he read it?"

"I don't know." Leo escaped into the kitchen.

The blacksmith opened his smithy earlier than usual and noticed a slip of paper addressed to Señor Blacksmith lying across his tool belt.

Señor Blacksmith,

My name is Lea Tavio. I apologize I am not meeting you in person, but I work in the kitchen at the El Comienzo Tavern just across the street, and I am quite busy. I understand you are very skilled in your craft. I have somewhat of a strange request. I need four posts five meters in length with an opening ten centimeters by ten centimeters. If you would be so kind, send a bid for the job with my friend Leo, por favor.

Gracias, Señorita Tavio

Running his fingers through his thick beard, he chuckled as he considered the request. Seeing no Leo to send a message back to her, and quite intrigued by this Señorita Tavio, he went across the street to address her himself.

Upon entering the tavern, the blacksmith was instantly hit with the smell of something burning. Suppressing the impulse to cover his nose, he looked around, wondering who to approach.

If Señorita Tavio is cooking whatever I smell, I don't have a great deal of confidence in her abilities. In the years he'd lived across the street, he'd never set foot in the dark and unimpressive tavern. He debated if he should just leave.

A middle-aged, fleshy woman finally greeted him. "Buenos días, señor. May I interest you in some refreshment?"

"No, gracias. I am here to see a Señorita Tavio. I understand she works in the kitchen."

A severely pocked, red-headed boy peeked around the corner from the back of the room.

"Uh, si. I am Señora Consuela, the matron. She is quite busy at the moment. Is there something I can help you with?"

Sensing a power struggle and not appreciating her condescension, the blacksmith leaned a little closer and said, "I would like to speak with her myself. We have some business to discuss."

Pursing her lips together, Señora Consuela finally muttered, "Have a seat," and motioned him to sit before she walked away.

"Lea, it seems you have a visitor." Señora Consuela startled Amalia, and she spilled some water from the pot she'd just filled from the well.

Bending to wipe the splashed dirt off her apron, Amalia was pulled off-balance when the matron grabbed her by the arm and growled, "Have you been sneaking out of the tavern?"

"Of course not. Who is it? I'm not expecting anyone."

"I don't know what you're up to, but I will not tolerate any nonsense. I have told you many times that no one should see you in your condition. It isn't proper."

Amalia almost laughed but successfully stifled it. *Does she know how ludicrous she sounds?*

"The blacksmith from across the street says he has some business with you."

Amalia smiled. "Gracias, señora. I asked Leo to deliver a letter requesting the blacksmith's help on a small job for one of my recipes. Do I have your permission to speak with him? I'm sure it won't take long."

Señora Consuela considered it for a moment. "You certainly work fast, señorita. It was only an hour ago that I spoke to you about helping Rana."

Amalia wiped her hands clean. "This is a meal I have a lot of experience making. It seemed natural to start preparing for it immediately."

"You can see him," the señora conceded, "but we will not pay for whatever he is making. You can see him back here behind the tavern. You have five minutes."

"Gracias." Amalia wiped her face and straightened her cap. Weeks had gone by since she'd spoken with anyone outside of the tavern.

A tall, burly middle-aged man with short, dark hair and scruffy beard, the blacksmith looked stern when he appeared around the corner, but Amalia's racing heart calmed when she saw kindness in his eyes.

"Buenos días, señor. I did not expect you, but gracias for coming to see me. Did you have a question about my request?"

He gaped at her a moment, mouth slightly open, as if stunned. Finally, he found his voice. "Buenos días, Señorita Tavio. I am José Rendón. Pleased to meet you." Holding the letter in his hand, he walked closer and continued, "I don't have questions. I was merely curious about the request, considering you work in a kitchen. I'm not implying you don't know your own business, but I . . . I thought I should meet you before filling your order." He shoved a chicken away with his foot.

"I am prepared to pay for your work if the amount is agreeable. I need the posts to make a special dish. If I don't have the amount of money you need, I will have to consider other options. I'm not actually the cook yet, but just this morning, I was asked to help Señor Rana with some new dishes."

Studying her with a crooked smile, he ran his fingers through his beard. "I believe I can make the posts for you fairly quickly with scraps from other jobs I have done. That should keep the cost down. I'll send you a message with the amount in a few days." He chuckled and winked at her. "I am actually relieved it wasn't your cooking I smelled wafting through the tavern."

Amalia giggled behind her hand. "Si, I'm hoping to change that. Believe it or not, it's better than it was."

Señor Rendón tipped his head. "Buenos días, señorita."

Amalia smiled. "Gracias, Señor Rendón."

Señora Consuela had been watching the exchange from a distance. As soon as their conversation ended, she approached Amalia. "You seem extremely happy."

"Like I said, I asked him to do a project for me, and it sounds like he will help me."

"Just this once, Lea. I don't like you going behind my back. Who knows what Señor Guerra will say about this."

"I promise you will not be disappointed."

Señora Consuela scoffed. "We will see."

Buttercup

CHAPTER 24

TO AMALIA'S DELIGHT, Señor Rendón delivered her posts only a few days after her request and only charged her a fraction of what she thought it would cost. It was time to turn the tavern upside down.

When Amalia entered the kitchen, Leo had on his apron, chopping vegetables at the preparation table, and Cook grumbled next to him, working some dough for the baguettes. Another young man she'd never seen before sat in the corner, looking confused. He also wore an apron.

Walking up to him, she introduced herself. "Buenos días. I am Lea Tavio."

"Buenos . . . Buenos días, Señorita Tavio."

When he offered nothing else, she stepped over to Cook and whispered in his ear, "Pardon me, Señor Rana, I wondered if you could tell me who the young man is over there in the corner."

Cook threw down his dough and punched it a few times. "He's your new kitchen help. This is your kitchen now, señorita." His tone brimmed with sarcasm.

"My kitchen?" She tried to downplay his cantankerous mood. "I'm only here to help *you* with the cooking and add a few new recipes to the list we already have."

Cook grunted, "That's not what I understand. You better start giving orders, or we won't have anything to serve the patrons when they come."

A plan already formulated in her mind, Amalia squared her shoulders. "Once the dough is set to rise, slaughter a pig and get it cleaned and ready to cook this evening, por favor."

"What parts of the pig do you need?"

"All parts. I want the whole pig. Just discard the large intestine. Set the other innards aside in a pot, por favor."

"What do you need a whole pig for? That's a lot of meat, señorita."

Amalia just smiled at him.

He finally shrugged his shoulders and said, "I hope you know what you're doing."

A whole pig *was* a lot of meat. Having thought it through, Amalia figured the pig would need to cook in a pit through the night to be ready for the afternoon rush the next day. If all went to plan, the pig would change everything for her, but the timing had to be perfect.

"With our attention on the pig today and through the night, I think we should do a simple variation of torrejas for this morning," Amalia said. "It's a delicious bread pudding I learned how to make from . . . from a friend I met last year. No more throwing out perfectly good bread."

Rana rolled his eyes and pursed his large lips in a grimace.

She continued, "Now that the vegetables are ready, Leo, I have some instructions for you. Meet me outside with your friend. Señor, start on the vegetable stew for later. I'll make the torrejas."

Amalia grabbed a pail and walked out to the barn to milk the cow.

A voice interrupted her rhythm. "José and I are here, Lea. What would you like us to do?"

"José, is it?" Amalia stood from her three-legged stool and offered her hand. "Welcome to the kitchen. I need you and Leo to dig a large hole in the ground on the other side of the garden, por favor. It needs to be about this big." Amalia used her foot to draw some lines in the dirt. "Also, make it about two meters deep. Then I would like you to line the bottom with wood and fill it with melon-size rocks. Later this afternoon, we will start a fire in it."

Leo didn't have to say anything. His face said it all.

"I know it's an odd request, but I have a good reason. With the two of you working together, it will go quickly. Many hands make for light work." She winked at Leo before returning her focus to the cow.

As Amalia thought about the vegetable stew they would serve with rice for the next meal, her spirits lifted. She brought the fresh milk into the kitchen for Rana with a silly grin on her face.

"What are you smiling like that for? This is a serious business, and you're acting like a giddy little girl." Señor Rana scowled at her.

Amalia tried to scowl back. "You're right, señor. I will attempt to act more like you."

A huge fire burned in the spot Amalia specified. It would take hours for it to burn down to coals, so while they waited, Amalia and the boys gathered leaves from the elephant ear plants on the hill above the barn, which helped keep her mind busy. Señor Rana slaughtered the largest pig, and she suspected he did it to prove a point. *Por favor, God, let this work.*

"Fetch a large pot of boiling water, Leo, por favor. These leaves are toxic unless blanched first. José, will you ask Cook to get . . . Oh no, I can't believe I forgot one of the most important things we need to cook the pig." Amalia rushed down the hill, yelling over her shoulder, "Bring all the leaves with you and get the water boiling."

Spotting Cook near the shed, she sprinted the rest of the way. "Señor Rana? I need something to lay the pig on in the pit, so we can lift it out easily when it's done. At home, my father made me a wrought iron grate with handles. Do you have anything we can use to construct something like that? We also need a large slab with holes in the bottom to put the pig on so the juices can drain."

She stood, hands clenched at her side, biting her lip. Amalia wanted to cry. *I should have had the blacksmith make something. Everything will be ruined if we can't lift the pig out of the pit. How could I be so stupid?*

Having only cooked a quarter of the pig at a time to feed her family, she realized to her horror how unprepared she felt, but she couldn't possibly let Cook know that.

He scrutinized her for a moment, long enough to make Amalia's heart sink. "I'll see what I can find," he finally said.

Amalia wanted to hug him but refrained. "Gracias." Her mind spun again. *With the bones, I'll make a stock for the vegetable stew for the next day.* She wiped the sweat from her brow. She had no idea how much it took to run a kitchen. By the end of the day, she only wanted one thing: her bed. Her back and feet throbbed, but her bed would have to wait. One task still remained.

Leo and José stood by the charred pit, shovels in hand.

"I need you boys to dig out the hot rocks and some of the coals. I have prepared some wet rags for you to tie on your arms and over your nose and mouth."

"Where did you get the idea to cook a pig like this?" Leo asked.

Delighted with the question, Amalia said, "At home, cooking the meat underground kept my younger siblings from getting hurt by a spit or open flame. I always set the fire early in the morning before they were up so, by the time they were running around and playing, the meat was already covered in the ground."

Leo nodded his head and began to dig with his friend. Señor Rana approached her a moment later with a large tray woven with thin strands of wire to lay the pig on.

"This is genius, señor."

Hiding a smile, he grunted, "I'm going to bed."

"Actually, I need you for thirty more minutes."

"Will this nightmare of a day ever end?"

"Not much longer." Amalia tried to smile through her anxiety.

With the coals and rocks out, the boys placed the pig, wrapped with wet burlap and blanched elephant ear leaves, onto the wire cradle and lowered it just above the remaining hot rocks.

"Señor, hold these two posts straight while the boys fill the hole back up. I'll hold these two at this end." She moved to the other side.

He scowled at her.

When the last of the rocks, coals, and dirt filled in the pit, she said, "Well done, señors. I will take it from here. Sleep well."

For the first couple of hours, Amalia periodically poured water down the center of the posts. If her calculations were right, the pig would be ready just in time for la merienda the next day. Covered in soot and praying her risk would pay off, Amalia made her way to her room and fell into bed without changing her clothes.

Morning came too soon. Amalia ached all over. Her bed was smeared with black soot from the night before, and her mirror showed matted hair and smudges of dirt everywhere. *The pig.* Excitement filled her to the brim. She quickly shed her soiled clothes, scrubbed her face and hands, and pulled her hair back in a tidy bun with Gordy's whittled stick. The stench of the bonfire still hung in the air, but Amalia left her room without a second thought.

Señora Consuela confronted her at the bottom of the back stairs. "Señor Guerra wants to see you, Lea. He heard you killed a pig yesterday. You've been in charge of the kitchen one day and already spent more money than Señor Rana spends in a month. Prepare yourself for a severe reprimand. He may even dock your pay for the next month."

Amalia said, "What? I thought I was working off my first month's stay, but it's been a few months now."

Señora Consuela huffed. "You'd be surprised how much it costs to house someone for free. You won't see any money for a while."

Amalia's mouth dropped open.

Consuela scrunched her nose. "You need to take care of that smell. But not now. Vamos. Señor Guerra is waiting for you."

Amalia took a deep breath. Her insides squirmed like a thousand slippery worms. Taking slow steps toward the office, her hands began to shake and regret set in. She heard voices behind the door and paused before knocking. It was Señor Rana and Señor Guerra.

"Calm yourself, Rana. I'm angry about the pig too. Believe me, there is no telling how far I will go to make her pay for carelessly losing us money. Consuela seems to think she has some potential, and we need her help. Our tavern is in trouble, Rana. We need a change whether we like it or not."

"I *don't* like it. There is something fishy about her. You ever find out where she's from?"

Señor Guerra said, "No, but I've got my suspicions. Listen, at this point, I really don't care if she can bring in some good money. Since she's been in the kitchen, business is better. We're actually *making* money for the first time in years instead of just breaking even."

"Not enough money to cover killing a pig a day. She's too insistent, telling me what to do and batting those beautiful green eyes at me to get what she wants. It's maddening."

Laughing, Guerra observed, "You're just jealous she is a better cook than you."

"Don't be ridiculous. I'm not so stupid I haven't noticed the food is better, but you can't just turn my kitchen over to her. The way she is cooking this pig, I've never seen anything like it. It's going to be a disaster!"

Amalia couldn't listen anymore—not just the insults, but it scared her to think they were looking into her past. She knocked on the door.

"Well, don't just stand there." The intimidating man, behind the oversized, cluttered desk, stood to full height.

Keeping her eyes down, Amalia walked toward Señor Guerra but stopped just inside the door.

"Señor Rana and I have been discussing your reckless use of our resources. He seems to think you have lost us a great deal of money, so whatever money I lose today, I will take from your wages."

"But I haven't received any money since I've been here."

"Then you will hardly notice the difference."

Squaring her shoulders, she said, "I should be compensated for my work. You hired me."

"Don't talk back to me." Guerra looked at Rana. "I see what you mean."

"It isn't right for you to have me work with no pay. I was willing to work the very first day I arrived here, but Señora Consuela insisted I stay in bed until my sickness passed. It's been months since I started working in the kitchen, so what I owed should have been reconciled by now. And if this meal is to your liking, I should get a percentage of the sales for my hard work. It is only fair."

Guerra mumbled under his breath, "Consuela. Thickheaded, that woman."

Amalia felt sick to her stomach. She looked between the two men who filled the office with just their bodies. *They don't respect Consuela either. Men. It's always men who stop my progress.*

Señor Rana folded his arms and smirked at her.

"May I be excused?"

Señor Guerra waved her away. "Get out of here, and I don't want to see your face for the rest of the day. You better pray this pig is edible."

Fists at her side, she left. Amalia hadn't *stopped* praying. Entering the kitchen, she found Leo and José chopping vegetables. Neither of them dared look up at her. It seemed they already knew what was at stake if her plan didn't work. Amalia chose not to let them see her trepidation and started preparing the torrejas for breakfast.

Time crawled mercilessly until they could finally unbury the pig. Nerves raw, Amalia instructed the boys on their duties. Trying to look more confident than she felt, she pulled her shoulders back and led Señor Rana to the results of her impending fate.

A space of time between rushes allowed Señora Consuela and Señor Guerra to also join them near the pit. The boys struggled lifting the pig out of the pit, so Señor Rana and Señor Guerra had to help.

"Por favor, set it on the ground here. It needs to sit for several minutes before we can cut the leaves and burlap off." Amalia pointed to a spot on the ground near the kitchen.

"Should we just carry it straight to the trash?" asked Rana.

He got a weak reaction from everyone waiting as anxiously as Amalia was to see the result. Amalia stood, staring at the large bundle of flesh and wringing her hands. When the seconds turned into minutes and the minutes dragged on to the point everyone got irritated, Amalia finally gave the order to cut the covering off the carcass. A mouthwatering aroma hit them all at once, and an audible *ahh* escaped everyone's lips. Amalia's heart skipped with joy, knowing as soon as she cut into the skin of the animal, the meat would fall off the bones.

She beamed at the wide-eyed, speechless group staring back at her. "Señors, if you would kindly bring the pig into the kitchen." She led the way but stopped just inside the door. "Oh no, the pig will take up all the counter space, leaving no room to prepare the plates." Ignoring the bitter mumbles and curses aimed at her, Amalia had them retreat back outside. "We'll have to cut large portions of the meat and bring it into the kitchen to make up the plates. Señor Guerra, will you allow us to use another table outside so we don't have to prepare the meals on the ground?"

Guerra nodded his assent and excused himself, grabbed Consuela by the arm, and pulled her away.

Eager to have Cook and the boys try the meat, knowing it would be an experience they'd never forget, Amalia prepared a plate for each of them.

"Please sit here, señors." She pulled out a chair at the corner counter for Leo. Two other chairs sat ready for Rana and José. Amalia made up three plates of rice, roasted vegetables, and succulent pig. The boys licked their lips, lusting at the pulled pork and juice-soaked rice, but Señor Rana acted like he wanted nothing to do with her work of art. Grudgingly, he picked up his fork. All three stared at their plates as if wondering what to do next.

"Take a bite. I promise you've never tasted anything like it. Go on," Amalia urged.

Leo looked at José then Rana before putting a forkful in his mouth. He closed his eyes and groaned with pleasure.

José didn't waste time. He ate a huge mouthful and mimicked his friend's satisfaction.

Rana still remained stoic.

"Try it, Rana. It's really delicious," Leo encouraged him.

The two boys cleaned their plates in minutes and anxiously asked for more. Señor Rana, however, took one bite and left his food, removing himself from the kitchen without a word.

Amalia's mouth turned down more from frustration than sadness. *Two out of three isn't bad.* As far as she was concerned, the project worked, despite a few miscalculations on her part. It would go smoother the second time with the kinks all worked out.

Amalia made a plate for herself, ate a few bites, and rattled off some instructions to the boys before making two plates for Guerra and Consuela and excused herself to serve it to them.

Approaching Guerra's closed office door, she heard what sounded like slapping. Amalia lightly knocked and opened the door to see Guerra and Cook stepping away from each other as if they'd been embracing. Cook mumbled something as he excused himself, but a touch of a smile hit his eyes as he brushed past her. "I'll see you in the kitchen."

Confused, she addressed her boss. "Pardon me, señor, I have made a plate for you and the señora to try the dish before we start serving it to the patrons."

Señor Guerra replied, "How very thoughtful of you, señorita."

Heat rushed to her face. He and Rana were acting very strange. Both Guerra and Consuela sat expectantly at Guerra's quickly cleared desk. Placing the meals in front of them, Amalia quickly left, not needing to stay for their approval.

Upon reentering the kitchen, she noticed Cook's plate missing from the counter. When he came to ask her a question about the roasted vegetables, Amalia saw a kernel of rice and pork juice on his chin. Obviously, he had eaten his meal in a rush, hoping she wouldn't notice. She kept a straight face as he spoke, but her heart was dancing with joy. She chanced a glance Leo's direction, and he looked like he was trying to swallow his fist; José couldn't hide his grin. Amalia had to bite her lips to keep from smiling.

By the end of the day, the bare carcass outside was evidence of their success. The boys helped clean up the kitchen, allowing Amalia to retire to her room earlier than usual. She hadn't seen either Guerra or Consuela before retiring, but she was too tired to care. Her back hurt, and her feet protested every step, but she slowly made her way up the stairs, hoping for a bath. Leo and José took it upon themselves to provide hot water for her. So touched by their kindness, Amalia sank into the warm water and, unable to contain her emotions, began to cry. It felt good to let go of the burden she had been carrying.

Her door flew open. She grabbed for a towel, but it was out of reach on the bed, so she covered what she could with her hands. "What is going on?"

Señora Consuela didn't seem to notice Amalia sitting naked in the small metal tub, crying. "You're still up. Bueno." She did, however, see the dirty clothes from the night before lying in a clump at her feet. "You have some wash to do."

"Is there something you need?" Amalia found it hard to keep her voice level.

"No, I just thought you should know how lucky you are that stunt of yours paid off. You better be more careful in the future. I can't save you from every bad choice you make." The woman pointedly looked on Amalia's round belly. "Buenas noches."

"Señora, it sounds like the day was a success. I expect that my pay will increase now. We probably earned enough to buy four more pigs for the future."

"You would think that wouldn't you. Well, I spoke with Señor Guerra, and we only earned enough for two new pigs, so your wages won't be what you think you deserve."

"What I think I deserve is fair pay like everyone else."

Consuela huffed and slammed the door behind her.

Agitated by the unexpected visit, Amalia could no longer enjoy the warm water. She got out of the tub and dressed in her sleeping gown. "As soon as I am recovered from your delivery, I will seek other employment, amorcito. This tavern is no place for you to grow up."

Rubbing her belly, she felt a kick and laughed. Each time her baby moved, Amalia thanked God she would always have someone to fill the hole in her heart.

HOLLY BROUGH

"We need you to come up with six more special dishes for the other days of the week," Señor Guerra insisted.

Amalia and Rana stood next to each other in front of Guerra's unorganized desk.

"It's gotten too busy on Thursdays since we made it *pig* day. We don't have the room to seat that many people in one evening. Customers are waiting for as long as an hour to be seated."

Rana moaned like a child. "Will we still be serving my meals, or are we throwing my whole menu out?"

"We'll still serve some of the meals we've offered for years, but we need something special for the other days of the week to even out the crowds." Señora Guerra ran his hand down his face. "Do you have some ideas, señorita, or have I put my faith in the wrong person?"

Señora Consuela spoke as she entered the room. "I told you she would only end up disappointing us."

Amalia bit the insides of her cheeks to keep her focus on what she wanted to say. "I have several ideas. First, I need rabbits brought in to make my blood sausage. Also, a French dish called quiche is easy to make with the things we already have access to. I'd like to make paella with a few variations instead of mussels and cuttlefish every time. I've made it with shrimp and squid. We can use the remaining pork and add chicken and rabbit. I also suggest we start cooking with bomba rice instead of senia. Bomba is less likely to overcook." Amalia paused to take a breath. No one interrupted, so she continued, "Leo grows fine onions, which would make a delicious onion soup and—"

"Onion soup? That sounds disgusting," Señora Consuela interjected.

Amalia shot daggers the señora's way, and the woman shut her mouth. "And another thing . . . I am struggling to get the necessary spices for my dishes, like saffron and paprika. Because we use it so often, it runs out quickly."

"And?" Guerra asked.

Amalia looked sideways at Consuela. "I'm not allowed to leave the tavern to purchase these items, and Señora Consuela is too busy to go."

"Is that so?" Guerra leaned back in his chair and looked directly at the defiant woman, who in turn glared at Amalia.

"Consuela?"

"Si?" She looked innocently toward him.

"I suggest you take time from your *busy schedule* and purchase those items immediately."

Señora Consuela huffed and walked out.

Addressing Amalia, he added, "Before we serve any of these dishes, I insist on tasting them."

"Of course, señor." Amalia smiled at Cook.

Rana avoided her gaze and grumbled as he often did, "Keep your smile to yourself. If you fail, at least *I* won't be out on the streets." He turned on his heel and walked out the door.

Rose

CHAPTER 25

HER SHAWL WRAPPED tightly about her, Lady Huntingdon and her husband watched just outside the grand entrance of Hodcott House, awaiting their son's arrival. The weather was a little chilly, and the flowers hadn't blossomed to their full brilliance yet, but nothing could dampen her excitement when her precious cargo finally pulled to a stop directly in front of where they stood on the gravel driveway. Her handsome boy alighted his horse and took only a step before his mother enveloped him in a warm embrace.

"Son." Tears pooled in her golden-brown eyes, which she immediately dabbed at as they parted. "There were times I thought I would never see you again. You've been gone far too long, príncipe."

"I have a surprise for you." Smiling at his mother, Joshua walked to the carriage that had pulled up directly behind him and opened the door to retrieve Abuela, but a hand he wasn't expecting took hold.

"Such a gentleman, Hastings. Thank you." Channing stepped out of the black carriage with a silly grin on his face.

Joshua tossed his hand away. "When did you get into the carriage?" He muttered "fopdoodle" under his breath and shoved Channing aside to reach for a giggling Abuela.

Channing returned the quip with "drate-poke" before giving his attention to Joshua's mother, Lady Huntingdon. Bowing in his lavender frock coat and removing his matching top hat, he took her hand and said, "My, how you brighten even the sunniest of days, Lady Huntingdon."

A full grin lit up her face. The soft wind blew wisps of her dark hair into her eyes, and she brushed them aside. "Channing, such a pleasure. I see you haven't lost your sense of style . . . or your humor."

"Never, my lady, never." Again, Gil dramatically bowed over her hand and quickly added a kiss.

Lord Huntingdon took his wife's hand from Gil and cleared his throat. "Channing."

Gil clicked his heels and bowed his head, all jest aside. "Your Lordship."

Joshua finally had Abuela in his grasp and pulled her out of the carriage. "Gracias, amorcito."

Lady Huntingdon took Abuela into an embrace the moment she set foot on the ground. "Cousin."

"Darling, Martha. It has been too long."

Lord Huntingdon stepped forward. "Cousin Eulalia, it is an honor to welcome you to our home."

Abuela patted his cheek. "Gracias, Walter."

Sonia was kindly helped out of the carriage and welcomed by a member of the staff who showed her to her quarters while the rest of the party made their way into Hodcott House.

Gil nudged Joshua. "It's good to be home, isn't it, Hastings? I love this place."

"You've spent enough time here. Does your family know you're back in England?"

"I plan to send them word as my second order of business."

"What is your first order of business?"

"Something to do with blankets and a pillow, I think."

The party entered the cavernous entrance hall, their footsteps echoing off the marble floor. A crystal chandelier hung from the high ceiling embossed with floral designs and gold overlay. Footmen took the shawls, hats, and traveling cloaks from the party before walking into the spacious morning room directly to the right of the entrance hall.

The sun shone uncharacteristically bright outside, so the heavy curtains were pulled open to let in as much sunlight as possible. Joshua loved the morning room. Pale green floral fabric adorned the walls from the chair rail to the white cornice. The colors his mother had chosen for that particular room were calming and airy, so he spent as much time there as possible when he visited home.

Stepping over to the decanter tray, Joshua helped himself to a glass of scotch. He didn't drink often, but the stress of being home drove him to dull his senses. Tilting his head back to down the drink, he admired the embossed design encircling the chandelier.

Pulling her eyes off her tall son's frame, Lady Huntingdon addressed the butler, "Gregory, please have tea brought up."

"At once." The butler bowed his head and exited the room.

"I understand you come to us under duress, Cousin Eulalia. I am sorry to hear it," Lord Huntingdon said to Abuela, motioning for her to take a seat on the settee near the unlit fireplace.

"I am afraid I come to you dispossessed and a beggar. I have little left and nowhere to call home."

Lady Huntingdon sat next to her. "Your home is with us now. It's long been our wish to have you join us in England. Living in that big house by yourself without Sebastián must have been lonely."

"I've struggled to leave him and my sweet Lucita behind. But in truth, they aren't there. They are here." She touched her heart.

Joshua sat in one of the green velvet chairs across from the ladies and watched his father squirm at the emotional sentiment.

Lord Huntingdon changed the subject. "We've arranged a welcoming party in your and Hastings's honor for this Friday evening. You must meet our friends and begin your transition to English culture."

Lady Huntingdon turned a sharp look toward her husband.

"Uh, that is, if you are agreeable," he added.

"Certainly, Walter. Gracias. Now, if you don't mind. I would like to retire." Abuela got up to leave, and everyone stood with her.

"Yes, of course . . . Gregory?" Lord Huntingdon gave a side glance at his wife. "We've prepared the room with a beautiful view of the gardens. We hope you will be pleased."

"I'd be pleased with a cushion in that corner. My joints are screaming mutiny."

Joshua smiled at Abuela's humor.

Bowing, Gregory motioned for her to follow. "Right this way, Most Illustrious Lady Domingo."

Just at that moment, the tea was brought in, but Joshua's mother seemed upset by her cousin's abrupt departure and waved the housemaid away. "She's tired, Walter. I told you Friday would be too soon for a party."

Lord Huntingdon ran his hand down his face. "I'm sorry, Martha. I didn't mean to upset her."

"Mother, with a little rest, she will be feeling much better." Joshua replaced Abuela's seat next to her and took her hand. Channing remained standing near the largest window, enjoying the drink Joshua gave him.

"You haven't aged a day, Mother."

"Oh, darling." She patted his hand. "I'm worried for her. I know this is a difficult adjustment."

"Yes. She lost everything. She came to England with little but the clothing on her back."

"When I heard you were coming, I had some of her favorite shawls ordered and delivered here. I hope she will be pleased."

"I insisted on purchasing a few things for her before we left, but she didn't allow me to get much." Looking at his father, Joshua continued, "I must say I'm not interested in socializing myself just yet."

"It is expected, Hastings. You have been gone for years. People need to see for themselves you weren't lost at sea. Besides, all the young ladies who were too young before you left are now ripe for the picking. You will have plenty to choose from."

Lady Huntingdon shot her husband another warning glance. He shrugged his shoulders and mouthed, *What?*

Joshua couldn't listen anymore. "Please excuse me. Channing?" Joshua cleared the room in two strides.

"A pleasure to be with you again." Gil bowed, put down his drink, and followed his friend out of the morning room.

Joshua held his tongue down the entrance hall and into the gentlemen's morning room, which had been adapted into a parlor of sorts, before turning on his heel to say, "Blast it! The young *Viscount* Hastings on display for everyone to ogle at. My parents know how much I despise playing the host to a bunch of self-absorbed braggarts and their silly daughters."

"I can't say I feel sorry for you, old chap." He smacked Joshua on the back. "Now, if you will excuse me. There is a pillow upstairs calling my name." Gil dashed around the corner and up the stairs before Joshua could stop him.

Friday came too soon. Stuart, Joshua's valet, couldn't seem to find a pair of cufflinks to suit his mood. He searched through every box in the top drawer of the chest, but Joshua declined them all.

"Here is a pair with emeralds to match your waistcoat, my lord. Very smart." Joshua stared at the jewels in a trance.

"My lord?"

He let out a heavy sigh. "I'll wear the black onyx cufflinks, Stuart."

"Very good, my lord."

"Please call me Hastings. I know it's been a few years and things have changed, but we needn't adopt the formalities." Joshua tugged at his waistcoat, anxious for the evening to be over. He stared at his reflection in the mirror and wondered why he'd come home. *I need to find Amalia.*

"Are you well, my—uh, Hastings?" Tall and muscular with dark-blond hair and hazel eyes, Stuart had only five years on Joshua. He came to their service when Joshua was ten. They grew close over the sixteen years he'd been in the family's service, even sparring and grappling with him and his younger brother, Charles.

Joshua took a deep breath. "I've been out of the social scene for so long I've gotten used to doing my own things and being my own person. At these parties, I have to act a part I'm not comfortable in anymore."

Finishing the last touches of his cravat, Stuart said, "I don't see why you have to play any part. Be you. No one expects more."

"Everyone expects more." Joshua sat in a chair by the mirror to have his shoes tied. "Even you. I have tied my own shoes and put on my own boots for almost five years now, and here you are, tying them for me."

"If it would put you in a better mood, I can double knot them for you."

He smiled at Stuart in appreciation for his humor. "Maybe not too tight tonight. I'll be anxious to throw them off as soon as the party is over."

The two men spoke often over the years about the duties each adhered to. They couldn't escape the order of things, and both felt trapped where they stood, yet they'd agreed not to let it interfere with the friendship they'd developed.

Joshua rose to his feet, shook out his arms, and rolled his neck.

Stuart smiled. "You look good, Hastings. Be yourself."

By the time Joshua joined the large gathering in the ballroom of the great house, people from all over the county had arrived to greet him and Abuela. Of course, every eligible young lady stood at the arm of her mother, awaiting introductions. He hadn't seen so much color and glamor in one room for so long, his eyes struggled to adjust. Overwhelmed by the stuffy, suppressive atmosphere, Joshua greeted a few of the young ladies, making sure his parents observed him socializing before slipping out into the north gardens where tall hedgerows created large allies for visitors to stroll even in winter and not experience the harsh winds that often accompanied a storm. Plus, they made the perfect hiding place.

Rushing down the stairs, Joshua checked behind him to see if anyone noticed his escape and stumbled into someone.

"Ouch. Careful, amorcito." She clung to him like a hawk does its prey.

"Abuela? Is that you? Are you alright?"

"Si, si."

"How did you get away?"

"I asked for a drink, and when they weren't looking, I sneaked out. I'm a terrible guest, I know."

"Not at all. I'm sorry they rushed you into this madness. It can be suffocating."

"Príncipe, you must accept your duty to your family someday, and there is no time like the present. I, too, must accept my new situation."

"There is one purpose my parents have in mind, but I can't endure the attention of such flirtatious, silly girls"—Joshua searched her eyes for understanding—"much less give my heart to one of them."

"Perhaps because your heart is already taken?"

Joshua almost stumbled back. "I don't know what you mean."

Abuela cocked her head and gave him a knowing smile.

"But I . . . I . . ."

She reached up and patted his cheek. "I see you languishing over her."

Joshua opened his mouth to respond, but she stopped him. "I know who you long for, and you must do something about it. Not just for you, but for me as well."

Carnation

CHAPTER 26

A MALIA'S ROOM WAS so oppressive and hot she could hardly breathe. "Stop touching me, you wretched woman! I hate you touching me." Señora Consuela's presence for the delivery made Amalia wish for her mother, something she never expected to feel.

"Si, si, one more push. You can do it. Push."

"I can't. I'm too tired. Isn't there something you can give me for the pain?"

"I'm no medicine woman. Now push."

Amalia moaned as she gave one more effort.

"There you go. Oh, there you go." Señora Consuela laughed in delight. "I was right. You have a fine boy, Lea. Bueno. Listen to him wail. Strong lungs." The birth string tied and cut, she wiped off some of the blood and waxy substance all newborns have on their skin before wrapping him in a clean sheet.

"Let me see him." Amalia reached for her bebé. Overcome with such joy and love when she first looked into his splotchy face, she could not contain it, and tears ran down her cheeks. He immediately took to her breast.

"What will you call him?"

Amalia looked up to see Rana and Leo standing at the door, hands clasped in front of them in reverence. José peeked around the corner. Señora Consuela gathered the soiled sheets and pushed past the men.

Modestly covering herself, Amalia smiled at them. "Alejandro. It means *protector of man.*"

Rana stepped forward. "That is a fine name. How are you feeling?"

"I'm tired but happy. Gracias for your kind help, all of you."

Leo looked at José over his shoulder and smiled. Rana shuffled his feet.

"It was nothing much, just cloths and water," Rana said.

"Still, I am grateful."

"Our pleasure. Leo will bring up a nice meal for you shortly, and I asked Guerra to give you a four-week break from the kitchen. We'll take care of things, si?"

Amalia smiled and absently rubbed the wet, dark tufts of hair on Alejandro's head, amazed at the transformation in Rana over the months they'd worked together. Everyone on the kitchen staff had grown to be quite fond of each other. Rana learned the recipes Amalia showed him. It took time for him to get it right, but she was patient. The boys took more responsibility in the kitchen when Amalia no longer possessed the strength or energy to do her job well. They doted on her, often encouraging her to sit and rest or giving her a snack to energize her. When her water broke, the men were just as apprehensive and excited as she felt—as if they were having the baby with her. She almost wished it had been Rana and Leo who assisted her in the delivery instead of the wretched woman, Consuela . . . almost.

Amalia's strength came back quickly. Though she felt fit to return to the kitchen after a few days, she wanted to spend as much time with her son as possible. His cooing melted her heart, and over the weeks, Amalia marveled as Alejandro grew chubby. He wrapped his dimpled fingers around hers when he nursed, and she knew the very moment his eyes showed recognition at her face.

Relishing in his every new discovery, Amalia would place him in the crook of her knees and watch him for hours. His cheeks resembled the soft dough she often shaped, and she couldn't resist kissing them over and over. Alejandro tried to latch on to the tip of her nose, making Amalia giggle with delight.

"You are my príncipe. I'm grateful you don't look much like your father."

After four weeks of recovery and two weeks of very limited work around the tavern, Señora Consuela decided it was time for Amalia to return to full-time work. She made that very apparent when she barged into Amalia's room during siesta one day with a voluptuous woman at her side. Amalia did not recognize the woman and was extremely agitated they interrupted a tender moment between her and Alejandro. Her heart plummeted to her toes before Consuela said a word.

"Lea, now that you are recovered, Señor Guerra and I have decided it is time for you to go back to the kitchen full time. I will not hear any complaints." Moving to the side to let the other woman step forward, she said, "This is Esperanza. She will be your wet nurse and care for little Alejandro, so you can start earning your keep again."

Amalia held tighter to Alejandro. "What do you mean?"

Esperanza had flawless dark skin and rich brown eyes. Her hair stylishly pinned up on top of her head, she wore a smile on her face Amalia immediately hated.

Señora Consuela practically ripped Alejandro out of Amalia's arms and placed him in the arms of the intruder. Tears burned Amalia's eyes as she jumped out of her bed toward Esperanza, only to have Consuela step between them.

"How could you do this to me? Haven't I done everything you asked? Have I not earned some respect?" Amalia wailed.

"Respect? It's respect you want?" the wicked woman mocked. "You will earn respect when you stop complaining and get back to work. It costs money to run a tavern, and this isn't a free ride, señorita."

Esperanza looked at Amalia with pity as she put Alejandro to her breast, clearly delighting in him. Señora Consuela pulled Esperanza out of the room, and Amalia crumpled to the floor, clutching her chest in a vain effort to keep her heart from breaking again. It was no use. Something inside her died.

Her feet felt like lead as she dragged them along the floor, moving from one station in the kitchen to the next, absently stirring the rice or cutting a carrot. The hole in her heart grew with each passing moment Alejandro wasn't in her arms, which was most of the day. Only when there was a lull between meals could Amalia hold her child, and even then, it was in the presence of Señora Consuela or Esperanza. The longer they were apart, the fussier Ale got in her arms.

"You know he is only going through a phase. When Esperanza's boob isn't available anymore, he'll be just as happy to be with you as her," Señor Rana said.

"You shouldn't talk like that, Rana," Leo said.

"What? Your innocent ears tingling?"

"No, I just don't think you should be so disrespectful."

Rana threw a piece of meat into the lard. "I was only trying to make Lea feel better."

Amalia dropped her spoon. "Did you hear that?" Her eyes were wide with excitement, and a grin brightened her face. "There it is again. He's giggling." Amalia ran toward the sound and peeked around the corner to see Esperanza holding him on her lap and pulling him up to blow on the nape of his neck. Amalia quickly pulled back out of sight, her back to the wall where only the men in the kitchen could see her. She clutched her chest, as if to stay her heart. "He giggled for her. He's never giggled for me."

Glancing the men's way, Amalia excused herself and ran through the back door, past the garden, and behind the shed, where she allowed herself to cry in private. Gasping for air, Amalia wished she wasn't familiar with the pain of a broken heart. Leaving Thomas behind almost killed her. *This is worse. I can't live like this. God help me.*

A few moments later, she heard someone approach. Leo. He squatted beside her and offered a handkerchief. Saying nothing, Leo sat down with his back against the shed and put his arm around her shoulder, allowing Amalia to bury her head and cry.

Finally, she spoke. "I don't know how much more agony I can feel for my son before my heart shrivels up. There have been times when I would rather die than have him so close yet so far away."

Leo nodded his head as if he knew how she felt and let her cry.

Later that day, Esperanza sneaked into the kitchen to grab a crust of bread while bouncing Alejandro on her hip. She glanced toward Leo and saw a scowl on his face. He nodded in Amalia's direction, and Esperanza followed his gaze to a puffy-eyed woman staring at a pot of boiling rice.

Understanding, Esperanza walked over to her. "Lea, will you take Alejandro for me? I need a private moment."

"Oh, of course. Leo?" Overjoyed at the request, Amalia gladly gave up her spoon to Leo and reached for her chubby bebé. Alejandro fussed for a minute but quieted down as Amalia pressed him to her. She nuzzled her face into the soft, velvety folds of his neck and kissed him. He giggled. Amalia's heart skipped. She did it again, and he giggled again. Delighted with the result of their interaction, she laughed and twirled him around.

Leo stood, watching their exchange with a silly grin on his face, and nodded his appreciation to the wet nurse.

"Have a seat, Lea." The large owner loomed over her. "Señora Consuela and I are taking a holiday to Nice, France for a few weeks.

With the tavern doing so well, the timing is right. You may be wondering who will be in charge while we are gone. Of course, Señor Rana will run the kitchen, but I want you to oversee the tavern."

"Me? You are asking me to run the tavern?"

Señora Consuela spoke up. "I think it is a terrible idea, but we don't have a choice. Rana is too valuable in the kitchen."

Señor Guerra shot a look toward Consuela that shut her up immediately. "We aren't asking, señorita. However, *I've* decided that if things go well while we are gone, I will consider making you a partner."

"Me, a partner?" Amalia couldn't believe it. "Does this mean I would get a pay raise?"

"Only if—"

Señor Guerra held up his hand as if to smack the intrusive woman. "Certainly."

Amalia beamed. *I may be able to leave the tavern sooner than I expected.*

The four weeks Guerra and Consuela were gone, things relaxed in the kitchen and with Esperanza. Everyone was eager to see Alejandro, but no one more than his mama. Esperanza came in often so Amalia could enjoy his company and play with him. A family feeling took over, and everyone started calling Esperanza, Anza. The tavern ran so smoothly that people started commenting on how the establishment was one of nicest places to dine in Mahón.

Time passed too quickly, and the day after Guerra and Consuela returned from France, Amalia was summoned to Guerra's office.

She knocked and peeked in. "You sent for me?"

"Come in and sit down, Lea. It's been reported things went smoothly while we were gone, and our books indicate business has increased tremendously." Her burly boss folded his arms and leaned back in his chair.

Amalia smiled expectantly.

"This is good news because we now feel we can adopt more ways to improve our business. While in France, Señora Consuela and I had our eyes opened to a new business opportunity."

Her smile spread to a grin. *Are they opening a new business in France and letting me take over here? Or making me a partner, perhaps?*

"I have decided to make some changes around here by moving you out of the kitchen and up to the front of the tavern welcoming patrons and showing them to a table. Since you've recovered from your delivery, you've grown into a very comely woman. You know this business almost as well as we do, and with you as greeter, more people will perceive you as the face of our establishment, which I believe will draw more customers. In addition to this change, you and the other girls will share your rooms with . . . lonely travelers needing a place to stay for the night."

"Share my room? I don't understand." Amalia's smile disappeared, and she sank into the chair behind her.

He raised his eyebrows.

Amalia's eyes grew wide. "Surely you don't mean for me to—"

Señora Consuela cut in. "Don't be such a prude. You're no saint. Think of how much money you could make."

"You're not serious. I cannot believe you would suggest such a thing. I thought you were going to make me a partner when you came back. That was our agreement when you left on your holiday—not this abominable idea." Amalia's stomach twisted in pain.

Señor Guerra spoke up. "I said I would *think* about making you a partner. You need to prove yourself, Lea. You need to be willing to do whatever it takes to make this business the best in town. Since being in France, we realized there is a lot more money out there."

Amalia's knuckles were white from gripping the arms on her chair.

"This is not a request, señorita. And if you don't cooperate, we will send Alejandro to a workhouse where they can keep and train him until he is old enough to work off your debt to us."

"My debt? I don't owe you anything, and I forbid you to send Alejandro away. I'm his mother."

"Don't forget who saved you from the streets and gave you a job. We've risked our reputation by housing a *puta* and her illegitimate child. You owe us a *great* debt. He's practically ours anyway. We're the ones who have raised him, not you." Consuela couldn't keep her mouth shut.

"That's not fair. I have tried to mother him, but with the hours I have to work—"

"That's right. You were never up to the task. That is why we brought in Esperanza. We knew she would do a far better job than you could, considering your past recklessness," Señora Consuela said.

Guerra laughed.

Amalia looked dumbfounded between the two disingenuous people in front of her. *This life I'm living is far worse than I ever imagined. How could I have ever let this happen?* "After all I've done for you, how can you be so cruel?"

"Ha, after all you've done for us?" Señora Consuela scoffed.

Amalia pressed on, "This tavern is a reputable establishment, and you want to turn it into a whorehouse and make me participate?"

Señor Guerra stood up behind the desk. "It's because of our savvy business sense that this tavern is successful, not you . . . and it will stay reputable. We learned ways to improve our bottom line, and we've witnessed how it can be done"—he paused for a moment—"tastefully. Our tavern will be the biggest and best in town, making us thousands."

Señora Consuela smiled at her partner, and he winked at her.

What happened between those two while they were gone? I've never seen them so agreeable with each other. Tears welled up in her eyes, and her throat tightened. "I think I'm going to be sick."

"You will not leave my office until we have reached an agreement."

"I will absolutely not agree to this. You can find someone else. I quit." She stood up.

Señor Guerra was around the desk before Amalia could take a step toward the door and held her shoulders in his large hands. "You will do no such thing." He pulled her close enough to whisper in her ear, "There is nowhere for you to go, and I will see to it you never find employment on this island. I know you are hiding from someone. If you don't agree to my terms, you will beg for my mercy after I decide what to do with you. Understand, señorita?"

His whiskers scratched her cheek. Shoving Amalia back into her chair, he again resumed his seat behind the desk. Amalia wiped angrily at the tears on her face.

"Oh, stop pouting. If you find yourself in the family way again, I have ways to get rid of the problem," Señora Consuela declared nonchalantly.

Shocked at her insensitivity, Amalia's brain worked fast. "I-I have my own methods of preventing that situation too." *What is my plan?* She needed time. "If I agree to this repulsive ultimatum, you must allow me to do this my own way."

Opening and closing his fists in agitation, Señor Guerra glared at her before acquiescing. "I don't care how you do it as long as our patrons leave happy."

I don't need to be a virgin to be virtuous. Alejandro will not have a whore for a mother. Amalia had an idea. "May I be excused?"

Guerra waved her off.

When out of sight, Amalia went out to the back of the tavern and located the Spanish Blue poppies she'd discovered growing behind the animal shed the year before. Carefully scoring the poppy bulbs, she left them to seep for a day. The next day, she scraped the dried pulp off and placed it in a tin before scoring a few more lines on each bulb.

Within a few days, she had enough pulp to brew into opium for sedating her nighttime guests—a recipe Amalia learned from her mother, who took it in her chamomile tea during labor or when suffering from headaches. Now she needed it to save her life and ultimately her son's. Just the right amount in some tea to calm her nightly guests would help prevent a compromising situation, while making sure those men also left feeling well rested and satisfied.

Evening came, but no one had requested her company, so she joined Rana and the boys in the kitchen to clean up for the day.

"I want you to know, Lea, I had nothing to do with the changes at the tavern," Señor Rana said after only one short week since the changes. The news spread like wildfire. "I told them things went really well while they were gone, but they had their minds set on this rotten idea, and nothing I said could change their minds." He took a pot from her to dry. "If there is anything I can do to help you—without them finding out, of course—I will."

"I cry myself to sleep every night thinking that if I don't do what they want, Ale will be sent away, and I'll never see him again."

"They threatened to send him away? But he's just a baby," José said.

Amalia started crying. "I know. I'm just grateful things haven't gotten out of hand with my guests so far. Ale doesn't deserve a whore for a mother."

"Poor Ale." Rana shook his head.

"Why do you stay if they don't listen to you?" Amalia asked. "I thought you were their partner too."

Cook shrugged his shoulders before hanging another pot on the ceiling rack. "I'm a creature of habit. Change isn't something I do well. Plus, cooking here instead of cooking on a ship is what I prefer. That's the only other life I've known."

"Lea," Señora Consuela called.

Amalia looked at her kitchen companions before walking over to the repulsive woman.

"Someone is requesting your company."

Removing her apron, Amalia nodded to Leo, his cue to find Esperanza and prepare some warm water to be brought to her room. Since Esperanza cared for little Alejandro, she didn't have to stoop to the level of whore. The friendship they'd developed while the owners were gone moved Esperanza with such compassion for Amalia that she was willing to do anything to help her not have to stoop to whoring.

Gazania

CHAPTER 27

SUMMER CAME, WHICH meant traveling to Holborn House in the heart of London for the peak of the season. The latest styles—chiffon, lace, pearls, and silks—could be seen in all their glory wherever they went. Joshua felt like a caged animal after several weeks of balls and dinner parties. It had been over a year since he last saw Amalia, and none of the young ladies who attended the events piqued his interest. Cluttered, smoky, and gray, the city held little interest for him. He longed for the fresh air of the outdoors. Even Hyde Park was no substitute for the wide open air he'd come to love at sea and in Spain.

One particularly dismal morning, Joshua's mother appeared in the spacious study of Holborn House to find him pacing.

"What is troubling you, Hastings? You haven't been yourself since you've been home."

Joshua stopped mid stride and stared at the hundreds of books lining the walls. "I tell you, in earnest, I cannot stay here another day."

"But you just got home." With a sigh, she gracefully sat in a single chair near an accent table and folded her hands in her lap. "From your youth, you've wanted to experience all the world can offer. Your father and I let you spread your wings, reckless as it was, but now it is time for you to stay home, find a wife, and start a family. Charles has found such joy with Christine, and they're expecting a child this September. As the eldest, it is your duty, your right to take over for your father someday."

"I know my duty." Joshua paused to say something he'd been considering for weeks. "I think I've found my wife, Mother. I didn't fully realize it until Abuela brought it to my attention at our first welcome party in Berkshire. I should have left months ago, but I worried about leaving you so soon after arriving home."

"Oh?" Lady Huntingdon kept a neutral expression.

Sitting on the edge of a settee near her, he said, "I need to go back to Spain. I need to get her and bring her back here with me. I've yet to hear from my contact in Menorca if he's located her, and it's driving me mad."

"Spain? Who is this fine maiden who has captured your heart, amorcito?" Though she only spoke her native tongue with him in private, Joshua loved hearing it.

He confided, "It's hard to explain. I only met her once, and our interaction was brief, but it was like lightning struck my consciousness, and I cannot get her out of my mind. I think of her unceasingly. Everything reminds me of her." He sat, still looking at the books in front of him. "She loves to read, you know."

"How did you meet?" Lady Huntingdon asked.

"At the port in Águilas, she was running from Señor Tudó when we ran into her in the shipyard." He absently smiled at the memory.

"Manuel Tudó?"

"Abuela and I think she is Lucita's daughter."

"Cousin Eulalia told me about her granddaughter, Amalia. It's extraordinary to think Lucita had a child. This Amalia is your true love?"

"Yes."

"She stole Tudó's valuable jewelry."

Joshua looked at her. *She doesn't understand.* "No . . . in part . . . but that was only to ensure she could take care of herself. She ran because

Tudó tried to force himself on her. What's worse is we've also considered she could be Tudó's daughter."

"Abominable. Cousin Eulalia also mentioned that. She showed me a sketch included with the jewels. It is Lucita's exact likeness, and Amalia looks almost identical?"

"Except Amalia's nose is smaller, and she doesn't have a cleft chin like Lucita. I actually have a sketch of Amalia. Wait here." Joshua walked over to a small table set by a wall of shelves to fetch it out of the tailcoat he'd discarded upon entering the study. "Here." He unfolded it and handed it to his mother.

"My, she does look like Lucita, but I see what you mean about her nose and chin. I wish I could remember what Anton looked like. Eulalia thinks she sees Anton in her, but that could also be wishful. We all wish it."

"I know."

"There is something about her eyes that concerns me. She looks defiant."

"I took this from a wanted bulletin Tudó posted of her. I suspect he sketched her that way on purpose. Amalia is certainly stubborn, but she has to be."

His mother repositioned herself on the red velvet chair she occupied. "I'm not comfortable with you getting entangled with Manuel Tudó. This sounds like trouble to me."

"It's not anything I can't handle, Mother."

Lady Huntingdon searched his face.

He resumed his seat across from her and reached for her hand. "Amalia is the most exquisite creature I have ever encountered. She has thick waves of hair and eyes the color of emeralds. Her smile could bring out the sun on a cloudy day."

Lady Huntingdon's mouth dropped slightly open, the corners of her lips turning upward. "My, I've never seen you like this. I don't mean to ruin your happiness, but you know she was in a family way, son."

"Yes."

"And that doesn't bother you?"

"No."

"A child by the duke of Cádiz," Eulalia said.

"How is that possible?"

"Mother, a noble on holiday seeking entertainment? Amalia was a victim. He took advantage of her youth for his own pleasure and then left. That is their calling card, you know that."

Looking down and brushing off her evening dress, she said, "Hastings, this is a lot to take in. She isn't of high birth and is having an illegitimate child."

"Amalia is the granddaughter of a hidalgo and possibly Princess di Bassano if she is Tudó's daughter. That should be noble enough for father."

"We cannot be attached to that wicked man. If she is Tudó's daughter, why would he want to molest her? I cannot fathom it. He is too wicked, no matter who you think she is."

"Mother, she has had little advantage in life. I am drawn to her like a magnet. I need to find her and discover her story. There is more here than meets the eye, I just know it."

"There are too many questions."

"Exactly, that is why I must go. Please understand. I haven't voiced these feelings with anyone, not even Channing, and now that I have, I can't ignore them any longer."

"You've been so focused on your education and then the navy. My heart rejoices in your happiness but also hesitates. I don't want to see your heart broken. Do you really understand the consequences of your choice? She is Spanish, so she will receive no welcome from your peers or their families. I struggled with that myself. And she comes with a child, assuming things go as we expect they should."

"Why does there have to be a social or cultural divide? It's maddening."

"I agree. As a son of a Spanish mother, it is all you know, but the adjustment was difficult for me and your father. It will be the same for you. And have you considered she may not want what you want?"

Thoughtfully, Joshua replied, "I understand your concern. But I'm certain all will work out."

After some companionable silence, Joshua took a deep breath and continued, "I've found my purpose, Mother, the adventure of a lifetime—to discover her true identity and give her the life she deserves." Joshua ran his hands through his hair. "She is why I am restless. I must save her from her uncertain future and bring her to England. Please. I wouldn't leave you again if it wasn't necessary."

Lady Huntingdon cupped his chiseled jaw, gazing into his marvelous blue eyes. "You are inspiring. You could never resist saving someone in need, always thinking of others. A true hero, querido."

"It's not about being a hero, Mother. Our destinies are linked. We are two halves searching for our whole. I must sound like a fool to you. I wish you could understand. I wish *I* could understand. I have never felt this way before."

Brushing a curl from his eyes, she replied, "I do understand. Love rarely makes sense. I hope you find the happiness you seek, amorcito." Lady Huntingdon's voice cracked a little as she spoke. "You deserve it more than anyone."

"Thank you for understanding, Mother." He kissed her cheek before leaving to find Channing. He was in the rose gardens visiting with Abuela.

Joshua approached and asked, "Will you excuse us a moment, Abuela?"

Channing bowed over her hand before Joshua grabbed his arm and pulled him away.

"I feel it is time for me to resume my quest to find Amalia and get some answers."

Channing replied, "I need to pay a visit to my family before following you back to Menorca, brother."

Fully expecting Channing to bid him a good journey and leave it at that, Joshua felt great relief knowing his friend would join him eventually.

"Thank you, Channing. I'm grateful. I could use your help."

"Pardon me, my lord. A telegram just arrived." One of the footmen held out a silver tray with an envelope.

Joshua stepped aside to read it.

Hastings,

I have finally located Amalia. She is at the El Comienzo Tavern on Del Sol Street in Mahón. You should know that Tudó is still offering a reward for her capture. I'm looking into it, but have nothing yet. D.

"Finally." Joshua handed it to Channing, who quickly read it. "Del Sol Street is a filthy part of Mahón. How did she end up there?"

Channing looked up. "What I want to know is why Tudó is still after her when he has his jewels."

"That *is* the question, isn't it?"

Geranium

CHAPTER 28

AFTER LIVING WITH the new arrangements at the tavern for months, a classy, tall, and slender gentleman entered the tavern with some of his friends, boasting how he would soon be a world-renowned artist. Amalia set her eyes on him. Alejandro was a year old, and Amalia wanted very much to have a miniature done of her and her son to send to Cisco. She felt he deserved to know they had a child together, even if he didn't care.

She seated the small party, keeping her focus exclusively on the artist, smiling as he spoke, and brushing arms with him as he took his seat. He watched her walk away, he watched her clean the nearby table, and he smiled when she made eye contact with him. Only moments after she situated herself on the other side of the tavern, Amalia saw him whisper something to his colleague. Pretending to busy herself with a smudge on the bar, she turned her back, anticipating his next move.

"Hm-mm." A man cleared his throat behind her. She continued wiping off the bar until she felt a light tap on her shoulder.

Turning, Amalia came face-to-face with the artist's friend. "May I help you?"

He looked over his shoulder at their table, got a nod to go ahead, and mustered the courage to speak. "Señorita, may I introduce myself. I am Rodolfo Diego. My friend has requested you come to him. He would like to make your acquaintance."

Acting as if she didn't hope for that very thing, she replied, "How nice. Who is this friend of yours?"

"He is just over here, señorita." He waved his arm for her to follow.

Discarding her rag, she wiped her hands on her apron and followed the young Diego.

They weaved through the tables crowding the tavern to reach his table. "May I introduce my colleague, Señor Carlos Luis de Ribera y Fieve. He just finished nine years in Paris studying with the French painter Paul Delaroche and is enjoying a short season of relaxation on this beautiful island."

With her most charming smile, Amalia said, "It is an honor to meet you, señor. I hope you find your stay pleasant." She curtsied before excusing herself. "Forgive me, but I have work to do." With a wink, she walked away before Señor Ribera could say a word. He'd follow her. No man could resist a chase; she knew it all too well.

It took another thirty minutes before Señor Ribera collected enough determination to approach her. With crisp white breeches and high boots squeaking as he walked, he stepped up with hands behind his back.

"Señorita, I was hoping to become more acquainted with you."

Amalia looked into his rich brown eyes shaded by his handsome top hat and stated, "I, too, would like to become more acquainted."

Señor Ribera smiled with relief but awkwardly asked, "How . . . how do I arrange for that?"

Pointing toward Señora Consuela, Amalia said, "See that woman over there? She would be happy to help you with the arrangements. You may join me in my bedchamber in ten minutes. It is up the stairs and down the hall, last door on the right."

"Gracias, señorita. I will see you momentarily." He tipped his hat and turned to approach Señora Consuela.

Amalia left immediately, informing Leo to have Esperanza bring up a pot of hot water. She straightened her floral bedspread and started a small fire with a dash of lavender. Taking off her apron, Amalia let down her hair and brushed through it quickly before splashing a bit of rose water on her neck. By the time Señor Ribera arrived, the room felt inviting.

"Welcome, señor. Come make yourself comfortable." Amalia led him to the chair she had placed near the fireplace and helped him out of his stylish bolero jacket.

"Gracias, señorita. I apologize if I seem nervous. I have never called on a woman this way before."

"Don't be nervous. I've been entertaining like this for several months now and only had a few uncomfortable situations present themselves."

As young as he appeared, Amalia doubted if he had yet called on a woman in *any* way. His kind eyes followed her every move. Under his top hat, the señor's greased, jet-black hair reflected the firelight, and though he was slender, his solid frame portrayed physicality and strength. Ribera's genuine smile intrigued her the most. If she hadn't sworn off men, she might have liked him.

"Relax, Señor Ribera. We are merely getting acquainted. In a moment, hot water will be delivered, and I will prepare you some tea. I find I have little taste for coffee."

"That would be most welcome." He loosened his cravat. "I-I feel at a disadvantage. You know my name, but I've yet to learn yours."

"I am Lea Tavio." Amalia walked to the door and opened it to relieve Esperanza of the pot of hot water.

Esperanza scrutinized Amalia until she smiled and gave her a reassuring nod.

Curious, Señor Ribera asked, "That appears to be more water than we need."

"I have a very special surprise for you, señor. I hope you're not ticklish." He chuckled and fidgeted in his chair.

"Will you tell me about your art?" She handed him some tea, then poured the water into a bowl that she placed on the floor at his feet.

"I had the great fortune to train under the historical painter and master Monsieur Delaroche in Paris. He took me all over Europe to paint different landscapes and people. I have lived in France for half my life but am grateful to be back on Spanish soil."

While he spoke, Amalia removed his well-polished boots and stockings.

Interrupting his own narrative, he asked, "What is this tea? It's very bitter."

"Chamomile. Do you not like it? Would you like something else?"

"No, gracias. I am fine." He sighed and settled deeper into his chair. "I'm feeling very relaxed."

Amalia placed his feet one at a time into the warm water. "How does that feel?"

"Wonderful."

"While your feet soak, I will rub your shoulders."

Stepping behind him, Amalia unbuttoned his shirt, lowered it to reveal well-formed shoulders, and kneaded his muscles. "What is it you enjoy painting the most, señor?"

It took a moment for him to respond. "Portraits, but I've been told I have a gift for landscapes and action scenes. I believe that is the direction I will follow, though I'll never give up portraits altogether."

Amalia moved to sit in front of him, used some soap Leo acquired for her to wash his feet, then removed one foot out of the water to dry it off. Señor Ribera looked at her with a silly grin on his face.

"This is my specialty." She returned the smile.

He leaned his head back and closed his eyes. "This is not what I expected, Señorita Tavio, but I find I am quite content."

"I'm pleased . . . because I have a confession to make."

His eyes remained closed. "Oh?"

"Si, I was hoping you could help me with something."

"Whatever it is, I will gladly obey."

This is easier than I thought it would be. "I would like you to paint a miniature of me and my son."

Señor Ribera lifted his head. "You have a son?"

"Si, his name is Alejandro, but few know him as my son. Most people believe he is my ward."

"I seem to recall a little machito scurrying around the tavern. Is that him?"

Amalia nodded before taking a glob of salve infused with eucalyptus, something else Leo purchased for her, and rubbed it into the arch of his foot, through each of his toes, and then worked her way up his calf muscle.

Señor Ribera laid his head back again and moaned with pleasure. "I'm having difficulty concentrating, señorita. Is this how you treat all of your gentleman callers?"

"If I said si, would you be disappointed?"

"No. I was just under the impression that this kind of entertainment is not what men are expecting when they pay for your company."

Amalia giggled. "I assure you it is not." She paused. *He seems trustworthy.* "May I tell you something in confidence?"

Ribera nodded.

"When Señor Guerra, the master of the tavern, ordered me to start *entertaining* men, I devised this plan of a relaxing massage to avoid compromising myself. I apologize for the deception, but my son will not have a whore for a mother."

"It is an ingenious plan. Does it always work?"

"Mostly. I've had some close calls."

No response.

"My son is actually of noble blood. Of course, not by me. I am no one, but I still have enough respect for myself not to willingly participate in such a despicable vocation. This is the only service you'll be receiving tonight."

"I'm happy to say I'm not disappointed in the least."

Amalia let out the breath she was holding. "Bueno. Also, I have another confession. I laced your tea with opium. That is how I get the men to relax. Most of them are already intoxicated and don't seem to notice the bitter taste. By the time they leave, they feel so good and refreshed they don't remember or don't mind that their service didn't match their expectations. I actually have a few regular callers who like to come for a good foot rub. Some men have terrible, disgusting feet, but I believe the alternative is far worse."

Señor Ribera chuckled and shook his head in disbelief. "I must say I am a bit jealous that I am not the only man you have treated this way. You are enchanting, señorita." He paused. "So back to business. When do you propose we do this miniature of you and Alejandro? Is this to be a secret?" He looked at her.

"Si, I was hoping you would visit me for a few evenings . . . however many you need to do this for me, and I will pay Señor Guerra my entertainment fee for you."

"I would be happy to, señorita. I will enjoy being with you and meeting your son, but I insist on paying my own fee."

"I cannot allow that, señor. I've hired you, and I intend to pay."

"I'll not hear of it. Rarely do I have the satisfaction of painting such a lovely subject anymore. It would be my pleasure."

"Gracias, señor. I wasn't expecting such generosity. Por favor, don't refer to Alejandro as my son. The owner wouldn't like it."

"Of course." Señor Ribera ventured a request, "May I ask you some questions?"

"You may. But I might not answer," she teased.

Amalia enjoyed Señor Ribera's company. He had a calming nature, kindness with no pretense—not to mention, very pleasant to look at.

"What happened to your husband?"

Color rushed to Amalia's face.

"I apologize. I can see it's an uncomfortable subject. You need not answer."

Amalia wanted to tell him. She wanted to confide in someone about the secret she'd guarded for so long. The temptation to talk about her past won the battle raging in her head. "I haven't spoken of . . . It happened in another lifetime. Promise you will never speak of it?"

"You have my word."

"I've never been married."

Señor Ribera didn't blink.

Amalia went on, "When I was barely sixteen, I had a brief affair with the man who is destined to be king of España."

That time, Señor Ribera sat up and took his foot away from her grasp.

Not wanting him to interrupt, Amalia continued, "I don't blame you for not believing me, but it is true. I was young and inexperienced with love. We were only together for a few weeks, but I gave him my heart." Avoiding eye contact, she said, "I gave him everything. He led me to believe he wanted to run away together, but I found out he was just having some sport before he turned his life over to the crown. His declarations of affection were untrue. I was a fool."

Taking a deep breath, he replied, "I can believe everything but the last of what you said. You are not a fool, and it's very unlikely he had no affection for you."

Resentfully, Amalia said, "His cousin made it very clear to me, and as you can see, I am here in this prison, and he's at court living a carefree life of luxury. My son, Alejandro, is a product of our affair. You can understand why I wouldn't want my son to think he was less of a person because his mother is not married. I may have lost my virtue, but I can still be a virtuous woman."

Señor Ribera sat, speechless.

"The reason I would like you to do this miniature is because Francis didn't know I was carrying his child. I want to send it to him so he will know he has a son, and . . . I would like for you to post it for me. I'm not allowed to leave the tavern, and I need someone I can trust to make sure it has a chance to get to him."

With a lopsided smile, he gave his foot back to Amalia and said, "I'm flattered by your trust, señorita, but what is it you're hoping to accomplish by sending this miniature to him, that he will help you? Even if he could, I don't believe he'd do anything for you."

She expected Ribera's response, but his anticipated rejection still stung, putting her on the defense. "I don't want anything from him. I just want him to know."

"Are you aware of the rumors about the duke and the queen?"

"What rumors?"

"Some people believe that Francisco and Isabella are not compatible, that he is too effeminate for her taste and possibly doesn't prefer women."

Amalia laughed. "Cisco acts like a fop with people he does not like, but that's just a facade. He's a romantic. He never aspired to be king. He wanted a life of freedom where he could be who he wanted to be."

After some silence, Ribera finally clapped his hands down on his thighs and said, "I will do this for you on one condition."

Amalia brightened. "Gracias, I will pay—"

He held up his hand to quiet her. "I already said I will pay my own fee. All I want when this project is completed is another foot rub."

"Señor?"

With a most serious look, he stated, "That is my fee."

Amalia smiled. "Then I believe we have an agreement, Señor Ribera."

Señor Ribera smiled back. "Por favor, call me Carlos. We are friends now, no? And before we end our evening, would you mind doing my other foot? I have never enjoyed such a unique evening in all my life."

Amalia laughed as she took his other foot. Closing his eyes and laying his head back, Carlos softly quoted the poet Francisco de Queredo. "'Soul by no less than a god confined, veins that such a blazing fire have fueled, marrow to its glorious flames consigned: the body will abandon, not its woes; will soon be ash, but ash that is aware; dust will be, but dust whose love still grows.'"

Another romantic.

Esperanza sneaked Ale into Amalia's room each night for their painting sessions. Carlos promised Alejandro a prize at the end of each session if he sat very still, and he behaved beautifully. Amalia cherished the precious moments she held her son close, giving her another reason to appreciate her new friend.

Señor Ribera's work was exquisite, capturing Ale's cherub cheeks and full lips. She even appreciated the way Carlos illustrated her vibrant green eyes and rich complexion. Amalia fell in love with the painting— so much so that she almost regretted sending it away. The keepsake would have been a treasure, but her desire for Cisco to know of their son drove her to part with it.

The painting finally done, Amalia treated Carlos to one last foot massage.

Before he left, Amalia said, "I am so pleased with your work, Carlos, and it gives me great pleasure to know Cisco will have a miniature of us, even if he doesn't receive it happily. At least he will know he has a son. Even if you *had* allowed me to, I could never truly repay you for your kindness."

"It has been my honor, Lea. I believe you will forever be the most memorable subject I'll ever paint." He shyly smiled before looking down at his feet. Stuttering a bit, he asked, "M-May I kiss you farewell?"

Amalia lightly placed her hand to his cheek and softly kissed him on the lips. "Buenas noches." And shut the door.

Days later, Carlos Ribera walked into the tavern, confident he was doing the right thing until he saw Esperanza carrying a pot of hot water up the stairs. Disappointed that Lea already had a guest, he turned to walk away until he noticed Esperanza put the pot down and trip up the stairs. Unable to resist, Carlos followed after her. Nearing the top, they both heard a scream come from Lea's room.

Running toward the commotion, he asked, "What is going on?"

Esperanza scowled at him.

Furniture crashed to the floor. Carlos burst through the door to witness a man on top of Lea, fumbling with his pants, and her struggling to push him off. Carlos grabbed him by the arm and pulled him off.

"I believe you are in the wrong room, señor."

Esperanza came up from behind and hit the unsuspecting man on the head with a pot. He fell to the floor unconscious.

"I guess that works too. Well done, señorita."

Lea slowly sat up, wiping at her tear-stained face and pulling her blouse closed. Looking at his knees, she asked, "What are you doing here?"

Esperanza spoke up. "I'll get some ice for your cheek. Señor, would you mind helping me with this guest?"

"Of course." Señor Ribera hefted the man over his shoulder. "I won't be a moment."

Lea nodded, so he quickly followed Esperanza to the back of the tavern and around a corner, depositing the unconscious man in a ditch. They returned to Lea to find she had changed her blouse and washed her face.

Handing her the ice, Esperanza excused herself. "I'll be just outside the door."

Biting her bottom lip, Lea avoided Carlos's concerned face.

"Lea, I wanted to see you one last time before I sailed back to España." Sitting down, he took her hand. "I can't express how sorry I am for what you . . . You deserve so much more." He sat for a moment, unsure what to say. "I wanted to give this to you and let you know I posted the miniature to Francisco. I happen to have a friend at court. I'm certain Francisco will get it."

She whispered, "Gracias."

"Open it."

Inside the tissue paper, an exact replica of the miniature he'd painted for Cisco looked up at her.

"Is this for me?"

"Si, I thought you should have one."

Her face lit up. That alone made his delay back to España worth it. "I can't believe it. I don't deserve this, but it is my most cherished possession." Wiping away her tears, she gave Carlos a timid smile. "You are too kind."

He leaned in slightly to kiss her cheek, but she winced away.

"I will never forget you," he said before quickly exiting her room.

Ivy

CHAPTER 29

"BLAST. THIS IS not what I needed today." Joshua stood next to his elegant two-wheel volante just outside Mahón, wondering if he could make it to the smithy before the wheel broke clean through.

Taking his place on the bench, he clicked his horse, Trudy, forward, keeping a slow pace. The smithy came into view, and Joshua sighed with relief, but the wheel snapped just as he pulled Trudy to a halt, throwing him off-balance. He jumped out and grabbed Trudy's reins to keep her from rearing up.

"Shh, we made it, old girl. It's alright." She threw her head back and pulled the reins out of his hand. "I'm sorry, did I call you *old girl*? I meant to call you *beautiful*." The horse nudged his chin with her lips and made him laugh. "Women." Joshua quickly unstrapped her and tied her to a post.

The blacksmith approached. "Hola, señor. Having a bit of trouble, I see."

"Hola. Si, the wheel is a total loss. Do you have anything to replace it?"

Wiping his hands on his leather apron, he offered his hand. "The name's Rendón."

"Hastings."

"Well, Señor Hastings, I have just the thing, but it will take some work. Should have it done in a few hours."

"I would be most appreciative."

Señor Rendón removed the wheel and set to work.

"Pardon me, señor, do you frequent the tavern or know the people who run the place?"

"Si. Señor Guerra is the owner. It's been in business for about fifteen years, but my wife and I never took a meal there until almost a year ago."

"Why a year ago?"

"A young girl named Lea showed up and single-handedly transformed the tavern into a reputable place. The food is delicious. Now they have people waiting in a line outside until a table becomes available. I've never seen a girl work as hard as I have seen that Lea work. She practically runs the place." He looked up and pointed toward the tavern with his hammer. "She oversees the kitchen, she's the hostess, she makes sure the girls are doing their jobs and the customers are happy."

"Really?"

The blacksmith beamed like a proud father. "She'd put most men to shame."

Joshua paused before asking, "Speaking of men, have you seen any strange men lurking around here lately?"

"You mean, other than you?" Rendón gave him a side glance.

Joshua shifted his weight. "I'm watching out for Amalia . . . I mean, Lea."

Señor Rendón stopped what he was doing. "Who's Amalia? Is Lea in danger?"

"I meant to say Lea . . . and she could be in danger. If you happen to notice something seedy going on, will you let me know?"

The blacksmith stroked his beard and considered Joshua before responding. "What kind of seedy? There are a lot of unfamiliar faces visiting the tavern lately."

"Anyone who comes and starts looking around or asking questions about Lea."

"You're describing yourself, señor."

"I am, aren't I?"

Señor Rendón went back to his work. "I'll keep an eye out."

"Gracias. I think I'll take a walk around."

Joshua visited the tavern but couldn't see Amalia. He did get a glimpse of her son sitting under a stool near the bar, gnawing on a piece of bread. He had thick, dark hair and bright green eyes, just like his mother. The poor boy was filthy from head to toe, wearing an old tattered shirt and cut-off trousers. *I could change that and give him the home he deserves.*

He made his way to the common goods store and looked around, finding a fine silver mirror and brush. Joshua couldn't resist. *She deserves something lovely like this. I'll have it delivered anonymously.* He imagined her surprise.

"When should we reveal ourselves to her? We've been to the tavern three times, and she shows no sign of recognizing us." Joshua asked his closest friend as they sat in the parlor of his family's home on Menorca. Unfortunately, the villa sat on the outskirts of Ciutadella on the opposite side of the island from Mahón. It took over an hour to get to Amalia each day. The travel didn't bother him, just the length of time it took to get to her.

He and Channing enjoyed the view while sipping some sherry before retiring for the night. The sun slipped into the water, changing the sky from a soft orange to deep blue.

"I think the sooner the better." Channing downed the rest of his drink. "All this sneaking around makes us look like voyeurs. If I'm going to devote so much time to observing a woman, I'd rather be honest about it."

"She seems quite content. I saw her son again today. He's a beautiful boy but very neglected. That is no life for an innocent child."

Standing up to look out the window, Channing observed, "A boy needs a father. You realize that could be you if you play your cards right."

"I do." Joshua downed his drink.

"And you're prepared to take on that responsibility?"

"I am."

"I never thought I'd see the day you settle down and become a papa. I'm quite looking forward to it."

"I'm sure you are. Good night, Channing." When Joshua reached his room, he walked over to draw the curtains but stopped to enjoy the magnificent seascape his wall-length window framed. He opened his glass door to let in some fresh air and sat at a small table near his bed, took off his boots, and opened his correspondence. One of his contacts on mainland Spain had a possible lead.

He sat back and tapped the letter on his leg, considering the possibility of finding another clue and admiring the hand-painted murals of nature his mother designed on the walls for him. It had been his room for as long as he could remember.

Penning another query to his correspondent, Joshua sealed it and called for a footman.

"You rang?"

"Si. Have this taken to the telegraph station first thing in the morning."

"Si, señor."

Rana sneaked up behind her at the bar and said in her ear, "I just saw a package for you on Guerra's desk."

Amalia looked over her shoulder. "What do you mean?"

"I mean there is a package on Guerra's desk addressed to you."

"To me, Lea Tavio?"

"Sometimes I wonder if you choose to be simple just to annoy me. Come."

She dropped the rag she used to wipe off the tables and followed Rana to Guerra's office. Amalia paused.

"It's okay. They aren't here," Cook said. He walked into the office and came out with the package in hand. "I'll cover for you."

Amalia took the package and ran up the stairs two at a time. When she reached her room, she shut her door and sat on the bed, holding the parcel to her chest. *Who would have sent this to me?* Apprehension filled her bosom, but she was too curious not to open it. Amalia carefully pulled back the tissue to reveal a silver hand mirror and hairbrush.

"Oh, it's beautiful." *Too beautiful. I shouldn't accept it, but who would I return it to?* Amalia stuffed it in her bag under her bed where she kept all her treasures and promised to revisit the mystery later.

Amalia was clearing a messy table when a voice from behind her asked, "Is it alright if we seat ourselves, señorita?"

Amalia's heart skipped. She'd never forgotten his voice, like warm honey. Spinning around to find herself face-to-face with none other than Captain Hastings, she noticed immediately he'd changed. Softer and kinder, his eyes sparkled when he looked at her, not at all critical or calculating. She finally discovered their color—turquoise blue, the color of the water near the coast. Joshua still kept his wavy, golden-brown hair tied at the nape of his neck, but a well-groomed goatee and strong jaw held her attention at his perfect smile.

In fact, she must have stood gazing at him too long because his smile waned. When he cocked a brow, she quickly found her voice. "Captain Hastings, si, help yourself. I will have someone with you momentarily."

Hastings tipped his hat and turned to seat himself. Instead of his military uniform, he wore a navy tailcoat and tan breeches that clung to his muscular legs. Amalia's eyes followed every movement until she heard a chuckle. Looking about, she noticed Commander Channing.

He donned a bright, royal blue tailcoat and matching top hat, which delighted Amalia. She admired a man who confidently made his own statement.

"Commander Channing? I can't believe it. How wonderful to see you again." She rushed forward to show them to a table herself, choosing one in the far corner.

"It is nice to see you too, señorita. May we inquire after your aunt?"

"Who?"

"Your aunt . . . Sonia, I believe." He glanced sideways at Hastings.

Amalia was at a loss. Then it dawned on her. *Oh no. My aunt Sonia—my reason for coming to Menorca.*

With a frown, she said, "Gracias, for asking. She died shortly after I arrived here."

Captain Hastings cleared his throat. "We're sorry for your loss."

A painful pause followed. Captain Hastings tilted his head at Commander Channing, so Channing quickly recovered the conversation.

"However, it's no longer captain, señorita. Hastings and I finished our commissions last year and are merely common folk. Well, I am. There is nothing common about Hastings here."

That comment earned a scowl from his friend, but Channing clapped him on the back with a smile before taking the seat Amalia offered him.

Noticing Hastings's frown and trying to hide her own smile, she asked, "What brings you here?"

The only thing different about Señor Channing was his full beard. He still flaunted his rotund middle and charming disposition. *Seems to me I've noticed these men in the tavern before but didn't recognize them because I've been avoiding eye contact with unfamiliar men. I wonder.*

"We're on holiday, staying at Hastings's place just outside of Ciutadella."

"I have not been there—Ciutadella, that is." *Or anywhere on this island.* "Is it beautiful?"

Señor Hastings looked at the table with a frown on his face.

"It is quite lovely, right, Hastings?"

He looked up to say, "Mm-hmm."

"That was despicable," Channing said to his friend after Amalia disappeared from view.

"She didn't seem very happy to see me," Joshua muttered.

"Mmm, yes, women usually ignore you when I'm around. I have a mesmerizing effect on the fairer sex."

Joshua rolled his eyes.

"Don't let it vex you. She just knows me better than you because I spent the most time with her on our journey to the island."

"Are you trying to make me feel more regret than I already do?"

Channing examined the perplexing man sitting across the table. "In truth, Hastings, she couldn't keep her eyes off you."

"Really? I didn't see it."

"Probably because you've been staring at that lovely knot in the table." Channing repositioned himself on the chair to lean forward. "Forgive me, Joshua, but you have not shown any semblance of affection toward this woman until now. Has something suddenly changed?"

"How has it escaped your notice?" Joshua retorted.

"I see how you spend an inordinate amount of time thinking about her safety and your obsession with Tudó, but I have not sensed much more than that." Seeing Joshua's frustration, he continued, "I apologize. I thought your fixation was in discovering her connection with Tudó in hopes of bringing him to justice. Of course, I noticed you were entranced by her vibrant green eyes and lovely figure. So was I. But if you felt any fondness toward her, you have not shown it, as far as I have seen."

Joshua considered his friend. "You're right. I haven't been entirely forthcoming. I only realized how I felt about her when we were in England. It seems unlikely, I know, but I think about her constantly because it's more than wanting to finally bring Tudó to justice. I . . . I think I love her."

Channing threw his hands down on the table, making a thunderous noise. "Bloody hell, Hastings." Laughing out loud, he congratulated his friend. "I knew it."

"Quiet, Channing," Joshua hissed. "You are making a scene."

"I'm happy for you, Hastings, but it complicates things, don't you think?"

"How do you mean?"

"Well, she's a . . . and you're a . . ."

"We don't know what she is. If anything, she is the granddaughter of a hidalgo."

"Is that enough?"

"I know you adhere to the hierarchy, but really? I didn't ever take you for a snob."

Channing considered him a moment before continuing, "I assume it would be alright for you because your brother has married well. You being the heir to the earldom, I would think you'd be cognizant of your responsibilities. I, on the other hand, am the fourth son of a baron. I have to marry well. Who would pay for my clothing? It costs quite a bit to make me look this good." Channing rubbed his multicolored silk waistcoat.

"Can we talk about something else? It doesn't matter anyway. Clearly, I didn't make a very good impression."

"Give it time, old chap. Give it time."

Joshua and Channing sat at their usual table, Joshua preferring to sit where he had the best view of the tavern—and Amalia.

Watching her approach, Amalia's smile beamed at him. *She is more beautiful than ever.* A strand of her coiffed hair had pulled loose, and dirt dappled her perfect forehead, probably from wiping perspiration away with the back of her wrist.

Joshua felt a nudge under the table. Amalia's smile was fading. He looked at Channing, and Channing lowered his head a little, cocking a brow. Joshua needed to say something.

"*Gachata, por favor.* Uh, I mean . . ." Shaking his head to clear it, he smiled nervously and spoke slower. "Can we get galleta and horchata, por favor?"

"I'll have coffee," Channing interjected.

Amalia was obviously amused by Joshua's blunder but managed to excuse herself before laughing. Her shoulders shook slightly as she walked away.

"*Gachata?* You frightened the poor señorita." Channing chuckled at his nervous friend.

"I don't know what came over me. I noticed how beautiful she is even with a smudge on her forehead and didn't realize she addressed me this time instead of you. Oh, I am a fool, Channing. I feel so muddled in her presence. I need help." Swallowing his pride, he leaned in. "Will you practice conversing with me?"

Channing widened his eyes but matched his tone. "Are you asking for my *help?*"

"You won't make this easy for me, will you?"

Fluffing his lacy cuffs, he said, "I'm flattered, Hastings, but I don't know if there is anything I can do. You're hopeless."

He knew Channing would tease him incessantly and sat back in a huff.

"Oh, come now, Hastings. You've hired the right man. Of course, my price is steep, but you look desperate enough to pay it."

It took some time for Amalia to finally bring their meal. So embarrassed by his earlier blunder, Joshua couldn't look at her. When she handed him his plate, their hands touched, and lightning shot between them so unexpectedly that Amalia dropped the plate before he had time to grasp it. He bent over to pick it up at the same time she did, and they bumped heads. Both moved to rub out the pain and made eye contact. Amalia let out a giggle. Joshua's earlier chagrin softened into a full grin, and he chuckled with her. *Her laugh is like a tinkling bell.*

Amalia stared at Hastings for a moment, then turned on her heel and rushed away.

Grateful for her hasty retreat, Joshua gulped his horchata. "Let's get out of here."

Channing threw some coins on the table and joined his friend. The silence between them back to the villa was deafening. To break the silence, Channing declared, "It will be my honor to train you in the fine arts of wooing the fairer sex. You shall not fail. Let's begin!" He threw his arm forward as if commanding an army to rally, and his horse jumped into a gallop.

Joshua couldn't help but laugh as he spurred his horse, Trudy, to catch up.

True to his word, Channing ran Joshua through ridiculous conversations until his head spun. Channing thought it wonderfully amusing until Joshua threatened to bring out his dueling pistols. Finally getting serious, his best mate used every opportunity to rehearse.

The following day, Channing greeted Joshua with his falsetto voice and curtsy when he entered the morning room. "Buenas tardes, Señor Hastings, how are you on this fine day?" He was wearing a ridiculous pink waistcoat and fluffy cravat.

Joshua took some toast and spread jam on it. "Not now, Channing. We have a lead."

"Oh?" Clearing his throat, he lowered his voice. "Oh?" Channing sat back down.

"One of my contacts has sent word that the Maritimo family traveled north near the southeastern border of France. It's a weak lead, but it is more than we have had for over a month." Looking out the window, he added, "This couldn't have come at a better time. I am afraid to show my face at the tavern again after my last blunder."

"It wasn't *that* bad."

"No, it was worse." Considering his friend, he added, "I think I preferred seeing you in your drab military uniform. That color is too bright, even for you."

"It makes me look fat, doesn't it?"

Lavender

CHAPTER 30

JOSHUA CROSSED PATHS with a wretched-looking wagon laden with various parcels, mismatched furniture, several children, and a cow in tow as he approached the small town of Benás near the border of France. After much travel and what seemed like hundreds of empty leads, Joshua finally made his way to the only available mercantile to see if Channing had sent him word on his progress farther southwest.

Though he desperately needed a warm meal and bath, Joshua had to inquire after Gordon Maritimo before businesses closed up for the evening. He made his way to a few open shops.

No such luck. The mercantile gave him no information, nor the apothecary.

The man can't have fallen off the face of the earth. Spotting a blacksmith at the end of the road, he hurried that way. No one could go without a blacksmith.

Joshua introduced himself to the man in a leather apron pounding some steel. "Buenas tardes, señor. My name is Joshua Hastings. I wonder if you could help me find someone? Have you heard of or do you know of a man named Gordon Maritimo, who may have moved to this village two years back?"

Putting the rod back into the fire, the blacksmith said, "Buenas tardes, Señor Hastings. Name's Abaroa. I don't know of a Gordon *Maritimo*. I know a Gordon Godoy, who took up residence here. I think it's been more than two years since he moved here, though. He and his large family had a small parcel of land a few miles west, near the border. If you follow that road as far as it goes and then continue on for a few more miles, you'll find the place, but I don't think he and his family are there anymore. They recently lost their land. A deal gone bad, I heard."

"Do you have any idea where they would have gone?"

"No, señor. Very private people. Señor Godoy seemed a pleasant fellow but refused to engage in idle conversation."

"Gracias, señor. I appreciate this information very much. Buenas tardes."

Hopeful, Joshua made his way to the only decent inn in town for a meal, bath, and bed. Morning couldn't come soon enough.

It took an hour for Joshua to find anything resembling a house, which appeared to be nothing more than a shabby dwelling among uneven rows of mysterious fruit trees. Chickens ran wild throughout the neglected grounds. Dismounting his rented horse, Joshua almost landed on a chicken and kicked it aside to approach the slightly ajar door. He knocked.

No answer.

Joshua peeked inside. "Hola, is anyone home?" Silence.

Dishes lay scattered on the table, remnants of partially eaten food rotted, and a chair had been turned on its side. The family appeared to have left in a hurry. In the room opposite the kitchen, a blanket lay thrown haphazardly into a corner. Something was hidden underneath, so Joshua went to investigate. A worn Holy Bible sat on the floor, the front cover pulled back to reveal several handwritten names. Among the most damning were the names Godoy followed by Maritimo. Farther down the page were the letters *AMA* scrawled in a child's handwriting just above the name of Gordon Maritimo Junior. AMA was probably short for Amalia. It appeared Joshua had found Amalia's family—or what was left of it—and their suspected connection to Manuel Tudó, the only living son of Manuel Godoy and Pepita Tudó.

Joshua reverently wrapped the Bible in the blanket and placed it in his satchel. Taking one last look around the empty house, he couldn't shake the feeling something needed his attention. He decided to take a look around the outside.

As Joshua rounded the corner, he heard some rustling in the bushes. Pulling his revolver from his belt, he turned. A flash of fur leaped from the brush and sunk its claws into his face. Joshua dropped his gun and wrestled to break free. In the scuffle, he experienced a sharp pain to his shin. Joshua barely registered what it was when the cat ran off.

Joshua picked up his gun and put it away before going after the little andrajoso machito who kicked him. As he approached a makeshift shed so crooked it looked like one push could topple it, he heard some movement in the shadows.

"Hola, niño. My name is Señor Hastings. I will not harm you. I want to help. Will you let me help you?"

More noise near the back corner. Joshua followed the sound and found a small boy, who looked to be no more than five or six years old, curled up in the hay.

Joshua knelt beside him. "Hola, what is your name?" Reaching to brush the boy's light brown hair aside, he whispered, "Let me help you. Where is your family?"

The little boy moved back from his outstretched hand and scrutinized Joshua for a moment before shrugging.

"Are you alone?"

The boy nodded.

"Where is your family?"

"They are gone, señor. They said I am a bad machito."

"A bad machito? Well, you certainly have a strong kick. My shin still aches. But I don't know if you are a bad machito. Will you tell me your name?"

"Thomas."

"Thomas." Joshua's heart skipped a beat. "That is a fine name. How old are you?"

"I am eight years old, señor."

He's too small to be eight years old.

"Are you hungry? I'm about to leave. Would you like to join me?"

"Si, señor. I am very hungry."

Joshua reached out his hand, and the small boy took it. With strength betraying his gaunt appearance, he deftly pulled himself up.

"Will you help me find my sister?"

Joshua proceeded to dust Thomas off. "If I can. Tell me about her."

"She is my oldest sister. My parents sent her away so we could live here. I miss her."

Pleased Thomas wasn't shy, Joshua replied, "I believe you. What is her name?"

"Ama."

The two walked to Joshua's horse. "Ama. That is an unusual name. Is it short for something else?"

"Si, her name is Am-al-ia."

Joshua expected his answer. "Well, Thomas, I think I can help you with that."

"Really?"

Lifting him up on the saddle, Joshua teased, "Si, but first we need to get some meat on those bones."

Thomas snickered behind his hand.

"Was that funny?"

"Your face is covered in blood and red welts, señor."

"Blast that stupid animal. My face also *hurts*. Of all the battles I've fought, never have I been bested by a feline. I don't know where she went."

"That's alright. She can take care of herself. She's a great hunter. Ama eats better than I do." Thomas became quiet, his face pulled into a frown.

"Is there something wrong, machito? I can look for her."

"No. Your face reminded me of something."

"Will you tell me about it while we ride?"

"Well, I switched my papa's shaving soap for my mama's fancy soap. They practically look the same, so my mama used it, and her face and hands got really red and blistered. I only thought it would make her smell funny. I didn't know she would get hurt. They didn't believe me."

Joshua processed the information and said, "Well, I am sure you learned your lesson."

"Si, señor," Thomas mumbled.

"As soon as we reach the village, I'll take you to the inn and order you whatever you want to eat. I'm afraid if the wind started to blow, you'd float away."

With Thomas as guide, it didn't take them long to get back to town. Once they arrived, Joshua led him into the spacious dining room to order the scrawny boy whatever he wanted. Thomas ate like a beast, proving he wasn't malnourished as a result of his appetite. Color filled his cheeks, and his countenance brightened, amazing Joshua at the transformation. He sat back with his arms folded, smiling as the boy gorged himself.

"So, Thomas, where is your family? How long have you been alone?"

Thomas took another bite of squid paella. A kernel of rice stuck to his chin, so Joshua handed him a napkin.

"They left yesterday morning. I don't know where they were going. I hid so they couldn't find me, and after a couple of minutes, they gave up looking. My mama didn't like me anyway. She called me a festering sliver in her finger." He shrugged his shoulders and went back to his food. "I don't care. I'm going to find Ama. She loved me. She gave me a kitten."

A festering sliver? What a terrible label. Joshua decided to focus on Amalia's gift. "She gave you a kitten? What did you call it?"

"I called her Ama. You met her. She was the one who scratched your face off." Thomas laughed with bulging cheeks full of food. "May I have your bread?" Thomas reached for it.

Joshua smiled as he handed over his roll. *What a precocious boy . . . and charming. It must have broken Amalia's heart to leave him behind.*

"Thomas, I would like you to come with me, but if you leave with me tomorrow, you won't be coming back here. You may never see your family again."

Stopping mid bite, Thomas said, "I thought we already decided I was coming with you."

"Well, excellent. That's settled, then." Joshua had been leaning back on his chair. He let it fall forward before getting up. "My comrade is in Erista waiting for us. I will send word to him that I found a scrawny little machito who needs some fattening up."

Thomas smiled.

"I think it is about time we put you to bed, machito. I'll make sure the room is ready."

Thomas's brow furrowed. He reached out and grabbed Joshua's wrist. "Will you be staying with me?"

"Si, if that is agreeable, or I could try to make other arrangements." *I don't know what those would be.*

Thomas smiled. "No, I'm glad you are staying. I don't want to be alone."

Ruffling Thomas's hair, Joshua said, "I won't be long."

He left the boy for a few minutes to arrange for a room and a tub of water. Thomas needed a good bath. Entering their room, Joshua thought he'd arranged for another bed to be brought up but instead a mattress lay on the floor. Uncomfortable having Thomas sleep on the ground, Joshua reconsidered the arrangements.

"I apologize for the mattress on the floor. Why don't you take the bed? You need to get a good night's sleep," Joshua offered.

"Oh no, señor, this mattress is much better than what I'm used to."

"You sure? I am happy to take the floor."

"Si, señor."

Joshua marveled at Thomas's good nature. He might have been mischievous but certainly not bad. Maybe time would tell a different story.

"Well then, I have ordered you a bath. Let's get you out of those clothes and clean you up. I asked the matron of the inn if she would provide some nightclothes for you tonight. In the morning, I will get you some new clothing that will fit you better."

A bit shy undressing, Thomas still did as he was told and stripped off his shirt and breeches. Joshua helped him in the bucket and knelt beside him. Large welts riddled Thomas's back. Pretending he didn't notice, Joshua took a rag and dipped it into the warm water to scrub the dirt away.

A few spots Joshua couldn't seem to rub clean, and poor Thomas winced in pain. Rinsing the suds away to try cleaning them again, to his horror, Joshua realized they were deep bruises on Thomas's forehead, chin, and neck. He took in a sharp breath.

"I'm so sorry. I didn't know I was hurting you. Why don't I help you with your shoulders and back, and you can do the rest?"

Timidly, Thomas replied, "Did I do something wrong?"

Joshua handed him the soap. "Of course not, machito. I'm just a bit tired from traveling. I'll be just outside the door if you need me."

After exiting the room, Joshua leaned back on the door and closed his eyes to steady his nerves. How could a parent treat a child like that? What kind of life was this boy subjected to? And what about Amalia? Joshua took deep breaths to calm his emotions, and when Thomas called for him, he adopted an impassive expression before reentering the room.

Finding Thomas struggling with the nightshirt, Joshua crossed the room to his side. "Here, let me help you with that. There, all better." He settled Thomas into the blankets on the floor mattress. "Dulces sueños, Thomas."

"Buenas noches, Señor Hastings."

As an afterthought, Joshua added, "And Thomas, leave your pranks for later, por favor. I am truly in need of a good night's sleep."

By the sound of his steady breathing, Thomas already slept. Joshua lay in bed, mulling over the new revelations of the day. According to the Maritimos' Bible, Amalia was not their biological child. Her name didn't appear anywhere except where Thomas scrawled it in. If Amalia's assumed mother, Luisa Godoy, was related to Manuel Tudó, perhaps that's how Amalia ended up in the Maritimo household, but that didn't reveal her parentage. Pulling his hands down his face, he thought, *I don't want it to be true, but she could very well be Tudó's daughter. Anton probably got himself killed trying to save Lucita. I can understand how he felt. I'm prepared to do the same for Amalia.*

Paprika

CHAPTER 31

JOSHUA ROSE EARLY and acquired clothing suitable for Thomas to travel in until they met up with Channing. The boy would need a full wardrobe, but resources were scarce until they reached their final destination: the coast.

When he returned to find his young companion still asleep, he pulled up a chair and ate an apple while skimming through the Maritimo family Bible. Studying the names at the top of the page, Joshua noticed it wasn't the Maritimo Bible but a Godoy Bible.

Miguel de la Grúa Talamanca de Carini y Branciforte, First Marquis of Branciforte, was married to Tudó's aunt, Maria Godoy. *Luisa Godoy is Manuel Tudó's cousin. That's how they're connected, but why is Luisa living in squalor married to Gordon Maritimo, a man of no name or privilege?*

Thomas finally woke, and Joshua ordered him a plate of sweet rolls and hot milk before starting their journey.

"I've hired a carriage to take us to a villa in Santander, which is on the west coast. Have you been there before?"

"I've never been anywhere, señor."

"Then you are due for an adventure, I think."

Thomas's eyes lit up.

"The journey will take a few days because we need to pick up my comrade on the way."

The scrawny machito nodded his head as he stuffed his face with food. Chuckling, Joshua set out his clothes and readied his things.

Two hours into their journey, the carriage hit a pothole, startling Joshua out of his doze. The same junk-laden wagon he'd observed on his way to Benás the day before sat off to the side of the road. Thomas sat up when Joshua hollered to stop the coach. Wiping the sleep out of his eyes, Thomas spotted one of his sisters sitting in the shade of a tree.

"No, señor." He gripped Joshua's arm and pulled him back. "That is my family. Por favor, don't give me back."

Grateful for the revelation, Joshua couldn't resist meeting them. "Hush now. I just want to see if I can help."

Thomas pulled harder.

Joshua patted his hand and reassured him, "Crawl onto the floor in the corner and put my cloak over you. I won't let them know you are here."

Thomas quickly obeyed, and Joshua exited the carriage.

"Buenos días. May I be of assistance?"

A scruffy man came out from behind a horse. "Buenos días." Wagging his thumb toward the horse, he said, "Old Gordita here has thrown a shoe and gone lame. This load is too heavy for my other horse to pull alone."

Joshua offered his hand and replied, "It would appear so. I'm Señor Hastings."

"A pleasure to meet you, Señor Hastings, but I don't know how you can help unless you have an extra horse hiding in that carriage of yours." The man laughed at his own joke.

Joshua looked at him with a smirk. "You didn't tell me your name, señor."

All joking aside, he responded, "I didn't, did I?"

Not liking the response, Joshua tipped his hat. "I will bid you farewell." And turned to walk away.

A horrible wail, like a cat in heat, rent the air from behind the wagon. Joshua spun around to see a plump, disheveled woman wearing too many ruffles come stumbling out to whine at her poor husband.

The sight was so amusing that Joshua had to cough behind his hand to muffle a laugh.

"How could you? You selfish, mean-hearted man! We need help. We have been here for two days!" She then looked at Joshua with her day-old makeup smudging her face and spoke with a syrupy voice. "Oh, señor, we are so grateful for your offer. Por favor, have mercy on us. See our poor, wretched children?"

How absurd. I only saw this sorry wagon yesterday morning. The town couldn't be more than a few hour's walk from here.

The over-indulged matron motioned for her two eldest daughters to join her; the girls giggled like chattering monkeys as they stepped forward, overwhelming Joshua with all the ribbons bobbing in their disheveled hair. He stumbled backward. Already, a resemblance to the Godoy family was blossoming before his eyes. Definitely Luisa Godoy. The woman displayed a manipulative, cunning nature like her cousin.

Señor Maritimo jumped between Joshua and his wife. "Stop, mi amor. You are frightening the man. My apologies, señor."

Joshua straightened his waistcoat and hat. "Gracias."

All the other children of the family had gathered in front of the wagon to watch. Joshua nodded at them and returned his attention to Señor Maritimo.

"I still don't know your name. I can help you, but I refuse to do business with someone whose name I don't know."

Raising his hands in surrender, he replied, "I am Gordon Godoy. This is my wife, Luisa, and these are our children."

Joshua tipped his hat. "Any relation to Manuel Godoy?"

"Why do you want to know?" Señor Maritimo snapped.

Señora Luisa quickly interjected, "You say you can help us?"

Disappointed he didn't get an answer, Joshua replied, "Indeed, it is your lucky day, señora. I happen to have a horse I would be willing to trade with you."

Señor Maritimo's eyes narrowed. "Do you think us fools? Where is it? In your pocket?"

"Just a moment, por favor." *I do not like that man.* Joshua walked around the back of his carriage and took the reins of the horse he had rented. A good horse but not properly trained, it took every opportunity to wander off. *Sonia told me Amalia loved Gordita. A good trade, I think.*

Señor Maritimo looked surprised. "I guess I didn't see that horse when you pulled up."

"How could you? You were behind your wagon on the other side of the road. I will trade this horse for old Gordita, as you call her."

Scratching his head under his hat, Maritimo stalled. "I don't know. What's wrong with your horse? Who in his right mind would trade that fine specimen of horseflesh for an old, fat horse?"

Joshua stood patiently while the man examined and salivated over his rental.

Maritimo muttered, "Gordita is like our family pet. I can't just trade her like that."

Joshua didn't reply.

Señor Maritimo ran his hand through his beard and looked between his family and Joshua. The incessant whining, especially from his wife, made up his mind.

"Alright, we'll trade. I'm getting the better deal, you know. No funny business. If this horse dies before the day is out, I *will* find you. I never forget a face *or* a name."

Joshua didn't appreciate the insinuation and looked Gordon Maritimo straight in the eyes. "If I ever see *your* face again, it will be all too soon."

The man winced back before carefully taking the reins from Joshua and grunted "Gracias" as he scurried away.

Joshua walked over to Gordita and patted her neck. Pleased at what he saw, he had to admit Maritimo knew how to take care of horses. If Gordita was as old as the man implied, she epitomized health and still had some good years in her. Joshua hummed in low, calming sounds as he carefully lifted her hoof to see the bad split. She nodded her head at him.

"It's alright, Gordita. I think you will make it just fine if we go slow to the next town. I'll take very good care of you." He patted her neck and said to Maritimo, "You've made a good trade, señor. I'll help you hitch up your horses before I am off."

Joshua removed his waistcoat and hat and rolled up his sleeves. He opened the door to the carriage and threw his things on top of Thomas, who was peeking out from under the cloak.

Joshua winked at him.

Addressing Luisa Godoy, he turned and said, "You have been blessed with a large family, señora."

With a curtsy, she said, "You are kind to notice, señor. We have . . . six children. Our two oldest boys recently left home to find lives of their own."

"You forgot Amalia and Thomas," a blond-haired, blue-eyed little girl said.

"Hush, child." Señora Luisa gave the little girl a nasty look before turning on her charm with false remorse. "Pardon me, señor. Our poor Thomas died, and it is difficult to speak of him."

Joshua stopped what he was doing momentarily upon hearing Amalia's name. He tried to keep a straight face as he helped Señor Maritimo and said, "I'm sorry for your loss. How old was he?"

"He was nearly nine years old, señor—too young to leave this life."

"Si. And your Amalia? Did she die too?" Joshua prayed Luisa was willing to share information.

She stepped toward Joshua. "No, Amalia was never truly ours."

Joshua's heart skipped.

"We raised her from an infant and loved her, but we only had her until she came of age, and then we sent her back to her true guardian."

He was almost afraid of the truth, and his heart threatened to beat out of his chest, but he pressed on. "It's quite admirable that you would take someone else's child and raise her."

The pretentious woman beamed at the compliment and moved close enough for him to smell her body odor.

"Gracias, señor. That is very generous of you to say, but it was a small thing to do for family." In a more hushed voice, she said, "The poor mother died in childbirth, and my cousin asked us to take her. He wasn't yet married and couldn't very well court a reputable woman carrying such baggage." She gave him a demure smile from under her fluttering eyelashes.

Clearing his throat, he voiced the hardest question. "I can imagine it was difficult to part with her after so many years. You were related to her, then? An aunt, perhaps?"

The men had almost finished hitching up the wagon, and he noticed Señor Maritimo becoming agitated by the conversation. Joshua held his breath, hoping for a little more.

"No, señor. We are not related, but we cared for her as our own. We have heard nothing from her since the day she left. Such ingratitude is hard to bear."

Joshua wiped at the sweat dripping at his temples. *Amalia isn't related. She's not Tudó's daughter. Why does he still pursue her?*

"You must love your cousin very much. Did you ever tell Amalia about her real mother?"

"Of course not. There was no need to upset her when we were raising her as our own."

"You never told her she wasn't yours? What a burden to carry all those years. She must have been devastated to leave your family, not understanding why." Joshua looked at the señora with false compassion.

Señor Maritimo's gruff voice finally interrupted, "You certainly are asking a lot of questions, señor."

"Forgive me. I have a soft place in my heart for abandoned or orphaned children."

"Oh, how very good of you, señor." Señora Luisa clutched her chest. "You are right, of course. It was a burden. I tried to be a loving mother to her, despite her indolence. I think she was just like her real mother, but my cousin never spoke of her—heartbroken at her loss."

"Very sad, indeed. May I ask your cousin's name?"

"Why do you need to know?" Señor Maritimo interjected.

"No need. I was merely asking because my family lived in España for many years, and my time in the navy has blessed me with many friends."

Señora Luisa said excitedly, "Oh, a military man. I should have known. You are so tall and strong." She then looked at her girls with a wink. "Are you attached, señor? As you can see, we have two beautiful daughters who would make lovely brides."

Señor Marítimo quickly said with a warning glare to his wife, "When did you serve?"

Joshua was grateful for the diversion. Señora Luisa undoubtedly had no boundaries. "My commission just ended. When did *you* serve?"

"How do you know I served?"

Realizing his blunder, he quickly said, "A military man is *always* as cautious as you are."

Taking that as a compliment, he stated, "About eighteen or so years ago."

Señora Luisa interjected, "You are so rude, husband. Why does everything have to be about you? I'm sure your family knows my cousin, señor. His father was essential in the Spanish court—"

Señor Marítimo interrupted, "We are all finished up here. Gracias, señor. You must be anxious to get on your journey."

"Ah, si." *I got most of what I needed.* He patted the rented horse on its back and turned to the family. "It was nice to meet you all. Buenos días." *I hope they aren't continuing to the same town.*

Taking Gordita by the reins, Joshua walked her to the other side of the carriage to secure her and tipped his head in a final farewell before getting into the carriage.

Señor Marítimo watched him leave, and Señora Luisa waved her handkerchief, motioning for her girls to curtsy.

Relieved when the family disappeared out of sight, Joshua pulled Thomas from under his cover. Lifting the red-nosed, bloodshot-eyed boy onto the seat next to him, he asked, "What's all this?"

"The voices got so close to the carriage, I thought they would discover me. I was so afraid you would give me back."

Joshua pulled Thomas closer and wrapped an arm around him. "I would never make you go back to that family. You will always be safe with me, machito. Always." He felt no reticence, apprehension, or contrition about taking Thomas under his wing and making him family. As far as Joshua was concerned, the Marítimo family was dead.

The boy relaxed into him, and Joshua got lost in his thoughts. If Amalia was not related to Tudó or Luisa Godoy, then maybe Anton was her father—or maybe Tudó just told Luisa there was no relation.

Ahh! I don't know. Could it be possible Lucita chose Anton over Tudó, and he killed Anton out of vengeance? He was a jealous man. He would do anything to get revenge. Joshua just needed proof.

Thomas interrupted his musings, "Are you alright?"

"Si, machito. I need to confess something." Joshua put some space between them so his young companion could look directly at him. "I met your sister Amalia about three years ago."

Thomas's jaw dropped.

"I'm sorry. I didn't know for sure she was your sister until I saw the names in your Bible. Maybe I should have told you sooner. After meeting your family, I am even more sure you should stay with me."

"Really?"

"Really."

Thomas gave Joshua a hug. "Where is Ama? Are we going to her?"

"She is on an island in the Balearic Sea called Menorca, but you will not accompany me. I need you to stay safe, so I am taking you to Santander until I can bring her to you. You need to get rested for our journey to England."

Thomas's eyes got big.

"You will like Santander. It is a beautiful city near the ocean. Luckily, my comrade, Channing, was able to hire a lovely lady named Señorita Camila, who will watch over you while I am away."

Thomas quickly looked out the window and took some deep breaths. He sniffed and wiped at his eyes but didn't look at Joshua.

"I promise you will like Señorita Camila. And you will love the beach. I like skipping rocks in the water. I'll teach you how."

The young boy focused hard on something in the distance.

Joshua sensed Thomas's fear. "Are you worried I won't come back for you?"

Thomas shrugged.

"I will always come back to you, Thomas. I am leaving you in Santander because I suspect it will be difficult to convince Amalia's employers to let her go. That is not something you need to worry about. I know people have broken your heart, machito, but you must learn to trust me. Where I am going, you cannot go. In Santander, I will know you are safe and taken care of."

Thomas nodded his head as he wiped another tear from his cheek.

Joshua tousled his thick hair and sat back to look out the window. *I am gathering my family. I can feel it in my bones. I just need the final piece. Please, Lord, guide me.*

Pomegranate blossom

CHAPTER 32

M ONTHS WENT BY without a visit from Señor Hastings or Señor Channing. Amalia didn't want to admit how much it troubled her. A week after she'd noticed their absence, she received a mysterious package, a book called *Mansfield Park* by a woman named Jane Austen. Written in English, of which she knew very little, she still cherished having her own special book—something other than the educational book Señora Consuela gave her about herbs and livestock. Amalia secretly hoped it was one of her captains who sent the package, and in the event one of them asked about it, she wanted to tell them gracias. But they never came back.

She tortured herself with a myriad of reasons why they stayed away, each one worse than the last, but eventually she accepted that they realized the kind of establishment the tavern had become and decided to take their business elsewhere. Reprimanding herself for allowing her feelings to venture beyond the hedge she'd built around her heart, she focused on work.

Amalia's anxiety didn't wane much when she found out Alejandro disappeared for hours at a time and turned up with a new toy or wearing new clothes. She asked him several times to tell her where he'd been, but he always said he didn't know. The tavern demanded so much of her time that it was impossible for her to keep an eye on her son, and Esperanza, who usually watched over him, had been given more responsibilities, so the almost three-year-old child spent much of his time on his own, doing things no one seemed to know.

"Buenos días, señor."

The blacksmith offered his hand to Joshua. "Buenos días, *stranger*. It's been months. I didn't think I would ever see you again."

"Been chasing down demons." Joshua tossed his thumb toward the tavern. "It seems business is as good as ever."

"Si, it is. Wait until evening. The patrons wait hours for a seat some nights. How have you been?"

"Well enough. I've been anxious to see how Lea is doing."

"Really? I thought maybe you had moved on by now."

"Moved on? No, I've been investigating some of her past to see how I can keep her safe."

"Her past? You told me she wasn't in danger." Señor Rendón took off his hat and wiped the sweat from his brow with the back of his hand. "Did you get what you were looking for?"

Joshua took a deep breath. "Some but not enough, I'm afraid."

"You are a man of means, a gentleman. You could have your pick of women. Why would you be interested in someone like Lea?"

Joshua looked at him confused.

"Don't get me wrong. My wife and I are very fond of her, but . . ."

"But what? Because she had a child out of wedlock?"

The blacksmith's eyes shifted. "You know there is more to it than that."

"Do I? What do you know that I don't?"

Señor Rendón shoved some iron into the embers and asked, "Have you enjoyed some of the many different services Señor Guerra provides at their business?"

"Many different services? What is there besides food and drink?"

Taking a deep breath, the blacksmith said, "I don't see how Lea ever sleeps. She's a favorite among the lonely travelers who stay there, if you know what I mean."

The color drained from Joshua's face. He could hardly speak. "Lonely travelers? What are you saying?"

Pounding the iron in his hand, Rendón responded, "Well, they try to keep it more like a side business, but I heard Lea had a tough time with one of the patrons the other night. It's none of my business, and I'm not her father, but I feel sorry for her. My wife says I shouldn't concern myself because she chooses to work there."

Joshua's mouth had gone dry. "And Amal—I mean, Lea told you this?"

Shrugging his shoulders, "She told me some things, but I don't know anything *firsthand*. I have my own place to stay . . . and a wife, but we don't go there for meals anymore."

Joshua stood, watching the steam rise into the air, speechless. *How could this have happened? How did I not notice? Did Gil notice?*

"I'm sorry, Hastings. I thought you knew."

"I asked you to watch out for her while I was gone. How could you let this happen? Why didn't you send word?" *I would have come back sooner. I thought she was safe. I could never have considered something like this happening.*

"Send word? Where?" Rendón raised his voice. "I didn't know where you went." Joshua ran his hands down his face and glared at the blacksmith.

"You can't blame me. You didn't come back. Nobody came asking questions like you implied they would. I can't control Lea or what she does. I haven't even spoken to her since my wife insisted we stop taking our meals there. Listen, I like you, and it's hard for me to say it, but Lea isn't who you think she is. She is a great cook and works really hard, but I'm sure you could do better."

Joshua made eye contact with Señor Rendón. "No, she is much more than what you think. I don't believe for a second she is a willing participant in this atrocity."

"You don't know how much I wish that were true."

Joshua mounted Trudy. "This will not continue another day." He spurred her to a full gallop back to the villa. He needed a plan before coming back in the evening. If Gil knew about what the tavern had become and kept it from him, he didn't want to think what he would do. *My best mate! How could he keep this from me?*

Joshua couldn't get back to his villa fast enough. The whole time, thoughts of what Amalia was having to do, and Gil . . . As soon as Joshua arrived, he dismounted before Trudy could fully stop and rushed through the door. He made his way to the study, where he knew Gil would be, and burst into the room.

Gil dropped his feet off the desk and stood to greet him but stopped short. "That bad, huh?"

Joshua asked as calmly as possible, "Did you know?"

"Hastings, what happened?"

Joshua stormed within six inches of him. "Did you know about the tavern?"

Gil winced back. "Did I know what about the tavern?"

"Did you know that the tavern had become a whorehouse? A brothel?"

Gil put a few more inches between them and spoke calmly to defuse some of Joshua's anger. "I didn't know. No one solicited me."

Running his hands through his hair to gather his thoughts, Joshua replied more subdued, "I wanted so badly for Amalia to be safe and happy that I tried to see the good in everything. How could I be such a simpleton? Months . . . it's been months she's lived like this."

Gil cautiously moved to a brown leather chair opposite the one he'd been occupying and took a seat. "Don't be so hard on yourself. It was not obvious, and we never went to the tavern later in the evening. How could we know? We aren't in the business of hiring entertainment."

Joshua held up his hand. "Please don't say that. I cannot hear it. I am sick with regret. Of course, we should have known. And to think I could have saved her from such a fate. What do I do now?" Joshua slumped in the chair Gil vacated.

Trying to steer Joshua back to his problem-solving mode, Gil let out a long sigh. "I guess we should pack up and leave."

Joshua looked up sharply. "What do you mean, leave? We can't leave now. I have to get her out of there."

Gil smiled. "Of course you need to get her out of there. Take your coin pouch and give that Señor Guerra an offer he can't refuse."

Joshua thought for a moment. "You mean, pay for her time?"

"All of it. She doesn't have to know the details. Just make sure her time is solely yours when you make the deal."

Joshua asked, "How much should I take? How much do you think it will take to buy her . . . companionship for, say, a month? I don't know how long it will take to convince her to come with me."

"I would take two hundred, just to be sure," Gil said in all seriousness.

Knowing Guerra would be a fool to refuse, Joshua made up his mind. "Right you are. Two hundred it is. Bid high or go home, right, Gil?"

"Right. Would you like me to go with you?"

"No, I need to do this on my own. Thanks for the offer, though. I can always count on you, Gil."

Gil smiled. "I love you too, old chap."

Joshua laughed. He crossed the room to his safe and pulled out a bag of coins. "Are you going to wish me good luck?"

"You don't need it." Gil gave a quick salute.

Saffron Crocus

CHAPTER 33

JOSHUA COULDN'T IMAGINE Amalia willingly sharing her room with a stranger, and he determined to prevent her from having to do so again. Upon entering the tavern, he found a barmaid and insisted on a meeting with Señor Guerra at the bar. He stood there waiting in disguise for almost an hour, rankling Joshua's nerves even more before Señor Guerra showed his face.

Offering his hand, Guerra said, "You wished to see me?"

"I am interested in the companionship of one of your señoritas." Joshua pulled his lapel aside to show a bulge in his frock coat.

"Oh, and who would that be?"

"I'm prepared to pay handsomely for the sole attention of Lea Tavio for the next month."

Señor Guerra did not hide his surprise. "Sole attention? Señorita Tavio is my most valuable employee. You cannot have her for that long. I have my business to think about."

Joshua tapped his bag of coins to make them jingle. "I am only speaking of a few hours each afternoon."

Señor Guerra licked his lips. "I don't understand what you mean by sole attention, then."

"I mean she doesn't entertain anyone but me, *even* when I am not here." Joshua emphasized the last part.

Tsking his tongue, he replied, "That is going to cost you handsomely, señor. I do not think you can afford it."

Joshua stayed quiet.

"I earn four escudos a night for that señorita. She is very popular with the patrons. What is your interest in her?"

Joshua hated hearing how popular she was but casually shrugged his shoulders and replied, "I guess I just like her. If I am willing to pay for her, what does it matter?"

"Give me an offer, and I'll consider it."

Joshua shook his head. "You give *me* an offer, and I will agree or disagree."

It was apparent Señor Guerra had a weakness for money, but he wasn't a good businessman. Looking around, he finally said, "I will be right back."

Before he could leave, Joshua said, "We will close this deal now, or I am gone. I have a bag of gold doubloons with me, but if you leave, I will take my money elsewhere."

Lust filled Guerra's eyes. Sweat trickled down his cheek, and he wiped at it as he leaned in, motioning for Joshua to do the same.

"Give me one fifty, and you have a deal."

Joshua said, "One hundred." He knew that was more than enough to cover her fee.

Guerra bit his lip and scanned the room as if trying to find someone. Joshua turned to leave.

"Wait . . . You have a deal."

Joshua pulled out his pouch and counted one hundred coins. He could tell Amalia's employer was annoyed he hadn't insisted on more. Along with the coins, Joshua handed him a handwritten document. "Please sign here, señor."

"What is this?" Señor Guerra grumbled.

"This is our contract." Joshua smiled but did not break eye contact.

After only a few tense seconds, Señor Guerra took the nice fountain pen Joshua offered and signed his name without reading it. Admiring the pen, Guerra moved to put it in his pocket, but Joshua snatched it from him.

"Gracias, señor. She is not to see anyone this evening. I want her well rested for tomorrow. If you break our contract, I will ruin you. I have people watching you. Do you understand?" Joshua stared him down.

More sweat dripped from Guerra's temples. "Si, si."

"I'll be here after la merienda to pick her up."

"Pick her up? She is not allowed to leave my tavern."

Pointing to the document, Joshua replied, "You agreed I would have her sole attention. I cannot have that if she is available to you while she is with me."

Señor Guerra let out a huff. "How do I know you'll bring her back?"

"You don't." Joshua tipped his hat. "Buenos días. Have her ready on time."

"It's done. I see her tomorrow." Joshua announced as he entered the parlor, threw his frock coat and hat on a chair, and poured himself a drink.

"I knew you could do it. So what is your plan to woo her? Will you take her to the beach?"

Joshua shook his head. "No, I'm too self-conscious about my feet."

"It might be a nice gesture to hire a nursemaid to watch over Alejandro while you are out, so she doesn't worry about him."

"Good idea. What other ideas do you have to soften her toward me?"

"Women love flowers. You could go on a walk in the country and pick her a bouquet of wildflowers as you go. She might like that."

Joshua shrugged his shoulders. "That is an idea."

"What about a picnic? You could pack a small basket from the kitchen with bread, cheese, and fruit. A woman always likes it when she doesn't have to prepare a meal."

"How do you know that?"

Gil's jaw dropped, "It is a simple practice of observance and deduction. A woman loves it when a man does something for her that she usually has to do herself or for others. Well, I guess English aristocrats don't do anything for themselves, so it wouldn't apply there, but with Amalia, for instance, she is constantly taking care of the needs of others. Knowing that, what do you think she would appreciate most from someone?"

"A day off . . . a break?"

Channing nodded his head. "Which you have already arranged for her. Now plan something meaningful."

As he pulled up in his volante just ahead of his planned arrival time, Joshua suggested to the nursemaid, "Why don't you go in ahead of me, Melisandra, and find the woman Esperanza? Lea's son should be close by." Joshua needed a minute to collect himself.

Taking a deep breath and muttering a quick prayer, Joshua checked to be sure everything was in order one last time. He dismounted and walked inside the tavern door with as much confidence as he could muster.

Upon entering, he spotted Amalia speaking with the matron of the tavern. Amalia didn't seem at all pleased with the conversation. Already, Joshua's heart started to fail him.

Amalia couldn't truthfully admit she liked seeing Señor Hastings again. He'd been absent for months. Having her feelings of abandonment conjured up all over again at seeing his perfect, tall frame immaculately dressed standing inside the door of the tavern made Amalia angry. It'd been so long. So much had changed. There was a time when she'd hoped Señor Hastings was her answer for escape. She tried not to invest her heart, but the effort seemed futile. He beguiled her.

Then the two men disappeared. It took weeks for her to reconcile the disappointment she felt. *Now I have no choice but to leave the tavern when all my supplies to protect myself are here? I thought he was an honorable man, not self-serving. What if I was wrong?*

She slowly made her way toward Señor Hastings, who tipped his hat with a smile. "Are you ready to leave?"

Her mouth went dry, but she heard herself squeak, "Seeing as I have no choice, I guess I am ready." She cleared her throat. "I'd like to make sure my ward, Alejandro, is watched after."

Stopping her before she could turn around and leave, he said under his breath, "Your son is well taken care of."

Amalia stiffened, and her eyes shifted about the tavern.

Señor Hastings quickly added, "Forgive me if I upset you. It's just that I have observed you with him, and I recognize a mother's love for her child, and he looks just like you. Rest assured your secret is safe with me. You need never hide anything from me. You can trust me, Lea."

Looking into his eyes, Amalia tried to sense his sincerity.

He continued, "I hope you don't mind, but I have hired a nursemaid for him."

"A nursemaid? I already have someone who takes care of him for me."

Señor Hastings tilted his head and shrugged. "I'm sure she tries, but she has other things demanding her attention. My nursemaid can care for Alejandro with no distractions. She's sought him out already."

Wanting to see this woman for herself, Amalia mumbled, "I would like to check on him, if you don't mind."

Smiling, he waved his arm forward. "I'll accompany you."

"If you insist."

When they reached the back room, Amalia heard giggling and searched to find her son. At a table in the corner, Alejandro sat on the lap of the kind-looking woman who had a toy in her hands, a cute little duck with a string attached to it, holding it just out of reach to make him try harder to retrieve it from her. Ale laughed with delight when

HOLLY BROUGH

he finally grabbed it. He hopped down and pulled it along the ground as it wobbled behind him. His heart was easily won.

Amalia walked up to the woman and said, "I am Alejandro's guardian, Lea. Gracias for watching him while I'm gone. Please keep a close eye on him, though. He has a tendency of disappearing for hours at a time, and no one knows where he goes."

"Si, señorita. I'll watch him closely. He is a wonderful machito."

Amalia turned to Señor Hastings and shrugged with a half smile. "It seems he's in good hands. I'll meet you outside in a moment."

"You are disappointed," Señor Hastings stated.

"No, I'm fine," she huffed. "I'll meet you outside in a moment."

"As you wish." Bowing his head, Señor Hastings turned and left.

Amalia stood, quietly watching her child when Señora Consuela sneaked up behind her. "What are you doing? Your gentleman is waiting. Vamos!"

Amalia turned to her. "I haven't left the tavern for years, let alone with a man. Will I be safe?"

"Of course, what do you take us for?"

"I'm not feeling well."

"Don't you dare make excuses, señorita. I can see you are fit enough, a bit pale in your cheeks, but your eyes are bright with excitement."

"But Alejandro—"

"He looks to be very happy."

Amalia looked at her, pleading, but Señora Consuela slapped her on the cheek. Amalia touched her cheek in surprise. The señora slapped her promptly on the other cheek. Tears burned Amalia's eyes.

"Wonderful. Now there is fresh color in your cheeks, and your eyes have a beautiful sparkle to them. Get out of here." Señora Consuela shoved her toward the door.

Wrestling with the flow of tears ready to stream down her cheeks, Amalia quickly walked out of the tavern.

Pushing himself from the volante, Señor Hastings said, "I was beginning to wonder if I should come in after you." Suddenly, his eyes grew big, and he moved to brush a tear from her cheek but instead lightly touched her shoulder. "Are you alright? What happened?"

Amalia helped herself up to the plush bench of the opulent two-wheel volante. She did not look at him or answer his question. Dropping his hands, he let out a sigh and shifted his weight as he watched her get comfortable. The señor's face hardened.

Amalia noticed and gave him a smile. "I am fine, gracias."

Joshua turned around and looked at the tavern, the muscles in his jaw tightening. Clenching and unclenching his hands, he walked around the volante and got in. At that moment, more than anything, he wanted to whisk Amalia away from the tavern even if it was against her will, damn the consequences. But in his desire, he erred. Amalia had been forced to do things against her will all her life. Taking her from the tavern without her consent would turn her against him. Leaving with him would have to be her choice, so getting her to like him was paramount.

Joshua clicked the horse to move. "The weather is perfect for an outing today, don't you think?" Sonia had mentioned Amalia loved the outdoors.

Amalia didn't say anything, but it was clear she reveled in the open air. Putting her head back slightly, she closed her eyes. Joshua saw her move and looked over to watch her lean back and stretch her neck. Her skin glowed like an angel's, flawless down the curvature of her neck, seamlessly blending below the loose opening of her blouse and . . .

Someone hollered, and Joshua pulled his attention back to the road. Somehow, he'd steered Trudy toward a shop and almost hit a man and his produce stand. He quickly righted the volante, but Amalia's peaceful moment ended abruptly. She grabbed the handles and looked at him with wide eyes.

Joshua cleared his throat. "Sorry. I was . . . distracted by the beauty of my surroundings."

Amalia looked around. There was the butcher's shop with carcasses hanging from the portico, the bakery with baskets of bread, and the apothecary.

"Really?"

Joshua gave her a side glance before clicking the horse on.

Once they left the confines of the small town, lovely foliage surrounded them on both sides of the road. Buttercup flowers flecked the ground. A yellow orange-tipped butterfly lazily floated past their gaze, and a smile lit up Amalia's beautiful face.

Joshua was pleased with her simple, unforced grin as they rode to the spot he'd previously chosen for their picnic. Finally reaching the small overhang of private beach, Joshua slowed the horse to a stop. He quickly dismounted from the volante and rushed to help Amalia down, but she beat him to it.

Blast the woman. Can't she allow me to be a gentleman? Grabbing the picnic basket and blanket from the back of the volante, he caught up to her just as she reached a spot with a perfect view of the sea.

The water moved with the gentle breeze. Joshua took a deep breath and turned to look at his lovely companion. She had so much of her mother in her. He couldn't imagine a more beautiful scene—Amalia looking peacefully toward the horizon with, dare he say, hope? Longing to run the back of his hand down her soft cheek, he barely caught himself from doing so and instead spread the blanket out on the ground.

"Will you join me?"

Amalia was so taken by the beauty of the ocean that she startled at Señor Hastings's voice. Close enough to feel his breath tickle her skin, he softly touched her back and motioned for her to sit on the blanket he spread out for them. A tingle ran through her. She tried to ignore it, but their eyes met, and his look penetrated her soul. Lost in the depth of his eyes, she noticed his pupils were surrounded by golden sand caressed by deep turquoise water. She had never seen eyes like his, guarded and mysterious, full of longing for something illusive.

Apprehension gripped her when Señor Hastings sat next to her and pulled out the delicacies hidden in his picnic basket—cheese, strawberries, and something wrapped in paper. *How do I keep this casual?* Expectation filled her companion's countenance as he carefully unwrapped his surprise.

Chocolate? It was chocolate. Amalia tried to swallow, but her throat constricted.

Señor Hastings's hands lowered to his lap. "Are you unwell?"

Amalia didn't reply. She looked around, hoping for a hole to crawl in. *Of all the things he could have brought, he had to bring chocolate!*

For a moment, Señor Hastings sat silent, observing her. "It's chocolate. Have you tried it before?"

She willed her heart to slow and spoke through a choked throat. "I have, actually."

Señor Hastings's shoulders slumped as he exhaled. "I'm sorry. I thought you would like it."

Darkness filled the edges of her vision. *I can't do this. Por favor, God, get me out of here.*

"You don't look well, Lea. Should I take you back to the tavern?"

Amalia whispered, "You would do that for me?"

"Of course." Repacking the basket, he stood and offered his hand to help her up. He remained silent, as if knowing words would just make things worse. Amalia wiped at a tear and walked toward the volante with her head down. Thoughts of the way Cisco kissed the chocolate off her lips under the carob tree . . . That dream had turned into a nightmare—her life, a shattered mess.

What will Señor Hastings tell Guerra when we return so early? What should I do?

She wrapped her arms tightly around herself. "I apologize, señor. How can I make this up to you? I know you paid for my time, and I have ruined our outing."

Hastings gave her a sideways glance but kept his eyes on the road. "No need. I only wanted to spend time with you and get to know you better. I will see you tomorrow."

"Tomorrow?"

"Si, tomorrow."

"I don't understand. Why?"

"The señora will explain it to you. Here we are. I'll help you down." Señor Hastings jumped down and rushed to Amalia's side, but she had already helped herself and walked into the tavern.

Sand Viper's Bugloss

CHAPTER 34

A TELEGRAPH CAME FROM Guillermo Duranté the next morning. It explained that he and his partner, Señor Juan Engaños, were sailing to Menorca. He'd intercepted a message at their office in Águilas that a woman with Amalia's description lived in Mahón, and they were coming to verify her identity. Duranté vaguely indicated he had information Joshua needed to hear.

"Blast the secrecy."

"He has to keep his cover."

"I know *why* it's necessary to keep his message ambiguous. I still hate it." Joshua paced.

"What information is it, do you think?" Channing pressed.

"It could be anything. Maybe he knows where Tudó is hiding out, or he could know her paternity. I don't know, and I feel like I'll go mad if I don't see her soon."

"Then go. No one says you have to wait till late afternoon. Go now before you pull all your hair out. I believe there's a bald spot beginning just there." Channing pointed to the crown of Joshua's head. "Go before I kick you out."

The same fancy two-wheeled volante pulled up in front of the tavern earlier than expected. Señora Consuela insisted Amalia go out and greet him.

He looked exceptionally smart, wearing a burgundy waistcoat, navy breeches, and polished high boots. Standing straight as a pin and with a tip of his head, Señor Hastings greeted her, "Another lovely day, wouldn't you agree?"

Melisandra walked past Amalia with a smile.

"Why are you here again? Wasn't yesterday bad enough?" she asked briskly after the nursemaid stepped out of earshot.

He looked deep into her eyes. Though she tried to look back to show he didn't intimidate her, Amalia had to look away. *I hate it when he does that. He is far too endearing for his own good—for my own good.*

Offering his hand to help her up, he said, "I thought we could give it another try."

Amalia shrugged her shoulders and stepped up to take a seat, ignoring his offered hand. A small bouquet of wildflowers lay next to where she sat, and she quickly brushed them onto the floor. Señor Hastings bent to pick them up when he joined her, but Amalia stopped him.

"Por favor, leave them there. They bring back sad memories."

Hastings couldn't hide his concern, but he nudged the flowers onto the ground with his foot and clicked Trudy to go without another word.

Amalia began to relax as the time passed peacefully between them, but as they drew closer to a small grove of trees, she recognized them as carob trees filled with vibrant red blossoms. A horrible feeling of nostalgia deflated her. Several bouquets of wildflowers dotted their destination, and she took in a sharp breath.

I've worked so hard to put the memories of Cisco and the life I hoped for away, but Señor Hastings keeps bringing those ghosts back.

A detailed picture of Cisco leaning against their tree, a bouquet of wildflowers in his hand, rushed to her mind. Amalia gripped the bench and shut her eyes to force her thoughts somewhere else. Heart racing, she felt the weight of the ocean suffocating her. Joshua stopped the volante and grabbed her by the shoulders to turn her toward him.

Her reaction made him pull his hands back and immediately apologize. "I am so sorry. I just . . . Are you ill? Should I summon a physician? Por favor, tell me, A . . . A . . . Lea."

When Amalia just stared at him with wide eyes, he begged pardon again. "Forgive me. I should never have touched you like that. It was wrong of me. I just want to help." He slumped against the bench. "You look like you've seen a ghost. You're shivering." He moved to take off his outer frock coat.

She flinched, and Joshua stopped mid motion before looking toward the carob trees, clearly uncertain what to do.

Amalia's heart slowed, and she finally found her voice. "I'm sorry. It looks like you planned a lovely day, but I . . . I do feel a bit fatigued. If you could take me back, I would be grateful." Seeing his disappointment, she quickly added, "I'm still happy to entertain you there."

Joshua winced, and his ears turned red. Seemingly agitated by her offer, he took the reins and clicked his tongue for the horse to move.

Amalia tried to rub away the throbbing in her temples. Going back didn't make her happy, but staying with Señor Hastings was not an option. Something didn't add up. He'd only asked a few hours of her time during the slowest part of the day, and not once had they been together for more than half an hour. Yet he hadn't tried to put any unwanted moves on her and didn't complain when she asked him to take her back to the tavern. *He's not like the other men. Why is he so different?* Against her better judgment, she liked him.

Joshua rode back to his place in Ciutadella, again disappointed he hadn't made any progress with Amalia. Grateful for the long drive, he needed some time to think . . . or not think. Actually, he felt numb. Joshua had done everything Channing suggested a woman liked:

chocolate, pleasant conversation under the shade of a tree, flowers—all of which Amalia clearly did *not* like. He searched his memory of what he knew about Amalia.

Joshua threw off his tailcoat and hat upon entering his villa and sought out Channing.

Finding him in the small library near the back of the house, he announced, "You are no longer my courting counselor."

Channing looked up from his book. "What do you mean? Are you sacking me?"

"Yes, I am. Nothing you have suggested has softened Amalia toward me. In fact, it has pushed her further away."

Putting his book down, Channing said, "I see. She is not a typical woman, then."

"She may have been at one point but not any longer. That damned cad Francis. It isn't fair I have to compete with her past when all I want to do is give her a better future. Well, the hell with him."

"Hear, hear!" Channing held up his drink. "What is it you plan to do?"

Joshua paced. "I have to come up with something I know Amalia will like, something that will not remind her of her past. It has to be unique, not the typical thing a man would do to win a woman's affections."

Channing sat back and put his feet up. "Well, your knowledge is incomplete at best. The only things we've heard about Amalia are from stories Sonia and Thomas have divulged."

Joshua wagged his finger in thought. "We have to recollect that information and use it to help me woo Amalia."

Amused, Channing watched his best friend deliberate. Offering a suggestion, he said, "Doesn't Amalia have a love of horses? That is why you traded for Gordita, right?"

Joshua lit up. "I know of some fantastic stables in Mercadal I could take her to. It would be a long drive, though. She hardly speaks to me. It can be so quiet between us. You have no idea how much I wish she would confide in me."

"I know, but you need to be patient a little longer. I think your idea to take her to the stables will be a great diversion for her." Channing tapped his finger on his lower lip. "But what would she wear? I suspect she doesn't own a riding habit and boots. Amalia can't very well ride in the clothes she wears every day. The suggestion is reprehensible . . . though I know you would love to see her bare ankles." He grinned.

Joshua did not like how Channing knew his thoughts. "Perhaps you are right. What if I purchase some riding clothes for her and have them ready if she decides she'd like to ride?"

"You could, but what if they don't fit?"

"I have an idea." He moved toward the door. "I need to make some arrangements."

Channing dropped his feet to the floor. "Do you mind if I join you? I admit that I am feeling a bit bored sitting around here all day."

"Of course, sorry I didn't think of it."

It took the rest of the day to make purchases and plans, but Joshua finally felt like he was moving in the right direction. Thinking Amalia could use a break from seeing him for a day, he hoped that not going the next afternoon would make her realize she missed him.

No horse-drawn chariot pulled up at the appointed time the next day, and Amalia felt disappointed, even though she knew it was for the best. She hoped he wouldn't give up on her, but it appeared he had. Señor Hastings's absence did not escape Señora Consuela's notice either, and she wasted no time finding Amalia in the kitchen.

"Your gentleman did not show up today. It seems you haven't the ability to keep a man like him satisfied. I knew you were out of your league, but Señor Guerra would not listen to me. No matter. Since you are free this evening, there is a man who is interested in your company. I will let him know you will be available for him."

Amalia looked at Rana, who looked as alarmed as she felt. Leo removed a large pot from the counter and left to fill it with water, and Amalia removed her apron before going to find Ale.

Esperanza bumped into her. "Where are you going in a hurry?"

"It appears I've driven Señor Hastings away, and I'm entertaining strangers again," Amalia said.

"I'm sorry."

"Me too. I thought . . . Never mind. Where is Ale?"

"He was in the kitchen with Leo."

"No, I just came from there." Amalia looked around the back area.

"It sounds like he has disappeared again. He's a slippery one."

"He isn't yet three and already has too much freedom." She took off toward the stable.

"Maybe he is playing with the kittens," Esperanza yelled after her. "I'll check in the garden."

Amalia rounded the corner of the tavern to see Ale talking to a man crouched down to his level. Something furry hung from his grasp. At first, she thought the man might be Señor Hastings and almost yelled for him, but then he stood and handed something to her son. By the way he moved, she knew it wasn't Hastings. She backed out of sight and watched Ale reach around the stranger's leg and hug him before the man straightened to full stature and walked away. Amalia couldn't discern his face because his face was shadowed by a wide brimmed hat. Her heart began to pound. Something familiar about him made the hairs on her neck stand on end. That used to happen when Manuel Tudó plagued her life, but she was certain it wasn't him. The man stood too tall.

Amalia hid herself around the corner. She struggled to still her heart until she made herself known when Ale's little footsteps approached.

"Who was that?"

Startled, he snapped his hands behind his back.

"Ale? Who was that?"

He hung his head and said, "I don't know?"

"What do you mean? What did he give you?"

Ale didn't move. Amalia squatted next to him, pulled his arms out, and forced his fingers open. He was holding two reales, one in each hand.

"What is this for? Tell me now."

Alejandro struggled free and ran into the tavern through the kitchen. "You can't make me."

Esperanza found Amalia staring after her boy. "You don't have time to chase after him. You have a guest to prepare for. I'll be up shortly."

It took longer than expected for Esperanza to get the hot water Amalia required. She heard weeping as she approached Amalia's room. Opening the door, she found her friend sitting against her bed on the floor in her sick.

"What happened?"

Amalia's clothes were torn, and Esperanza instinctively knew. The mysterious guest succeeded in taking everything Amalia had fought so hard to safeguard.

"He was too strong," Amalia whimpered. "I tried. I tried."

"I'm so sorry." Esperanza rocked Amalia in her arms and mourned with her.

Joshua was grateful he'd chosen not to go to the tavern the next day because Durante showed up at his villa unexpectedly.

Joshua stood. "What news do you have for us? You were perfectly vague in your telegraph."

"I apologize, but you know the reason for my discretion." He pointed to the decanter tray.

"Help yourself. However, my patience is at its end. Do you know why Tudó continues to pursue Amalia?" Joshua looked at his guest with apprehension as Duranté walked over to the crystal decanter and poured himself a drink.

Gil chimed in. "I'll have one too."

After handing Channing a glass, Duranté said, "I do, and you're not going to believe me." He took a long drink.

"Out with it, man."

"Si, si." Duranté positioned himself on the edge of the offered chair. "A week ago, when Señor Juan Engaños, my partner, had too much to drink, I was able to glean from him why Tudó is obsessed with Amalia. And I do mean obsessed. He is determined to have her or end her."

Joshua brought his knuckles down on the desk, making Gil and Duranté jump. "Have her?"

Duranté continued, "Many years ago, Tudó was enamored with a beautiful young señorita, Abuela's deceased daughter, Lucita."

Joshua nodded for Duranté to continue.

Taking a deep breath, he went on, "But Lucita loved a young man named—"

"Anton. We know," Joshua interrupted.

"Will you let me finish?" Duranté asked.

"I apologize, continue."

"Tudó tried to win her heart by giving her extravagant gifts and promising a comfortable life. You know all this. Of course, the heirloom emerald jewels were included in his bribes. Strange that Amalia would steal those particular jewels."

Joshua nodded.

"He was furious when he found out Lucita was carrying Anton's child."

"Anton's child?" Joshua sat in the study chair. "I knew it."

Both men looked at Joshua incredulously.

"Go on."

Duranté said, "So Tudó kidnapped them when they were together one evening and tortured Anton to death. They say Tudó mutilated Anton's body in a most cruel manner in front of Lucita."

Joshua let out a deep breath. "I came upon his body behind his father's shop. I was very young. I covered it the best I could with my coat and ran to tell my parents. We were on holiday visiting Abuela. When Lucita and Anton disappeared, we came immediately to comfort and help her and Sebastián. My parents told me never to tell anyone what I saw."

"You can tell us," Channing said.

"His face remained untouched, but the rest of his body . . . grotesque. That is Tudó's mark. He breaks every bone in the body, or close to it, until his victims die from shock or internal bleeding, but he leaves their faces unblemished."

"So you're saying he has done this before?"

"A few times, unfortunately. I can think of three other times. All people who undermined his authority."

Channing stood and got himself another drink. "I believed you, Hastings, when you said the man was the vilest of creatures, but that is beyond my imaginings."

Nodding his head in agreement, Duranté said, "Tudó made Lucita endure the torture of her lover to punish her for refusing him. Then he took her up north by the border of France."

Channing spoke up. "Was the town called Benás?"

"Si. How did you know?" Duranté asked.

"That is where Hastings found Amalia's brother Thomas. Tudó must own some land there, or at least he did. The Maritimos relocated there after sending Amalia off only to lose it. We don't know where they are now."

Duranté resumed, "Tudó kept Lucita under his watch until she gave birth to a little girl. Engaños said Tudó was delighted the bebé was a girl. He said he would wait until she came of age and then he would have Lucita's daughter, pure and undefiled."

Though Joshua's blood boiled, his face turned green. The future Tudó envisioned for Amalia nauseated him. "What will he do if he finds out about Alejandro?"

The narrative continued, "Tudó took Amalia from Lucita and gave her to his cousin, Luisa Godoy, until Amalia turned fifteen. That's why she worked for his household."

"Do you know how Luisa Godoy ended up with Maritimo?" Channing asked.

"Actually, I do. Evidently, Maritimo abandoned his post in the Spanish Navy because he and Luisa fell in love. She found out she was expecting. The navy caught him, and he was tried for desertion. Tudó saw an opportunity. He somehow bribed the judge and saved the man from execution. Changing his name from Felipe Martinez to Gordon Maritimo, he agreed to claim the bebé as his own until Tudó called for her. Tudó made a clergyman perform the marriage ceremony and record Amalia as the twin of their unborn bebé. They went into hiding so Amalia would appear to be their child. Tudó promised the young couple a large plot of land and money when they gave Amalia back. I believe you know the rest."

Joshua shook his head. "So this is the missing piece of Amalia's story."

Duranté slumped back in his chair as though he had just exerted a great deal of energy. "I have never known a more disturbing person. Tudó won't rest until he has Amalia to himself or until she is dead. I think he is ignorant of the child. I will do everything I can to keep Engaños from finding her, but I think it is only a matter of time. She is in danger, Hastings. You need to get her somewhere safe."

Joshua replied, "I'm working on that, but it is not as easy as it sounds. Amalia has been forced into situations her whole life, and winning her trust, let alone her heart, is very difficult. I haven't even told her I know who she really is or of my intentions to take her away from this place. I've thought about taking her against her will, but I can't justify it. Even if my motives are well intended, she would never forgive me. I just need more time."

Duranté downed the rest of his drink. "That, unfortunately, is in short supply. You must hasten your efforts."

"Where is Tudó?"

"France. It wouldn't take him long to get here."

Joshua looked at Channing, who said, "He's right, old chap. It sounds like Tudó is knocking at the door. We may need to come up with a different plan. If you are not able to make progress with Amalia tomorrow afternoon at the horse stables, then we need to do something a little more drastic to get her to leave Menorca with us. I'm sorry, Hastings. This is not good news."

Spanish Bluebells

CHAPTER 35

FEELING BROKEN BEYOND repair, Amalia welcomed mournful gratitude that Señor Hastings had given up on her. She could never face him again. While trying to find solace in her room, Señora Consuela barged in uninvited to confront her yet again.

"Your caller surprisingly showed up today. Get out there."

"What? Por favor, don't make me go."

"Oh, poor señorita. Too tired from your activities last night?" Señora Consuela laughed.

Amalia bit her lip to keep from crying and made her way downstairs to Señor Hastings, who smiled from ear to ear. She stopped short, disturbed by his jovial demeanor. They couldn't have been more polarized than at that moment.

Señor Hastings greeted her. "Are you ready? I'm assuming my nursemaid has already arrived?"

"Did she?"

"I believe so."

He lightly placed his hand on the small of her back causing her to flinch a little, but Señor Hastings didn't seem to notice and led her to the volante. This time, Amalia made no attempt to get in without his assistance. She had little energy to keep his company or anyone's; instead, she wanted to crawl in a hole and disappear.

Finally, Señor Hastings broke the silence. "Am I such bad company that you cannot find anything to say to me?"

Amalia closed her eyes, willing the tears to stay put.

Señor Hastings said, "It is a beautiful day for riding, don't you agree?"

Her forehead creased with confusion. How could he be so happy when her whole world had turned upside down?

"I have made plans for us to go to some stables in Es Mercadal. They have some fantastic horses there I think you might like."

That actually sounds nice. Amalia wondered how to respond. *I'm tired of this game he's playing. He knows what I am, so he can drop the facade.*

"Why are you doing all of this, making all of this effort? You paid for my time. I am guaranteed company, señor. You don't have to do anything but show up."

Hastings furrowed his brow. "It isn't like that for me."

So you're not like every other man? "I don't know what you mean. You paid for my time like every other man who wants my companionship."

Pulling the horse to an abrupt stop, he said, "Believe it or not, that has *never* been my intention. I'm sorry if I gave you that impression."

"What else am I supposed to think?"

"I only wanted to give you a reprieve from the tavern. If you'd rather I take you back, I will."

Amalia sat silent, mulling over the options. She folded her arms in resignation. "I don't want to go back to the tavern." *Ever.*

Hastings clicked the horse on.

The thought of seeing horses made her want to smile, but she didn't. *Don't forget who you are.* Thoughts of the night before crept in, and the frustration she felt at Señor Hastings's absence consumed her.

"Why didn't you come yesterday?" Her throat clinched painfully.

He didn't reply right away. "Perhaps I thought you needed a break from me and my blundering ways, but I came today because I never let my discouragement keep me down when something important to me is on the line."

Amalia sat in silence. *Does he mean I am important to him? He doesn't know me.*

When she remained quiet, Hastings left her to her thoughts. It wasn't until the stables came into sight that she perked up. A few horses grazed in the fields, and she pointed out her favorites. "That is an Andalusian over there. Oh, look, she has a foal."

Hastings chuckled at her delight. "Look at the chestnut Arabian over there. He is impressive."

Amalia looked in that direction and let out a sigh. "I have missed the smell of stables. The Tudó estate stables were immaculate with the soft, raked dirt and fresh hay. I visited as often as I could."

Hastings looked at her sideways at the mention of Tudó, but her mood hadn't soured.

"I had a horse growing up. Her name was Gordita. All of my siblings could ride her without any worry. She somehow sensed her precious cargo."

"Horses are smart animals." Pulling up to the stables, Hastings rushed to help Amalia down, but again, she beat him to it. This time, it wasn't to rankle him. So enamored by the animals, she merely forgot to wait.

"Oh my." Amalia walked up to a sleek black stallion. "This is the most glorious horse I have ever seen. Look at his wavy mane and tail, like someone unwove several braids. He looks like an Arabian, but he is thicker around the girth, and his face is a little broader in the jaw."

"You know your horses. I'm impressed. This is a new breed called American Morgan. Superb."

Amalia whispered under her breath, "American Morgan. His sleek coat just gleams in the sun."

"How do you know so much about horses?"

Amalia stepped closer to the horse and blew in his nose. "My father took me on his journeys to sell our produce and told me about the different horseflesh being sold at the docks." She ventured a look his way. "Some of them were secret markets only a select few knew about, so I saw a variety of other animals too, like monkeys and, my favorite, a striped cat called a tiger—exquisitely beautiful but terrifying."

Joshua nodded as if he knew what she meant.

"But horses were my father's favorite. He trained them for the military." Looking back at the stallion, she added, "I read some books about horses. I love the larger ones like the Breton and Spanish-Norman, but I also like the sleek look of the Arabian." Amalia watched the horse move about anxiously. "Gordita was a Spanish-Norman."

Hastings looked like he wanted to say something but instead showed her into the stables. "Shall we?"

Ten stalls lined each side of the spacious building. Amalia took her time walking to each stall, looking at its occupant, and making note of their names.

Following at a respectful distance with his hands behind his back, Joshua asked, "What do you think?"

Amalia turned to him with her brilliant smile and replied, "I can't put it into words. These horses are magnificent. They're obviously well taken care of."

"The owner of the stables is a good man." Hastings walked up to a dapple gray Andalusian mare and clicked his tongue. She immediately accepted the carrot in his open hand.

"Would you like to offer a treat?" Joshua presented a carrot to Amalia, and a flash of Tudó offering her a carrot struck her. Amalia forced her eyes shut to block out the memory.

"Are you alright?"

She took a deep breath and looked up at him. "Si, gracias."

Amalia lingered in his gaze. He gave her a lopsided grin, and she realized she'd been staring at the perfect curve of his lips too long. Quickly taking the carrot from him, she walked to the next stall. It contained a gorgeous blue roan with a black face, mane, and tail.

Looking at a shingle next to her stall, Amalia read out loud, "Bellflower. What a perfect name for a blue beauty such as you. Oh, you are wonderful."

The mare walked up to Amalia and nibbled up the carrot she offered, giving Amalia the opportunity to reach up and rub Bellflower's velvety forehead and blow into her nose. Bellflower earned a giggle from Amalia when she flapped her lips near her face.

"I like this horse very much." She smiled at Hastings.

He smiled back. "You have very good taste, señorita. She is an American Quarter horse. They are strong, good-natured beasts."

Bellflower nibbled at the hair on Amalia's shoulder, pushing her off-balance and making her laugh. "Am I ignoring you, sweet Bell?" She reached up with both hands and scratched her jowls. "You are a good señorita, aren't you?"

When Amalia turned back to Joshua, he had a silly look on his face. "What?"

Clearing his throat behind his fist, he turned his attention to the horse. "Nothing. It's just nice to see you happy."

I am happy. But her heart sank when she remembered herself. *I don't deserve happiness.*

Seeing the slight change in Amalia's mood, Joshua quickly asked, "Would you like to ride Bellflower?"

Amalia's heart skipped at the thought. "I would."

"Just a moment." Joshua hurried off.

She patiently waited until he returned with a large box. "I took the liberty of getting you a riding habit and boots. I hope they fit."

Amalia took the box. "What is a riding habit?"

"It's something you wear when you ride a horse."

A crease formed between her brows. "I'm afraid I will not know how to wear it."

"Not to worry. The owner's wife will gladly help you. Follow me."

Amalia trailed after him. "If you insist." *What am I doing? I'm trying to be someone I'm not—that's what I'm doing.* The weight in her heart got heavier.

Leading her through an archway, Joshua showed her to a door that led into a quaint house behind the stables. A kind woman stood waiting.

"This is Señora Cortés. Meet Señorita Tavio. I'll leave you two. You'll find me back at the stables when you are ready." Joshua tipped his hat before leaving.

As she and the owner's wife took the costume out, Amalia was dazzled by the supple fabric. Feeling it between her fingers, she muttered, "It's so fine."

"Si. The señor seems very fond of you."

Feeling self-conscious, Amalia bit her lip as she admired the full, pale-blue gown with a high waist and plenty of room for free movement. The beautiful royal blue spencer jacket had three large buttons down the front. White satin swirls were embroidered in the fabric along the lapel.

Amalia pulled a length of fabric out of the box. "What is this?"

"That is a scarf, or *cravat*, to wrap around your neck," Señora Cortés said.

"Look at these." Amalia held up soft-blue kid gloves from the bottom of the box.

"Your señor has also included a bonnet and boots." The woman turned to retrieve them and held out the bonnet for her. "We will secure the bonnet with this scarf."

"They're very pretty, but I don't like wearing hats, and the boots are too big. I'll just wear my shoes."

"As you wish."

Having put on the dress, Amalia held the sides of the gown out, turning side to side. It fit perfectly. *How many times have I wished for such fine clothing? Now it just feels wrong.* "I look foolish dressed up like this." *He's going to see right through me.*

"Hush now, señorita. You look perfect."

Señora Cortés led Amalia back to Joshua, and by his reaction, he was pleased with her appearance and didn't seem to care that the bonnet was missing.

"You look wonderful, Lea. Do you like it?" he asked.

Amalia held out the fabric. "It's beautiful. I've never worn anything so fine."

Joshua assured her, "You will soon get used to it. It isn't much different than the full skirts you wear. You will find it is very comfortable to ride in."

"Are you speaking from experience?"

That earned a blast of laughter from him as he showed her to Bellflower. Amalia stopped when she saw the sidesaddle.

"Is there something wrong?" Joshua asked.

"I'm sorry. I've never ridden sidesaddle. May I straddle her?"

"How will you ride straddle in a skirt?"

Amalia declared, "Like you said, the skirt is full."

He cocked his head, looking at the horse, before nodding to the groom to change the saddle. Finally ready, Amalia gladly used the knee offered to mount Bellflower. She swung her leg up and over easily.

He chuckled under his breath at her deftness. He stopped short at the sight of her bare ankles. Staring a little too long, Joshua focused on adjusting the stirrup. "Did the boots not fit?"

"No, they were too big. I hope you don't mind, but I decided my shoes would be fine," Amalia replied. "I'd rather ride barefoot."

Joshua's eyes widened, but he quickly mumbled, "The shoes will be fine," before walking to his own horse—the Morgan they met when first arriving. His name was, fittingly, Fuego. The horse high-spirited, Amalia could tell Joshua was up for the challenge. He looked regal atop Fuego, straight-backed, little movement in the saddle as the horse danced under him, eager to run.

Amalia barely waited for Joshua to settle on his mount before spurring Bellflower forward. She heard Joshua laugh, so she urged her horse faster. He soon caught up. Looking at him with a smile, Amalia kicked her horse into a full gallop, so Joshua leaned forward and followed suit with a robust "Hah!"

The wind whipped at them as they climbed the rolling hills above the stables. Exhilaration flowed through Amalia, cleansing her soul and lifting an oppressive weight from her chest. Tears blurred her vision, so she closed her eyes and gave her horse free rein, leaning her head back and spreading her arms wide. The floodgates opened, and she found herself gulping in sobs. *I should let Bellflower ride on forever and never come back. Alejandro is better off without me.*

"Lea! Where are you going?"

Lush vegetation cracked and split under Bell's trampling hooves, so Amalia couldn't understand his muddled words. She listened harder to his voice.

"Lea, slow down. Lea . . . Amalia!"

Hearing her name was like a stab to her heart. Amalia righted herself, wiped at her eyes, and grabbed for the reins. *Did Señor Hastings call me Amalia?* Looking over her shoulder, she realized how close he was and steered Bellflower away from him, kicking her to run faster.

Despite her efforts, Hastings caught up and grabbed Bellflower's bridle to slow her to a stop.

"You're going to kill yourself riding like that."

Amalia kicked at him, but he deftly dodged out of her way. "How do you know my name? Stay away from me!"

Keeping hold of Bellflower, he confessed, "There is much to explain."

The horses danced around each other. "You've been lying to me!"

Seeing her pain, his voice cracked when he admitted, "I knew you when I first met you on the docks in Águilas."

Amalia took in a sharp breath, her eyes frantically searching their surroundings. *What do I do?*

"Amalia—"

"Don't call me that. I am Lea." Breaking free from Joshua, she spurred Bellflower on. *Is he here for Tudó? Who else knows my real name?*

Basil

CHAPTER 36

JOSHUA CHARGED AFTER her. Lining up alongside Bellflower, he grabbed the reins again, but then he jumped from his horse mid stride and pulled Amalia off her horse.

"Let me go." Amalia labored to break free.

"Listen to me. You need to calm down. I'm not going to hurt you."

Amalia forced enough distance between them to kick him in the shin. Joshua doubled over. *Lud, that hurt. Now I know where Thomas gets it.*

"So, you're not like other men?!" Amalia screamed over her shoulder as she waddled through the tall grass in her long riding habit.

Joshua limped after her, easily catching and tackling her to the ground. "Will you give me a minute? I need to talk with you. Lud, you are feisty."

Amalia whimpered, "Por favor, don't hurt me."

She lay rigid under his weight. Seeing the terror in her eyes made Joshua quickly pull her to her feet and put some distance between them. "I would never hurt you. I . . . I . . . You need to hear what I have to say." *Please, God, get her to listen to me.*

Amalia slumped to the ground, covering her head in her hands. "I am so tired of being afraid all the time. I can't trust anyone. Not even you."

"I know you're scared. I just want to help you." Joshua crouched beside the woman he loved, knowing the truth he and his friends had uncovered would only add more pain to her broken heart. Amalia looked so vulnerable. He shifted to brush a strand of hair off her face but thought better of it and let his hand fall limp to his knee.

"I am really sorry, Amalia. I shouldn't have lied to you. There is so much I could have done differently. I just didn't know how to tell you, and there never seemed to be a good opportunity."

Amalia gave him a side-look.

"*And* I shouldn't have grabbed you like that. I regret handling you . . . more than you know." He grimaced at the pain in his shin as he slowly took a seat next to her and took off his boot with an exaggerated moan. "You kick *really* hard. I believe I feel a bruise developing right here. Can you see that?" He looked at Amalia, hoping to see some pleasure in her triumph.

She risked a glance but then quickly looked the other way. She wasn't fast enough, however, and Joshua saw it. A smile touched her lips.

Amalia remained silent, so Joshua pressed on, "You are Amalia Maritimo. You grew up near Puerto Lumbreras. I know everything about you. I know you have been betrayed many times—by your father, by Francisco, and by your employer."

Her head shot up. "How do you know so much?"

"Since the moment I met you, I have spent much of my time trying to discover how you are connected to Manuel Tudó."

Amalia sucked in a sharp breath.

"He is the worst of men. I know his treachery, but I don't pretend to understand why he does what he does. When I was only ten years old, I watched my cousin try to choose between two different men—a young man her age named Anton and the other, Tudó. She chose Anton. Her name was Lucita."

Amalia's eyes grew wide.

"Abuela's daughter." Joshua looked into her eyes.

"You're related to my Abuela?" Amalia quickly corrected herself, "I don't mean to say she's *my* Abuela. She asked me to call her that. She allowed me to stay with her for a few days after I ran from Tudó. I've never known such kindness. She loved me like her own. I miss her." She wiped away a stray tear.

It took excruciating self-control to keep from reaching for her. He braced himself for Amalia's reaction to his next revelation. "Lucita was carrying Anton's child, and Tudó took their love as a betrayal. He murdered Anton and hid Lucita away until she gave birth. He killed her as a message to anyone who tried to make a fool of him. Tudó got away with both murders."

Amalia whispered, "I know the story. I can't hear any more of this. Señor Hastings, I ran from that life and have a child to protect. I pray every day I am not discovered, but now you know who I am, I fear you are not the only one." Amalia quickly got up. "I need to get back to Alejandro."

Joshua got up as well, but he assured her, "Alejandro is fine. He likes my nursemaid."

"Just the same, I feel I need to get back to the tavern, por favor. I am overburdened by your story. I need some time."

Reaching for her arm, Joshua touched it just enough to get her to turn his way. "Amalia, I have more to tell you. It is very important." He hopped on one foot to get his boot back on in the event she ran again. Amalia watched him, arms wrapped tightly around her, as if trying to hold herself together.

"I don't know how to say exactly what I need to, but there's no other way except telling you without beating around the bush."

Amalia nodded her head, visibly nervous.

"I have searched long and hard to find out the story of your life. At first, I didn't understand why I felt such a need to continue my quest. You and I had only met once, and you were a fugitive from the law, or so I thought. But when I realized how obsessed Tudó was with you, even after I returned the jewelry you stole, I needed to know more."

"You returned the jewelry?" Amalia asked.

Joshua paused.

"Do not stop now, señor."

Joshua took a deep breath to calm himself. His head felt fuzzy.

"Are you alright, señor? You've gone pale."

"Por favor, call me Joshua." He put his hands on his hips and squeezed his eyes shut. *What is wrong with me?*

"Señor?"

"It's Joshua. Give me a moment, por favor."

Biting her bottom lip and tapping her fingers, Amalia looked away to give him some privacy. "Por favor, señor . . . uh, Joshua, you are making me nervous. Do you have some bad news for me? Is it about Abuela? What is it?"

"Abuela is the Doña Eulalia Domingo, and she *is* your real abuela. Lucita . . . was your mother."

Amalia gasped. "What? What proof do you have that Lucita was my mother?"

"The proof is written on your face, your manner, your whole body. You are Lucita's daughter."

Amalia searched his face with her piercing green eyes.

"That's not the thing I wanted to say to you."

"There's more?"

Joshua took a deep breath and blurted, "What I have to say to you may not make sense, but I . . . I would like you to be my wife."

Amalia's mouth dropped open.

"I know it is sudden, but I would like to marry you." Lowering his head, he tried to calm his racing heart. "I apologize. For some reason, I am feeling a bit unsteady." *This is absurd.*

Color rushed to her cheeks. "I feel like I've just been trampled by a horse from all this information, and now you say you want to marry me? Your intentions are completely implausible. I am me and you are you. I am broken. Things have happened to me that would . . . nevermind. You don't know me like you think you know me. I am not the person you met three years ago. I am not honorable like you, my very presence brings shame to others. And what's more, I am Spanish and you are English. In many circles, we are enemies."

"Si, that part is true for some Englishmen, but not for me or the members of my immediate circle."

After a pause, she asked, "Have I ever done *anything* to lead you to believe I have such feelings for you?"

"No." Joshua felt deflated.

Amalia could not let this go any further. As painful as it was, she and Joshua could never have a future together. It was impossible. *Last night, I became a whore! He is goodness, and I am filth.*

On the verge of heartbreaking anguish, she lied, "I have no such feelings for you. And you could not possibly have those feelings for me. I am less than congenial company. You know that from our failed outings, and I am . . . I am . . . You cannot be serious."

Joshua stood his ground, his eyes bright and earnest. "I assure you I am serious. I know you better than you realize. Believe it or not, I have fallen in love with you. I know you don't have feelings for me, but I ask this of you because I can think of no other way to protect you. I find I can think of nothing else but you and your safety. I can no longer stand watching you live in misery when I could protect you and provide for you and love you the way you deserve to be loved. I beg you, consider me if not for yourself, then for your son . . ."

After taking care of everyone else, she hated to admit it would be nice to have someone take care of her. Hadn't she been trying to find a way to get herself and Ale out of their current situation? But he was a good man. She couldn't ruin his reputation by agreeing to this ludicrous proposal. He couldn't possibly love her.

"Señor Hastings—"

"Joshua."

"*Señor Hastings*, I have been taking care of myself for years and done a fairly good job, despite what you may think." *I've gotten good at lying, even to myself.*

"I do not ask for your answer today. Think on it, por favor. I can give you a new start in England, a safe place to live and comforts you have never known. Amalia . . ."

Her emotions simmered under the surface. "Why would you want this? You are throwing your life away by choosing me. You must know other women more suited to your lifestyle, your traditions, and the expectations of your family. Why me? I cannot understand your reasoning." Amalia's feelings boiled over, and tears streamed down her face again. "I am filthy and despicable. If you truly know me the way you say you know me, I should be your *last* choice." She turned her back to him.

Joshua took her shoulders and gently turned her in his direction. "You are not despicable. You are lovely. Amalia, none of that matters to me. Por favor, all I ask is that you think on it."

He lowered his hands, but his touch lingered on her skin. *What's happening? I can't consider this.*

Joshua continued, "I'm sorry for all you have seen and experienced at the hands of others whose purpose was for their own gratification. I don't presume that your trust is easily earned, but it's my greatest desire that you trust me and feel you can confide in me. It takes more than words to win your confidence, I know, but have my actions been honorable toward you? I ask you to judge me by what you have seen of me. If I've acted in any way that has not been for your good welfare and that of your son's, then I do not deserve your trust."

"It isn't that, Joshua, I know you're honorable. *That* is the problem. I am what I am, and you are what you are. We cannot be together. We are like oil and water." Amalia wiped aggressively at her tears, angry that they wouldn't stop.

Both stood looking at their surroundings, anywhere but at each other. Amalia was mentally and emotionally exhausted.

"Who you are is more important to me than what you do," Joshua whispered.

Amalia shook her head in disbelief. Her day had started in despair, but now a small sprout of hope threatened to push through the barren ground of her heart. She let that happen once before, when she was innocent and naive, but she'd grown wiser over the years. She couldn't give her heart again, knowing Joshua would realize his mistake and abandon her like the other men in her life.

The silence grew longer, both instinctively knowing it was time to head back. Deep in thought and forgetting herself, Amalia took the arm Joshua offered, and they walked to the horses lazily grazing under a cork tree. Amalia felt the strength of his hands around her waist when he lifted her to the saddle. Yearning to feel his closeness a little longer distressed her.

He will take me back to the tavern, and I'll never see him again. Of course, that's how it should be.

Black Cumin

CHAPTER 37

UPON ARRIVING BACK to the stables, Joshua quickly dismounted to help Amalia down from her horse. His hands fit perfectly around her waist, causing fervent feelings of desire to well up inside him. He breathed her in. *Roses.* Her petite frame molded to his for only a moment as he lowered her carefully to the ground. Enjoying the closeness, he regrettably put some distance between them, but his body despised the separation. *How can I possibly take her back to that prison, placing her in danger? I may never see her again. How can I live my life without her?*

Having quickly changed out of the habit, Amalia returned it to Joshua despite his protests, and she sat quietly the entire ride back to the tavern. With all the things he'd told her, Joshua didn't want to say anything else to upset her. After what felt like an eternity, Joshua pulled up, and Amalia moved to get down. Hearing a release of breath from her driver, she looked at him and slowly sat back. He smiled and quickly hopped down from the volante, moved to her side, and offered his hand to help her down.

Reminding him of who she had become, Amalia said, "To make up for a disappointing afternoon, I'm happy to entertain you in my room."

His ears turned red. "Uh, I will bid you farewell and anxiously wait for your answer. I'll see you in a few days?"

Amalia watched him drive off. *What is it about him? He wants nothing from me, expects nothing from me. Certainly, when he gets to know the real Amalia, he will turn on me.* But that bud of hope in her heart was trying to push through the barren ground. She closed her eyes tight. *Foolish, foolish girl. Being with him is a dream, Amalia. This tavern is your life.*

Her thoughts were interrupted when she heard a shrill scream come from within the tavern. *Alejandro?* Amalia picked up her skirt and ran through the door to find her son sprawled over Señora Consuela's lap, his tiny bottom bared and swatted mercilessly with a wooden spoon. Welts had already appeared on his tender skin.

Panic pushed her forward, lunging for the spoon. "What are you doing? Stop. Stop it!"

People laughed at the spectacle when she tripped and fell to the floor. Scrambling with all her strength to rescue her screaming child, she successfully took hold of his hands and pulled him free. The wooden spoon turned on her with a vengeance, and Amalia found herself trying to defend from the blows aimed at her.

Amalia reached around the wretched woman. "Alejandro, run to my room. Run as fast as you can. Vamos."

Esperanza waited for Ale near the stairs to take him away from the commotion. Finding her feet, Amalia got a grip on the spoon and tried to yank it free from the madwoman, but a sharp pain pierced her side. She heard a crack, and the injury crippled her to the ground. The beating continued until Amalia curled into a ball and gave up all her fight.

Joshua didn't go far. Turning around, he went back to the tavern. *She'll have to do more than that to scare me away. I can't leave her there any longer. Amalia can decide to marry me or not while she's under my care.*

Upon entering the tavern, he saw Amalia on the ground in the fetal position and patrons laughing as they walked away from what seemed to be a horrible thrashing. Joshua ran to her side just as Cook Rana reached her.

"Shh, pequeña, I have you," Señor Rana said as he gently lifted Amalia off the ground.

"Get her out of here. Take her to the smithy. I'll get Alejandro."

"He's upstairs in Lea's room."

Joshua took the stairs two at a time. Checking in each room, he finally found Esperanza sitting on the bed with Alejandro. Both were in tears.

"Grab Amalia's things. We're leaving."

"Me too, señor?" Esperanza asked.

"Yes, you as well. It's not safe here."

Alejandro started whining. "But I don't want to go. I'll miss my friend."

Joshua ignored Ale's protests and searched the room for anything Amalia might need. Throwing it all in a carpetbag, he motioned Esperanza to follow him.

She remembered Amalia's treasure box under the bed. Taking Ale by the hand, she said, "We need to go. Everything will be okay."

Señor Rana was standing at the bottom of the stairs with the two kitchen boys. Each held a heavy pan in their hands. The tavern had been cleared except for four thugs guarding the front doors.

Rana said, "We're here to escort Esperanza and Ale out of the tavern. It looks like maybe you have something to settle with Guerra over there."

"Si, it appears so."

Joshua stood at the bottom of the stairs and watched Rana take them out the back door. He overheard Rana reassure Esperanza that they would be okay, and she need only watch over Amalia and her son.

Guerra spoke up. "You can't take my best employee and successful pickpocket without paying handsomely for them. I won't allow it." Both he and Consuela stood in the corner with smiles on their faces.

"I see. And you aren't man enough to exact it from me yourself?"

"I'm no fool. I know you could best me. That's why my friends are here. Hand over your coin purse, and I'll tell them to be gentle with you."

Joshua chuckled. *I'm in the mood for a little sport. I probably should have dressed down a bit, though. My new shirt is going to get wrinkled, probably bloodied. Wouldn't be the first time.*

Removing his hat and frock coat, Joshua rolled up his sleeves. "Shall we get on with it then?"

The men spread out.

Joshua took note of his assailants. The long-haired man to his right had a limp. The man to his left was short and stout. Toothless in front of him brandished a knife, and the smelly man behind him thumped a club against his palm.

He didn't wait for them to attack first. Leaning to his left, Joshua kicked Gimpy's bad leg, buckling him to the ground, just as Stinky swung his club, which flew over Joshua's head, narrowly missing him. He grabbed Stinky's outstretched arm to swing him into Toothless when poor Shorty tried to get involved, but Joshua stopped him with an elbow to the side of the head, sending him to the ground.

Stinky and Toothless got back up and moved to attack. Joshua bent over as if injured, slowing both men just enough on their approach for him to take advantage. He swung his fist up, hitting Stinky in the groin, who then tripped Toothless in the process of crumpling to the ground. Joshua used his knee to remove the last remaining tooth in Toothless's mouth.

With his assailants moaning on the ground, Joshua brushed his hands off, grabbed his coat and hat, and walked over to Guerra. "I believe we're settled. Buenos dias."

Consuela stood with her mouth hanging open, and Guerra looked at his shoes. Joshua tipped his hat and left.

Amalia could hardly breathe. "Where were you? Where was Melisandra? Someone was supposed to be watching him."

Esperanza got defensive. "I was out back getting some water from the well, Lea. I work too."

Trying to fix her position on the sofa, Amalia cried out in pain.

"You need to hold still." Esperanza used a wet cloth to wipe Amalia's face clean. "Earlier, Señor Guerra threw Melisandra out because she slapped a man for touching her inappropriately. Before she left, she said the tavern wasn't the place for a child and insisted on taking Alejandro with her, but Guerra threatened her life."

"This is madness." Amalia started to remove her blouse to see the damage, but stopped short when she heard Joshua storm into the shop.

Esperanza said, "I think we should have a physician called."

"I sent for the physician, but with all the excitement going on, you and your party should leave right away." Señor Rendón escorted Joshua to Amalia.

"I agree. Do you have a horse I can use?"

"I'll come with you. Esperanza can ride a horse with the boy. You drive Lea, I mean, Amalia. I'll follow." Señora Rendón spoke up.

"Do you think that is wise? What if they decide you are a threat to them?"

"She's right. We don't want to jeopardize your livelihood."

The blacksmith spoke firmly, "Don't you worry about us. We will be fine." Rendón turned to his wife. "This is the right thing to do."

"Excuse me. Do I have a say in any of this?" Amalia took in a sharp breath.

Both men said "no" at the same time.

Ale reached for his mama. "They hurt you too."

"Si, angelito, but I will feel much better if you give me a little kiss."

He gently took her face in his tiny hands and kissed her cheek before taking Esperanza's hand.

Just then the doctor walked in.

"I'm sorry, Doctor, but we need to leave right now. Can you give her something for the pain?" Joshua asked.

"Allow me a quick evaluation. It won't take long."

Joshua didn't move.

"Por favor."

The group left the room for privacy. Rendón readied two horses.

In addition to the deep bruises on her arms and back, Amalia's right ribs were indeed cracked, which explained why she struggled to breathe. He wrapped her torso and gave her laudanum to ease the pain for the ride to Ciutedella.

Bougainvillea

CHAPTER 38

THE RIDE TO Joshua's villa was bumpy and miserable. Amalia couldn't get comfortable sitting on her own with no support. Eventually she half faced Joshua and allowed herself to rest her head on his shoulder. Sleep overtook her as they pulled up to the large house. A protest escaped her as Joshua lifted her from the volante.

"I'm sorry. Not much farther, and you'll be able to rest comfortably."

Channing greeted them at the door. "What the hell happened, Hastings? Did she fall from the horse?"

Esperanza, Ale, and Rendón followed in after him. "Hola, Señor. Name's José Rendón. I'm the smithy in town."

"Si, Hastings has told me about you. Why are you all here? What is going on?"

The butler interjected, "I'll have some food and drinks brought out."

"Gracias," Channing said. "Should I have a doctor summoned?"

"The doctor has already seen her, but she will need more pain medicine to stay comfortable."

"Is someone going to tell me what happened?"

"Si, but this machito is tired. He needs a bed, and I'm quite exhausted myself." Esperanza held a sleepy boy in her arms. "We've had a very stressful day. Lea and Ale were beaten by Señora Consuela."

Channing motioned toward the morning room. "Beaten?"

"Ale was caught pickpocketing a patron. Señora Consuela beat him with a wooden spoon, and when Lea came upon the scene, she tried to save him only to have Consuela turn the spoon on her. Some patrons joined in hitting and kicking her. Joshua got there just as the beating ended. Lea is badly injured."

The butler returned with a housemaid and a few trays full of refreshment.

Joshua walked in after them. "Gracias, Carlos. Is anyone hungry?" He took a sweet roll from the butler.

Esperanza said, "I think Ale and I just need a bed, if that is okay with you."

"Of course. Carlos?"

"I'll show her to a guest room directly, señor." The butler motioned for Esperanza to follow.

"Gracias, señor."

"Will you stay for a while?" Joshua asked Rendón.

"I must get back. Keep me informed as to how Amalia fairs."

Peacefully sleeping, Amalia became aware of a squeaking sound. Her eyes were heavy from the laudanum the doctor gave her, but she pried her eyes open a crack to see someone sneaking into her room through the glass doors facing the ocean. Waves muddled the sound. Maybe it was her imagination. Then the strong smell of body odor permeated the air. Amalia's heart began to pound in her ears.

Someone grabbed her shoulder. She opened her eyes to see Tudó glimmer in the moonlight.

"No!" Amalia tried to move away from him.

A red-faced Manuel Tudó brandished a nearly empty bottle of bourbon. "So, Amalia, we meet again. Though, I must say I'm a little disappointed that after denying me, you go and offer yourself to anyone who is willing to pay a few reales." He tsked his tongue. "Very disappointing, indeed. I should have known you'd turn out like your mother. That boy of yours is gold, though. I look forward to raising him as my own."

"What? How do you know Alejandro?"

He smashed the bottle on the wall, splashing alcohol everywhere. Holding her side, she yelled for help, but no one came.

Tudó laughed. "You betrayed me once before, Lucita. You will not do it again."

"Lucita? I'm not Lucita." Amalia reached for the pitcher on the nightstand.

"I will not be made a fool, Amalia." Tudó raised his arm.

The pitcher was just out of reach. She turned to distinguish the glint of sharp glass in his hand and turned her body just as Tudó slashed across her shoulder and collarbone. Amalia fell to the floor. Tudó yanked her injured arm, bringing her ever present. She screamed. Unable to do anything but succumb to her impending death, she hung in his grasp, watching the shard of glass glimmer in the moonlight.

"If I can't have you, no one will."

"Mama?"

Both Tudó and Amalia looked toward the door to see Alejandro staring wide-eyed at her.

"Run, Ale, run!"

"Manny!" Alejandro ran, but he ran the wrong direction.

Tudó wrapped him in his arms. "Aw, machito. So good to see you."

"Leave him alone." Amalia moaned.

"I don't think so. Ale here is going with me, aren't you, el joven." Ale looked at Amalia then at Tudó. "Si, Manny. I go with you."

"Bueno. Here you go." Tudó gave him a coin. "Say buenas noches."

"Noches, mama."

"Ale, no." Amalia could hardly speak. She was losing a lot of blood. Trying to get up, she fell hard. They were gone.

It felt like hours before someone came to her aid. In her dream, Amalia knew Joshua could only be a means to an end. She would not give in to her feelings for him because he deserved better than she could offer, but visions of his perfect mouth and the way the loose wisps of his hair curled around his ears filled her mind.

"Out of my way!" Pushing past Hastings, the doctor pulled Amalia's blouse open to reveal a gaping gash across her collarbone. "I must act quickly. Everyone out."

"Joshua?" she breathed.

"Will she be alright?" Joshua didn't want to leave.

"How long has she been like this?"

Joshua looked at Channing and Esperanza, "I . . . We don't know. I don't know."

"Time will tell. Out."

Duranté joined the group in the morning room after being at the Civil Guard Headquarters to send word Alejandro had been abducted.

"I'm sorry to say Tudó is probably halfway across the sea," he said.

"Damn him to hell!" Joshua cursed.

"How's Amalia?" Duranté asked.

Channing spoke for the group. "We don't know."

Duranté looked down at a notice he'd started reading.

Esperanza read it over his shoulder and sucked in a sharp breath.

"What is it?" Channing asked.

Duranté said, "They found Engaños dead in a ditch just outside Mahón."

"That's not all," Esperanza cut in. "Duranté has just been decommissioned. If he's seen in Menorca again, he will be arrested."

"I'm sorry, Duranté. Do they know what happened to your partner?"

"It doesn't say."

"You are welcome to join us in England, maybe as my private security," Joshua said.

"That's very generous of you."

"I'm serious. Do you want the job?"

Duranté smiled. "Of course, I do."

"Then it's settled." Joshua leaned back in his chair. "You sent word to all my contacts back in España and France to have the magistrate post a warrant for Tudó's arrest?"

"Si. We'll find him."

"I've been thinking you and Channing should go ahead of us. Amalia can't travel in her condition. We'd be faster on the jump if you two were already on the mainland. What do you say?"

"I'm willing if you are, Channing."

"I'll do anything to get Ale back safe and sound. We'll leave first thing in the morning."

"Esperanza, are you alright with staying here with me and Amalia? I could use your help with her." Joshua looked at her. Pain filled his features.

"Señor Hastings, are you alright?" she asked.

He looked at her for a moment before asking, "How did you become involved with the tavern?"

She glanced at Señor Duranté, who nodded for her to answer. "My husband died overseas when I was expecting our first child. I gave birth two months early, and my child died a week later. Sorrow consumed me, and I secluded myself from society. Though few people knew of my loss, somehow Señora Consuela knew, like she'd been watching me. Right after I buried my bebé, she contacted me and asked if I would be a wet nurse for a woman in her employ. I almost felt guilty taking over Ale's care, but he filled the hole in my heart immediately." Esperanza paused before continuing, "I think somehow they discovered Amalia planned to find employment elsewhere. After she took over the kitchen, their business brought in massive crowds. If she left, they would probably lose their business. They told her they would make her a partner eventually."

Channing spoke up. "A partner?"

She nodded. "That is what they told her so she wouldn't leave. They offered her a lot more money, and she told me she was hoping to save enough to sail to England for a fresh start. She ran the place for a month while Guerra and Consuela took a holiday in France."

"That's a lot of responsibility for someone so young. They must have really trusted her abilities," Duranté said.

Esperanza agreed. "The tavern was a well of undesirable folk until Amalia took over. People respected her. Until the owners came back and made the girls entertain at night, it was a reputable place to dine. Luckily, they didn't make me receive guests because I cared for Ale."

Joshua confessed, "I am ashamed to admit I didn't become aware of the *arrangements* at the tavern until recently. I did what I could to keep her from having to do that."

"If the tavern was doing so well, why would the owners want to turn it into a whorehouse?" Duranté asked her.

"They thought they could do it 'tastefully' and bring in more money. Those were Señor Guerra's words. They saw all the money whorehouses were bringing in in France and wanted it for themselves."

Changing the direction of the conversation, Joshua said, "I feel childish saying this, but despite my efforts, I can't get Amalia to warm to me. Has she mentioned anything to you?" He felt more foolish after hearing himself admit his concerns out loud.

Esperanza laughed. "She is fond of you. That's the problem. She is ashamed of what happened to her and doesn't feel worthy of your affections."

Joshua looked at her. "What do you mean?"

"A couple days ago, the night you didn't come back to the tavern, something happened."

All three men asked, "What happened?"

Esperanza didn't speak at first, and Joshua's heart pounded.

"I don't know if it is my place to tell you." She looked at Joshua, who looked desperate for information. She gave in. "You must be patient while I explain. Don't judge her harshly, por favor. When the owners told her she had to share her room, Amalia devised a plan that would help prevent her from compromising herself, and for the most part, it worked really well. Because I had fewer obligations, I helped her. There were some close calls, but nothing too serious except the day you didn't come, and Consuela made arrangements for her to entertain another man."

"Guerra broke the contract?" Joshua said.

"I don't think he knew about it."

He bit his knuckle to keep from letting out a string of expletives. *I know what happened next, but I still need to hear it. Oh, God, forgive me. Why didn't I just tell her Tudó was coming for her? She would have come with me right then.*

Nervous to continue, Esperanza took a deep breath. "The man who joined Amalia in her room was angry and aggressive with her. I thought I recognized him—tall, muscular, bulging eyes, black hair—maybe a Civil Guard, but he was wearing civilian clothes, so I wasn't sure."

"Engaños," Duranté muttered under his breath.

"You think it was Engaños?" Esperanza asked.

"Your description fits him."

"He succeeded in taking advantage of her, and I found her on the ground in her room, sitting in her sick, utterly defeated."

"Maybe Tudó found out what he did and killed him," Channing interjected. "Didn't you say he swore Amalia would be his or no one's?"

Pale as a ghost, Joshua stared at his comrades, feeling like he'd been kicked in the gut.

Esperanza finished, "That's why she can't accept you, señor. She lost the little shred of dignity she had left. She was devastated that, after all her effort, she'd become a whore anyway."

"I could have prevented this," Joshua mumbled. "This is my fault." He pressed his palms to his burning eyes. All his well-intentioned efforts to protect Amalia culminated in one catastrophic failure. Physical wounds were easier to recover from than emotional and mental ones. His throat was so tight he had to cough in his hand to gain control of his emotions. *I allowed this to happen. I facilitated her rape by my pride. Unforgivable. I am no better than the men who've hurt her before.* "Pardon me," he said before exiting.

Esperanza looked at Duranté. "Is he angry?"

"He's furious."

"Surely not at Amalia!"

"No, at himself," Channing said as he followed after his friend.

"But he didn't do anything wrong. He saved her life."

Duranté took her hand. "Because he loves her, and he didn't protect her."

Chamomile

CHAPTER 39

A MALIA COULDN'T OPEN her eyes. A familiar voice tried to calm her. *Who is it? Is it Mother? No, that woman was never my mother, and my real mother is dead.* A warm hand touched her forehead. She tried to speak but she felt heavy. A horrible memory invaded her thoughts—an intruder . . . Tudó and a shard of glass. Her son was gone. She tried to scream, but no sound came. Amalia felt a prick in her arm, and sweet darkness consumed her.

Growing aware of his beautiful baritone voice—like soothing warm honey—Amalia remembered hearing Joshua sing to the melody of a mandolin intermittently as she came in and out of consciousness. Finally, bright sunlight streamed through her eyelids. Joshua's tall figure stood at the door.

He moved to her side and took her hand. "How are you feeling?"

"My head aches and my shoulder hurts." Amalia smacked her lips. "May I have some water, por favor?"

"Certainly." Joshua looked around for the pitcher.

Esperanza entered the room. "You are awake." She poured Amalia a cup of water.

Helping hold Amalia's head up to drink, a drop of water escaped and ran down her chin. Joshua moved to wipe it away but instead handed her his handkerchief.

"I'm so clumsy."

Joshua simply stared at her, the deep, blue sea of his eyes washing over her.

"Nonsense." Esperanza reached around him and took the cup from her.

Amalia wanted to say something, anything to Joshua, but he stood and left.

She looked at Anza for understanding.

"He blames himself for what has happened. We almost lost you."

"Ale is gone. Tudó took him." Tears welled up in her eyes.

"Shh. Don't work yourself up. Hastings had Duranté go to the Civil Guard and post Ale's abduction. Tudó's face will be everywhere in France and España. He will be found."

"How long have I been asleep?"

"Six long, torturous days."

"Almost a week. It seemed only a few hours."

"Well, now that you're awake, we can start making plans to meet the rest of our party in Barcelona."

"What do you mean?"

"Señor Hastings sent Duranté and Channing to España to help with the search and join up with some others."

"I don't know what I would do without their help. How could I ever repay them for how they have helped us?"

"You should say that to Señor Hastings. He needs to hear it."

"I . . . I wouldn't know what to say."

"Just what you said to me."

"I can't. I feel so uncomfortable. He asked me to be his wife the last time he dropped me off at the tavern. The same day he also saved us.

I, of course, told him I can't marry him. He is a good man and noble. I am used and nothing."

"You are not nothing. Or used. You were taken advantage of. That wasn't your fault. None of this is your fault."

Amalia shook her head in disbelief.

"No, listen to me." Esperanza stopped her protest. "You are a survivor. You are strong and smart. You are barely over twenty, and you ran a tavern on your own for over a month. It's because of you, your hard work and your recipes, that the tavern was successful. It was *the* place for people to spend their evenings. Not to mention, you have a beautiful little boy. You love him, and he knows it."

"What is happening to him? Will we ever find him?"

Anza took her hand. "I worry as you do, but I know Joshua will spare no expense to get him back. Ale will be found. Despite how hard it was to share him with me, you have made me a part of your family. You filled the hole in my heart and are the sister I never had. I love him as you do."

Amalia chuckled, "I hated you when we first met."

"Si, you did, but you overcame that and showed me love. You are strong and have overcome so much. Amalia, por favor, be gentle with yourself and think of all the good you have done."

Amalia grew silent. *Could what she is saying be true? Am I more than the sum of my mistakes?* "Gracias, Anza. I need to rest now."

"I'll leave you to your thoughts then." Esperanza left to find Joshua. Sitting next to him, she said, "I thought you would be right back to sit with Amalia. You've hardly left her side until today. Now she needs you more than ever."

"I'm sure you were able to calm her down." Joshua pinched the bridge of his nose with his fingers. "I can't face her now. I fear Tudó knew where she was this whole time, and I did nothing but enable his retribution."

"If he knew where she was, why would he wait to come after her? She'd been at the tavern for almost four years."

"Unless his target was Alejandro all along."

"What?"

"Is there any better way to get revenge on Amalia than to manipulate and purloin her son right under her nose?"

"I know it's hard, but you can't blame yourself. No one could have foreseen this."

Built within walking distance of the sea, Joshua's villa featured large windows across the backside of the house, welcoming the sunlight and framing the exquisite beauty just beyond them. Amalia stayed in the northwest room, where the view of the sea was unencumbered. Its walls featured hand-painted frescos of seascapes and nature, creating its own personal haven. Just beyond the door was a lovely, manicured walk out to the beach and beautiful blue water—the color of Joshua's eyes.

The sound of waves lazily lapping up the sand relaxed and lulled Amalia to sleep. Though Amalia wished otherwise, the doctor informed her she would remain in the land of the living. She was haunted by the possibilities of what Guerra had done to her son and what Tudó might still do. Tudó came with a curse, and somehow his life and hers were indelibly connected to each other with no possible escape. *I think he said he looked forward to raising my son. Over my dead body.*

The harrowing memory of Tudó barging into her room to kill her and take her son brought on another fit of terror and anxiety, moving Amalia to tears. She struggled to control her breathing and think of something happy when Joshua walked into the room with a tray of sweet cakes and fresh horchata. His visits since she'd regained consciousness were strained and sparse, and Amalia wondered if he had realized what a mistake he'd made asking for her hand.

"I thought you could use some refreshment," he announced.

Always in the latest fashion—creased breeches, polished boots, conservative blue waistcoat, and cravat—his broad shoulders and upper body filled out his shirt so well; Joshua's muscular physique put most men to shame. Amalia watched him as he approached, wishing she knew how he felt toward her. He must have sensed her discomfort because he put the tray down and hurried to her side.

"Are you in pain?"

Amalia shook her head slightly.

"Haunted again?" he asked.

Tormented by so much more than her mortal enemy, she chose to avoid the subject of their relationship. "I can't recall much of that night, but if I think about it, the fear consumes me. I was so afraid—I'm still afraid." A tear slipped down her cheek.

Joshua sat beside her, pulled out his handkerchief, and wiped the tear away before handing the handkerchief to her.

Moved by his unexpected tenderness, she allowed the tears to fall. The stabbing pains in her ribs took her breath away, but she'd been suppressing her feelings for so long she couldn't control the flood.

"He has my son."

Joshua reached for her hand. "I know. We'll find him. You need to focus on getting better. As soon as you are well enough, we will join the search. I promise." Joshua retrieved the horchata. "Here, drink this. It will help you calm down."

Amalia shook her head, but he insisted, "Trust me. It will help. My mother encouraged me to drink something when I couldn't stop crying—when I was very young, of course. It always worked."

She took a sip, and her gasping sobs stopped. "You used to cry?"

"Well . . . si. Everyone cries. One would have to be heartless never to cry."

"I was beginning to wonder."

Joshua flinched back. "What do you mean by that?"

"You've been so stoic over all that has happened, even distant lately. It's like you are a different person."

"I've had a lot on my mind. I'm concerned for Ale."

Amalia's heart wrenched. "Have you heard any word?"

"No. Would you like to talk about it?" Joshua asked.

"No."

Getting the plate of sweet bread, Joshua took one and motioned for her to take one too. "I fear you are starting to waste away. Eat up, or there will be little of you left to take back to your son."

Amalia smiled. "I *am* a little hungry. Gracias."

Joshua stood to leave.

Before she could stop herself, her hand shot out and caught him by the wrist. "Stay with me."

He tentatively resumed his seat at her bedside. "Of course." He didn't let the silence between them last. "I understand you like to read."

"Si, very much. I used to sneak books from Tudó's library all the time, but I have had little opportunity to read since. I received a book from a mystery person in Mahón. Esperanza brought it with us. It's called *Mansfield Park*."

"I have heard of that book."

"I suspect you have." She tried to sense any sign that he sent it to her. *Face as stone—definitely a tell*. "Unfortunately, it is in English, and my English is very poor. Will you read it to me?"

Joshua's eyes lit up. "I would be happy to."

Amalia nodded her head toward the dresser. "It is in the top drawer over there."

Joshua looked at her as if she wanted him to enter a den of snakes.

She giggled. "Don't worry. All of my personal items and clothing donated by your staff are in the lower drawers."

Acting as if it was of no consequence, he moved to the dresser and pulled out the top drawer. Holding up a miniature painting, he said, "I couldn't help but notice this miniature of you and Alejandro. It captures you perfectly. Who is the artist?"

"Carlos Luis de Ribera y Fieve. He had just finished his studies in Paris and stopped in Menorca for a short holiday. He came to the tavern, and when I heard he was an artist, I asked him to paint it for me. Actually, that is a copy of his original work. The original I had him send to the duke of Cádiz."

"I see." He put the miniature back where he found it and retrieved the book.

"Francisco de Asis is Alejandro's father."

Joshua nodded, and Amalia heard him say something like "blasted cad" under his breath.

She wondered what it meant but chose not to ask.

"It's a good likeness." He sat next to her. "Shall I begin?"

Disappointed he didn't seem interested in her declaration about Ale's father, Amalia let out a heavy sigh. "I guess."

He began reading the first chapter, but after a few pages, Amalia interrupted him, "Why don't you ask more questions? I just announced the father of my child. Are you not at all curious?"

"Curious about what? What does it matter who his father is? Alejandro is not Francisco de Asis. He is *you*, and that is all that matters to me. Your future is what concerns me, not your past." Joshua looked deep into her eyes. When she remained silent, he asked, "Is there more you want to tell me or should I start again from the beginning?" Marveling at his goodness, Amalia shook her head.

"Very well." Joshua turned back to the book.

Every evening after that, Joshua visited her to read from *Mansfield Park*, explaining the story as he read. He opened the glass doors of her room so the light breeze could come in and freshen things up. He seemed to know just what she needed.

Listening to the soothing tones of his voice became her favorite part of those evenings. Joshua read until he could see Amalia getting too sleepy to pay attention. Silently, he would sit and look out the window with her until she fell asleep. Inevitably, he would fall asleep too, and she loved waking to see him slumped in his chair. She'd come not only to recognize but savor the fresh scent of cologne. The fragrance stirred things inside her she hadn't felt in years. If only they would receive news of Ale.

Daffodil

CHAPTER 40

A S THEY WALKED together behind the Hastings family villa, Amalia said, "Joshua, I've been thinking."

"Si?"

"I want to change my name. I know it sounds foolish. It isn't common to change one's name, and I seem to have made a habit of it, but I keep hoping that if a name can define who we are or hope to be, maybe the name I choose will give me a better future."

Joshua stopped walking again. "I've been thinking about that as well, but for a different reason. Changing your name may be one more way to protect you from Tudó."

"I hadn't thought of that."

"Amalia, I don't mean to be insensitive about your feelings on the subject, but I think we are more in control of our lives than the meaning of our names."

Amalia tried to protest, but Joshua held up his hand. *He's so endearing when he does that.*

"Names can be very significant, but in any circumstance, good or bad, it is not our name that defines us but how we conduct ourselves in that moment. You are so much more than a name."

Amalia whispered, "I wish I could see what you see. I have done terrible things. I struggle to feel like I deserve a second chance."

Joshua matched her tone. "You deserve it more than anyone." He lifted his hand to brush her cheek but instead lightly touched her shoulder. "Have you already been considering names? I have, actually."

Amalia pondered his last observation.

"Amalia?"

She looked up at him. What did she see in his eyes? Yearning? Heartache?

"Any ideas on names?" He rubbed the back of his neck, clearly uncertain about something. "Have . . . Do . . . Uh, have you considered changing your name to Hastings?"

He still wants me? How he could still feel this way, she would never know, but deep down, she needed him. She wanted him. She yearned for him, but she also knew it couldn't be love. Maybe he felt an obligation.

Doubt filled her tone. "You still want me after all you know about me?"

"Si, Amalia, but will you have me after how much I have failed you?"

"Failed me? Joshua, you saved me." Her heart beat boldly in her chest. She watched his Adam's apple move up and down in his neck and his jaw muscles tense nervously. *Should I accept him, knowing he's ruining his life choosing me? I don't deserve happiness, but I will do it for Ale. That is a noble reason.*

Amalia took a heavy sigh. "Hastings . . . si, I want the name Hastings."

"Truly?"

She turned to him and said in English, "Yes, and I want to learn better English. I don't want any more of this life. There is little happiness here, and I want a fresh start."

Joshua took her hand and turned it over to place a tender kiss on the inside of her wrist, sending tingles through her whole body. "Amalia, te amo. I want nothing more than to be your husband, but if you don't think you can find joy in our union, I will not have you trade one prison for another. I want to be with you all the rest of my days, but I couldn't go through with it if I thought you would never be happy with me. My greatest desires have always been for your happiness."

The feel of his lips lingered on her hand. "I . . ." Not knowing how to voice her feelings, she looked into the deep sea of his eyes. "I hope I can make you happy, Joshua. I worry you are making a terrible mistake with me, that I will ruin your future happiness. I have everything to gain and nothing to offer you in return."

Joshua stepped closer and caressed her cheek with the back of his hand. "You are everything I want. You are my other half, Amalia. I am incomplete without you. I've known it from the moment I watched you walk off my ship into Mahón. I will do everything I can to assure you of my love. I do not expect anything from you, but I hope, in time, you will find happiness in your choice. I promise to love and protect you all the days of my life. You will want for nothing." Joshua brushed a hair from her forehead and whispered, "I have never been happier than at this moment."

Amalia released the breath she was holding and closed her eyes. "I do not deserve you, but I am very happy." She dared lean up and kiss him on the cheek. Lingering for just a moment, Joshua turned his head slightly and kissed the corner of her mouth. Tempted to turn her head just enough to meet his lips fully, she hesitated too long, and he moved away. The moment was gone, but the sensation of having him so close felt exhilarating, like running a horse at top speed.

Opening her eyes, she saw Joshua wearing a crooked grin. He looked so endearing, and Amalia laughed.

That earned a dazzling smile in return. "I will send word to my mother immediately."

They enjoyed their walk a while longer on the uneven slate path woven through the flower gardens. Fresh air filled Amalia's lungs but heaviness pulled her heart down again.

"I miss Alejandro. I feel guilty for being happy when he is with that evil man. I can't imagine the fear Alejandro is suffering right now. You know, the moment I took him into my arms, I thought my heart would burst with joy. The first month we spent together was the best I've ever known. But when Esperanza took over as his wet nurse and nursemaid, everything changed. Now he is gone and I feel helpless and lonely for him all over again. Am I meant to merely see glimpses of happiness only to have it torn from me?"

Joshua answered, "Life's unfair, but you're resilient and full of courage despite your challenges. I want you to know you can't go so far in the darkness that God cannot find you. He hasn't forgotten you, Amalia. We will find Ale and bring Tudó to justice. I have notices and men all over España and France. Don't lose faith."

Longing for the warmth only Joshua could provide, she took his arm. "What is Tudó doing to my son? Guerra taught him horrible things. Before you came to rescue us, I heard what he had Alejandro did for money. I was oblivious to it. What kind of mother am I?"

Placing his hand on hers, he asked, "Por favor, don't be so hard on yourself. You did the best you could do."

Amalia was silent.

"What things did he do?"

"Alejandro throws rocks at kittens and kills them for money. What's worse is that he likes it. And he picked pockets for Guerra too."

Joshua looked out to the water. "I heard about the pickpocketing."

"That's why Señora Consuela whipped him with a wooden spoon. One of the patrons caught him stealing."

"And you tried to stop the beating only to be beaten in his stead." Joshua let go of her hand and turned away. "I should have walked you into the tavern that day when you offered. I did not want you to think I expected anything from you after my proposal. I was foolish."

"I made you feel uncomfortable. Don't blame yourself. I know you do, but por favor, don't. You saved us."

Amalia was well enough to travel, but anxiety was her constant companion. Channing had sent word they got a weak lead, but a lead nonetheless, that Tudó was seen in Lleida headed west.

Joshua stopped by Amalia's room early in the morning to make sure she had everything she needed.

"May I have a word with you?" he asked.

"Si, what is it? Is something wrong?"

"No. I'm hoping this will lift your spirits a bit."

Amalia smiled.

"I should have told you sooner. I don't know why I didn't, but I'm done holding back."

"Por favor, Joshua, just say it."

"I have a few surprises for you in Barcelona. You remember when I was looking for answers about your past and your family?"

She nodded.

"Well, I found Thomas."

"What? Where? Is he well? Can I see him?"

"Calm yourself, Amalia. Let me finish. He is fine. He is wonderful actually. I adore him. I found him abandoned at your family's property near the border of France. He was half starved, but he's healthy and thriving now. We will see him when we get to Barcelona."

"But where has he been all this time? It's been months."

"He was with a governess in Santander until a week ago. Also, I have your old horse, Gordita."

Amalia grabbed her chest. "I can't believe it. How? My father loved that horse. I can't believe he would give her up."

"I'll tell you about it on our way to España. Are you ready?"

"More than ever." Amalia smiled and took Joshua in an embrace. He melted into her, and the feeling was luxurious. *He is so wonderful, so I will forgive him for his secrets this last time.*

Joshua, Esperanza, and Amalia boarded a ship called *Phoenix*, the ship that would take them to mainland España, Alejandro, Thomas, and Gordita. So many emotions filled her heart. It felt like forever to get to port. Heavy wind blessed their journey, however, and within a day, their party made port at Barcelona.

Just in the distance, Channing stepped out holding the reins of her childhood horse. Thomas jumped from Gordita and ran into Amalia's outstretched arms. Amalia fell to her knees, taking his head in her hands and covering his face with kisses. Thomas giggled with delight.

"Oh, how I've missed you, angelito. Let me look at you. You are so grown up and handsome. Are you really my Thomas?"

"Si, Ama. It's me."

"Be careful, Thomas. Amalia is sore from . . . She's just sore. Be gentle."

"Si, señor."

She pulled him into another embrace and sobbed tears of joy until the rest of the group joined them. Gordita would not be left out. She nuzzled up to Amalia until Amalia rose to scratch behind Gordita's ears.

"I missed you too, my old friend." Amalia turned to Joshua and whispered under her breath, "This is almost more than I can bear. Why didn't you tell me sooner? My heart has longed for Thomas for years."

Joshua stood looking like a scolded child. "I'm sorry."

"No more secrets, Joshua. Secrets are like unspoken lies to me. I don't like them, and you have kept many secrets from me."

Duranté rushed forward and took the luggage from Esperanza. Amalia noticed he greeted Anza with a wide smile. making her blush.

Staying the night in Barcelona, the group left early the next morning to travel to Pamplona. Sitting in a carriage for several hours caused Amalia terrible discomfort despite the soft velvet cushions. Her ribs and back ached from all the rocking, so she didn't enjoy the beautiful landscapes as much as Esperanza did. Thomas chose to ride on Gordita alongside Joshua. Amalia couldn't believe little Thomas's transformation over four years.

They made it to Pamplona in no time. Everyone was anxious to get settled and start the search for Ale themselves.

"I've always wanted to experience the excitement of festivals, but the timing couldn't be worse. How will we find a little boy in this sea of people?" She looked at Joshua with wide eyes. Festivities for the celebration surrounded them at every turn, and people from different countries gathered to enjoy the variety of foods, shows, and bullfights.

Esperanza said, "Everything is so grand. I've never seen anything this grand before."

"We'll find him." It pricked Joshua's heart, realizing he'd upset Amalia with his surprise. It hadn't occurred to him she would react that way, but he should have thought it through, considering the deception she'd had to endure throughout her life. Not ever wanting to feel that regret again, he vowed to tell Amalia about his other two surprises waiting for her in England.

After walking the city looking for any sign of Ale, they had a late supper and headed for bed.

"We'll start first thing in the morning. Try to get some rest. Amalia, can I have a word?"

"Joshua, I'm so tired. Can it wait? I need to put Thomas to bed."

"Si, I guess he is tired."

"I see his obvious affection for you and Channing. That pleases me very much."

"Amalia, I would like to tell you something in private."

She yawned.

"It won't take long."

"Esperanza, would you mind taking Thomas with you a minute?"

"Not at all. Vamos, machito."

Joshua led her to a chair in their hotel lobby. "I regret that I have a few more secrets I've been keeping to myself."

Amalia tensed up. "Why would you do that? I don't understand."

"It's because I wanted to protect you from possible pain and help you heal unencumbered."

The silence between them got thick. Joshua fidgetted with an invisible thread on his trousers. "I also found Sonia before the Tudó household left for Paris. She is with Abuela in England."

Her eyes welled with tears, and she looked down. "Sonia is dear to me, and I have struggled with the fact that I left her in an abusive situation where she was vulnerable and helpless. You didn't think that information could have given me peace? And why is Abuela in England?"

Joshua mumbled, "Tudó had her house burned to the ground."

Amalia gasped.

"Duranté was there and witnessed everything. Channing and I came upon the house when it was fully engulfed in flames. I found Abuela on the ground behind the house with a terrible gash on her head. That is when she asked me to retrieve the jewels, so I could have them returned to Tudó."

"She lost everything. Is she in good health?"

"Si, both are very well. Sonia is Abuela's lady's maid, and they are very happy together."

"I'm so grateful they are safe. God is good, but I don't know what to say to you. After Thomas, I said no more lies. You've hurt me deeply, Joshua." Amalia sat silent for a moment as if all the wind had gone out of her.

"I'm sorry." Sorrow filled his features. "Forgive me, por favor."

"I need some time . . . and some rest. Noches, Joshua." Without a glance back, Amalia left him sitting alone.

Poppy

CHAPTER 41

THE CARNIVAL ATMOSPHERE already bustled at its height when the group made their way to the main road early the next morning. Red flags hung from windows and across the streets. The vibrant Fiesta de San Fermín, one of the most popular traditions in España, began with the dangerous running of the bulls.

Two loud rockets rent the air, and a cheer rang out from the hundreds of anxious people craning their necks to see the bulls as they charged down the street. Heavy hooves hammered forward, causing Amalia alarm when the large animals rounded the corner at full speed, chasing men called toreros wearing white shirts and red sashes.

The excitement escalated. It was impossible to see with so many people gathered around. Pulling his eyes off the thunder rolling their way, Joshua spotted a small, dark head peeking through the legs of a gentleman on the other side of the cobblestone street. It was Alejandro.

Then to his horror, he saw Ale dart into the middle of the street. Time slowed. Every detail was acutely defined as Joshua watched the scene unfold. Toreros sprinted away from the bulls and past Ale, but he stood motionless staring at the huge bulls running toward him.

"Alejandro, run," Joshua yelled.

Tudó emerged from the crowd toward the boy, but a bloodcurdling scream rose above the roar of the crowd, stopping everyone. Amalia peeled her eyes away from the rushing bulls only to discover her son standing in the middle of the street.

Amalia screamed, "Alejandro!"

She moved to run after him, but Channing held her back, seeing Joshua and Duranté had reached the edge of the crowded street. Joshua surged forward, barely reaching Alejandro and throwing him toward Duranté's outstretched arms before pain shuddered throughout his whole body. Concern for Ale kept him from staying on the ground long. But he didn't get out of the way fast enough. A sharp stab penetrated his left armpit, goring him through his shoulder and exiting near his neck. An anguished cry escaped him as he hung like a rag doll, unable to get his feet underneath him.

In a desperate attempt to free himself, Joshua reached his right fist around and hit the bull several times in the eye and nose. The bull threw his head back, pitching Joshua up and over, releasing his arm, and rolling him down its long back. The cynical laughter of a man rang out just before Joshua landed headfirst on the street. Some of the runners were able to distract the bull and direct him away from Joshua so people could give him aid. Other brave men formed a semicircle around his limp body to steer the remaining bulls toward the arena.

Amalia watched in horror. Her mind took in every detail, the noise becoming a distant hum. When Joshua hit the ground, Señor Channing's grip on her loosened. Shock registered in his eyes. Thomas still held fast to Señor Channing's other hand, staring pale faced at the motionless body of his hero. Amalia's eyes fell on Alejandro in Duranté's arms. He struggled to break free and run to Joshua. Chaos reigned the streets.

Somehow, Amalia found herself standing over Joshua's bloodstained body. Noise suddenly blasted into her ears as she was pushed and jostled out of her trance. Amalia covered her ears and gaped at the amount of crimson soaking into the spaces between the cobblestones.

A large man shoved Amalia aside, shouting instructions to a few other men close by. She looked up momentarily to watch a familiar figure walking away from the scene. Her heart caught in her throat. *It can't be.*

Feeling light-headed, Amalia finally registered someone was yelling at her. Señor Channing pulled her hands from her ears and shook her. "Amalia, you must follow them. Vamos!"

The men who gingerly picked Joshua up rushed toward a small building at the end of the street. Alejandro ran to Amalia, but Señor Channing whisked him into his arms, grabbed Thomas by the hand, and quickly followed after them. Esperanza and Duranté each took one of Amalia's arms and dragged her along.

Amalia found her own feet and pulled away, running through the doors of the large medical building of her own accord into a spacious entryway. To her left, a door led to what appeared to be a small sitting room. Mahogany stairs lead to a second floor to her right. The clatter of rushing feet echoed off the marble floors as the men rushed down a long hallway to lay Joshua down on a cot in the far room. With hats in their hands, each expressed their condolences as they passed. Amalia followed a trail of blood to Joshua's limp body.

Immediately, nurses and doctors attended to his injuries while his friends watched in silence. All color had drained from his face. Blood matted his hair; his mouth hung slack. The left side of his upper body was scraped from contact with the cobblestones, and his left arm appeared to be torn from its socket. His clothing was torn so badly it took little effort for the doctor to remove it completely.

Seeing Joshua's bare torso under any other circumstance may have been pleasurable, but his injuries were alarming. Unable to believe what she'd just witnessed, she stood, staring at the body of a courageous and good man who just saved her son's life, praying he had the strength to fight for his own. An indescribable sorrow settled in when she realized she had opened her heart to him, and again, it was on the verge of being torn from her chest. *He doesn't know how deeply I care for him. Our last conversation, I was cruel to him.*

A nurse escorted the small, disheveled group to the sitting room near the front of the building, where they could wait until more information became available.

Amalia felt an anxious mess. *What if he dies? I should have told him I forgive him.*

Alejandro pulled her from her thoughts. "Mama."

Taking him in her arms, she nuzzled him and said, "Amorcito, I have been so worried. Are you alright? Did he hurt you?"

"That man is hurt." He pointed his little hand toward Joshua.

"Si, he is. Are you hurt?"

"No."

Amalia looked at his head and lifted his shirt. No sign of abuse. "Mi amor." She kissed him all over, but Ale struggled free.

A cannon fired outside, making everyone jump.

"That was the final rocket, indicating the bulls are safely inside the bullring corral," Duranté explained.

"I want to go see the bull fight!" Ale yelled. "Manny was taking me. He promised."

"Who's Manny?" Channing asked.

"I believe it is our old friend, Manuel Tudó," Amalia whispered to him.

"No, machito. You will stay here with us. We've been looking for you. You left your mama very sad," Esperanza said.

The group sat patiently for almost an hour, trying to entertain two young boys and wondering what the physician was doing to Joshua. No longer able to sit, Amalia paced the floor. *I just need to know he's alive.*

Just as Amalia decided to seek out a nurse, a nice-looking woman came out of a room and made her way to Amalia. "Are you the group who came in with the injured señor?"

Channing stood and approached the woman. "Si. May we inquire after Señor Hastings?"

"He lost a lot of blood. As you know, he suffered a serious head injury and has not regained consciousness. The doctor reset his dislocated shoulder and stitched it up, along with the gash in his head. Thankfully, he should regain full use of his arm in time."

Amalia forgot to breathe. She asked, "Will he wake?"

"If he wakes, he may have a chance at a nearly full recovery. Only time will tell." *Nearly full recovery? It cannot be.* Amalia stared at her hands in shock.

"My name is Señora Tapia if you need anything. In an hour, the doctor will allow you to see him. Try to make yourselves comfortable."

Amalia excused herself to the lobby, sat on a chair, and allowed herself a good cry.

When someone came to get the group, Amalia's energy drained even more to see Joshua bare from the waist up, bandages covering most of him; the rest of him was shrouded in purple and red bruises. He appeared to be sleeping peacefully, but his broken body did not invoke peaceful thoughts.

A nurse placed a chair next to him where Amalia could sit and observe his chest move slowly up and down. *Oh, Joshua, what have we done to you? You don't deserve this.*

He didn't wake the next day. Amalia thought a little color had come back to his pale features, but no one else saw any change. Señor Channing sent for their luggage and acquired a nice place for them to stay across the street from the hospital. Amalia couldn't sleep. She sat with the boys, playing word games and singing songs, but her mind kept drifting back to Joshua's horrible accident and him lying motionless on the small bed across the street.

"Mama, Mama?"

Amalia was pulled from her thoughts. "Si, amorcito?"

"The matador kisses the bull after he stabs him dead. Manny told me."

Amalia hated to hear of the things that fascinated Ale. Thankfully, Thomas already slept. "Your eyes need to grow heavy and bring you dreams."

Ale cuddled up next to her. She sang him a lullaby, then tried to stay up for Esperanza to join her, but the effort proved too difficult. She eventually slept too.

Buttercup

CHAPTER 42

A MALIA WAS UP, dressed, and over to Joshua's side before the cock crowed. The doctor seemed to think Joshua had improved through the night, and she asked if she could wash his feet. With no objection from the doctor, the nurses gathered some towels and prepared warm water for her. Slowly and carefully, she used a rag to clean away the dried blood crusted between his toes. Asking for some salve and with his feet free of blood and dirt, Amalia massaged the liniment into the balls of his feet and calloused heels, humming while she worked.

Roses. Joshua knew Amalia had returned. Her sweet voice calmed him, and her delicate touch did miracles for his soul. *If only it could take away the pain in my head. Why can't I open my eyes? I need to tell her I saw Tudó, and I need her near, but this infuriating pain in my head . . . Ahh! Make it go away, please! I need help. No, don't stop singing. Please don't. No! Don't leave! Don't leave me, Amalia. I need you.*

Joshua could hear screaming, and he felt his body thrashing around, out of control. *Make it stop! Make it stop!*

Suddenly, Joshua kicked the water bowl to the ground. A terrifying sound rent the air as his body thrashed in torment.

Amalia yelled, "Help! He's dying! Save him, you must save him." She threw her body across his to keep him from hurting himself, but it did little good. She said in his ear, "Joshua, don't leave me. Stay with me, por favor. I . . . I . . ."

Strong hands pulled her off as Joshua stiffened. His eyes rolled back in his head and spittle came out of his mouth.

"No. What's happening?"

A doctor and some nurses shoved her out of the way to attend to him while she stood, watching his life slip away. *I can't watch him die.* Amalia backed out of the room and into a corner of the waiting room. Slipping to the floor, she put her head between her knees and hummed to block out the noise.

Joshua's face filled her mind—his honey voice, the deep blue of his eyes, his crooked smile when she said something that amused him, and the way he brushed his hair aside with his clean, manicured hands. *I can't imagine my life without him.* The anguish of his loss threatened to swallow her, and she whispered a prayer in desperation.

"I need him. I know that now. Por favor, don't take him from me. He's my protector, my savior. He's sacrificed everything to save us all with no thought of his own life. I . . . I love him, and if he dies, he will never know how much we all need him. Let me die in his place. His life is so much more valuable than mine."

Gradually, Amalia grew conscious of Señor Duranté, his thick, straight hair falling into his face. Squatting beside her, he said, "Señorita Maritimo, are you alright? Come, you need food and rest. You've hardly slept or eaten for two days."

"No," Amalia protested. "I cannot look into his lifeless eyes. Por favor."

"What are you talking about? Did someone die?"

She was confused. "What?"

"Are you referring to Señor Hastings? He is not dead. He is doing quite well, actually. There was some pressure in his head the doctor had to relieve. It's a risky procedure, but Hastings is doing much better. I think it would be good for you to see him."

"Is he awake?"

"No. He hasn't opened his eyes, but the doctors and nurses say he is responding well. They've moved him to his own room on the second floor."

A tentative hope filled her heart. "Take me to him."

Upon entering Joshua's room, Amalia was tackled by a red-eyed Thomas and frantic Esperanza.

"Where have you been? Are you hurt?" Anza asked.

"No."

"Come sit by the hearth."

"Where is my son? Where is Ale?"

"Señor Channing is having a talk with him. He's not been very nice to Thomas."

Amalia called for Alejandro. "Come here and tell me about what is going on."

The boy obediently walked over to Amalia and sat on her lap. "I got a toy, and Thomas wanted it too."

Thomas started fidgeting next to Esperanza.

Amalia said, "Thomas, did you want your own toy?"

He pointed at Joshua. "I am worried about Señor Hastings. Something's wrong."

Everyone's attention turned to Joshua. It was true. He did not look well at all. Instead of pasty, he appeared feverish, and perspiration drenched his bandages. Channing leaned over and felt his head.

"Damn! He's burning up. Duranté, get the doctor. Esperanza, take the children back to their rooms. Amalia, you should join her."

"I will not leave him."

"Amalia, you need your rest. Vamos, Esperanza. I will stay with him," Channing urged them with as much patience as he could muster.

"But—"

"This is not a discussion! Go with Esperanza now. Bueno, the doctor is here. Vamos!" The days had taken their toll on everyone, but Channing had always remained calm until then.

Señor Duranté steered Amalia out of the room. "Channing has never spoken to me like that before," she said. "What's happening?"

Once the door was closed behind them, Señor Duranté pulled her into an embrace, allowing her to cry into his shoulder.

After a little sleep, Amalia waited for what seemed like hours before she felt it was safe to slip out of her room. She stopped a moment to look at her little angels. A cherub when he slept, Alejandro had such beautiful skin, long eyelashes, and soft, wavy hair—the one thing he inherited from his father, wavy locks of dark hair.

Then sweet Thomas—quieter than she remembered. He'd become so sober; she missed his playful nature. Brushing his cheek, she thanked God He brought them back together, kissed him, then left the children to their dreams.

Entering Joshua's room on the second floor, she saw Channing slumped in a chair near the hearth, and Joshua in his bed, tossing his head back and forth, hands clenched at his side.

He cried, "I'm so sorry. I should have saved him. Please forgive me. I shouldn't have hesitated. I'm so sorry. I'm so sorry."

She rushed to his side. His eyes were closed. She touched his forehead. Hot. Amalia ran to Channing and woke him.

"Channing, Joshua . . . he needs to be cooled down. Por favor, let the nurse know and get some cold water."

Señor Channing burst into action. "Blast, we thought his fever had broken."

Amalia went back to Joshua's side. She took his hand and whispered in her rudimentary English, "Joshua, all is fine. Alejandro is fine. You saved him. He is well."

He cried out, "I'm so sorry I didn't save him. The poor boy. I shouldn't have hesitated. Please forgive me."

While the nurse pulled off Joshua's sheets and laid a wet blanket over him, Amalia said, "Hush. Alejandro is fine. You saved him."

Señor Channing approached her. "Can he hear you? Is he responding?"

Tears in her eyes, she abandoned the English. "No. He keeps saying he is sorry he didn't save Alejandro. I've told him he did, but he can't hear me."

Joshua spoke again. "I am so sorry. He is dead because of me. I hesitated. I shouldn't have hesitated."

Amalia brushed the wet hair from his brow and tried to comfort him. "Shh. Joshua, por favor, hear me. You saved his life."

Señor Channing handed a wet cloth to Amalia. "He's not speaking of Alejandro."

"What do you mean?"

Channing let out a sigh. "It was years ago, when Joshua and I were at school together, at Eton College. He and I took a holiday for a few days in London's West End . . ." Shaking his head at the thought, he continued, "I knew the accident upset him, but . . . everyone saw there was nothing he or anyone could have done."

"What couldn't be done?"

Channing sat silent for a moment. "A young boy, maybe four years old, saw a shilling in the road and ran right in front of a hackney carriage. The boy didn't have a chance. Joshua saw the entire scene unfold. He hesitated for only a moment, but a moment was all it took for the boy to be trampled. Joshua blamed himself for hesitating, but if he had tried to save the machito, they both would have been killed. He vowed to never hesitate again, and as you know, he kept his word."

Amalia's heart broke for Joshua. "He has been carrying such a burden." She wrapped her two hands around his and lowered her head to kiss his fingers. "Joshua is in agony. I wish I could ease his burden." She wiped his brow.

Channing replied, "I hate to see him suffer also. Such a proud man . . . he'd be mortified if he knew you've seen him in his drawers and bare feet. Hastings's very self-conscious about his feet, you know."

The hint of a smile touched her lips. Channing winked at her, and Amalia looked away to hide her amusement.

"Why don't you work your magic and massage his feet and hum a tune for him?"

"What?"

"The nurses told me you have very healing hands." He dropped down into the overstuffed chair in front of the hearth and closed his eyes with a smirk on his lips.

A nurse nudged Amalia to move. With help from another nurse, they lifted the wet sheet, fanned it in the air a couple of times and laid it back on him. Another nurse brought some ice, and another took over wiping Joshua's brow. A chair had been placed at the foot of the bed, and Amalia moved down to occupy it, took some salve, and worked it into the arches and balls of his feel. Joshua's body relaxed. The ritual seemed to have a healing effect on them both.

Again, Amalia marveled at his beauty—his thick, long eyelashes, square jaw accentuated by a few days' growth, his complexion slightly tanned by long days in the sun.

Joshua's breathing slowed, and finally, he slept, giving her solace in his peace.

It took another few hours before Joshua's temperature broke and his color returned to normal. The next day, he opened his eyes to see the beautiful face of his Amalia. *She brought me back.*

"Joshua?" Amalia's smile spread from ear to ear. She took his face in her hands and kissed his eyes, his cheeks, his nose, and finally his mouth.

HOLLY BROUGH

Abruptly pulling back, she said, "Oh my. I am so sorry. I . . ."

Joshua pulled her close with his good arm and said, "It's nice to see you too." He wiped a tear from her cheek and smiled.

She kept his gaze for a moment, basking in the warmth of his touch. "Would you like something to drink?"

"Si, gracias."

She reluctantly got up to fetch some refreshment, and Channing came into view, momentarily serious. "You gave us quite a scare, old chap."

Joshua grimaced.

Reverting back to his foppish ways, he said a little louder, "I would appreciate it if you'd put on some clothes." Channing fluffed his lacy cravat. "With you half naked, the women don't even look my way. You're ruining my prospects."

Joshua tried to shift his position. "How long have I been out? Is Alejandro alright? I threw him pretty hard."

"He's fine, Hastings. And it seems you will be too. Thank God for that."

"Gil, Tudó . . . Keep a close eye on everyone."

"No one has seen anything of him."

"He was at the running of the bulls."

"Ale said Tudó was going to take him to the bullfights."

Amalia approached and offered Joshua a drink. Alejandro and Thomas, squealing with delight, scurried into the room with Duranté and Anza. Thomas ran to the bed and bumped it.

Joshua moaned.

"I'm sorry." He stepped back with his head down.

"I'm still a little bruised, machito."

Amalia pulled him to her.

"I'm happy to see you awake. I've missed you," Thomas said in a tight voice. He gave Alejandro a side glance and ran his arm along his nose, trying to stave off his emotions.

"I've missed you too, machito. How are you faring these days?"

Thomas shrugged his shoulders.

Alejandro jumped up and down. "Now you're awake, can we go see a lady shot out of a cannon."

Amalia reached out to prevent him from bumping the bed too.

Joshua said, "I'm so relieved to see you safe with your mother. Maybe in a few days, I will feel better, and we can get a churro together, what do you think?"

Alejandro seemed disappointed. "Okay," he said as he slipped from Amalia's grasp and walked over to a corner to play with his toy.

Joshua couldn't move very well, but he put his free hand on Thomas's shoulder. "Everything is okay. I promised I would never leave you, and I never will, Thomas. Soon we will be on our way to England. Would you like that?"

Thomas nodded.

"Very good. Now, I am feeling quite hungry. Is there anything to eat around here?"

Amalia smiled at his returning energy. Channing, Duranté, and Anza all laughed, and soon everyone joined in.

Channing herded the others out the door. "I'll see if I can find some soup for you to eat."

Joshua looked at Amalia and asked, "Will you ever forgive me?"

"Forgive you for what?"

"Forgive me for keeping secrets from you."

"Oh that. I hope you never keep things from me again, no matter how much you think it will cause me pain. But, si, I have forgiven you."

"Gracias. I am so grateful."

Amalia smiled. "You are the best of men, Joshua." Her voice cracked. "When you were in a coma, I thought you would not come back to me, to us. I was so afraid."

"I will never leave you without giving advanced warning. You can't get rid of me that easily."

Rose

CHAPTER 43

J OSHUA COULDN'T FORGET Amalia's kiss and hoped for
another, but the opportunity hadn't presented itself again. Two
more days went by with slow progress. At his insistence, Amalia finally
consented to go with the others and experience her rich heritage and
maybe gain an appreciation for it before they traveled to England. With
Channing and watching out for the others, he felt they would be safe.

Coming out of a light doze, he heard a soft squeaking of shoes in the
room and wondered if Amalia had come to visit him. Hoping to catch
her by surprise, he kept still and cracked open his uncovered eye. The
silhouette of a large man in a black cloak crept slowly toward him. *Tudó.*

Joshua's heart threatened to jump out of his chest. His left arm still
strapped to his torso to prevent any movement, Joshua tried to recall
the design of the room and things near the right side of his bed. *I'm at
a terrible disadvantage, and he knows it.* Joshua listened for any other
sounds. Not even the usual clangs and buzzing of the hospital could
be heard. *Is he alone? Has he silenced everyone? What about Amalia and
the others?*

The rustling of his cloak got closer, even as close as Joshua's bed before it stopped. He could hear Tudó breathing and smell his pungent body odor, then the heat of his body radiated near his head.

"You've meddled too much in my affairs, Señor," Tudó whispered in Joshua's ear.

Maybe he thinks I'm still in a coma.

"Life is so unfair. I thought I'd ended Amalia's life. And yet she lives. She will still pay for her sins. You may have Ale back, but not for long. He will be the son I always wanted with you out of the way. Alejandro and I have bonded in a very special way, you know. Raising him as my son, I'll finally have my vengeance on that puta, Lucita. She'll be tormented for all eternity after she sees what I do with her family." He chortled.

More rustling made Joshua perk his hearing. *Is he moving away?* He could still feel Tudó's threatening presence.

The timing has to be just right. Be patient . . . Now!

Joshua opened his eyes right when Tudó thrust a knife toward his chest. His reflexes caused his body to turn and block it with his good hand, stopping the blade inches from his heart.

Tudó's eyes widened in surprise. "I thought you were . . ." He pressed down harder on the knife and grabbed Joshua's bandaged shoulder. Joshua cried out.

Tossing his head back in boisterous laughter, Tudó said, "You are no match for my strength."

"Si, you're a real champion when your opponent is near death, you coward," Joshua said through gritted teeth, stars shooting across his vision.

Tudó's features contorted and flushed with rage. "You are a dead man!"

"No." Amalia stood in the doorway, a sugar-coated churro hung limp in her grasp. "Leave him alone. It's me you want."

Their mortal enemy turned in her direction. "Ah, Amalia, come to see your lover die?"

She looked between Tudó and Joshua then suddenly, her manner changed; she lowered her voice and relaxed her posture. "Manuel, let this man be. I'm here now. We can run away together and never look back."

"Lucita, mi amor?" The crimson of his anger turned into a look of longing.

Amalia's eyes shifted slightly, but she kept her focus on him, hesitating only a moment before responding, "Si. I was foolish to choose Anton. You have always been the one for me. Can you ever forgive me?"

His grip loosened on Joshua's shoulder as he straightened his back and dropped his knife. Tudó moved slightly toward Amalia. "I-I thought I lost you, Lucita. We have a daughter. I kept her safe."

"You did a fine thing, Manuel." Slowly walking toward the mantel, Amalia stepped in front of the fireplace and felt for the poker hanging from the tool rack. She spoke over the noise as she gripped it in her hand. "I've seen her. She's lovely. What did you call her?"

"I named her Amalia. You like that name, si?" Tudó's eyes had gone childish, his manner timid and gentle.

Joshua grabbed of the knife discarded at his side and watched them closely—aware of Amalia's plan—and searched for something to distract Tudó long enough for her to take a swing at him.

She paused, and Tudó stopped his progress, cocking his head.

She quickly added, "Amalia is a lovely name. I am so grateful to you for watching over her. Let's be a family. Would you like that?"

There was a flick of her eyes, and Joshua took that as his cue. "Now!"

Tudó flinched at his voice, and Amalia lunged forward, swinging the poker at his head. She missed and hit him across the shoulder, causing him to fall to one knee. Amalia wound up to swing again, but Tudó caught the poker midair. The two grappled and tugged to gain control; however, his strength quickly overpowered her. An angry glint lit his obsidian eyes, and he laughed as he rose to his full height.

Amalia let go and scurried over to Joshua, laying across him like a mother lion protecting her cub.

"What are you doing? Run, get out of here." Joshua tried to shove her away, but she wouldn't relent. He felt helpless, unable to protect her. *Please, God, give me strength to save her.*

"No, Joshua. I'll not lose you. The world can do without me but not you, and I refuse to be a victim anymore." Amalia looked into Tudó's eyes, unwilling to be intimidated by him.

"Kind sentiments. Just like your mother. She was a stupid, silly girl too. She chose the wrong man, and he died a pathetic death. No one can stand up to me."

"She didn't choose you because you are a fool, Tudó. No one could love a coward like you."

He yelled in rage and raised the poker at Amalia. Joshua exerted the last of his strength and threw Tudó's knife. It hit him just under his left collarbone. Dropping the poker, Tudó pulled the knife out just as a force thrust him to the ground. Duranté's fist came down hard, hitting Tudó in the kidney. Tudó's hands pinned underneath him, he had no way to defend himself while Duranté rammed his head into the ground over and over. The beating continued until Channing pulled him off. Three Civil Guards surrounded Tudó and tried to revive him.

"Is he dead?" Amalia whispered.

Channing yelled, "Take him out of here!"

Blood was everywhere. The three men quickly picked Tudó up and left Joshua's room.

Once he was gone, Amalia slipped to her knees at the side of Joshua's bed and cried into the sheets. Joshua laid his good hand on her shoulder, finding it difficult to control his own emotions.

It was difficult for Joshua to let Amalia out of his sight after the drama of the day before, but she insisted on getting him a treat. To their great excitement, the boys finally got to see a woman shot out of a cannon. It seemed a great weight had been lifted from their shoulders.

Amalia entered his room with joy written all over her face and presented Joshua the first churro he'd had for months. Savoring each taste, crystals of sugar coated his lips, and no matter how much he tried, he couldn't lick his mouth clean.

She laughed at his attempts. "I'll be right back."

Before she could get too far, he reached out and grabbed her arm, pulling her to him. Their faces inches apart, he looked deep into her bright green eyes, savoring her fragrance. *Roses. I love roses.* Joshua couldn't tame the pounding in his heart as warmth filled him from head to toe.

"You saved my life," he whispered.

"You saved mine."

He hesitated for only a moment. With a sigh, she closed her eyes, and Joshua bridged the distance between them, tenderly brushed his lips at the corner of hers. Amalia turned her head to move her lips over his. She was intoxicating, and he couldn't resist kissing her fully, the feelings in his heart overflowing when she leaned her body over his. Taking Amalia's head with his good hand, he held her there, savoring every taste of her.

The barrier built between them seemed to melt away, and they indulged their longing for each other until the echo of footsteps interrupted.

Amalia stood abruptly and wiped at her mouth.

Joshua licked his lips. "Hmm. All clean. I believe that is an excellent way to get rid of any lingering sugar. Don't you agree, señorita?"

Heat rushed to her face, and Amalia stifled a giggle.

Taking the hand at her side, he pulled her in for one more kiss before the guests arrived. "Amalia, you are my joy. Te amo."

"Te amo, Joshua. Te amo."

It was a welcome change to prepare for their sail to England. The doctors agreed Joshua had healed enough to make the journey, even though he still wore a sling on his left arm and a band around his head.

Waves crashed against the ship as the couple enjoyed watching the boys run about, pestering the crew. Walking along the deck, the clean breeze and warmth of the sun healed them in ways nothing else could. They enjoyed their newfound freedom.

"Have you thought of a new name?" Producing a wrapped gift from his coat pocket, he handed it to her. "I looked up a few and marked them, but of course, you should choose. I found a name that means *peace. Alanna.* It happens to be a family name on your mother's side. Lucita's favorite aunt's name was Alanna. I know it is not a name you were considering, but it is beautiful and unique, just like you. Maybe it will help you achieve that peace you seek in your life."

She unwrapped the paper and read, *What's in a Name? Names and Their Meanings.*

"Where did you get this book?"

Brushing away a wisp of hair caught on her eyelashes, he said, "I ordered it right after I heard about the book your friend Sonia shared with you. I thought you might like one of your own."

Tears welled up in her eyes, and she whispered, "Thank you, Joshua. I will treasure this."

"You never have to look back, Amalia. Only forward. Anger, hate, regret—those things only eat at your soul. I know from experience. I also know if you cleanse yourself of those feelings, learn to forgive not just others but yourself, you can find peace in your heart."

She admitted, "I want that."

Joshua kissed the inside of her wrist, "Tudó is gone. We can move on together."

Just then, a burst of energy knocked them off-balance. A giggling Thomas grabbed hold of their legs, and Joshua and Amalia wrapped him up.

Amalia laughed. "Where is Alejandro?"

"He is playing some dice game with some of the crewmen. They promised him a shilling if he got a seven."

Amalia felt an emptiness for her son, who seemed a stranger to her in many ways. Her gaze shifted to Joshua whose concerned expression troubled her further. She smiled, though she knew it didn't reach her eyes. Amalia quickly shifted her focus to the sea and her future, holding on to the hope that their life together would somehow bring her son back to her.

This is our chance for a fresh start. The name I choose is Alanna.

Names and Their Meanings

José (Hose 'a)—may Jehovah give increase, 187, 190–92, 195–98, 209

Josephine—may Jehovah give increase, 2, 6

Joshua—Jehovah saves, 129, 133–34, 137–42, 149–74, 201–7, 218–23, 234–38, 240–60, 262–69, 272–73, 276, 278–80, 282–86, 290–302, 304–9, 311–14, 316–35, 337–51

L

Lea Tavio (Lee' a Tov' e o)—tired eighth, 107, 110

Leonardo—lion, bold, he had red hair, 178

Lucita (Loo 'see ta)—light, x, xii, 111–12, 114–18, 121–22, 127, 138, 154, 156–57, 203, 219–20, 251, 259, 283–85, 296–98, 310, 346–47, 350

Luisa (Loo 'ee sa)—famous in war, 1, 251–52, 254, 256–58, 285

M

Majestad—majesty, 45

Manuel Tudó (Man 'hwell Too doe')—God with us, his parents were grateful for his birth, 31, 118, 127, 154, 160, 168, 219–20, 246, 251–52, 281, 296

Maria—bitter, 2, 6, 252

Mariana (Mar ee 'a na)—bitter, 40–41

Martha—Lady, 202, 204

Melisandra (Mel 'iss on' dra)—determined, 269, 277, 306

Morales (Mor 'al is)—morality, 16–21, 23–27, 29, 34, 37–38, 41–42, 44, 47–48, 57, 64, 93, 100–101, 162–64, 166

P

Pepita (Pe 'peet a)—nugget, 25, 121, 246

R

Rana (Ron' a)—frog, 147–48, 176–80, 182–84, 186–87, 189–97, 199–200, 209, 211, 213, 217, 237–38, 281, 304

Rendón (Ren 'done)—bold, daring, 187, 189, 235–36, 262–63, 306–9

Rodolfo—famous wolf, 225

S

Sabina (Sob 'een a)—ambitious, independent, 133, 136, 138–39, 145, 155

Sebastián—venerable, revered, 117–19, 203, 284

Sonia Vela—wisdom, watchful, 17, 59, 168

T

Taddeo (Tad 'day oe)—courageous, 75–76

Tapia (Top' ee a)—wall, 335

Thomas—twin, 3–8, 11–12, 15, 27, 30, 97, 119–20, 148, 177, 212, 247–53, 256, 258–60, 279, 284, 295, 327–30, 332–33, 336, 339–40, 343–44, 350

V

Valdez—brave, 16, 41, 161–64

Valeria—valiant, 40–41